Blood Fugue

By

Amber Anthony

Copyright

Copyright © 2020 Amber Anthony.

All rights reserved, including the right to reproduce this book or portions thereof in any form whatsoever. For information, address the publisher.

All rights reserved. This book or parts thereof may not be reproduced in any form, stored in any retrieval system, or transmitted in any form by any means—electronic, mechanical, photocopy, recording, or otherwise — without prior written permission of the publisher, except as provided by United States of America copyright law. For permission requests, write to the publisher at "Attention: Permissions Coordinator" at the address below.

Thank you for respecting their intellectual property.

eBook ISBN 978-1-3934094-7-2
Paperback ISBN 978-1-7343822-1-1
Library of Congress Control Number: 2020933015

Blood Fugue is a *work of fiction*. Any references to historical events, real people, or real places are used fictitiously with terrific imagination. Other names, characters, places, and events are creations of the authors' imaginations, and any resemblances to actual events or places or persons, living or dead, is entirely coincidental.

Published by Amber Anthony
WriteAmberAnthony@gmail.com
March 10, 2020
March 21, 2020 Printing

Dedications

It gives us great joy when we get to this part of our project. This book is dedicated to those who have made our lives memorable.

To those who are still opening doors, seeking their destiny.

To Rusty's husband, Tim, who thirty-nine years ago, said the right thing at the right time. Whoever said love remains the same was wrong. Love is resilient; love is relentless; love is indisputably the wildest ride on this planet.

Thank you, Dorothy, have a great big party.

Acknowledgments

Nancy reflected on some family experiences and recollections for Harry's Army career.

Finally, because my husband and I own a neighborhood tavern, I have the chance to meet noteworthy people with intriguing stories. There would be no Harry VanAlt without Harry Bauer's years of Army stories from Korea. Thanks, Harry, for your service in the Army and your unending sense of humor.

Cover Credits
Cover Artist

Kelly Martin, kam.design.
We wish to formally thank Kelly Martin for her creative genius
on all of our book covers.

Cover Photos

DepositPhotos: Subbotina, sakkmesterke
Shutterstock: Akaphon, ninanaina
Period Images

Editor/Publisher Credits

Professional Editor Services
Published by Amber Anthony, Printed in the United States of America

MEMORANDUM
Date: January 1, 2003
To: Mortal Readers
From: Richard Hiatt, Vampire and Co-founder/CEO
Reference: Qualities of the Undead

It has come to my attention that many Mortals believe Vampires are a fable. This memo is to dispel this inaccuracy. Vampires are real. Literature and film have gone far to paint us with a violent brush. To be honest, we are like you. We have good and bad nights.

What's it like to be a vampire? We're the top of the food chain. What do vampires look like? We're like you, simply more stunning. We can walk in daylight, but we prefer night. We can drink wine and spirits. If we add a few drops of blood, we enjoy the flavor.

Are vampires killers? Are mortals? Our origins were mortal. What we become over decades is a refinement of who we were.

In the twenty-first century, most vampires thrill to feed, sadly some still kill to feed. Those vampires make us conspicuous and must be dealt with. Our government is referred to as The Council.

So, you say, "I've never seen a vampire." That's because of our Responders, our law enforcement, our healers, and our cleanup crews. Our Responders are skilled at thralling. Had an ugly interaction with a fanged hellion? The tech in the blue jumpsuit will spellbind that nightmare. Sweet dreams, you're welcome.

We are stronger, faster, and more perceptive than mortals. We don't fly. We don't shape-shift. (That's a horse of different color). Our senses are more acute, and each of us has different gifts. We may be clairsentient, precognicient, telepathic, or some of us are gifted to scent the past. What we aren't is omniscient, but that would be aces.

In the world of the twenty-four-hour news cycle, our existence requires us to relocate and reestablish our identities periodically. Ever been in a museum and seen a face in a portrait from the 1500s that you swear you've seen on the street? Bingo! Vampire.

We can be killed. Stake us; we're immobilized. Shoot or stab us, we heal. Silver will poison us, we can recover, but it's not easy. Fire will immolate us. Beheadings are forever.

A well-fed vampire is stunning. Our skin is luminous. Our eyes mesmerize, our physiques are jaw-dropping.

Back to the thrilling to feed part… The skilled vampire's bite is orgasmic ecstasy. In 1923, we radically reduced feeding deaths with the origin of the exclusive vampire club, The Gaoler. Willing mortals exchange their blood for the exhilaration of our bite. More adventurous donors engage in consenting acts of BDSM. A bit of well-dispensed pain in exchange for a colossal orgasm. Great fun.

We're not recruiting. *Don't ask.*

Chapter One

January 6, 2003

…Not the Beginning

The streetlight in front of the house flickered, but with vampire sight, Harry could plainly see the couple struggling in the taxi's back seat. A woman's screams advertised her horror.

Harry didn't just open the door, he yanked it off the hinges and grabbed her attacker around the throat with one powerful hand. He hadn't expected the creature he pulled from the car.

Opalescent eyes and wicked fangs tipped with blood greeted him under a cab driver's cap. Straightaway, the game changed. The attacker fought Harry for his undead life. With the element of surprise and martial arts training, Harry subdued the wayward, dining vampire.

In subtones, unheard by mortals, Harry warned the struggling bloodsucker. "I don't know where you're from, but the streets of Los Angeles are not your buffet. I can snap your neck, or I can turn you over to the Responders." The driver snarled back a non-answer. "Do I interpret that as you'd like the Responders to pick you up?"

"Lemme go. It's not even my cab. Lemme go."

Harry brought the miscreant nose to nose, pulled out his phone, and hissed, "Smile." The vamp shook out of Harry's grasp and vanished in the night with Harry calling after him. "They will be hunting you, and they have a very nice photo for the BOLO."

Harry straightened his clothing and reached a hand toward the wide-eyed woman cowering against the cab's far door. "He won't be back. You're safe."

Her shaking hand grasped his. She breathed deeply. "What the hell just happened?"

Harry pulled her to her feet. "You're welcome."

"No, seriously, what just happened?" She ran both hands over her wildly disheveled tendrils of hair.

Harry wrapped his handkerchief around two fingers and dabbed at the blood on her neck. "Looks like he cut you a little. Are you okay? Do you want to go to the hospital?"

She arched her neck toward him. "Does it look like it needs stitches?"

Oh, A-Positive, ovulating, healthy. "Mmm, not to me." *With a good lick, I could seal that closed.* He glanced around. "Do you live here? The guy said he stole the cab. Do you want the police?"

"What's the point? He's long gone now. When I get up tomorrow, I'll report a cab abandoned in my driveway. I'm a criminal profiler, and I know the prints will still be there in the morning when I wake up."

No living being's prints.

She walked around the cab, noticing the door several feet away. "You pulled the door off. Where's your phone booth, Clark Kent?"

Harry ducked his head. "Adrenaline?"

The woman narrowed her eyes as her gaze swept her block. She turned back to Harry. "Did you see his eyes? I saw his eyes." She dug in the back seat for her purse and hung it over her shoulder. She scrutinized him. "I saw yours, too. Nobody's that strong. What are you? A super-soldier?"

"Seriously, that door was hanging on by a rusty hinge. I'm just a crime writer. I was waiting for your neighbor to come home for an interview. I caught the cabbie off guard. He focused on you, and I got the upper hand."

"Unh, huh." She looked toward the house. "So, Eddie Cartwright knows you?" Harry nodded. "You want a drink? I need a drink." She handed Harry her house key. "I can't put a shoulder into it tonight, would you do the honors?" He looked at her askance. "The door sticks in damp weather."

Harry nodded. He took the steps up the Craftsman style porch and scented for other intruders. When he opened the door, he made an effort to make it look tricky. Harry reached in for the usual living room light switch and illuminated a nineteen-forties time capsule of a living room. He stepped back to allow the woman into her home.

Extending his hand, he volunteered. "I'm Harry VanAlt, your local Superman." *...and valiant vampire.*

She accepted his hand with a smirk. "I'm Lizbet Mitchell, your local crime statistic." She slipped out of her raincoat and hung it on the adjacent hall tree. "Have a seat, welcome to my refuge."

"I sense a theme going on here." Harry gestured to the décor.

"I think the 1940s were far more stylish than today. Plus, I made the high bid at an estate sale. Most of this was the original grouping."

The vampire closed his eyes and visualized a post-war widow in her nineties as she wrapped each tchotchke carefully for sale at auction. Harry admired the brightly polished wood floors and the floral chintz drapes that complimented the dominating tropical print of the sofa. He paced around the seating group, taking in the matched pair of sea nymph lamps. "Mom had a set like this." Graceful sea-green figures swayed in the elegant waves. He denied the urge to pick one up and check the trademark. Harry nodded, and with his hands planted on his hips, he smiled. "Man, this takes me back to my Granny's house. This stuff is killer diller." He felt her scrutiny.

"Unfortunately, the dictionary for that era's slang did not come with the furniture. Does that mean you like it?" Lizbet walked the short distance to a built-in cabinet and retrieved two glasses and a bottle of Bulleit Bourbon. Holding up the bottle, she smiled. "Bourbon, okay?" Harry nodded. "It would have been that or buttermilk." He grimaced. "Bourbon it is." She poured and brought two glasses to the coffee table. Harry waited until she took her seat before he took his opposite her.

Lizbet sat back on the nubby boucle sofa and tucked one slender ankle under her thigh as she demurely smoothed her skirt. Her stockings were reinforced toe; her toenails were bright red matching her active length fingernails. Before she lifted her glass, she released her mussed chignon and shook her head, releasing raven hair tumbling past her shoulders. She gave Harry an assessing glance out of emerald green eyes. Her smile widened in approval. "Here's to rescuers in the night."

Harry nodded, his brow rose as his lips curled humorlessly. "Here's to friendships forged by alcohol." She chuckled, and Harry considered it the most delightful sound he'd ever heard.

♦♦♦♦

Her gaze consumed the man on the chintz chair opposite her, one booted foot resting casually on his knee. There was quite a lot of manspread going on with his sleek black dress trousers. His sport coat hung open to reveal braided black leather braces. *When is the last time I saw those?* His dress shirt was impeccably pressed at eight o'clock at night, and pearl buttons secured the tailored fit. A hint of an athletic undershirt peaked out of the open neck. *Where is his necktie?* She struggled for something to say. "You're interviewing Eddie? Where's your camera crew?"

He laughed easily. It was a provocative sound. "Not television. I can't remain the enigma I am with cameras."

She nodded, her brows knit. "Enigma, oh my. Are you the real Lamont Cranston?"

One of his shoulders shrugged. "I could be. But I enjoy telling tall tales too much. So I write the drama, I don't live it."

"Have I read any of your work?"

"If you're a criminal profiler, my guess is yes."

Her gaze turned to built-in bookshelves. "I don't believe I've read anything by Harry VanAlt."

He pointed at a volume. "M. C. Westmacott, *The Bitter Pill*. My third book about murderous wives."

"I loved that book. I bought that hardback as a birthday gift for myself."

He nodded judiciously. "Good to hear. Your neighbor, Eddie Cartwright, was a robbery detective during The Biltmore Heist. I'm hoping he has some scraps of info or quirks that I can spin. The police reports are mighty dry."

"Was he expecting you at this hour?" She looked at her watch. *It's after eight.*

"He said he might be late; he was coming from his granddaughter's honors assembly." He rose and moved the curtain aside with one slender finger. "But his porch light isn't on, and I don't see his car. I should wrap it up for the night."

She joined him at the window. "It's starting to rain again. You don't want to leave in the rain, especially after you've had a drink."

He shrugged. "I'm okay."

She left his side and nestled into her place on the sofa.

Harry turned and gave the room a long glance. "Well, I didn't notice that piano when I came in. Wow, a Steinway upright. Is that the original finish?"

Her grin was innocent. "It came with the rest of the furniture. I couldn't bear to separate them."

"Do you play?"

"No… I sing a bit, and I always thought I might take lessons. But I don't have the time to practice."

"You'll never get to Carnegie Hall."

"You're right. I'm stuck right here."

He warmed his hands and flexed his fingers. "Is it in tune?"

She waved him toward it. "I have no idea. Have at it." She sat with her back against one end of the sofa to watch him play a series of scales with practiced flair.

He winked. "Not too bad." His brow rose. "My repertoire is a little dated. My Gran was my teacher." He began playing Cole Porter's, 'You're the Top.'

Lizbet leaned back. His voice put Ol' Blue Eyes to shame. She excitedly jumped up to join him.

His voice was a smooth baritone, and as he sang the first verse of the song, she realized she didn't know the lyrics.

When he got to the chorus, she recognized it and joined in. "You're the top."

Harry's grin spread as he sang. "You're the Coliseum." With each line of the lyrics, all she could do was repeat the chorus, "You're the Top." His talented personality shone through Cole Porter's lyrics.

Three quarters through the song, there was a rap at the door. Lizbet jumped. "Is that nutty guy back?" She shrank behind Harry and the piano. Harry threw back his head, settling his dark brown waves that had fallen in his face from playing and singing. In his sudden stillness, she watched his nostrils flare.

"Eddie." Harry dropped his hands into his lap.

"Eddie?" She watched him go to the door and open it.

Lizbet's neighbor, the retired detective, was a ruddy-faced man with a receding hairline and ears that elongated with age. He stood, hands in pockets. "At this time of night, you guys are singing about Ovaltine? I don't think that's what you're drinking." He pointed to the empty glasses on the coffee table. "I can vouch that this lady here is far better company than me." He shook Harry's hand in greeting and nodded to Lizbet. "When I saw your car and heard the ivories, my detective second nature sent me here. You two sound pretty good together. Harry, is it too late to give you that interview?"

Lizbet's reserved persona returned. "I need to let you gentlemen work. Harry, thanks for rescuing me. May I invite you back for a homecooked dinner some night?"

Eddie's head went up in alarm. "Rescued you? Is that why there's a taxi parked in your driveway and a taxi door on your lawn?"

Harry looked up for heavenly help. "I guess the party's over." By the time explanations were given, Eddie was dialing the police.

Chapter Two

The tow truck driver labored to get the door into the cab's trunk. As the red flashers spun, the tow truck disappeared into the night. An officer from the Los Angeles Police Department knocked on Lizbet's door. After collecting their statements, the officer sought to reassure Lizbet, "It was a crime of opportunity. I doubt the guy will come anywhere near you. It looks like you have some good protectors on your side." He signaled to Eddie and Harry. He left with the careful admonition, "Detectives will be in touch. Remember to keep your porch lights on and always lock your doors." And he was gone.

Harry turned to Lizbet. "Are you going to be okay here tonight? Is there someone we can call? Do you want me to drop you off at a hotel?"

Eddie asked. "Where's your car?"

Lizbet gave an exasperated sigh. "I had trouble with it earlier today and had it towed to the dealership. I don't expect to have it for a few days by the estimate."

Harry processed her frustration. "Why don't I take you to the airport to rent a car?"

"I can make the call in the morning; they'll pick me up. That's nice of you to offer rescue *and* livery service." Lizbet approached her neighbor and laid a light hand on his forearm. "I'm sorry this incident wrecked your interview."

Eddie's expression was hungrily curious. "The important thing is that you are unhurt. I'll keep my eye on your place tonight. I wouldn't want to stay here alone if I were you." He turned to Harry. "Knowing your part in the rescue has made you more intriguing."

Harry shrugged off the compliment. "Why don't we try and do this interview again same time tomorrow?"

Eddie shook Harry's hand, nodded to Lizbet, and took his leave.

Harry looked down into her nervous green eyes. "Are you sure I can't take you to a hotel? The car rental services can meet you there as easily as here." Her lips curled sadly. "I have an alarm system. Of course, it wouldn't have helped earlier tonight. But, I want a bubble bath in my tub and a nightcap in my bedroom. I'll switch on my security system."

"Good night, then." He closed the front door behind him, silently disagreeing that she would rest. *That doesn't mean you'll sleep. You'll sit up all night listening for odd sounds.* He drove to a nearby parking lot and locked up his car for the night. *I'll rest easier knowing she's safely locked in.*

The neighborhood was tree-shrouded and dark as he walked back toward her bungalow. In the back corner of the yard, stood a small potting shed. There was no lock on the door; it contained bags of mulch, topsoil, and a tarp. He left the door cracked and unfolding the camp chair; he settled in for the night.

Harry dialed the Responders from his cell phone. "I'm sending you the image of a rogue vamp I had an encounter with tonight. The LAPD has impounded the cab he stole and took his description. Be on the lookout for a dead cab driver. Get this guy the hell out of here."

♦♦♦♦

Lizbet snapped out of a daze at the sound of her Ragdoll cat, Minka's plaintive meow. It was her hungry cry mixed with her peeved whine. Judging by the echo, she was inside Lizbet's box springs. Lizbet rolled on her stomach and looked under the bed. "There's nothing to eat in there unless you dragged it in. You'll have to come out to eat." Lizbet ruffled the rug next to the bed, and Minka batted at her fingers. "Come on, kitty, come to Mummy." Minka jumped onto the bed with an indignant barrump and threw herself on Lizbet's lap. "I'm happy to see you, too. We can cower in fear together." The Ragdoll gave her a sympathetic look. "Why didn't you come out to meet Harry? His jacket needs some cat hair." She went nose to nose with her kitty. "He's too perfect, isn't he? But you don't care about him; you missed dinner last night." Lizbet trudged out of bed and shuffled, turning lights on ahead of her, moving through familiar rooms like they were dungeons. She poured kibble into Minka's bowl and watched her settle down to munch. "If you cuddle next to me, maybe we can both get some sleep."

Lizbet checked the kitchen clock. Three AM, she had to be up at six. She turned off the light and stood, waiting for her eyes to acclimate. Peering into the backyard, she asked herself, *Is anyone out there?* Eddie's fastidious security lighting leaked into her jungle, creating horrific shadows. It was a few days since the full moon, so she could clearly see her white patio table and four chairs left as she'd stacked them last week. *Great, nobody is lurking in my back yard.* "Minka, I have to get a grip. I'm sure the police were right, and this was a crime of opportunity."

The back yard was a landscaping disaster because her desire for landscape design was more significant than her interest and physical abilities. *I'm too dang tired to work in a garden after ten-hour workdays. The mulch will keep. It's in the potting shed.* Lizbet peered closer out the window. *I closed up that shed Sunday afternoon. Why is the door open a crack?* She double-checked the locks on the back door and propped a chair under the doorknob. Wrapping her arms around herself, she worked to counter her hyperventilation. She picked up the cat bowl, much to Minka's distress, and shook it at the cat. "Come back to bed, kitty." She skittered to the safety of her bedroom, closed, and locked the door.

No matter how brave I am at work. My sense of safety is shattered, at least, for now. Lizbet briefly considered calling into work today. *Maybe I can sleep during the day?* She rejected the thought. The last thing she wanted to do was stay by herself. She climbed back into her mound of pillows and pulled the duvet up to her neck. *Yes, I'm shaking.*

When she opened her eyes, the clock said 5:45. The tension she carried since last night cramped her muscles. Her limbs protested as she sat on the side of the bed. Minka looked at her indignantly from the pillow. The cat raised a back leg and slowly groomed herself as if to say, "What, you can't do this?"

"Would you mind if I brought home a big burly German Shepherd?" Minka blinked and meowed. "That's a no?" Minka shook her head and repositioned on the pillow, tail tucked under her chin. "Silence gives consent."

♦♦♦♦

The elevator door opened at The Gaoler; the exclusive Vampire dining club secreted under the Consort Group International building on Wilshire. Matt Brenner, the club's co-founder, waited to get on as Harry waited to exit. Perennially young, with classic good looks, Harry's mentor greeted him. "Eating late before going to ground?"

Harry took the ribbing good-naturedly, but Matt was always nosey. "I'll have you know I was securing the secrets of the undead."

Matt drew a thumb across his bottom lip as his brow rose. "Yeah? Care to elucidate on that one?"

Harry scanned the hallways. "Mind if we talk somewhere less conspicuous?" Matt tucked a large envelope under his arm and nodded, pointing the way to the bar.

The Gaoler was founded in the Prohibition era in response to violent deaths caused by careless vampire feedings. Since its inception in 1923, vampires and willing mortal donors exchanged blood for the orgasmic thrill of the vampire's bite. There were always unfortunate accidents, but the number of vampire-related deaths dropped ninety-nine percent when vampires and mortal donors met in this speakeasy styled retreat.

Donors were vetted for healthy lifestyles, and vampires were likewise vetted for respectful behavior. There was no playing with your food. It was elegant dining. Everyone left happy. This morning Harry came to the subterranean hallways for a glass of freshly drawn O Positive. No bite, no swooning mortal. It was the undead's fast food.

Pre-dawn, the bar styled like an Irish pub was empty. The bartender recognized Matt and his protégé with a nod. Harry leaned across the small table. "Have you heard any more about that motorcycle gang the Blood Kings? I could have sworn the scummy little creep I pulled off a mortal last night was wearing motorcycle boots. I thought they headed back to Fairbanks after they got their hands slapped for picking fights with mortal gangs."

"MCs are unpredictable. Their members don't like following their own rules any more than they like following society constructs. You alerted the Responders?"

"Yeah, I snapped a photo of the wormy guy and sent it on. But, I'm concerned about the woman."

Matt threw up his hand. "That's what the Responders do. Don't take on a charity case."

"But, you didn't see the look on her face when I pulled that bastard off her."

Matt lowered his head and drew in a deep but unnecessary breath. "Pretty mortal, vulnerable, a set of stems that went all the way to her shoulders? Fill in the blanks, blond, brunette, redhead… etc., etc.?"

"This was different. I was waiting to interview Eddie Cartwright for my next book. He's a retired detective…"

"All the more reason to let LAPD watch your special project."

Harry laid both hands flat on the table. "Special project? She's mortal. Her name is Lizbet Mitchell."

Matt dropped back his head and slapped his forehead. "Never get their names. Have I taught you nothing?"

Harry scowled. "I respect the hell out of you, Matt, but you don't understand. She is going to see me again when I go back to talk to Eddie tonight. As a matter of fact, we have a lot in common. She's a criminal profiler."

"Oh, cheese and crackers. I believe you look for opportunities to interact with mortals in a nonfood environment."

"Well, what if I do? What's wrong with mortals?"

Matt's blue-eyed gaze sharpened. "We've had this discussion. It doesn't end well for them. They have a shelf life. They are curious. If you like them and want to protect them, stay away from them. Every vampire woman isn't a dominatrix. You could have an easy time of it, mingling for the evening at the theatre or symphony."

"But Lizbet is nostalgic for the 1940s. She's got a different vibe. She's an old fashioned girl."

"And how did you find that out?" Matt bore into him with a half-lidded irked gaze.

After a beat of silence, Harry shrugged. "I wanted to make sure her bungalow was clear. I opened her door; she invited me in for a drink…"

Matt pointed at Harry. "Which you can't taste without blood."

"Then, I played…"

"Dear God, I don't want to hear what you played…"

"Piano, she has a Steinway. I played Cole Porter. Hey, Matt, that's not the international signal for 'I'm a vampire'. Then Eddie showed up, and they towed off the cab, and we agreed to meet tonight for his interview."

All the while, Matt's gaze narrowed. "Then why do you smell like soil?"

Harry bit his bottom lip and sighed. "I couldn't leave her; she refused to go to a hotel." Matt's gaze darkened. "I parked my car around the corner and watched the house from her backyard potting shed. That was all."

"Make sure that is all, Harry. You and she won't end well."

"Yeah, yeah, I know you're right. I won't see Lizbet again."

"You know there are lots of lovely vampire women who are as ordinary as you are. Find one. In the meantime, let the Responders hunt for rogues."

"Sure, Dad. Can I order now? I'm famished." Harry's fangs dropped long, and he pushed the chair on to its back legs. With a nod, the bartender pulled the tall tumbler of O Positive and brought it on a tray.

"And you, Mr. Brenner?"

Harry gestured to Matt. "Have anything with a dose of Valium in it?"

With a shake of his head, the bartender retreated.

♦ ♦ ♦ ♦

Lizbet sat at her breakfast table, phone in hand. The car was easy to rent and have delivered, but she canceled it when they said she'd have to give the man a ride back to the auto center. Too soon to ride with a stranger. She checked her watch, eight in the morning. *This isn't an indecent hour to call Eddie; he did ask if he could help.*

Chapter Three

When Harry drove past Lizbet's house, he noticed the bland white rental car in the drive. He wondered how she was doing, but honored Matt's advice and resisted the urge to check. Being in the potting shed last night, he felt her anxiety as she turned on the kitchen light and stared into the shadows of the backyard. When the light went off, her presence lingered, keyed up with dread. Nothing would have pleased him more than to wrap her in his arms and make her feel secure. Still, he could appreciate Matt's warning. What if she got attached? What if he did?

He shut off the engine of the 1960 Buick LaSabre convertible. If she nervously watched the street, she'd know he was next door at Eddie's. It wasn't as if one of these exotic babies was on every corner. Matt liked cars, but he was not the connoisseur Harry was. The aerodynamic chrome, the space age lines, the two-tone leather, and suede interior. This LaSabre was a one of kind, and Harry loved it. "Can't you drive something a little less conspicuous?" Matt had asked. *No, I won't.* Let Matt fool around with that conservative Jaguar if he wanted, Harry knew classic auto chic.

Eddie greeted Harry on the porch. "You mind if I take a look at this cherry classic? Can I get you to pop the hood?" The hood raised with a metallic groan and Eddie stared at a tricked out engine meticulously chromed. "You know, I had one of these babies when I made detective. Man, I loved that car! Wasn't like this, though." He got low to admire the shine. "Looks like you barely drive it."

"She's my baby. She gets constant care." Harry enjoyed Eddie's appreciation of the fine machine. When Eddie stepped back, Harry lowered the hood with care. "So, Eddie, you made detective in 1960?"

The retiree straightened his shoulders and stood proudly. "Sure did."

"Then you must have had a terrific familiarity with the Biltmore?"

"Best hotel in town. If those walls could talk, my job would have been easier. Come on in the house. I'll make you one of my signature martinis, and you can ask all the questions you want. Ever been to the Gallery Bar, off the main lobby for a cocktail? While Eddie chattered about the bar's space formerly being a hallway until the hotel's main entrance moved to Grand Avenue, they ambled up the sidewalk. Harry's gaze wandered to Lizbet's bungalow. He kept his tone casual. "Have you heard from Lizbet?"

Eddie spoke while he chilled martini glasses and vodka. "She called me this morning for a ride to work. She's putting on a brave front, but she wouldn't be human if she weren't a little shook up. Thank God you were here last night."

Eddie led Harry to the den, each carrying their martinis. Before they could toast, Harry's eye drew directly to a large bulletin board on one wall devoted to news clippings and crime photos. Harry gestured to the board with his cocktail glass. "What's all this?" He studied the newspaper clippings, and in his head, he saw a smoky jazz club, his fingers on a piano keyboard. Beautiful women and dangerous men.

Eddie shrugged. "Articles on the Black Dahlia murder. Once a detective, always a detective. It's still unsolved. Keeps my cognitive freeway moving."

Harry stirred the olive around in his drink. "Were you on the force when she was killed?"

"I was a rookie. Fresh out of the Academy. Which is not to say I didn't do my share on the case. They had every cop on the force looking for that butcher. A damn shame, we never found him. Somebody died knowing the truth."

"I always wanted to write about her, but every time I turn around, there's a new release with a new-fangled theory. I didn't feel like I could do the story justice."

"You know, they say the last night she was seen alive was January ninth at the Biltmore. I could have sworn I was one of the people who saw her. I was part of a motorcade escorting the Governor, and I saw this young woman, looked just like her. She couldn't get out of that car fast enough. She caught my attention because she looked up as we stopped. She looked right at me with those brilliant green eyes. Damn shame."

Harry spoke wistfully. "Her eyes connect right to her soul."

Eddie poked him with an elbow. "You talk like you knew her, son. You weren't even a spark in your daddy's eye back then." Eddie pointed to a series of scrapbooks. "I could bend your ear all night about Elizabeth Short, but that's an amateur interest. Let me show you what I've got on the heist."

♦ ♦ ♦ ♦

Harry collected the quirky stories he sought, closed his notebook, and rose to leave. As Eddie packed up the crime binder, the phone rang. "Excuse me a second." Eddie pressed the speaker button on the ringing phone. "Cartwright."

Harry heard both sides of the conversation clearly. "Eddie, this is Lizbet. I apologize for interrupting your night. But, I'm embarrassed to say I just can't make myself go outside alone. I need my briefcase to go over court testimony tomorrow, and it's in the trunk of my rental. If I stand at my living room window and use the clicker to pop the trunk, would you bring it to me?"

Harry gave Eddie a thumbs up and headed for the door.

♦ ♦ ♦ ♦

Lizbet was surprised to see a tall, lean man with dark hair head toward her rental car. When the porch light caught his profile, at once, she recognized Harry VanAlt. She opened the door before he even rang the bell. "Harry!" Lizbet pulled the belt tighter on her oldest chenille robe, wishing she'd dragged the pretty one her aunt sent her for her birthday out of the closet instead. She ran self-conscious fingers through her wet hair and sighed in defeat. "I didn't interrupt your interview, did I? I can't believe I did that twice in a row."

Harry waved away her concern. "I was just leaving when you called. You okay, Lizbet?" She shrugged. "No one would fault you for feeling a little spooked after last night."

Lizbet sighed. "I wish I could tell you all my training made me less vulnerable. I can say I realize the reaction I'm having is run of the mill post-traumatic stress. Doesn't make it any less uncomfortable." He passed the briefcase to her, and their hands brushed. "How many cold beers did you drink? Your hands are like ice."

15

He laughed. "Cold hands, warm heart, I guess." He placed a comforting hand on her shoulder. "Is there anything else I can do to help?"

She chuckled grimly. "Wanna spend the night on my couch, so I'm not alone?"

"I'm not doing anything tonight. Why not?"

Her mouth dropped open. "Are you serious?"

"Are you?"

"Kind of."

"Me too. I'll bet you didn't sleep much last night."

She drew in a deep breath. "You're right about that."

"And didn't I hear you have to testify tomorrow?"

"Yes. I was going to go over my notes in bed and then try to fall asleep."

He nodded once. "Bring me a pillow and blanket and go do your thing. I'm sure I can find something to read around here."

"Oh, but Harry, I can't ask you…"

"You're not asking me; I'm offering."

"I'm accepting, make yourself comfortable, have a drink, raid the fridge." She shook the briefcase. "I have to tend to this paperwork for a while. Don't be afraid to disturb me." She picked up the television remote and placed it on the end table. When she walked toward a back bedroom, she looked over her shoulder at him.

♦♦♦♦

Focus, lady. The whole point of asking for help was to get this paperwork done. But who can concentrate on work with a guy like Harry VanAlt in the living room? She touched her damp hair and winced at her reflection in the mirror. *I look a wretch.*

Lizbet slid the files out of the leather satchel and shrugged. *By the time I dry my hair, he'll be asleep. Focus, work. Now.* She read the same paragraph over three times with no comprehension.

I can't sit here with wet hair. She felt the drip slide down her spine. *It's going to look like I wet myself.*

Drying her hair upside down gave her the rosiest cheeks, and then she switched into the pretty robe and stuck her head around the corner to spy on her guest. Harry flipped through the DaVinci Code like a speed reading demon. *Is he even scanning the words? Maybe he's already reading it and searching for his place?*

When Lizbet walked out with two pillows and a fluffy blanket, she noticed his empty glass, ice melting with the dregs of the bourbon. "I don't know what time you usually go to bed. I don't want to put a foot in your schedule." She dropped the bedding on the hassock.

"Don't worry about me." He gave her a disarming smile that went all the way up to his eyes. "I'm a night owl. I get more done after midnight. How's your court prep coming?"

She shrugged and walked to the liquor cabinet. "I can't concentrate." She held up the bottle. "Want a refill? I'll join you."

"You look tired, Lizbet. Alcohol isn't going to help you sleep. Do you keep chamomile tea?"

She poured Harry another two fingers of bourbon, poured her own, sat slowly on the sofa and propped her head on the back of it. "I think I got a gift box of tea. But I'd have to boil water."

Harry closed the book, walked over to her, took the glass from her hand, and placed it on the coffee table. He pointed to the cushion beside her, and after her smile of consent he sat next to her. He patted his shoulder. "Put your head here. Just relax."

She gave him a curious smirk but did it. *He smells woodsy like cedar and sage.* It was a comforting scent. Her protector stretched his arm across the back of the sofa, and she burrowed into him with her feet drawn up. He comfortably sat back in the corner, creating a nest for her to relax against him.

"Do you enjoy campfires? Being outdoors where the crickets and the night birds sing? There is a certain music in the owls calling to each other. The forest settles in, and if you breath in rhythm with the breeze running through the pines, it's comforting."

She imagined him across a campfire, wearing flannel and denim, burning marshmallows with that wicked grin of his. She sank deeper into him. He pulled the blanket over her, and she closed her eyes.

◆◆◆◆

Without disturbing Lizbet, Harry picked up a National Geographic and read more than he ever wanted to know about Sargassum, the seaweed that floats freely through the Caribbean and supports its own microcosm. When his brain was full of brown seagrasses and tiny pufferfish who sought refuge there, he felt Lizbet jerk and felt the vibration of her low moan. *Nightmare.* He caught her shoulders. "Lizbet, you're having a nightmare, time to wake up." Her eyelids fluttered, and she dove deeper into his embrace. Her breathing settled, and he scented her relaxation.

If she stays in this position all night, she'll wake up cramped. He waited until she was deeply asleep again and carried to her bedroom. He laid her on one side of the bed and folded back the duvet to cover her. She turned into the bed's center and cuddled into the pillow.

Chapter Four

Harry slipped silently to sit in the bedroom chair in front of the window. A small table held a lamp, a scented candle, and a paperback copy of *The Alchemist. She certainly is a reader. There are books everywhere.* He imagined her lighting the lavender candle and sitting in the peace of this chintz explosion of a bedroom. *Ah, Lizbet, you are a riddle.*

The streetlight sent horizontal slats of illumination into the room. At the sound of a car hitting a pothole, he lifted one lath of the blind and watched the disappearing taillights haloed by fog on the empty street.

Lizbet stirred at the sound of the car. She rolled on her back and fought out of the duvet to stretch her hands above her head. A flash of ice crossed his spine like a goose walking over his grave. Only Harry's grave stood empty.

The chair was soft and smelled like Lizbet. Looking across the room, he noticed a solitary perfume bottle on the chest of drawers, not the usual woman's collection of fragrances. The classic Chanel N°5 bottle sat centered on a glass tray with her discarded watch and earrings. The now and forever floral fragrance toyed with his vampire's senses. When he ran both hands along the stuffed chair's arms it woke the sensual and enveloping fragrance of her femininity. *She sits naked in this chair.* Her pleasing tang filled his nostrils, and he shifted in the seat, increasing the titillation until the pressure became too much and he stood abruptly.

He was here for her comfort, not seduction. It was her spirit that called him, in the waves of her ebony hair across the pillow, in her delicate arms framing her face as her breasts rose and fell with mortal breath. Smoothing the front of his trousers, he gathered his resolve and left the bedroom. *Snap out of it.*

♦♦♦♦

Lizbet woke with a start before dawn. Her duvet cocooned her, and she felt for her clothes. Her robe was still loosely tied around her waist. *Harry. What a guy.* She heard noises from the kitchen, and when she peeked into the living room, the blanket and pillow sat folded precisely as she gave them to him. Harry's sport jacket hung on the hall tree hook.

Half concerned for her appearance, Lizbet slipped into her bathroom and made a few fussy touches. Hair combed, teeth brushed, with her robe retied, she followed the smell of coffee.

Harry turned from the stove, holding a spatula, a dishtowel tucked into the front of his trousers. "I figured you had an alarm set. What time is your court appearance?" He lowered the heat on the burner and covered the omelet pan.

Lizbet ran her hands through her hair and leaned against the doorframe. "I'd be willing to call out sick if I could convince you to stay with me."

Harry raised a brow, and his face broke out in the most endearing smile she'd ever seen. "You don't want to get mixed up with a guy like me. Superman never managed to keep a girlfriend."

"But Lois had Clark."

"I'm more complex than Clark. Trust me. You're better off going to court."

Am I not his type? Is he already involved? "Then, I have to be in court at ten."

His eyes pierced the distance between them, and then he winked. Lizbet startled with the slow burn of rejection in the pit of her belly. *Don't get discouraged. When you get a no, on the first try, try another approach. Don't box Harry VanAlt in.*

The coffee maker was full, and he'd pulled her favorite coffee cup, the latte mug. "Can I get you a cup? All this work, aren't you eating?" She moved around the small kitchen to the coffee pot and poured her cup. She was amazed at his grace at flipping the omelet onto a plate.

"I have a breakfast meeting with a colleague; I hope I put the right stuff together. You had ham, spinach, and some cheese." He threw the dishtowel over his forearm and balanced the plate on his fingertips. "Have a seat; I'll bring your English muffin over in a snap." He lowered the muffin in the toaster and moved to the fridge. While he was bent into the refrigerator, she appreciated the sight of his fine ass. She sat frozen over her coffee cup. "Apple butter or butter or both?" Her gaze traveled down the backs of his legs to his stocking feet. He wore taupe and blue argyle socks. "Both?" His repeated word snapped her out of her reverie.

"Both." As in, he had to have the most exquisite buttocks she'd seen in her kitchen in many a day. Not that her kitchen was a parade ground for well-built buttocks. "You're not even having coffee, after all your work?"

He placed the hobnail butter dish and the jar of apple butter on the table and held out his hands, his fingers, long and graceful. "Coffee gives me the jitters, can't drink it. See these hands, steady as a surgeon." Yes, and she wondered what else he could do with those hands? "Do you feel safe enough for me to leave in a few?" His attention traveled to the kitchen window, and the indigo sky turning orange.

Lizbet realized her jaw hung open, and she quickly swallowed a gulp of coffee. She nodded and put down her cup. "I've already taken up your time, Harry. I can't thank you enough. Now, you absolutely have to let me cook a meal for you."

Harry carried the toasted muffin on a saucer and took the seat across from her. When he smiled an infectious smile, his elbows on the table, she noticed his handsomely fashioned dress shirt. *Was it bespoke*? Both sleeves crisply folded back twice revealed well-defined forearms. But she was staring, and she blinked hard and buttered her English muffin. *How did he sleep in those clothes?*

"That would be very kind of you. I won't stand on tradition. I'll leave my number, and you call me when you get your car ironed out, and your life calms down." Harry stretched his long legs out to the side of the table and sat back in the chair. Now she noticed his hands and the yellow gold monogram ring on his left hand. *Nice to see he isn't married, I hope.* The ring had the patina of jewelry worn daily for decades. *His father's?* He pulled out his wallet, produced a business card, and slid it across the table.

Lizbet swallowed her bite of exceptional omelet and wiped her hands with her napkin. *His card is classy, a heavyweight, thermographed card stock like my college graduation announcements. Just his name, Harrison VanAlt, phone number, and email.* "So this means, good morning and see you real soon?"

Harry drew back his wildly colored stockinged feet and shrugged. "Have to say good-bye, if I'm going to see you again." Lizbet felt an instant's squeezing disappointment. "I'd be a hell of a long term house guest." He scratched at his morning scruff. "I use a lot of ice." He stood and stretched, retucked the bit of a shirttail that slipped from his trim trousers and placed a cool hand on her shoulder. "You don't have to walk me out, but call me if you need a sentry."

"Oh, Harry, at least let me see you to the door." She chewed, swallowed, and felt his hand linger. Their gazes met, and she stayed seated. His head bowed closer, and before he could retreat, her lips locked on his. His cool lips kissed her back. And what started as good-bye became an invitation of unknown promise.

She rose, caught her footing, and fervently pressed against his lean, muscular form. His arms embraced her and held her even closer. When they broke the kiss, they were both wide-eyed. She fell back, and his hands splayed against her back caught her. *He has the most haunting blue-green eyes.* "Thanks, Harry, for everything." She whispered.

They slipped out of their embrace, and he cupped her shoulders, admonishing her in a humorous tone. "Now, sit there and eat everything I slaved to cook."

As the door clicked and she heard the automatic lock, she sighed. *They aren't making them like Harry anymore.*

Chapter Five

The parking garage stood in broad levels, minimizing the available natural light, creating an ominous flickering fluorescent mood. As an officer of the court, Lizbet had a reserved parking space near the elevators. She waited briefly in the car, wishing other people would join her on her walk inside. *When will this anxiety end?*

A woman in a sharp dark suit locked her black Mercedes and shouldered her briefcase. She walked purposefully, eyes straight ahead, heels clicking the concrete. When Lizbet saw her comportment in a vulnerable space, she admired the woman's intense posture and air of command. *She must be a judge.* Lizbet got out of her car and hurried to catch up to the woman to share an elevator.

The lady wore her ebony hair slicked into a tight bun on the top of her head. When she hesitated to check her watch, Lizbet heard the scuffle of sneakered feet. A scruffy man, a real tweaker, bolted toward the judge before Lizbet could yell. Lizbet froze beside a parked car and held her breath. Her own assault played through her mind in flickering scenes. The tweaker jogged, head down, and stiff-armed the woman to yank her briefcase off her shoulder.

With unreal speed, the 'judge' slipped away from the thug. She bent at the knees and dropped her head. Within a flash, she yanked the man's shirt collar, rolled into him, and tossed him over her shoulder to the concrete. Her speed created such a force when the man hit the ground; his shoulder appeared deformed.

The space filled with a hell of a shriek and a man's guttural cry. Lizbet, cell phone in hand, expected bloodshed. The thug lay on the ground; his shoulder dislocated. He cried out. "Demon, be gone," and held up an ornate crucifix from around his neck.

Despite wearing high heels, the woman in the business suit maintained her defensive martial arts pose as she grabbed her bag strap out of the man's impotent hand. When her dark head rose and swiveled to survey her surroundings, Lizbet noticed the woman's opalescent eyes and pale veined complexion as the lady's tongue swept over exceptionally long canine teeth.

Still on his back, with his crucifix held as high as the chain allowed, he crabbed away from her with his feet. "Devil, the power of God, compels you."

With a disparaging glare, the woman kicked at his hand holding the crucifix, and the gold religious symbol arced several aisles away.

Lizbet gasped, and the woman froze. Now observed, the woman dropped her head and smoothed her stray hair back into her updo. When Lizbet next made eye contact, the woman's eyes were once again doe-eyed brown. Her lipstick was perfect, and her manner composed. Lizbet made her way forward on shaky limbs. "Are you alright?" Her voice shook almost as badly as her hands.

"Perfectly fine, thank-you." The dark-haired woman's voice was genteel with a bayou lilt. "I expect we need to call the police."

Lizbet dialed twice before she could stop shaking enough to connect the numbers. "I'm sorry, I usually don't react so fearfully." Within seconds several officers poured from the elevator, and the hapless thief was placed in an ambulance. The mystery woman and Lizbet were led to a conference room inside the courthouse.

♦♦♦♦

Lizbet smiled at the young officer who looked down on her with professional detachment. "I'm due to testify at ten." She checked her watch; it was nine-thirty. "Can I do the police report after the trial?" The officer nodded.

The woman in black, who identified herself as Venus Aquillius, remained cold as marble. Unblinking, she sat with delicate hands folded on the table before her. Not one hair out of place, now. She turned concerned brown eyes Lizbet's way. "Are you sure you're quite alright, my dear?"

Lizbet blushed with embarrassment and waited for the officer to leave before she spoke. "Please forgive me. I feel ridiculous. You see, I was attacked by a man in a cab two nights ago. He tried to kill me and if a stranger hadn't happened by... I wish I could have reacted as you have."

The woman's bayou accent comforted Lizbet. "My daddy always believed a woman needs to know how to defend herself. I'm fortunate, I've had several opportunities to exercise my defense skills. After a while, it becomes second nature. Nor was this creature much of a challenge."

Lizbet recognized how Venus's eyes resembled her attacker's. Harry's eyes were the same, but that could have been a trick of the light. Still, Lizbet, wondered which of them was 'the creature'. Lizbet sipped at the glass of water the woman poured out and handed to her. "I'll be enrolling in a self-defense class as soon as I can get myself together a little more…"

"My dear, it's clear you've suffered quite a trauma. Believe it or not, I've worked with many women who've endured similar circumstances. You do whatever you need to do to help yourself feel safe again. But I assure you, that thief never touched me, nor will he cause me a moment's concern."

◆◆◆◆

Lizbet sought the bright lights and the scramble of people in the grocery store. Her workday was shorter than usual, and if she was going to burrow inside her home, she needed food to binge on. She pushed the cart through the wine department and picked up a trio of Malbec wines from different vintners.

She ended up in the bakery, asking what pastry went best with fruity red wines. The teenaged clerk gave her a look of pure confusion, but the woman's pale blue eyes unnerved her to the point that she did not pursue the question and walked away.

If only she could walk away from her memories as effortlessly. Lizbet shivered at the translucency of Venus's eyes. Their luminosity brought back the image of her terrifying attacker. His stench, his icy breath, his unbreakable hold on her gave her the shivers. Standing in the freezer aisle, she wrapped her arms around her waist and shivered.

An older woman pushed by and chuckled. "One of these days, you'll stand in the frozen food section just to catch a break from the hot flashes."

Yeah, they were cool, they were all unusually cool. Her attacker, Harry, and the oddly composed Venus. Lizbet had managed to talk herself out of her own observations the night of the attack. They couldn't have just been men with icy white eyes, translucent skin, and super strength. These misconceptions were understandably brought on by the stress. So how did she explain Venus? She decked a guy without breaking a nail in a pencil skirt and high heels. Where had she told the officer she worked? Consort Group International? That was a vague name. Lizbet had accused Harry of being a super-soldier. What if Consort Group dabbled in genetic engineering? Because what could explain the specific similarities, she'd seen in these three people?

Lizbet grabbed premade salads and two frozen pizzas, then headed home to bar the door, turn on all the lights and do a little Yahoo research.

Chapter Six

Harry pulled the long, lean LaSabre into his parking space in the underground garage and spun the keyring on his index finger. He couldn't get her touch and taste out of his mind. That kiss ignited something hidden within him. Something dangerous. He had to leave. He'd ask for the keys to Matt's cabin at Big Bear and head up there to write. Nice place, Big Bear. Lots of vampires enjoyed seclusion in the cool mountains and lakes. Lots of willing mortal donors, too.

Harry poured a tumbler of bagged blood. Not his favorite meal. It was filling, but not satisfying. He wore Lizbet's scent, and he regretted having to shower it away. If he ever loved her the way he wanted to, his scent would be a beacon to the undead brethren, "Lay off, she's mine."

He disrobed, showered, and sought the peace of his mausoleum.

♦♦♦♦

That evening, unconsciously spinning his keyring on his index finger, Harry paced the reception office of Consort Group International. Matt's secretary covered her headphone mouthpiece and waved Harry in. "He's back there. He knows you're coming."

Harry strolled into Matt's office, working to look casual, but failed as he scented Lizbet on Venus. Matt looked up from the signed courthouse papers. "Where have you two been?" He tapped his nose. "I scent a mortal in common. In fact, a very vulnerable mortal."

Venus's brow rose, and she pulled the second chair in front of Matt's desk closer. "Have a seat, Harry. Tell me about her."

Venus Aquillius, the Corporate Secretary for Consort Group International, had been involved with The Gaoler from day one. She and the three principal men had agreed to combine their skills and begin the company after the vampires lost their businesses to arson. Vampires Rick Hiatt and Matt Brenner conceived the business model of vamps thrilling to feed. Venus was the expert in domination and submission, which fit perfectly in the new feeding paradigm. Dragon Shifter Adam Lachlan was the real-estate rainmaker who brought the vampires to their present Miracle Mile location.

Harry pocketed his keys and sat heavily in the chair. He felt intense scrutiny as he sat back and crossed his foot onto his knee. "Lizbet Mitchell?"

Venus leaned her elbow on her chair arm and rolled her eyes. "Don't tell me, let me guess. You were the rescuer. But why is her scent so strong on you this morning?"

Matt pushed back his chair and buried his face in one hand.

Harry spilled. "You told me not to do it. I went back out for Cartwright's interview. She was too spooked to go back out to her car, I volunteered, and I just couldn't leave her. She was hurting."

Matt nodded. "A huh. Did you call the Responders?"

Harry hung his head. "Why bother them when I could stay and make her feel safe? How would she feel safe with strangers she can't place from a mortal organization? How would I explain them to her?"

Venus gave a low laugh. "You know, Harry, this would not be the first time Responders have dealt with mortals." Venus turned to Matt. "The woman was in the garage this morning when I was attacked. From the look on her face, I think she's beginning to put the numbers together. You probably won't like the math."

Matt hung back his head as his hand moved from Venus to Harry. "Within seventy-two hours, this mortal has had three interactions with the undead. All three vamped out." He glanced at Harry. "If she's as bright as you say, she'll figure it out soon if she hasn't already."

"That's why I'm here." Harry's lips straightened. "I'd like the keys to your place in Big Bear. I've got a book to write, and even at vamp speed, I wouldn't be able to avoid her here. Time for me to disappear until she forgets about me."

Matt got up from his chair and went to a painting on the wall, swinging the frame out he pulled a ring of keys from a hidden rack and closed it. Holding the keys back from Harry, Matt chided him. "She's seen you twice; now it's time to be a figment of her imagination. Go write a best-seller. Leave today. And by the way, keep that gold monstrosity in the garage. You are far too visible in that thing. There's a conservative Mercedes sedan waiting for you. Drive that while you're up there."

Harry took the keys along with the tongue lashing. "But, Dad, I love to drop the top."

Venus rolled her eyes at both of them as Matt went back to his chair. "Harry, don't make the Responders drop your top."

♦♦♦♦

Lizbet cleared her calendar for the rest of the week. She dug out her yoga clothes and turned on all the exterior lights. Locking every window and door, she opened a bottle of Malbec and popped a pizza into the oven. Snacking on a Greek salad, she booted up her computer. She entered the keywords, white eyes, translucent skin, fangs, cold to the touch, and let America Online sweep her into a world that posed more questions than it answered. She got responses from WebMD about signs of death. She found book listings for horror and fiction going back to 1764. But the most intriguing reference was 'traits of a vampire'. That didn't begin to slake her thirst for more knowledge.

The salad was an afterthought. The pizza was half-eaten, and she poured the third glass of wine by the time she discovered a chat room on the thirty-third page of her search. It had the bizarre name, 'My Night with a Vampire'. Vampire? *It was too fantastic to be possible, but… Vampire?* She had denied what she'd seen from her attacker and Harry, put it down to the trauma of the moment. Then, she saw it again this morning with Venus. *What could this mean? Have I developed some kind of isolated psychosis?* That didn't seem likely. She wasn't delusional in any other area of her life.

Do I have vision problems? Maybe some aberrant vision in low light? She'd seen other people in low light since it happened. They didn't have opalescent eyes and fangs.

What does Occam's Razor say? The simplest explanation is usually correct. Her attacker, Harry, and Venus are vampires.

So, this discussion board was for people to chat about their night with a vampire. It was initially a bland site that required registration to login into their chat boards -- no tantalizing art, nothing that hinted at the romance of Dracula.

Lizbet pulled up the registration page, ready to join. The page cheerfully greeted new registrants with 'Welcome to The Gaoler. Please provide your Donor Number'.

Gaoler? Donor number?

Lizbet reconfirmed the definition of gaoler, someone who guards prisoners. *Prisoners?* Scrolling down, down, down the list of other responses she found, The Gaoler with a Wilshire Boulevard address. She popped onto their page and found an austere, black, and white website that appeared more like an error message than a web address. *Damn. I thought I had something. Where did Venus work? Consort Group?*

Typing into the search bar, she found Consort Group International, an entertainment and resort company. Their lavish offices were established in London, Berlin, Shanghai, Rome, Paris, Amsterdam, as well as Los Angeles, New York, and New Orleans.

Well, Venus did look like a showgirl. She was a knockout. It doesn't sound like they'd be making super soldiers. The Los Angeles location was on the Miracle Mile on Wilshire. She drummed her pen on the desk, and her eye caught Harry's business card over a folded arts section of the newspaper. There was a book signing for his latest offering tonight at …The Bridge. 'Los Angeles's premier spot for jazz, cocktails and small plate dining'. Her eyes rounded; it was the same Wilshire Boulevard address as Consort Group. Lizbet was always suspicious of too much coincidence.

She'd dress to the nines, drop her keys with the valet, and sprint from her car to the front door. It would push her comfort zone, but to get answers, she would handle it.

The front elevation of the Consort Group International building was a ninety-year-old Italianate edifice. The plaque on the entry stated they opened as the supper club, The Phoenix, September 1, 1923. Now the ornate dining rooms were upscale clothing, jewelry, and luggage shops. Original photos were posted from place to place, celebrating singers and bands who entertained while tony guests enjoyed candlelit dancing and dining.

To the left of the entrance was The Bridge. Deep blue tones of velvet and suede dominated the walls and furniture. Relaxing indigo leather bar stools dotted the curved bar—people clustered in groups enjoying their fanciful drinks. Dynamic art deco sconces illuminated gold etched wall coverings and cast a candlelit glow that softened many a complexion.

To the left, a table and standing sign announced M. C. Westmacott, Best Selling Crime Author, The Bikini Murders. Shiny large hardback books were stacked by fours in front of an attractive older gentleman wearing tweed and a bow tie

Bronze Art Deco gates stood open at the bar's entrance. The host at the podium greeted her in Gatsby's style. "Good evening." Along with a discrete, "Are you dining alone tonight?"

Lizbet looked around the podium for Harry. "Yes. I'm here for the book signing, but I thought I dine first. When will Mr. Westmacott arrive?" The maître de bowed stiffly. "Why, that's Mr. Westmacott with the bow tie."

Lizbet squinted at the older guy. "I think I'm looking for his son, Harry VanAlt."

The stiff host picked up a menu and gestured. "This way, madam."

Lizbet stepped behind him. "Can you seat me with a view of his table?"

He bowed crisply again. "As you wish."

♦♦♦♦

After a day of gnoshing at home, she picked at stuffed mushrooms as people moved through, snapping photos and getting their books signed by this imposter. She purposely waited to be the last person in line. She stepped up authoritatively. "You're not M.C. Westmacott."

He gave her a superior look down his nose. "I beg your pardon."

"I said, you're not M.C. Westmacott. I know Harry VanAlt. Who are you, and where is Harry?"

The man with the clipped speech looked to the left and right and behind Lizbet. As she fumed, his brow arched, and he stuttered a reply. "I don't know what you're talking about."

31

Lizbet noted the man displayed every sign of a liar. She pulled her city attorney's office I.D. out of her bag. "I'm talking about I know Harry VanAlt, this is his pen name, and this is his book. What I don't know is who you are or why you're impersonating him." She bent nose to nose with the man. "I will find out even if I have to call the police."

The nervous man startled. "The police? Wait a minute. I'm an actor. I've played this role for Mr. VanAlt at the launch of every book."

Lizbet stood her ground. "Where is Harry?"

The impersonator fumbled in his pocket. "I have no idea; his agent hired me for this gig. This is his agent's card. I'm sure she could take a message. Please don't call the police. I'm on social security. This gig means a lot to me."

She snatched the card from his hand. "Okay, this will be our secret. And I'll talk to his agent."

Chapter Seven

Spitting mad, she turned and dug for her valet ticket as she clipped out of the bar. At this hour, the lobby was empty. Before she exited the building, she stopped and contemplated her next move. The elevator dinged, and a porter pushed a cart with a couple of suitcases, two copier paper boxes, and a large stainless steel cooler. The porter made a direct line for the dark sedan parked under the porte-cochere. Her gaze followed the porter, nearly missing Harry walking behind, reading his Blackberry.

She stood, fists at her waist. "Harry." Her sharp tone echoed off the terrazzo floor and stone walls.

He turned and looked like he'd been caught pants down. "Lizbet? What are you doing here?"

"I came to get M.C. Westmacott's autograph, but when I saw it was your Grampa, I passed."

"Oh, yeah…" He scratched at the back of his neck. "I guess you met Virgil. He's a big fan, knows my books inside and out. Loves to talk plots and characters. The fans love him…" He petered out, watching her brows connect over slitted eyes. She watched the porter stand beside the sedan door, watching them.

"You goin' somewhere?"

"I, I, have a place… where I write. I concentrate better there."

Lizbet made a step closer to him and whispered. "I have some questions for you, and I'm afraid they won't wait till you publish that next bestseller."

Harry found himself leaning back. "Oh? I'll ask the driver to wait. We can catch a drink next door." He gestured back to The Bridge.

Lizbet waved him off. "I have confidential questions. You *will* want more privacy." *Unless this building is full of vampires.*

Harry shuffled from foot to foot, bowed his head, drew his thumb over his bottom lip, and then winced. "I live upstairs." He offered lamely.

"Go ahead, tell the driver to park it." *I'm about to follow a vampire into his apartment.*

♦♦♦♦

The elevator door opened on the twenty-eighth floor. *I feel like I'm being sent out to pick a switch.* Harry ran a hand through his hair and bit his top lip as he entered the code to his door lock. *Bloody glasses washed? Trash emptied? Is the mausoleum door closed or wide open?*

Lizbet passed him through the doorway, walked to the kitchen, opened the fridge, shook her head, and leaned on the island. "Harry, are you a vampire?"

He unconsciously rubbed his palms on his backside to warm his hands. "Why would you think that?"

"I told you that night, I saw your eyes, I saw your skin, and I saw his. I also felt his fangs." She exposed her neck and pointed to the healed scratches.

Harry lowered his voice and spoke in his most reasonable tone. "Lizbet…"

She covered her eyes dramatically. "I watched Bela Lugosi mesmerize his prey. That's not happening with me. Don't step closer until you tell me the truth."

Harry spun away on his heel to hide his smile. Now, his hands were on his hips, head down and shaking he almost broke into a laugh. "I think I have more style than old Bela."

"You admit it then." She pointed an accusing finger.

"You're a reasonable woman. You know there no such thing as animated undead."

She crossed her arms over her breasts and screwed up her face at the term. "Animated undead? Who does your PR?" She snorted. "Animated undead. Three days ago, I would have said there's no such thing. Until this morning, I would have said it was a fluke. Today after seeing Venus in action, all bets are off."

Harry struck a casual pose, but his voice tightened. "You know Venus?"

"I watched her pull a man's arm out of the socket because he grabbed her briefcase strap." She shook her head for emphasis. "The guy pulled his crucifix out and started an exorcism right there. She kicked that crucifix across three aisles of cars. Didn't break a nail."

"Venus has --"

"Of course, that account does not include the white eyes, pale skin, and fangs I saw until she …" Lizbet made a circular motion around her face with her finger. "Morphed back, changed back, whatever you call it."

He held up his hands in surrender. "Have a seat, Lizbet. You got me." Her anger spent, Lizbet's defiance deflated as he gestured her into a seat. "Now that you know, what are you going to do?"

Lizbet looked at him blankly. "Do? What do you mean?"

"I mean, the fact that you encountered three members of the undead family in flagrante within three days is a million to one thing. You should buy a lottery ticket. Many people go their entire lives without finding a fang."

"One of your family tried to kill me."

Harry pinched the bridge of his nose in distress. "I apologize for that. Not all of us are house-broken. That guy was a rogue. He's been found and put down."

"Put down?" She squeaked. "Like a rabid dog?"

"Vampire justice moves faster than mortal justice. We have to protect our secrecy."

She gestured widely. "How can you maintain secrecy when an entire community of vampires live among us?"

"We live among you, but we're segregated."

"So do the Amish, but they don't break out and kill people."

"You've got statistics on that?" He asked. "Because vampires follow a strict code. We're bound by a higher court where deviants are dealt with quickly."

"Like the bogus taxi driver?"

"Yes. Now one of those rulings is we don't cultivate relationships with mortals."

"Oh, you don't play with your food?"

Harry chuckled and planted his hands on his hips as he paced the length of his glass doors. "We have willing donors who are compensated for their blood. It's a business arrangement, not personal. And right now, I've told you more than you need to know to be a nice mortal acquaintance. Vamp-mortal relationships never go deeper than that."

She bounced up from the sofa and followed his pacing. "But you kissed me this morning."

"More correctly, you kissed me." His voice was deep and a degree or two unsteady.

"I didn't notice you fighting me off. Those were your arms around me, weren't they?"

Harry sighed deeply. "Lizbet, I never said vamps weren't ever attracted to mortals. We simply don't act on the attraction. You're a beautiful woman in the best years of your life. You're a professional; you're warm and engaging…"

"Yeah, thanks for the squeal of approval, I'll use that when I fill out my Match.com profile."

He wiped his face with both hands and hung his head. "Look, what I'm trying to say is, I'm sorry you ran into a rogue vamp. I like you, and I wanted to help you over a rough patch. It can never go further than that."

"I see." She shrank back from him and stared out into the light dotted night of Los Angeles.

"Forget what happened in the taxi, that was a fluke. Just relegate the last three days to a fever dream." He walked to his front door and watched as she pressed close to the floor to ceiling window and spread her hands on the glass. She looked down twenty-eight floors and across the vista of his apartment's view. Then she stepped back, dropped her head, and followed him to the door.

"So, a relationship between us would be like the Montagues and the Capulets?" Her posture straightened; her dark head held high.

He sucked in a breath between his teeth, and his brow rose. "More like the bloody Hatfield's and the McCoy's. Have a good life, Lizbet."

He watched the elevator doors close from his doorstep. She was gone.

Chapter Eight

Lizbet clutched the steering wheel like Cruella Deville on a puppy run. Her conversation took both sides of the debate. "So how did you become a vampire? How old are you? When did it happen? Why can't we be friends? We can't. Have a nice life, Lizbet."

How does vampirism affect the ego? How does it affect the hierarchy of needs? Are vampires basic mortals who live forever and drink blood? Or is there more? What is the psychological makeup of a vampire? The Paradigm of Vampirism. Now that would be a great doctoral dissertation. A desire bloomed in her to learn more about homo sanguis.

♦♦♦♦

Tuesday, January 28th, 2003

The host at The Bridge led Lizbet to what she'd come to consider *her table.* The small round table with two plush chairs wedged in the corner gave her a view of everyone coming and going in this vast indigo room. She could watch people parallel to her in the mirror behind the long curving bar.

She paid particular attention to the heavy drinkers. She watched people arrive in groups and pair off and leave. She watched couples meeting other couples. But she was most curious about those who never ate. These beautiful people fairly glowed in the golden light. When her ice was melted, and she was done stirring the Old Fashioned, she'd raise her head, and the server took away the watery drink and replaced it with a fresh one. No questions asked. Each night, she paid cash and left by ten-thirty.

The bar manager appeared before her tonight, and she looked past him as he towered over her. He harrumphed and got her attention. "Martin, the bartender would like to know if there's something wrong with your drinks? You order them and keep them till they melt and then order another one. You're here from around six until ten-thirty, you nurse two drinks and leave. You're more dependable than some of my employees."

Lizbet raised a brow. "I thought all I had to do to enjoy this ambiance is to pay for my drinks."

"It's also implied you might enjoy those drinks. Unfortunately, if you've come for the jazz, our trio performs Thursday through Sunday."

She smiled. "Yes, I've heard them. Very nice."

"Are you hungry, may I send over a variety of our small plates?"

"I've eaten. Thank you." She looked around him as another trio of boisterous drinkers left the bar. She lowered her voice, almost to a whisper. "Have you heard of a club in this building called The Gaoler?"

♦♦♦♦

Now Lizbet held the fresh Old Fashioned to her lips, enjoying the tang of the bitters and the citrus of the fresh-cut orange on the small cocktail pick. In the subdued chatter of the large room, as a striking-looking man filtered between the close tables, heads nodded, and he waved like a celebrity. The tall man in the tailored suit drew closer, his whiskey-colored eyes meeting her gaze. All she could do was hide behind the glass and adjust her jaw as he drew nearer.

If Harry was handsome, this guy owned the room. As he strode, he unbuttoned his suit coat. Then he presented himself directly before her, his hands deep in the pockets of his pleated trousers as he rocked on the balls of his John Lobb loafers. A wry smile invaded his perfect features, and his grin drove directly to the pit of her stomach.

"Good evening, Ms. Mitchell. I understand you've made an inquiry about The Gaoler?"

The drinkers in the room went out of their way to not be caught watching. "I did, and you are?" She put down the drink and folded her hands before her on the table.

The man looked around the room as if his gaze could dispel their audience. Folks went back to their conversations. *Wow. Okay.*

His fingers combed through the errant hair that had fallen over his forehead, and he stood even taller if that was possible. "Rick Hiatt, at your service."

Her shoulders shook in subdued response. "What services would that include?"

"You asked about my club. The Gaoler?"

Then her look grew challenging. "Please, have a seat."

He stood there, nostrils flaring, his brow rising higher than hers. "This is not the place for that discussion."

"Well, we're not going to have this discussion anywhere else."

He took an appraising stance. His chin rested on his thumb and fingers as he buried a chuckle. "Do you always top from the bottom?"

"I could be a Domme for all you know, but I don't play those games. My communication is straightforward."

Rick took a casual stance, his hands resting on his slim hips. "Then why would you be interested in The Goaler?"

"I'm a psychologist. I'm interested in your clientele."

Rick pulled out the chair and sat leaning toward her, speaking softly. "The activities of The Gaoler are confidential. Dr. Bonner studied our clientele for Dom/sub interactions for use in game theory years ago. You could look him up."

"What's the breakdown of your clientele? Is it seventy/thirty or sixty/forty?" Rick's gaze narrowed. "Mortals versus vampires?"

He slapped his palms on his thighs and stood. "This is not the place for that discussion."

"Then, I guess this discussion is over. Because I told you before, I'm not leaving with you."

Rick bowed slightly, his hand over his undead heart. "You wound me, Ms. Mitchell. I strive to comport myself as a gentleman. I will never besmirch your honor."

Lizbet bowed her head regally. "It's Dr. Mitchell, and it's not my honor I'm worried about."

"Indeed, then what is troubling you?"

"My life --" Lizbet was interrupted when she saw a tall silhouette approaching. When the leather-clad woman stood before them, she recognized Venus.

"I regret having to interrupt you, Rick, your presence is required in the demonstration room."

Lizbet stood. "Venus, you look so different. I didn't realize how long your hair was." The woman in four-inch spiked heels wore her hair in a high braid. The end brushed at her trim waist.

"Good evening, Dr. Mitchell." Her greeting was icy.

Rick raised a brow. "Venus, I didn't know you two were acquainted. I was trying to convince *Dr.* Mitchell to accompany me to The Gaoler. She has some questions."

"I'm not sure she'd be the right fit." Venus's gaze trailed between Lizbet and Rick. When her hand fell on Rick's shoulder, she leaned closer, and her lips went to Rick's ear. Those red lips moved without sound.

Lizbet gathered her handbag. "Has no one taught you, it's rude to whisper in public?"

Eye to eye, Venus purred. "You wouldn't want to hear what I was saying."

Rick rose and buttoned his jacket. "Ladies, please allow me to escort you below." Lizbet drew her purse closer, straightened her shoulders, and nodded assent.

♦♦♦♦

Rick led them to a bank of elevators and approached the last one, which required a key. Before he keyed the car, Venus took her usual obstinate pose.

"You have a problem, dear?" Rick queried casually for the benefit of the mortal in their presence.

Venus spoke in subtones, "Look, Rick, I know I made an egregious error to go off in the parking garage. Stake me for forty-eight hours, but don't take her down there."

Rick's brow rose as he minimalized his lip's movement. "Was it chance that she saw three vamps in three days? Does she look like a tattletale? Some people are destined to be acquainted with the undead."

Venus lowered her gaze as she shook her head, her braid swooshed with her negative response.

♦♦♦♦

The elevator door opened, and the trio entered. A press of the button marked Consort started the car on its descent. As the overhead numbers

40

descended past Basement, Rick touched his hand to a security pad. Directly, the lights dimmed to a deep red glow. The temperature dropped precipitously, and the canned elevator Muzak converted to the thrumming of a human heartbeat that reverberated against the walls and all through Lizbet. She worked to disguise her shudder; however, Rick and Venus shared a look between them. *Did their lips move in some silent amusement?*

The elevator doors opened with a discrete swoosh, admitting them to the hallway of many doors. Lizbet combed her gaze over the crimson leather wallpaper and thick, black carpet. The lights were muted, meant to mimic flickering carriage lanterns. *Who was their designer? Jack, the Ripper.*

"Venus, would you escort Dr. Mitchell to my office while I handle the dustup in the demonstration room?"

Venus nodded, and Lizbet found herself led past high and wide solid doors. The vibes from the different doors collided in her psyche. She'd read of the BDSM fetish, but never been this close. It was like passing a train wreck. She wanted to watch, but should she? She snuck a look at Venus, who marched onward with a superior smirk on her face. When they were in the hallway, Lizbet noticed the crop in a holster lashed to her thigh. Venus's hand rested on the handle like you would caress a kitten. Lizbet almost ran into Venus's back when she stopped in front of a door and keyed a code at the knob.

The office was Art deco elegance. A large partner's desk dominated the room with two entirely different styles of order. Venus pulled a club chair closer to adjoin Rick's desk. Lizbet circled the exotic chair before she sat on the ivory leather seat. She sat erect, fighting the chair's invitation to sink into the comfort and rest her arms on the wide, shiny laminated wood. Lizbet's inspection of the sumptuously decorated room was interrupted by Venus.

"Would you like some coffee, Dr. Mitchell?" Venus's offer was incongruous with the severe black leather outfit and crop.

Lizbet's answer was interrupted by the opening of the door. Rick strode in, large and in charge. His gaze passed from Venus to Lizbet, and his index finger pointed between them. "Did she offer you coffee?" He sat back in his chair and chuckled. "Vampire or not, she loves the espresso machine. Humor her; take an espresso." Lizbet nodded, and Venus was gone. Rick watched Lizbet examine the photos on the wall, the art, and the sculpture until Venus returned with a steaming espresso. Then Venus left, leaving Lizbet with the tiny cup and saucer and Rick Hiatt.

"Oh, you don't have to drink it." He pushed a coaster toward her side of the desk.

Lizbet was speechless. "I… I… like… espresso."

Rick sat back in the leather desk chair and picked up an ornate fountain pen. He rolled it between his thumb and fingers like a cigar. "What prompted your sudden interest in vampires, Dr. Mitchell? I say sudden because I would have heard about you before."

"About a month ago, I was attacked in a taxi outside my home. Strangely enough, another vampire saw this creature, and he yanked a door off its hinge and sent the guy packing."

Rick's chuckle resonated deep within his chest. "Oh, you're the one."

"Yes, I am. But it didn't end there. Within seventy-two hours, I watched Venus take down a thug in the courthouse parking garage." Lizbet's hands framed her face. "Her eyes, her complexion, her fangs… were all out for me to see."

Rick's chair bobbed a few times while they stared each other down. He looked to the ceiling, and then his lips drew a straight line. He bit his bottom lip momentarily, and then his grin replaced his austere expression. "Harry stayed at your place, didn't he?"

"What does that have to do with it?"

Rick dropped his feet to the floor, and he leaned across his desk, hands folded. "You like him. He's fascinating; he generates the energy that feeds your vibe."

Lizbet's mouth hung open. "What?" She blushed furiously and put down her espresso. A rise of heat flew up her spine and she fell back into the comfort of the chair.

"So, you decided to study us, but you don't want to feed us, I assume you don't want to become one of us. All because of Harry?"

Lizbet found herself mesmerized by the bronze statue on a pedestal, behind Rick. Two angels, nude in an embrace. The name Harry snapped her back to reality. "I… I…"

Rick folded his arms on his blotter and took a more casual pose. "You know, Lizbet, there are two philosophies in the vampire family. One, mortals are for food and nothing else. The other is, we were once mortals, so why can't we enjoy them?" Her emerald-eyed gaze widened at his jovial presentation. "We live for impossibly long lifetimes. When the first man was made, it was said, it was not good to be alone. I've been alone far too long. But if you think marriage vows of 'till death do us part' are damning, just consider being together for eternity."

"Humph."

"You should probably also know; Harry sometimes comes here for a bite or blood on tap. But he doesn't partake of the other activities."

"Why would you tell me that?"

"Because Harry is just a guy with different dietary needs…"

Lizbet held up a halting hand. "What, ten minutes ago, you were a corporate looking mogul stalking me in a bar. Now you're Dolly Levi?" Then Lizbet pointed. "Did you say blood on tap? Like you put a spigot in the watermelon on the 4th of July?"

Rick comically screwed his smirk. "You mortals are sort of twisted. No, we do it blood bank style. God's nightgown. What kind of books are you reading?" He sat back, reclaiming his corporate posture, calling this meeting again to order. "Thanks for stopping by Dr. Mitchell. If there's nothing further…" He stood, and Lizbet, at a loss for words, followed. "May I ask your professional courtesy of complete confidentiality?" He walked around the desk and placed her hand inside his elbow. She nodded mutely. "May I walk you out?" She nodded again. They rode the elevator back to reality, and when they walked into the lobby, she heard the raucous sound of the late-night drinkers from The Bridge. "Do you have a valet ticket?" He extended his hand for it, and they waited together at the curb. When her car was delivered, he got her settled and as he closed the door, he winked. "Confidentiality?"

Lizbet nodded. "Of course." She fumbled with the ignition and watched him standing there in her rearview mirror. *What the hell just happened? Who would believe me If I did tell them?*

◆◆◆◆

Rick returned to his office and sat in his chair, palms on his blotter. *The night I was turned, I never expected to find the life I've been given.* He picked up the phone and dialed Harry in Big Bear.

Chapter Nine

It was almost eight-thirty in the evening when Harry ambled from his mausoleum to the darkening twilight on the porch overlooking Big Bear Lake. He carried his laptop and a mug of O Positive, looking fondly toward writing as he watched the sun disappear into the depths of the water.

He opened his laptop and scrolled to the last paragraph he'd written.

December 28th, 1946

Caught in the club's smoky haze, as he played, 'Give me five minutes more'… Frankie was caught up at the sight of a raven-haired miss…

Harry was stumped. He crafted his heart-wrenching tale of an Army Officer coming back from the war to find his girl married to a chump. This wasn't the book he intended to write. He meant to create a fictionalized account of The Black Dahlia murder through the eyes of those who knew her. How had Frankie become the main character? He'd never had a character take the wheel. It was unnerving.

Harry heard the garage door open and close, taking his mind off the book entirely. Expecting Matt, he was surprised when he heard Rick Hiatt call out from the kitchen.

"Are you parched out there, Mr. Hemingway?"

Harry turned from his laptop and smiled at his company. "There's half a bag of O Positive in the fridge…"

Harry was waiting for Rick's opinion on his breakfast.

"Drinking ice water again? How can a man nourish his creative juices with O Positive? How is O Positive like sex in a canoe… because both are fucking near water." Rick appeared with a bottle of scotch under one arm and two crystal rocks glasses of AB Negative. "Why am I here with such a delicacy? Because we need to talk."

"What did I do now?" Harry asked petulantly as he closed the laptop.

Rick took the chair next to Harry and poured a wee bit of scotch to top off the glasses. "Nothing, you did nothing." He handed the glass to Harry and raised it to toast. "Cheers!"

"You drove up here with AB Negative just for me?"

They sipped for a few moments as the sky darkened to deep purple. Rick got comfortable in an overstuffed wing chair and sighed. "I love this place. I'm so glad Matt let me talk him into buying it."

Harry drank and mined his thoughts for why Rick Hiatt was here. "Who did he buy it from?"

Rick grinned larcenously. "Me. I'm getting back at him for all the coaching he needed in those first ten years. But let's talk about you."

"Me? What did I do?"

"I told you, you did nothing. However -- I did receive a visit from Dr. Elizabeth Mitchell."

Harry tensed. "Lizbet came to see you. Why?"

Rick put his glass down and smirked. "She didn't come to see me. It seems she's spent countless nights, from six to ten-thirty sitting in The Bridge watching people. Buys her two drinks and lets them melt to bleh, pays her bill in cash, and leaves. Who's she looking for, Harry?"

"Me?" Harry flinched. "Rick, we had the talk."

Rick waved his hand. "I know, the Brenner talk. However, she was asking about The Gaoler. Why would she ask about that?"

Harry held up a pledging hand. "We never discussed anything remotely close to The Gaoler. I never figured out how she got my address... She came to the book signing and caught me while I was leaving."

Rick folded his hands in his lap. "Some people become fascinated after they discover vampires are real. With all our fangs and faults, I think she's got a crush on you, Harry."

Harry rose and paced with his drink in his hand. "I told her…"

"Of course, you did. That made it all the more exciting."

Harry stopped in front of Rick. "She's a special woman, Rick." He sighed deeply. "What would you do?"

Rick shrugged. "You like her?"

Harry turned and paced in front of the view of the dark horizon. "I know I shouldn't. But I haven't enjoyed a woman's company this much in decades. I played the piano, and she sang, and I was mortal all over again. I don't have to tell you how beautiful she is."

Rick leaned closer. "Do you have a type, Harry?"

"Not that I'm aware of. Do you mean, mortal? Because I've never sought that."

"No, I mean a physical type? Do you like Snow White or Sleeping Beauty?

Harry squinted at Rick.

Rick blew out a breath. "Dark or Blonde?"

Harry's downcast eyes signaled his uncertainty. "You know, I don't remember the women I dated before this." He gestured to his canine teeth. "All I know is, she sends me."

Rick nodded encouragement. "Then, my boy, go cherchez la femme."

"Look for the woman?" Harry's brows knit. "But Matt says…"

"She's had three encounters with vampires in three days. Don't you think this is destiny? If she were going to out us, she would have done it the day she was with Venus. She protected us when she whitewashed her account of the garage crime."

Harry took a long drink from his glass and nodded as he swallowed. "But who's protecting her?"

Rick shot a finger at him. "She has your scent on her, but not your mark. It's the mark that protects."

Harry inclined his dark head. "I'm not talking about physical protection, Rick. I'm talking about emotional protection. Nothing good happens for mortals involved with vampires. They lose every time."

Rick laughed. "What a load of manure. Is that the Brenner point of view? Because I can tell you stories of dozens of women who benefited by interactions with us. Helen, you know our donor manager. She fed me for ten years. She never asked to be turned, but our relationship gave her a damn good job, and she loves the life she leads."

Harry's jaw dropped. "Did she ever marry, have kids?"

Rick waved him back. "That's not every woman's dream. Helen's been around the world; she lives on a houseboat. She's more adventurous than most women. From what she tells me, mortal men disappointed her, vampires never did."

Harry's jaw dropped. "She's forty-five-ish. Is she going to work for you until she dies?"

"Helen told me she'd rather be carried out feet first than to be sitting watching tv. That gal has instincts I don't have. And don't forget the Marquis. Six hundred years old, he adores Helen."

Harry bit his lip. "I never thought about that."

Rick shook his finger. "We were fortunate to be turned in the flower of our youth. If you were turned at fifty, you think you'd want a *relationship* with a college cheerleader? Would you want that at your age?"

Harry was silent in thought for a few minutes. "So, not every vamp-mortal relationship ends badly for them?"

"Hell, no." Rick raised his glass. "Do you think I was turned by appointment to King Henry the VIII? No, Tsura was magnificent. We had two hundred and twenty-five years together, and I miss her every night." Rick's gaze drifted into the dark sky. An owl called and broke the silence.

Harry drank and thought. "Have you ever turned someone?"

Rick turned back to Harry. "No. I never met someone I wanted to turn." Reflectively, Rick gazed into the treeline. "But she's out there."

"You've given me a different perspective. It's going to kill Matt. But I don't know how she feels about me now."

Rick's lips curled in a mischievous smirk. "That will be your responsibility to decide. I'll handle your step-sire. I am the head of this family."

Chapter Ten

Harry unlocked the door to his stale apartment and went about airing out the place. With a knock, Matt was hovering. Harry threw back the sliding glass door in the living room.

Matt's question was tentative. "So, how's the book going?"

"For the first time in my life, I have writer's block, but that's peripheral."

"You have writer's block, but that's peripheral? So, what's on your mind?"

Harry grinned foolishly. "I'm in love. I think she is too."

Matt hung his head. "Rick sat me down the other night. I am not happy about this."

Harry turned from opening the balcony doors. "Not happy?"

"I've already given you the talk. What if it goes too far?"

Harry blanched. "Too far?"

Matt's face grew stony. "You'll have to watch her die."

"How about I watch her live and feel how good that is?"

"You'd turn her?"

"If she wanted it. We're nowhere near that point. But I won't know if I don't make that first call." Matt's frustration filled his expression. "Dad, I've got the Responders on speed dial. My training wheels are off. So, I'm going to see where this goes. And if the writing takes a back seat for a while, I have more than enough cushion to live on."

Matt's pacing slowed, and with a groan, he shook his head and said. "Good-bye."

♦♦♦♦

A week after she cornered Rick Hiatt, Lizbet's phone rang as she was coming in with groceries. She dropped them on the kitchen table and picked up. "Hello?"

"I'm calling from Rent-a-Cook. My records say you had one cheese, ham, and spinach omelet. Did your cook include the cleanup in his service?"

Lizbet's smile grew with every word. "He did not. He left a sink of dirty pans and dishes."

"That's regrettable, Dr. Mitchell. Please allow me to rectify that error. What can we do?"

"Send that representative back."

"When would that be convenient?"

She looked at the kitchen clock, nine-thirty in the evening. She was tired from the workweek, but nothing perked her up like Harry's baritone chuckle. "You better get him over here tonight. I've got some words for him."

"We guarantee satisfaction. Our representative will be there at ten P.M."

♦♦♦♦

Lizbet spun into action. *Twenty-nine minutes and he'll be on my doorstep?* First, she took a speed shower. She brushed her teeth like she was going to the dentist. It was a snap decision to apply blush and brow gel. In her closet, a new sundress hung with the tags still attached. The full skirt had a flowy petticoat underneath it, and roses bordered the hem and the pleated bust area. The red roses were electric against the yellow sateen, so she opted for pearl earrings and black flats. *He's going to sweep me off my feet.*

Lizbet was walking through a cloud of Chanel N°5 when she heard his huge automobile bump into her driveway. She smoothed her skirt, took a final glance in the mirror. *I defended a dissertation on malignant narcissistic personality disorder in violent criminals; I can date a vampire.*

She closed her eyes and stood in the bedroom, waiting for the doorbell. *When it rings, amble to the door.* The bell rang, and she ran, nearly out of breath. Her flats slid on the rug, and she hurtled into the door. She opened it with as much composure as she could gather. "Harry, you look well." She stood back. "Is this where I ask you in? Have I asked you in before?"

"You handed me the key and asked me to open it."

Lizbet covered her face as it flushed pink, and he entered her home.

50

"I put a dent in your bourbon on my last visit, so I thought you might enjoy this. It's a small batch bourbon." He held out the bottle, and she felt like the homecoming queen accepting roses.

Harry held a hardback book and stood grinning like a freshman. "I thought I'd bring an autographed copy of my new release since you accept no substitutes on the autograph." He held it open to display, "All my best. Love, M. C."

Lizbet hefted the thick book and the liter of liquor, looking like she'd just won the Kentucky Debry.

"I've never seen roses take a second to a woman's beauty, but Lizbet, they pale in comparison to you."

"Oh, Harry, you have a way with words. Can I get you something to eat?" Then it hit her. "Oh, good God. Why don't we open this wonderful bourbon?" She led him to the small bar area between her living and dining room. "I'll get the ice if you get the glasses." She left the book on the dining room table, and her knees knocked all the way to her freezer. *Why am I even like this? He's slept on my sofa, cooked me breakfast…*

She returned with a small chrome and walnut art deco ice bucket with silver tongs. She stood on the dining room side of the cabinet and placed it between them. Harry pointed to the container. "Silver?"

"Oh, no, chrome." She removed the lid, and inside, the tiny tongs rested on ice.

"Silver?" He pointed a long finger at the utensil.

"Oh, damn, yes… You're going to have to give me vampire lessons." She picked up the tongs and dropped ice into each glass.

Harry poured the bourbon, picked up both glasses, and gestured her toward the nubby upholstered sofa. When they were both seated, he handed her the drink and raised his glass. "Here's to breaking the rules."

"That makes it all the more exciting."

Harry sat back, resting the glass on his knee. "Are you excited to see me? I thought after our last conversation, I'd be dodging silver bullets."

She sipped, and her green eyes brightened. "You've got a real problem with silver, don't you?"

Harry nodded. "Yep. Probably need to run down a danger list tonight."

When Lizbet sat next to him, she crossed one leg over the other, tilting toward him. She held her glass up and rested her hand on his shoulder. "What a sharp charcoal suit." She placed her drink on the coffee table and turned to him. "Thank you for the bourbon and the book." She leaned in and gave him a chaste kiss on the mouth. His arm swept around her.

"I shopped for the bourbon myself. I think I can taste it on your lips."

She grinned hugely. "Really? Let me try." She leaned in again, and this time her tongue swept his full lower lip."

That was all the invitation he needed. His mouth descended on hers, hungrily in a kiss that stole her breath and warmed his cold blood. Her skirts rustled as he pulled her onto his lap. With one arm around her shoulders and one arm pulling her hips toward him, they melted into each other. A tangle of arms moved to their melody of sighs and whispers.

Harry slid Lizbet off his lap and into the corner of the sofa. Like a boss, he stood up and slipped out of his suit coat. Noticing the blinds were up, Harry held up a finger to delay her impatience. He dropped the slats and dialed them closed, then elegantly returned to corner her on the sofa.

Lizbet watched him, amazed at his grace and economy of movement. Her tummy fluttered at the memory of his first deep kiss.

"You have excellent foresight, Mr. VanAlt."

He gave her his best-crooked grin. "I *was* a Boy Scout."

"It shows. What other good deeds would you like to do?"

He sat beside her and swiveled her legs over his lap. They sat very close. Her arms caught him and pulled him over her. His knees pinned her between them, and when he slid her flat, she totally fell under his spell.

"I do have a bed; you watched me sleep in it."

With preternatural speed, he was off and sitting at the other end of the couch, looking nonchalant. "I don't want to move too fast. I want to remember every second of our first time."

She sat up and moved her skirt over her knees. "Would you like to dance? I have some Glenn Miller albums."

"I'd love the honor of that dance."

"The Nearness of You" was the first song when the needle dropped. Ray Eberle crooned as Harry held her, and they embraced on the open wooden floor between the living and dining room. She succumbed to his grace, her hand in his and his arm around her. In the space between them, his baritone hum chilled her with his cool breath.

She looked up into his blue-green eyes and laid her head on his shoulder. "Are you always like this?" She squeezed his chilly hand.

"I told you I use a lot of ice. But, after I feed, I'm warmer. Unless you can warm me up."

They swayed, their hips impossibly close. *Why did I wear a dress with a crinoline?* "Warm you up? How can I do that?"

Without breaking concentration, he dipped her. While she was bent back, his naughty smile broke into the conversation. "There are four things that warm me up. He drew her back with a snap and spun her out and then spun her into him. He ran a finger from her chin down her neck. "Do you want to guess what those four things are?"

She pressed her hips into his and bent back to see his wry smile. "I'm a bad guesser. We could be here all night. Why don't you just tell me?"

Harry looked up to the ceiling and briefly away. "Excuse my language." When a new song began, he moved them into another dance. "It's a little naughty."

"I like naughty."

"I warned you. I get warm when I vamp out…" His hip bumped hers.

"Ooh, like when you pulled that guy off me?"

"Yup, fighting does that. Feeding does it; fleeing does it and..." His head tilted to her bedroom. "Fucking. That makes me hot."

She stopped dancing. "That's incredible. What a coincidence, it makes me hot, too!" His head fell back, he laughed uproariously, pulled her into an embrace, and then tucked her head under his chin.

"I have no idea how I found you."

"It was suggested to me that we were destined to meet." *Are we destined to be together?*

"You got the talk from Rick, right?"

She playfully drew her hand down his jaw to the divot in his chin. "I certainly did. Right after Venus flipped out on him bringing me down to Jack the Ripper's paradise."

"Ah, you been to The Gaoler. It's not my thing."

"He had the nerve to ask me if I topped from the bottom."

Harry stopped dancing and looked down at her with interest. "Do you?"

"Of course, I don't. I don't play games."

Again, he caught her impossibly close to him and sighed. She felt the rumble within him, and her tummy quivered again. "There are a few things I have to be straight about." He led her back to the sofa and sat on the chair facing the couch. He held both her hands as he gathered his thoughts.

"You're scaring me, Harry."

Chapter Eleven

"That's not my intent, but vampires can be quite rough. We don't mean to; it's just that we move faster and are many times stronger than a mortal."

Lizbet bit her top lip. "Okay, ah, what does that mean?"

"Being naturally faster and stronger, I have to remember to treat you like a delicate treasure. I promise to take my time. It's been a while. You've excited me since we met."

"Well, it's been a while for me too. I dropped this total jerk last year, and I've spent nine months alone." She watched a smile spread to Harry's eyes.

"Nine months? Yeah." He nodded. "I dated a vampire woman for a while, but she took a job in Amsterdam, and it's been about that long for me. However, what I meant was the last time I made love to a mortal woman was 1951."

"Oh, dear God, I hope it wasn't one of my relatives."

"I doubt it, but within that week, I was turned and never went back into mortal society. It's just recently that I got out of my regular circle."

"Is that because of me?"

"In 2001, I began interviewing mortals about books. But, you, there's something about you that unlocks a door deep in my heart."

She rose from the sofa and settled on his lap. "Do you want to unlock your destiny tonight?"

He held her close, his head resting on her breasts. "More than anything, Lizbet. Yes."

She rose and turned out the lights and left the stack of records to play. When she crooked her finger, he followed.

◆◆◆◆

Her bedroom held the cloud of cologne she'd walked through earlier. He could tell where she applied it daily. He told himself not to scare her on their first night. *Don't bite her; bite myself when the time comes. Turn away and hope the darkness covers my transformation. I wish there was some way back to mortality. She deserves a warm body in her bed. Or perhaps, she'll come to my side?*

The blinds were down, sending slits of the streetlamp onto the floor. Hobnail milk glass lamps sat on each nightstand, nightlights glowing pink from the bottom globes. The low light was no deterrent in seeing all of her beauty. He slid out of his shoes as she drew back the duvet. Then he crooked his finger and turned her around. He murmured on cool breath in her ear, "May I unzip you?"

"Well, of course!" She turned to him and caught his handsome face in her hands. "May I undress you? Did women do that back then?"

Back then? Cheap walk-up apartments. Bare light bulbs hanging in the middle of the room. Spending a rapturous night on a full-size bed and waking to milk delivered on the doorstep...

"Harry? You in there?" Her hands rested on his trouser button.

"Every part of me is in there. Most parts want to get out."

With his nod, she lovingly unbuttoned his soft wool trousers. She held his slacks open, and her eyes widened. "Harry, where did you get these?" She snapped the waistband of his retro yoke front white cotton boxers. "If you have sock garters on, I am going to lose it!"

Harry deadpanned. "They keep my socks up." He laughed and stepped out of his trousers, revealing the garters holding up his black and yellow argyles.

She shook her head, still holding up her unzipped dress, and lowered her voice to a husky purr. "Wait until I tell you about elastic. It's in everything these days."

He began removing his cuff links. "Don't be a tease; you modern women are bewitching."

She loosened his necktie, and her smile grew wry. "If you think elastic is hot, wait till I tell you what Cosmopolitan says about oral sex."

Harry stood as she removed his shirt, leaving him in his retro boxers and gartered socks. "Oral sex? Is that where we read out loud to each other?" He winked.

"Harry, please don't frighten me. You've been on ice, not in a coma."

"Okay, explain these strange rituals of which you speak. Which book are we reading that has sex in it?" She dropped her dress, revealing her lacy ivory bra and her Betty Page styled knickers. Harry's eyes widened at the four tiny buttons on her hip. "Oh. Baby. You're making me work for my prize." *Please, God, give me the ability to slow down. It's 2003, but I am back in my happy place.* "You're incredible, every part of you. From that pink polish on your toes to the top of your glorious black hair."

Her fingertip ran down the center of his muscled chest and hooked into the front of his boxers. "May I have a peek?"

"But, of course, it would be awkward to stand here like this all night."

She hooked her thumbs into his waistband, and his boxers hung up on his interested flesh. "Oh, let me help you with that. I'm being thwarted." She freed the fabric. "I can see why." She admitted breathlessly.

He drew her to him and unhooked her bra with two fingers. "You wouldn't believe the trouble I got into learning this technique." She dropped her arms and the lacy brassiere joined his white boxers on the floor. "We're down to two socks and your knickers, who can get out of them faster?"

"I'll take that as a challenge. What do I win?" She smirked at the four buttons on her fancy undies.

Harry sat in the chair behind him and released the garter clips. He was totally naked before she got the last button undone. "Need some help?"

"You won, what's your prize?"

"That oral thing you spoke of; you're going to read to me?" He posed like a matinee idol sheik on a throne.

"Oh…that reading part was to appeal to your intellectual side. Right now, I want to show you some appreciation for your talent in undressing."

She knelt before him and ran her fingertips lightly from his knees, along his thighs and on to her ultimate prize.

Harry gasped. His arms fell limply onto the sides of the chair, his head rested back, and his eyes closed. The scent of her arousal combined with her cologne left him trembling urgently for her touch. Her mortal warmth awoke a myriad of sensations within him.

"Oh, my God!" She murmured. "You're magnificent!"

In his mind, Harry saw his book's character, Frankie, with a beautiful woman. Black-haired, jade-eyed, and stunning.

Harry groaned, feeling Lizbet's warm fingers embrace his aching length. Her warm tongue traced a path around his crown. Harry shook.

Lizbet's welcoming mouth engulfed him, and Harry cried out with the overwhelming sensation of her velvet heat. Her wicked tongue circled him as she sucked a steady tempo against him. Harry gasped, on the verge of orgasm. Harry's fingers dug into the arm of the upholstered chair.

Consternation at his failure to release stymied him until it slowly came back that he needed to bite. Lizbet's green eyes watched him as she drew steadily on him. He waited for an all-important blink, and as soon as her eyes closed, he turned his head and bit his wrist. He erupted like a roman candle with long, extravagant swells of sensation that left him panting. Lizbet continued to swirl her tongue, catching every bit of him. She rested her cheek upon his thigh as they both basked in the moment.

"Incredible, you're a vixen. My raven-haired vixen." He murmured. "Now, when do you read?"

She impishly swatted at his leg. "It's your turn to read to me."

Harry grinned. "I'll do my best. This is the moment I'm glad that I'm undead. Because I can go all night. C'mon, Betts, let's hit the sheets."

Chapter Twelve

Harry relaxed against the mattress, one arm over his head, the other arm cradling Lizbet against him. *Who knew this marvelous mortal woman was the cure for writer's block?* Throughout the hours, as he and Lizbet made love, in the background, there were oddly intrusive visions of the visceral emotional connection building between his characters. If only he had a second self who could separate and record it all. His mind was ready to write, but his heart and body weren't prepared to leave her bed.

In vampire homes, beds were optional recreational equipment. Granite was the rage in catafalques. But what harm would it do to put a nice comfy mattress on top of his slab? It wouldn't be as cool as the marble or granite. He thought about that. How about a large freezer on its back, a twin mattress set inside?

I wouldn't have to chill an entire room. This is brilliant. Why hasn't some vampire done this and made a mint? This will be my legacy; no one will think of me as a writer; I'll be known for changing the face of going to ground. I'll make a fortune on double wide freezers. My brain is moving in a million different directions. This woman has unleashed me.

He must have been thinking too loudly. Lizbet stirred beside him. *She must be exhausted.* Harry caught her in both arms and brought her face to his. Her eyes were heavy, and her lips over-kissed. She melted to him, and he sighed in happiness. He nuzzled her neck and inhaled deeply.

Her voice was drowsy. "Can you smell my blood?"

Everywhere her flesh touched his, he tingled. "Yep. A Positive, healthy adult female. Also, tired."

She stretched her warm, lithe body against his. "But satisfied."

Her wildly loose tresses framed her radiant face. As light crept into the room, it amplified her glow. He relished their joy. "That's good to hear. Want a little more satisfaction before I leave?"

"Leave? Where are you going?" Lizbet threw her leg over him.

Their morning wrestling match ended when he rolled her under him and kissed her soundly. "I have to go home, Betts." His cool fingers stroked her ivory neck and rested on her breast. "You don't have a pint to spare. I believe you've had a workout in the past eight hours." She frowned and pooched her bottom lip at him. "Remember I told you I use a lot of ice? Well, before the sun is high, I need to chill."

"You're about the most chill guy I know."

He cuddled her, and his regret grew. "Betts, I rest on a slab, a marble slab. We call it going to ground. It's dark and cold, and my mind turns off until the sunset triggers me to life."

"But if you're in the dark, how do you know?" She propped up her chin on her hand. "If it's dark, how *do* you know?"

He touched his chest. "It's my circadian rhythm. It's how you know to wake up every morning."

She winced. "You're right."

He was in the process of pulling himself out of their nest when he fell back into her spell. "Besides, I don't know any mortals who want to sleep on a slab of marble in a cold dark place."

She cringed. "Okay. It took me weeks to find this bed."

He moved back to her and kissed her forehead. "Perhaps you're the reason I was turned, to be here with you in this bed." His fingers combed through her shining raven hair. He drew a lock of it to his nose and held it close, mesmerized by how she wore his scent.

Her gaze traveled the room and then back to him. "Then I'd agree with Rick Hiatt; this is our destiny."

"Do you mean I'm welcome back?" Harry drew her chin toward him, pressing light kisses along her face.

Lizbet's fingertips trailed down his chest, tapping at his navel. "You'd better come back. Or I'll go vamp hunting."

He gasped. "Egads. We can't have that. How about I bring over my collection of vintage erotica, and we can read each into orbit."

"Do you have a bedroom? Would you be more comfortable at your place?"

"I could have a Murphy bed installed in the den. It would take a few days. Do you mind?"

"Are you kidding? It's Saturday morning, and I'm trying to figure out if my feet will touch the ground, I'm flying so high."

Please don't bring up eating, I beg of you.

"I'm anxious to see your vintage erotica. Speaking of vintage, how old are you?"

He looked askance. "Well, that was quite a change of subject. How old are you?"

Lizbet wiggled out of his embrace and turned to squirm her buttocks against his hip. "Now you're going to be difficult. I'm thirty-four."

Harry feigned a grave expression. "That old?"

"Yes, that old. Didn't you tell me the other night I was in my prime?"

He kept his deadpan expression. "Yeah, but I had no idea…"

She rolled back toward him and slugged him on the arm. "How old are you?" He opened his mouth, hesitatingly. "Don't ask me how old I think you are."

In mock defeat, Harry shook his fist. "Damn." He pushed himself up in the bed against the headboard and motioned for her to join him. He whispered in her ear. "I'm eighty-two."

"Wow, you get around great for your age. How old is Rick?"

Harry cocked his head. "I've spent all night giving you everything I've got, and you're asking how old my grand-sire is?"

She ran her hands through her wild dark hair and grinned at his jealousy. "You realize I'm a scientist. I'm curious. When is your birthday?"

Harry nodded. "Vamps have two birthdays. Those of us who are happy to be undead generally celebrate both. Those of us who did not choose this life, well, let me say, I celebrate my original birthday."

"Harry, you didn't choose this?"

"Betts, it's a long dark story. I need to eat and go to ground." He slid, naked out of bed, and began retrieving his clothes."

"I'm sorry." Lizbet left the bed and moved to embrace him. "I hit a nerve, didn't I? I didn't mean to."

He pulled her close, and they passionately kissed. It was a goodbye kiss. "I'm not upset with you, Betts. It is a long story. I'll tell you tonight. Believe it or not, you wore me out."

She playfully caught him by his shoulder. "I don't believe that."

♦♦♦♦

The sky was a myriad of pinks and purples against the horizon when she watched the boat of a car back out of her driveway. Harry was the kind of guy who was hard to hide; everything about his personality was larger than life. His car, his clothes, his musical talent, his velvet voice, and his indescribable touch. *We keep this up, and the neighborhood will think I'm a hussy. I'm sure Eddie noticed that boat of a Buick in my driveway.*

Chapter Thirteen

Lizbet washed and put away her dinner dishes, tingles of anticipation making the routine chore much more pleasurable. Every time she thought about their night together, her heart raced with pleasure. Tonight, she paid scrupulous attention to her grooming but kept her look casual. Shorts, halter top, and sandals. When you have a new man, he's seeing everything for the first time.

She dried her hands, fingered the new silk robes she bought for herself and Harry, and stopped to slather some Chanel N°5 lotion on her hands and arms. She paced. It was a good hour before he was due. What would she do with the time? Her phone rang, jolting her out of her happy place. She grabbed it up and answered cheerily. "Hello…"

"Lizard? I'm in town for the weekend, how about a little reunion? I'm not far from your place. I've brought back a bottle of tequila. I remember how we'd get revved up with a few mar-gar-ritas…"

While Roy went on ad nauseum, Lizbet inhaled and exhaled to maintain her peaceful center. "It's good to know you're alive. When you disappeared nine months ago, I thought perhaps you were pregnant and wanted to deliver in seclusion."

"Ouch, I didn't think you take it so personally."

"Roy, we dated for two years. How was I supposed to take it when you evaporated? One week we're on a cruise out of San Diego, and the next week, your phone is not in service."

There was a beat of silence. "I got too close, Lizard. I was afraid. You know, at your age, women want to pair up."

Her blood began a slow boil. "Well, don't worry your little head about me. Just keep moving, like the shark you are."

"Seriously, Liz, I want to apologize, in person."

"Seriously, Roy, I don't. I have to go now; I'm busy this evening." She hung up the phone with a satisfied smile on her face. To get her head ready for tonight, she put on a stack of big band albums and settled on the sofa stroking her Ragdoll cat, Minka.

Her ear pricked up at the sound of the LaSabre's suspension on her driveway. Minka bolted off her lap and ran low to the ground all the way to the office. *Calm down. It's never good to appear too anxious.* She sprinted to the door and held it open before he climbed the steps. "My God, you are gorgeous. I'd love to see your closet."

Harry had a dimple she noticed for the first time, appearing when he buried his smile. "Closet?"

"I adore the way you dress." She inhaled as he got closer. "I could eat you up; you smell so good." She ran her hands over the shoulders of his royal blue suitcoat. "And it's double-breasted. Did you buy this at a vintage store?"

Harry basked under her admiration. "I've got a guy; he calls me when he finds a good length of summer wool."

She playfully swooned into his arms. "Take me; I'm yours."

He caught her up and carried her inside. "That's exactly what I wanted to hear. Get yourself gussied up; I'm taking you out tonight."

"I don't know if I can match you, but I'll try." She disappeared into her bedroom and closed the door for her metamorphosis.

♦♦♦♦

Harry paced the living room, holding a glass of bourbon, enhanced with a couple of drops of A Positive. It didn't smell as sweet as Lizbet's blood, but he wanted to stall any of that for now. His foot tapped to the music of Tommy Dorsey, and he stared out the front window waiting for his delectable date.

Outside there was a throaty roar of a car breaking. The engine glub-glubbed and turned off. A car door squeaked, and Harry's vampire sense caught the repetitive flip flop of a weighty guy in thongs. Harry gazed out the front door's small glass window. The man in the faded UCLA tee-shirt and jams carried a bottle of liquor. Compared to the size of the guy, the liter looked tiny. He was a walking mountain, probably a wide-receiver by the way he carried the bottle. *Is he delivering liquor? No one would show up at a woman's door like this.* There was the man's light knock.

Harry swung open the door. "May I help you?"

The man's head drew back in surprise. "Is Lizzie here?"

"Dr. Mitchell is preparing for the evening." Harry filled the open doorway. "Can I help you?" Stepping out to the porch, he nodded at the bottle. "Do you have a delivery?"

Standing toe to toe, the stranger had Harry by a few inches high and wide. "Did she put you up to this getup?" The guy waved the bottle at Harry's suit.

"I beg your pardon. My tailor put me up to this. I see you're still dressing from the casual collection at the student union."

The man squinted at Harry. "Have we met? I'm Roy Hannon. I'm Lizzie's boyfriend." He chuckled, hot alcoholic breath blasting down on Harry.

"Is Dr. Mitchell expecting you?"

"No, she said she was busy tonight. Didn't expect you here."

"Well, I am here, and I'll be here from now on. Do you have a parting message for Dr. Mitchell?"

The sandy blond ex-footballer stepped back and scratched his head. "You could give her this from Roy." He held out the tequila bottle.

Harry's gaze shot daggers. "She no longer keeps tequila on her bar." He made no effort to accept the gift. "Thanks for stopping by, you said, it's Roy?"

At this point, the gridiron hero was no longer confident. Harry watched him retreat, and Eddie Cartwright appeared, watching from his porch. "Looking sharp there, Harry. You and Lizbet going out?"

Harry kept an eye on the glumly retreating Roy and called back. "Drinks and dancing tonight, Eddie."

Once the muscle car motored off, the older man joined Harry. Eddie worked a toothpick in his mouth as he kept an eye on the retreating car's lights. "I heard his car. I don't trust that bastard as far as I could toss him. I was worried he'd think a man elegantly dressed wouldn't raise a fist to him." Eddie exhaled and shook his head. "He was a bad one." Eddie chuckled lightly and spoke. "I'd say Roy is like a boner in sweatpants."

Harry's brows shot up as he buried a grin. "Yeah, how's that?"

Eddie folded his arms over his Police Athletic League tee-shirt. "He's out."

Head down, Harry shoved at a pebble on the porch floor. "Eddie, that's colorful language from a retired detective. Ever think about writing?"

Both men snickered until Lizbet opened the door, appearing like a 1940s screen icon. Eddie wolf-whistled. "If I were thirty years younger, I'd give your young man here a run for his money."

Harry's gaze couldn't leave Lizbet's ravishing presence. "Eddie, I like ya, but I'd arm-wrestle you for her."

Lizbet's look was suspicious. What's going on?"

Harry was the soul of innocence. "Eddie and I were just chatting, isn't that right, Eddie?"

Eddie nodded. "Nice night for a chat. But I can see you two are ready for a great evening, and I've got murder clues to follow."

Harry turned to Eddie. "You know, I've kinda put the heist story on hold. I'm working on a book about the Black Dahlia murder. If you don't mind, I'll make another appointment and pick your brain. I'd be happy to credit you in the acknowledgments."

Eddie nodded as he retreated. "Anytime, son. You get out and cut a rug for me."

Lizbet watched him leave with a head tilted in curiosity. "Okay… No kidding." She ran her hands down Harry's broad lapels and gave him an appealing smile, with strawberry red lips. "What just happened?"

Harry moved closer and kissed the top of her head. "Got your purse?"

With a nod, the house was locked, and they were driving away, top-down. He paused to let her wrap a black chiffon scarf around her long, dark hair.

"You slay me with that halter dress, what is that, satin?

"Yes, black satin, no pesky petticoat tonight."

"You look like a dark chocolate covered strawberry. Is that wrap warm enough? I could put the top up."

"Oh, no, Harry. You have the heat on. I'm fine."

"I can't begin to tell you the appetites you stir in me."

"That goes both ways, handsome." Lizbet stroked the suede inset in the upholstery. "I love this car. It must have cost a fortune."

"Oh, not as much as you might think."

"Where are you taking me tonight?"

Harry winked. "I thought it was time for Vampire College. How'd you like to go to the bar at The Gaoler?"

"Jack, the Ripper's place?" She grinned. "That's what I call an adventure." She added more seriously. "As long as I'm with you."

♦♦♦♦

Lizbet leaned back into the butter-soft leather of the LaSabre and enjoyed Harry's playlist. "What actually happened on the porch?"

Harry ducked her gaze and checked his lane position, then bit his bottom lip. "Delivery to the wrong house."

"You know I'm a trained observer. I can detect lies. You and Eddie had noses a foot long. And you enjoyed it. What happened?"

"You know a guy named Roy?"

She threw her head back. "What did you do to him?"

"Me? I never laid a hand on him, even when he inferred I was less than masculine."

She gasped. "He did not!" She braced her arm on the dashboard and turned to Harry. "What did he say?"

"He accused you of making me dress this way." He snorted.

"I was always trying to clean up Roy."

Harry smirked. "I can believe that. Anyway, we had a little chat about you being busy tonight. I asked him if he had a parting message for you. He didn't."

"Was he drunk?" Her nail tapped the dash.

"It smelled that way. His posturing drew Eddie out, which was nice but not necessary. I don't think he'll be back unless you ask him."

"Ask him? He called tonight, and I told him to get lost." She ran her hand up and down Harry's thigh. "

"Harry, as long as you're on my dance card, my card and my life are full." Within moments, the long nose of the convertible turned into the valet station at the Consort Group building.

Harry grinned. "I believe this was the place you were investigating?"

67

Lizbet shrunk down in the seat. "Hey, I was curious. I was curious about you."

Harry handed the keys to the carpark. "Park it in my garage space, will you, John?" The man took the key and nodded. Harry jogged around the car to Lizbet's door. As he helped her out, he bent down, his voice lulling her toward relaxation. "Do the members of my family make you a little nervous, Betts?"

She swallowed and let her scarf fall around her neck. "If they look hungry, they do." She cast her gaze around the bystanders.

"We'll cure that tonight. I won't leave your side."

They moved briskly through the lobby, and Harry had her in the elevator before she could peek into The Bridge to scan the regulars.

As the car dropped below the basement level, and the heartbeat began, she huddled closer to Harry. "This just gives me the willies. Who thought this up?"

"Vampires find heartbeats musical. Everyone is different, and it sings to us."

Lizbet's jaw dropped. "You can hear heartbeats? Do you hear mine?"

He drew her close. "I do, Betts. I can scent your arousal too. I can tell the exact moment you're ready for me."

Her eyes grew round. "I'm not sure how I feel about that."

He barked out a laugh. "You'll grow to love it. Then you can send me signals across the room."

The elevator doors opened onto the corridor of playrooms. "Can everybody here do that?" She asked in a reticent voice. Harry pointed all the way down the corridor.

"I know exactly what's going on in every playroom, right now. It's the acuity of undead senses."

"I've been here before. I didn't hear a thing."

He hugged her next to him. "You're adorable."

Chapter Fourteen

Before Harry led Lizbet toward the bar, he checked his watch. Ten P.M. "Do you want to see a feeding before or after a drink?"

Lizbet gulped. "Feed who, drink what?" Harry drew her to the side of the hallway as a couple in full BDSM gear passed them. "Do they serve bourbon? Anything stronger?"

"We have Bacardi 151, or the vampire's favorite, Everclear, which is 190 proof."

She watched the humor grow on his face. "Can't you go blind drinking that stuff?"

"Kids on spring break drink it all the time. So, I guess you want a drink, and we come back to the eleven o'clock show?"

"Show? They show it?"

"It's quite titillating. It's a real appetite enhancer for many vamps, and it gets the donors in the mood."

"Oh. Let's have a few drinks. Is there a midnight show?"

She watched wide-eyed as they entered the bar. What looked like a charming Irish pub held a collection of vampires and willing donors, drinking before or after they fed. The door swung open with a pneumatic whoosh, and all heads turned. Predominantly, the female donors scrutinized their perceived competition from her ankle strap pumps to the chiffon scarf around her neck. Their vampire companions sniffed the air and nodded approvingly to Harry. His arm encircled her slim waist, and he pulled her toward an isolated booth in the back corner. They sat together in the circular booth with a view of the entire room.

Harry pulled out a pocket note pad and the smallest fountain pen Lizbet had ever seen. He carefully wrote in graceful longhand.

> "The vampires approve of you. For what it's worth, the mortals are jealous."

She looked at him and held out her hand for the pen.

> "Why are you writing this?"

Harry took back his pen.

"Because every vamp can hear your heartbeat, of course, they could hear our conversation."

Lizbet shook her head and whispered. "Is gossip that popular?"

Harry capped the pen and returned it to his breast pocket. "Rick says it's the second most popular hobby next to sex."

One of the more debonair vamps across the room ran a tongue over his fangs and nodded in agreement. "Isn't it impolite to eavesdrop?"

"Yes." He frowned toward the older vamp who should have known better. "So, what are you drinking? Something fancy or something strong?"

She played with the chain on her evening bag. "Well, I don't want to be out of it when I see whatever it is you want me to see."

His hand covered hers. "Good." He nodded, and the server arrived to take their order.

The tuxedoed server stopped in front of Lizbet. "Have you decided what you'd like?"

She whispered. "A whiskey sour, do you have Buffalo Trace?"

The server nodded and turned to Harry. "The usual?"

Harry nodded, and the tall man was gone. She craned her neck to see the bar behind the glass partition. The sounds of the shakers and the blenders were somewhat muted for the undead's sensitive hearing.

"Your usual? What's that?"

"Absinthe with a few drops of A Positive."

She smiled. "Oh, that's so sweet."

"One more reason I believe we were destined to meet."

Her lips curled downward. "Do you want to drink my blood?"

"When you're ready." He touched her nose and winked. "You are not food. You are my love."

Her hand found his, and his words played on her lips as she repeated them in a whisper. His arm encircled her shoulder, and she sat even closer to him. *You are my love? I am his love? How fast is this happening?* She had to acknowledge; her feelings were the same. She chided herself for overanalyzing and reminded herself to stay in the moment.

The bartender appeared within a few moments with two ornate glasses. "Good evening, Mr. VanAlt." The bartender gave Harry a cheery smile.

"Good evening, Gerald. Nice crowd tonight."

The bartender slid the most gorgeous Whiskey Sour in front of her. An orange slice and deep red cherries covered a golden cocktail pick.

Gerald's tray held a rocks glass with two fingers of the green liquor, Absinthe. He placed a small pitcher of ice water on the table, and then laid an odd-looking flat spoon over the glass. One sugar cube was placed on the slotted spoon, and meticulously, he let drops of ice water dissolve the sugar cube. With that done, he presented Harry a tiny bottle nestled in a gold base. He removed the stopper, and Harry sniffed, waving that one away. The second bottle was smaller, and the glass was etched. Harry sniffed and nodded. Gerald measured out five fat drops of dark A Positive blood, and Lizbet was mesmerized at how it dispersed in the cloudy green drink.

Gerald bowed away, and Harry lifted his drink in a toast.

She raised her glass. "But…"

Harry put a finger to his lips. "In a minute." With his nod, they toasted. "To love."

She became emotional at his toast, and a tear glittered in her eye. "To love." Her drink lingered on her lips, and she wanted to swallow down every ounce, it was by far, the most exquisite cocktail she'd ever had. "This is delicious."

Harry nodded with a twinkle in his eye. "Gerald's been tending bar for over two hundred years. He knows what he's doing."

Her hand covered her face and her girlish smile. "I'm trying to process all of this, but it's like living history."

He hugged her close. "I know what a shock it is at first. It's amazing what becomes commonplace."

Lizbet nodded wide-eyed. "Why do you even want blood in your drink if the liquor tastes so good.?"

◆◆◆◆

Harry smiled indulgently. "Being undead, we do not eat, nor do we need to. We can't taste or digest food. The alcohol warms me; when there's blood added, I taste the liquor's flavor." He put the drink down, and his hands rested on the edge of the table. "Think of something that you could never eat again. I'll never have another ear of roast corn slathered with butter. I'll never have another filet mignon." He waited, and her face expressed what her words could not. "You can taste everything you eat, or why else would you eat it?" She nodded. "Vampires taste only the blood; it is delicious to us. That's why we each have our preference for types. From your expression, I can see, I've just appalled you."

"Well…"

"But you don't taste what we taste. If you did, you'd understand, for instance; A Positive is as delectable to me as a well-prepared risotto."

"I'll understand with time." She hid behind the large brandy snifter of whiskey sour and sipped. He watched the gears spinning in her mind by the perplexed expression when her lips left the straw. "So, I've had my first revelation of the night. What's a demonstration?"

Harry swirled his glass in his hand, watching the legs of the alcohol coat the crystal. "One couple who is comfortable being on display performs a scene that will jump-start the feeding rituals of the vamp and donor pairs in the audience." Her hand flew to her neck, where the rogue vampire grazed her. "Not everyone there feeds. Some use it as an enticement to foreplay before an evening of sex."

She broke out in a cold sweat, he could see it, he could read it in her heartbeat. He put down his drink and wrapped both arms around her. She whimpered softly. "Oh, Lizbet, that night he tried to bite you, I pulled him away and his fangs grazed you. Do you remember me wiping your neck with my handkerchief?" She nodded against his chest as she held him. "Did you ever see distinct bites?"

She shook her and whispered. "No."

"He made no mark on you. When you ask me to bite you, it will be an ecstatic feeling. Seeing this demonstration, you'll understand why mortals ask for the bite."

"Really?" *Ask... what if I never ask?*

Matt Brenner entered the bar head down, and drawing closer, looked up with his gaze directly aimed at Harry and Lizbet. Harry put his head down. "Oh, here we go."

Lizbet tucked her head down to Harry, asking, "Where are we going?"

♦♦♦♦

A tall shadow fell over them, and when they raised their heads, Matt stood grinning broadly. "Good evening, son. Who is this exquisite woman?

For a moment, Harry was at a loss for words, and Lizbet stared at Matt, agog. Harry recognized that look. *Matt got it all the damn time.* He looked mid-twenties, well over six feet, gorgeously built, with dark hair curling around an impossibly handsome face. Harry cleared his throat. "Matt Brenner, may I introduce Dr. Elizabeth Mitchell."

Matt extended his hand. "A genuine pleasure, Dr. Mitchell."

Bright as a penny, she smiled and gestured at the empty seat next to her. "Please call me Lizbet. Won't you join us? How can you possibly be Harry's father?"

Harry muttered. "It's complicated."

Matt winked at Lizbet and shook his head at Harry. "Harry, you failed to tell me how charming Lizbet is."

Because all you said was don't do it.

Matt ignored Harry's scowl and turned again to Lizbet. "The way the two of you are dressed, I feel like you should be out stomping at the Savoy. Did he drop the top of the monster machine of his?"

Lizbet giggled. "I love his car. Don't you?"

Matt looked aside with a smirk. "Some people call that a condo on four wheels."

She playfully slapped Matt on the back of his hand and giggled again.

Harry looked at the two of them. *Who are you kidding?*

Matt drew his thumb over his full bottom lip and looked directly at Harry. "Harry, she reminds me of someone. I can't put my finger on it."

Harry asked with a grin. "Yvonne DeCarlo?"

Matt tapped the table. "That's right. You could be her twin."

Lizbet's eyes widened. "Did you know her?"

Matt sat back with his hands folded in front of him. "In my dreams. I've always been a nightclub owner and artist, and she was a movie star."

Lizbet nodded excitedly at the painted mural behind the bar. "That exquisite piece isn't that your work?"

Matt lowered his head modestly and then turned for a look at it. "Well, it meant a great deal to me when I first painted it. It's like an old friend now."

"It reminds me of the artwork in The Bridge. Do you own the Bridge, too?"

Matt nodded cheerfully. "It's one of our properties." Matt looked at his watch and stood. "I'm sorry to leave such good company; I have to get ready for the demonstration." He looked directly at Harry. "You are bringing Lizbet to the eleven o'clock demonstration?"

"We were discussing that."

Lizbet's eyes widened and sparkled with cautious curiosity.

Matt took her hand in his and artfully stroked the back. "This is your first time to a demonstration. There's truly, no need to be afraid. It is a beautiful thing. This is a safe place, and no one is ever hurt."

Harry's face was a blank mask. *Unless they ask.*

Matt patted the back of her hand. "Will I see you there?"

Lizbet ducked her head shyly. "I think so."

Harry's brows knit. *Stop charming her, dammit.* "Thanks, Dad, see you later."

Matt turned back and pointed to them. "I'll reserve seats for you."

Chapter Fifteen

Fortified with another whiskey sour, Lizbet walked with Harry to the loveseat reserved for them in the demonstration room. They found themselves in front of center stage. As time grew closer to the feeding, couples eagerly settled into the seats around them.

An elegantly tall Viking of a man with chiseled good looks and a fit, muscular body gazed down at her from the raised round stage. His golden blond good looks were impeccably groomed. He wore tuxedo trousers, a formal pleated shirt, open at the neck, and an air of complete command.

Lizbet sat up straight, catching her breath. *Each man is impossibly better looking than the last.* She twisted her hands in her lap, reluctant to meet the gaze that said, 'Look at me'.

"Good evening." The man's voice was deep and resonant and brooked no denial. Lizbet's gaze snapped over to Harry.

"Are you alright, Lizbet?" Harry whispered, more for her sake.

"Uhuh." *Oh, God, Harry can smell my arousal, can they all?*

Harry gave her a knowing look and pulled her closer on the loveseat. "That is Adam Lachlan." She sank deeper into the loveseat. "He's coming over to welcome you to your first demonstration." *Oh, God! They all know.* Her face flamed, and she dared not pick up her drink.

With phenomenal grace, Master Adam stepped down from the stage and approached them. *His clothing seems painted on. I do not know how he moves.* She smiled oddly at Harry. "I'm going to kill you. With kindness, but I'm going to kill you."

Master Adam's blond brow rose quizzically as he arrived before them. Harry stood, and they affectionately shook hands, their arms adding casual embraces with stout smacks on each other's backs.

"Harry, you've brought a delicate rose to our garden tonight."

Harry drew in an exceptionally deep breath. "Master Adam, how am I going to impress Lizbet if you steal her away her first time here?"

A grin broke on Lizbet's face as she offered her hand. The Master took her hand and bowed from his considerable height to kiss the back of it. "Harry, if you can't keep her, she was never yours, to begin with."

Lizbet craned her neck to look up at the two men. Her gaze met Harry's. "I'm all yours, Harry. Aren't you a doll to bring me to meet all your handsome friends?" Harry made his introductions, it was white noise to Lizbet, awestruck within her surroundings.

Still holding her hand, Adam's aqua gaze penetrated her haze, "Dr. Mitchell, you may call me Master Adam." He placed her hand back on her lap and turned to Harry. "Did you come in tonight because of Matt doing the demonstration?"

Harry shoved his hands into his trouser pockets. "Not particularly." He scowled. "Just a Saturday night out."

Adam stood to his full six-foot, six inches, and smiled. "What lucky timing." He turned to see a woman place a long-stemmed red rose in a tall bud vase on a pedestal beside a broad and deep black velvet chaise. "We'll be starting in a minute; please excuse me." Adam left to go behind a drape, and the house lights dimmed to almost darkness. Lizbet sought Harry's hand, and he settled an arm around her and pulled her close.

The dim spotlight showed down on the harpist in the corner. There was a musical introduction, and a spotlight glowed on Master Adam. As he spoke, the theatre in the round stage became bathed in low light.

"Good evening, members and guests." His tone commanded.

A chorus of different accents and languages responded. "Good evening, Master Adam."

"This evening, we have something unheralded for a Saturday night demonstration. You'll notice we have music provided by an outstanding Harpist, Charity Saint Saenz, playing 'Adagio of Spartacus and Phrygia'. Our usual St. Andrews Cross is gone, replaced by a pedestal and a single red rose. And now, without further ado, we will welcome Matthew Brenner and his donor.

Ms. Saint Saenz delicately plucked the strings. The room filled with the elegantly syncopated rhythm of the adagio's developing theme as the lights fell to half-light.

With the sequence of the music's trills, a petite young woman, clad in a filmy toga, loosely tied at her waist, entered barefoot. The glow of a spotlight illuminated her silver-blonde beauty as her hair fell in waves around her shoulders. The donor waited; chin demurely tucked as Matt entered from the opposite side. The light danced on his chocolate brown waves of hair, the sheen of his silky shirt, and the satin stripe down his tuxedo trousers. Matt stood, nostrils flared, and his gaze momentarily flitted to Lizbet.

A slowly ascending scale played as Matt strolled, barefoot to the pedestal, and gracefully lifted the red rose from the vase. Drops of water fell dark as blood on the black stage. He met his donor, and Lizbet expected them to dance. Matt and his donor embraced elegantly, there was a turn, and she posed, waiting upon the chaise.

The strings eased into the famous 'love theme' for the first time as the room appreciated her pale, perfect body, in contrast to the black velvet. Standing behind her, Matt held the rose lightly, drawing its budding petals down her right arm and then back up. His arms framed her as he bent to scent her neck. Seductively, she swished her head, letting loose her platinum hair in response to his attention. They moved together as if choreographed in La Danse Apache.

The harp's delicate plucking of the strings accentuated the scalic movement, effectively adding to the atmosphere's intensity. The musician's command of the melody and counter-melody worked together to represent Matt and his willing donor.

As the intensity of the melody grew, so did their dynamics. The ferocity of Matt's hunger sent him to kneel at her feet. As Matt's graceful hand slipped under the gossamer of his donor's gown, Lizbet dropped her gaze to the floor. Harry held her hand, urging her to watch as Matt pushed back the donor's dress and ran the rose up the inside of his donor's leg. Her pale thighs spread with Matt's commanding hand.

Lizbet's breath caught, and she knew Matt heard her. It didn't stop him. The velour petals disappeared under the dress between the donor's legs as the donor fell back in a swoon against the tufted velvet. When he withdrew the rose, he held it to his nose, and the vampires in the audience released sighs of varying responses.

Harry squeezed Lizbet's hand and nuzzled her ear. As the intensity of the melody grew, so did the feeder/donor dynamics. As Matt sat back on his heels and hesitated, the music swept the room into a sensual spell. He rose and lifted the donor's legs along the length of the chaise. Matt's unbuttoned white silken shirt billowed with his movement to reveal his bare chest as he walked behind the chaise.

With a magician's grace, Matt's hands ran through her thick and lustrous hair. The woman's delight in his touch was exhibited by her lips gently parted in rapture. Matt buried his nose into her neck, caught her long hair in a twist, the donor handed him a clip, and her lovely, swanlike neck was pale and visible to the audience.

There was a gasp from the undead as Matt bent and licked from the spot behind her ear, all the way down to her shoulder. He lifted her hand, and his nose traveled her arm, his nostrils flaring at her cachet. The music and their responses exhibited a distinct feeling of call and response between them. Her developing aura enticed Matt's every move.

Matt lightly kissed her palm and returned to join her on the chaise. He sat facing the audience, his back against the velvet, his face a dreamy and sensual immortal sculpture. He dropped his head, and when he raised it, his vampire was in full bloom. His skin's translucent tone contrasted with her rosy complexion.

Lost within the harp's emotional score, Lizbet startled at the transformation. Staring at Matt's icy eyes, his full lips drawn back, revealing long, pointed fangs, she was unexpectantly turned on. Her belly quivered, and her thighs tightened. She felt more than heard Harry's soft chuckle at her response. She nudged him with her shoulder as if to say, *stop that.*

The woman clutching the rubine rose to her breast with one hand, draped her body into Matt's firm embrace. Their tension was two distinct timbres, creating this dramatic transition toward the expected climax.

Before Matt dropped his head to his donor, Lizbet felt his opalescent gaze. *Did his lips curl curiously on one side for show?* Matt's lips moved to the wrist where he would bite. The harpist plucked with greater fervency, and Matt's bite struck.

My God, did I actually hear him bite her? His lips massaged the blood from her wrist as the donor moaned in carnal pleasure. Her hair clip fell to the floor, but the harp played on.

Matt's tongue curled and cupped to catch her precious blood as he moved her arm into a different position. The undead audience stirred at the appearance of an errant drop on his chin. With the back of one practiced hand, he swept it off and languorously licked his flesh clean.

Lizbet sat agog, making a little squeak as she saw his curled tongue. His hand slipped around his donor's back, and he shifted closer to her, both of them settling deeper into the corner of the chaise. Now, embracing more urgently, Matt held the donor's wrist to his mouth and elicited what they had all come to see.

The translucent fabric allowed the spectators to appreciate the nearly nude donor's sensual flush of her building orgasm. As Matt masterfully fed, her legs shook, and her back arched in the ecstasy of his drawing bite. He caught her closer to him, her pale back exposed to the audience, her head on his shoulder, his fingers stroking her silken locks as she pressed her hips into his.

The tableau ended with the harp strings unifying the vamp/mortal's last swell together. The audience held silent for the donor's cry of culmination and her collapse against Matt's bare chest. After a beat, Matt held the donor's wrist high, exposing his well-placed bite. At the applause, he brought it back to his lips and generously laved his tongue over his bite marks to seal the small wounds.

Before Lizbet's eyes, the puncture marks healed to nothing. The lights went out, and she could barely see the ghost of Matt's shirt fluttering as he carried the woman off stage.

The audience made no sound. Matt returned, appeared under a spotlight, and bowed like a maestro. As he raised his hands in acknowledgment, his color was bright and robust. His chest revealed a sheen of light sexual perspiration.

Lizbet checked her jaw. She knew she was gawking. She dropped her head until the applause died, and Matt was gone

Harry gave her a minute, waiting as the others filed out to do what vampires and donors do. "Questions? Are you okay? Are we okay?"

Lizbet raised her gaze, emotionally overwhelmed. "I had no idea. I don't know what to think." She fell against him, closer than before, and whispered. "We are more than okay, but can we be alone? She patted her racing heart.

Harry kissed her forehead. "Of course, my sweet."

Chapter Sixteen

Harry pressed his floor number in the elevator and glanced down to Lizbet, listening to her racing heart. When they got to his door, he hesitated and capped his hands over her shoulders. "I know the last time you were here; it was not pleasant. Tonight, let's start again." He unlocked and swung open the door. "Won't you come in, Lizbet?"

She walked into his mid-century minimalist apartment and stood in the middle of the living room, eying everything. "I never would peg you for going mid-century."

Harry shrugged. "I bought the model. This is how it came. Is it bad?"

Lizbet grinned. It's not bad at all. It's very stylish. I didn't picture you here."

"Why not? Did you have me pegged for heavy wood and doilies?"

Lizbet laughed. "Not that either. I guess I saw you in something more traditional."

"Since I bought it, it's just been me. I'm easy on it and don't see the reason for change for the sake of change."

"You haven't had a woman in your life for a long time. Every lifestyle magazine has new colors every twenty-eight days." Harry winced, and Lizbet laughed. "Yeah, I'm not one of those people either." She walked to the coffee table and dropped her scarf and purse. "Do I get the nickel tour?"

Harry slid out of his double-breasted jacket and hung it in the closet. He loosened his tie as he walked to a switch and flipped on the water feature. The barrier between his kitchen and living room was a rocky wall fountain. Plants and small lights accentuated the rippling water as it traveled from the ceiling down to its reservoir and back again. The sound was restful. "This is my living room, complete with a view of the La Brea Tar Pits. During the summer, you wouldn't believe the Flintstone jokes I hear from the tourists."

"You're on the 28th floor?"

He tapped his ear. "Extraordinary vampire hearing, my dear." He opened the first set of patio doors, and there was a rattan chaise just like the leather one in the living room. A dense growth of ivy covered a cedar lattice to shield him from the sun along the thirty-foot length of the balcony. Inside, between the two patio doors sat a studio upright piano glowing in Birdseye maple. It illuminated the dark interior.

"No wonder you played so well at my house, look what you have." She sat on the velvet seat and turned, smiling at him.

His expression was blank. "It blends so well with the paneling; I forgot it's here."

"Oh, Harry, sure you did. What other treasures have you forgotten?"

On the way to his office, he led her past a wall of books and stereo equipment. "When I write, I need the resources of oddball details and a large music library." She looked at a thousand albums, a few hundred CDs, and books organized by subjects. "Come here." He opened the door to his writing room. The twelve by twelve room's walls were covered with maps, moon and sun charts, and various statistics. In the center of the room was a desk surrounded by several computer towers. Two monitors and more speakers stood like soldiers at attention on the desktop.

"Is this where you make your magic?"

He stood behind her and wrapped his arms around her waist, nuzzling her ear. "My agent thinks so. Didn't you tell me last night that I was a magician? Of course, that's a completely different skill."

Lizbet hip bumped back into him. "I have no words for what you do to me." He heard her stomach growl.

"Lizbet, when was the last time you ate? You had those two big drinks, but I hear a rumbly tummy."

She waved him off. "I had a perfectly fine dinner around seven. My rumbly tummy doesn't need a thing."

"Let me show you where I'm having the Murphy bed installed." He caught her hand and took her back through the living room to the hidden corner behind his kitchen. Pictures and furniture were moved aside, and preliminary carpentry was in evidence.

"This is fine for me, are you joining me out here, where do you sleep?" She curled into him, caught his suspenders, and ran her thumbs up and down inside them.

"With your permission, I'll stay here until you fall asleep, then I'll go to ground."

"Where is ground on the twenty-eighth floor?"

"It's my dark, quiet space. Nothing to see. We've talked about it before."

Lizbet shot him a skeptical glance, but let it pass wondering if he slept in a coffin.

"Would you like some tea?"

"You keep tea?"

He laughed. "I gave gifts to some of my editors and staff last year; I think there are peppermint or lapsang souchong tea bags. Join me in the kitchen." He had a minimalist kitchen with a microwave and a few tumblers and mugs. Two rotting lemons and a bottle of chardonnay sat in the wine cooler. He hurriedly tossed the lemons in the under sink trashcan.

"No fridge?"

He pressed a flat wood surface, and the door swung open, revealing bags of blood stored in an unusually presented refrigerator.

He felt her gaze as he pulled out a teabag and ran water into a cup."

"Boy, you're definitely not British. I'm bringing an electric teapot if I'm invited back."

"Sorry, think of this as camping." They stood, arms wrapped around each other while the microwave ticked. Within moments he had her settled on the modern curved chaise with her cup. He placed a light throw over them, and they cuddled while she drank the smoky flavored tea.

♦♦♦♦

Harry nuzzled her neck, which she was beginning to recognize as a preamble to more. She placed the mug on the table next to her. "Are you going to tell me what you thought of the demonstration?"

"Do you know that is one of my favorite ballets? Did you see the performance in the Hollywood Bowl last year?"

"So, you liked the music. We usually don't have music."

"That's a shame, live music adds so much." Her eyelashes fluttered as she relaxed.

He began to speak and stopped.

Her brows rose. "What were you going to say?"

"Generally, they're BDSM scenes with impact play."

"Ohhhh. Then I'm glad I was there for this one. I know what a St. Andrews Cross is for, just not interested."

Harry stopped to reflect. "The vamps tell me it's a rush, but it's lost on me. Aside from the music, what did you think?"

"I thought it was undeniably erotic." Harry opened his mouth and then hushed as she continued. "I also thought it was a good thing I met Matt before the demonstration in what I suppose was his usual charming self. If I had only seen him in the demonstration, I would have thought he was nothing but a predator."

"Well…"

"See, it's almost as if vampires are like Dr. Jekyll and Mr. Hyde. You have your near mortal presentation, which is very pleasant. And then you have the fanged predator."

"Do you think his donor felt preyed upon?"

Lizbet paused to consider. "Not at all. I do assume she is an experienced donor."

"Yes, Matt tends to keep dedicated donors. So they know each other quite well."

Lizbet went analytical. "So, familiarity, say between lovers would seem to increase pleasure and decrease distress."

Harry slanted her a serious look. "I think I can speak for every vamp in this building when I say, we would never want anyone receiving our bite to feel distressed."

"That takes the worry out of being close for them. What does this have to do with you and me?"

"You wanted to know about vampires. I'm a vampire. You had questions. I felt bringing you here tonight would open channels between us."

She caught his jaw and stared directly into his blue-green eyes. "You are tap dancing as fast as you can, aren't you, Harry?"

He sighed. "Why did I fall in love with a psychologist?"

"Just lucky, I guess." She rested her cheek on his chest and thought for a beat. "There really isn't anything ticking in there." She tapped his chest. "That's kind of spooky. I didn't appreciate how different you are until I observed your peers, and your peer's eating habits."

"But that's not really the elephant in the room, is it?"

"Do you want to bite me, Harry?"

"Yes, but let me tell you why." Her heartbeat escalated, her eyes dilated, and he felt a small tremor overtake her. "I don't want to feed from you. When we're intimate, your blood sings to me, and just the taste of it would share your feelings with me. It also allows me to climax."

Her gaze narrowed at him. "But, last night…"

"It was too soon to ask to bite you."

"It wasn't too soon for me to go down on you or to have you make love to me or for you to go down on me…"

Harry drew air between his teeth. "I see your point. But I knew it would be misunderstood, so I bit myself."

"I'm never closing my eyes on you again. You snuck that right past me."

"You realize the bite also enhances *your* orgasm. You saw the donor's response to feeding. Imagine that with foreplay? Coupled with the act of love, it's the ultimate union."

Lizbet was quiet for a beat. "Well, when you put it that way." She giggled. She gathered all her courage. "Okay, Mr. Romantic Vampire. Show me." She held up her wrist.

"Just like that?" His brows knit. "That's not the way I pictured your first bite."

She looked around. "What, you've got a garden tub, a champagne fountain? Violins?"

He caressed her and placed her head under his chin. "I want it to be special, something you'll remember for eternity."

♦♦♦♦

Rick lounged in his penthouse, watching Matt's demonstration by closed-circuit television. He switched camera angles to observe Harry and his mortal lover front and center to the action. When Matt bowed and left the stage, Rick sat up and rested his chin in his palm as he watched the vamps and donors moving around Harry and Lizbet. *She's the palest mortal I've seen this side of feeding. Oh, dear girl, don't faint on him.* He stood, thinking after that performance Matt was due for a critique.

If vampire blood could boil, Rick's circulated at high speed on the elevator ride down to their shared office. As Rick exited the elevator, he listened for mortal heartbeats. It would seem the dungeons were full. Well, after that peep show, he wasn't surprised. As Rick entered their office, Matt entered fresh from a shower in his playroom. Rick put a glass on each side of their partner's desk and poured brandy. "Have a seat, dear boy."

Matt ran a hand through his damp, dark hair and sniffed. Now dressed in his casual jeans and V-neck sweater, he was as robust a vampire as Rick had ever seen. On the streets, he would have passed as a mortal. The fresh feeding, coupled with the sexual foreplay, nearly had Matt's jugular pumping. "You have AB Negative left over?" Matt asked with a cocky grin.

Rick dispensed the drops into the glass as Matt swept it off his desk with gusto.

"What do you think you're doing?" Rick's expression drove the question home.

"I'm enjoying a victory drink for bringing something new to The Gaoler. All of us aren't into whips and handcuffs. I think they liked it." Matt sat down in his chair, self-satisfied.

"I have no quarrel with new types of demonstrations. However, that wasn't your primary goal, was it?"

Matt swirled his glass. "It was maybe also a chance to let little miss profiler see what she's getting into."

"So that was the purpose of your knowing gazes her way, your extra-long fangs and the audible bite you gave. Nice hesitation from your harpist. Did you have that planned, or did you hold your bite?"

Matt shrugged. "Happy accident. Really drove it home, didn't it?"

"Yeah, especially to a virgin who was attacked by a vampire a month ago."

"Hey, she can either deal with it or not." Matt's full bottom lip pursed as his brows rose. "Best to know upfront. Saves time; reduces vampire exposure." Matt lounged in his desk chair; his long legs stretched to the side as he considered his performance. "It saves us from vamp/mortal attachment."

Rick scowled and slapped his hand down on his desk. "Vamp/mortal attachment? Have you seen these two together? Have you scented her? He's done everything but bite her. She's been attacked by a rogue, observed Venus perform one of her famous takedowns, and Harry is in love with her. You think your little fang and rose show is going to separate them?"

"Well--."

Rick planted the heavy glass on his desk as he rose and leaned on his knuckles across to Matt. "Have you even considered how Harry will feel about you if you succeed in driving her away? How does it usually go when parents try to come between a romance?" Matt's expression grew wary. "I'll tell you; it drives them closer together. Do you want him living in her neighborhood? If you do manage to drive them apart are you ready for the resentment which might never be resolved?"

Matt's tongue wet his lips. "She's a nice girl for a mortal."

Rick shook his head. "She's thirty-four, she's a woman. I'm warning you, Matthew, stay out of this. Your one move is to be as supportive and positive as possible. You don't have to be a father figure; he's got fifty years in. Be a friend. This thing will work out, or it won't." They shared a beat of silence. "You don't want her pissed for an eternity if she joins the family."

Matt's head hit the back of his chair and his eyelids deliberately closed for a moment. "I never even considered that."

"Haven't I told you before, if you want someone to go your way, get on their side."

Matt sat back up, his hands between his knees, the glow of his performance dampened. "You think I should check on them?"

"Not until tomorrow. What about sending Dr. Mitchell a nice coffee and brunch cart around noon? Don't send a rose in a vase. Maybe we should invite her to tomorrow evening's dinner with the donors."

Matt nodded. "Yeah, okay. I'll arrange it."

Rick sat and swirled his glass. Looking at the ceiling, he quipped. "If you said that with some enthusiasm, I'd believe you."

Chapter Seventeen

"Let's table all this talk about biting. It's not an issue right now anyway." Harry rose and walked to his wall of stereo components. "Would you like to listen to some of my original seventy-eights?"

Lizbet bounded behind him. "You have seventy-eights?"

"Yeah, all mine from before I was turned. The original arrangements."

Lizbet held up a box set. "Oh, my God, this must have been Sinatra's first record album."

Harry grinned. "Let's put it on; you'll love it." He loaded the four heavy records into the post-war Capehart Flipover Changer Phonograph. "With these records being three and a half to five minutes each, we have about a half-hour of dancing time."

"Do you know all the old dances, handsome Harry?"

Harry led her to the patio and pushed the chaise to the side, giving them more room to dance. "I don't want to brag, but if I heard the music, the steps would come back." He placed his hand on her waist and drew her in. "I'm a little rusty. In fifty years, you're my first dance partner."

"Then we are both lucky I took ballroom classes. Haven't actually used it much because most men don't know how to dance." She pushed closer and looked up at him through her lashes. "Do you tango?"

He winked. "I can tangle just fine." Sinatra began, 'You Go to My Head'. Harry and Lizbet's chemistry melded perfectly with the song's harmonic movement. Their steps in unison moved intently on creating feverish intimacy. The drama of the past few days disappeared as their common interests drew them together.

By the time they reached the fourth song, Lizbet was amazed at how Harry's knowledge of dance enhanced the experience. Rather than distancing her from him, his embrace held her close against him. He stole her balance unless they leaned together and caused her to lift onto the balls of her feet. This was the position the ballroom instructor had always recommended, but she'd never had a real dance partner carry it out. It was heaven. No more guessing which way your partner was leading, Harry's hips and thighs guided her. She felt like Ginger Rogers, but Harry was far more seductive than Fred Astaire. Who knew dancing was a gateway drug? No wonder parents tried to keep young people off the dance floor.

Lizbet whispered. "Do you have anything here that plays music for an evening?"

Harry looked over his shoulder. "It won't have the high fidelity that this phonograph has."

Lizbet pulled on the front of his leather braces. "I was thinking about a more horizontal dance."

His face brightened. "The perfect reason for a full contingent of audio equipment. MP3s for the win." He led her back to the sofa. "Why don't you have a seat on the couch."

"If you don't mind, I'd like to freshen up for a minute." Harry directed her to one of the two closed doors in the apartment. *I wonder where the other door goes?*

The bathroom was extremely masculine and recently updated from the looks of the tile and cutting edge shower fixtures. She stood at one of the two sinks and held on to the granite counter. Staring into the large framed mirror, she took a deep, cleansing breath. *With all of my emotional responses this evening, from the feeding to dancing close, I hope he is aroused by my personal nervous scent.* She washed and dried her hands, patted her face with her damp fingers, and headed back out into the spider's web.

He doesn't look like a spider, she thought affectionately as she stood in the doorway. Harry grinned boyishly at her from the chaise in front of the wall fountain. The music was lower, slower, and the lights were dimmer. His tie was gone, and he stood, one hand in his trouser pocket, the fingers of his other hand unconsciously stroking the patina of the black leather chaise. "Care to take a break?"

"Are you trying to seduce me, Mr. VanAlt?"

Harry stalked to her, radiating vampire appeal. His usual crisp haircut was ruffled from dancing and nuzzling. His hickory colored hair fell adorably over his forehead. She could see muscles rippling under his superbly tailored dress shirt. His blue-green eyes deepened smokily, and Lizbet's knees went weak. She leaned against the doorframe for support as Harry moved in. His forearm above her head steadied him as he bent to whisper in her ear. "Is it working?"

"Oh, yeah."

"Then, may I have this dance?" He swept her up, and she squealed as he carried her to the wide curved chaise. Lizbet stretched on the length of soft tufted leather. Harry dropped his leather braces to the side and moved to lie facing her.

"You know, handsome, without these on your shoulders, your trousers might drop."

One arm swept behind her, and his other arm drew her to him. "I was counting on that."

Lizbet shivered under his spell, lost in his gaze. She pulled his waistband out and stared down. "There are parts of you still dancing."

He sniffed the air. "There's parts of you still following."

She flattened her hand as it dove down between his boxers and his cool flesh. "Gotcha."

His back straightened, and his hand moved under her full skirt to cup her panties. "Ditto."

"This is like some perverse game of Twister."

"We could make it easier by undressing."

"I'm not losing that contest again." She reached to her neck and pulled her halter's bow. "I'm down to one short zipper, how about you?" Lizbet felt the abrupt loss of his embrace, and in a blur, Harry was back beside her, nude. "What was that?"

"I told you, vamps are faster and stronger."

"So, I lost the game again?" She pouted.

His finger tapped her on her chin. "It wasn't a fair fight. You had no idea. So, you win."

"My memory is foggy. What do I win?"

He reached around her and slid down her dress zipper and pulled it over her head. "One complimentary undressing…" his hands moved to her bikini panties under her garter belt. "One replacement pair of panties."

"Replacement?"

He grasped both hips of her filmy panties and ripped.

"Oh!"

He pulled them to his nose and savored them. "May I have these?"

"They're yours."

Down to her garter belt and hose, Lizbet unbuckled and tossed off her shoes. The soft lighting of the water wall threw fingers of muted shadows across the room.

Harry pulled Lizbet across his hips, dizzy with the feeling of her warmth crushing him. "When I was at your house, I held back."

"Right, you didn't bite, that changes tonight."

"No, what I meant was, as aroused as I am after seeing that feeding, watching you, dancing, and holding you, I'm in my element here. I'm too strong to take the lead tonight. I need you to set the pace."

She nodded in understanding. A playful gleam came into her eyes.

"No teasing, I mean it." He held her hands in his and gazed hard into her eyes.

"Okay, handsome, no teasing." She tapped him on the chin. "I won't do this." She sucked in a breath of air at his ear and he shivered. "I won't do this…" She rolled his nipple between her fingers while she suckled the other.

The rumble in his chest built. "Two can play this game." He caught her hips in each hand, and amidst squeals of laughter, he slid downwards while he pulled her center over his lips. His words were muffled by her sex as the vibration of his words drove her crazy.

"Harry, no, too soon." She crawled back down and caught his face. "You know how that sends me. It's too soon. I want some of this first." She caught his hard length and stroked feverishly.

"Ah, I warned you. See how fast I can move?" His thumb stroked her center and she giggled to a squeal.

"Harry!"

Innocently, he stretched under her warmth. "What?"

She wiggled down to his thighs and lay flat on him, her finger drawing circles in his chest hair while she caught her breath. "I've noticed, you just breathe when you talk, which is great when you're down there owning a piece of me…but I need breath, so no tickling."

He sat her back up, astride him, and shook his head. "You're so strict."

With soft and serious lips, Lizbet claimed his mouth and caught his bottom lip in her teeth for a second. She felt his flesh quiver at her bite. Straddling Harry, Lizbet rose as high as she could and cupped his face with her hands; her fingers traced Harry's generous lips softer than a dragonfly. She placed another kiss on his mouth.

She guided him into her. "Ooh..." she sighed, moving rhythmically, answering his hip's motions. Harry's preternaturally cool hands gripped her as his long, leanly muscled body reclined along the undulating curve of the chaise, his dark head tilted back. Lizbet marveled at their fit, how their bodies dovetailed like yin and yang. A low rumble emanated from deep within his chest.

His mercurial blue-green eyes told her more than he uttered. She worked his length, riding him from tip to hilt. Her head fell back when she took all of him within her. Her lips oh'd, and she enjoyed the feeling of her hair as it caped her shoulders.

She found this her favorite position with Harry, the strength in his thrusts stroked her soul. No matter how many times they mounted the chaise, she'd work him hard with her slow, steady give and take.

Harry took over, holding her still as he rocked, fucking leisurely, extending their passion. At first, unintelligible words poured from her lips as her hands reached for his shoulders. The new angle introduced new shivers. The faster she stroked, the harder his thrust answered. They fucked, and she told him in a million ways she wanted to be bitten.

Lizbet rose almost to the point where her velvet grasp gripped only his crown to hesitate and lower, engulfing him to the hilt.

He cradled her in his arms when she came, and heat poured off her into him. She took a moment to catch her breath. Harry was still inside her, still hard as she squirmed and tightened herself against him shaking, panting, sweating, trying to hold on to that feeling, that thought, that moment. She closed her eyes finally and let go, collapsing into his arms, lost in the emotion.

His hands caressed her breasts, perfecting her round nipples between his fingers. Lizbet lowered her head; Harry's eyes still closed, when she said, "Who's fucking whom?"

♦♦♦♦

Their efforts in tandem were alchemy, turning what would be viewed as synchronized movement into gold.

The curve of her hip called him to hold her tightly. He never knew how their friction on the chaise could excite the scent of leather.

The unexpected taste of her aroused skin was so different from the flavor of her other emotions. Her singular bouquet sang as they whipped each other into a frenzy. All of this was compounded by the soundtrack of the trickling fountain water that set the pace of her rising and falling and rising again on him.

Her flat hands rested on his pecs. "You're right. You do get hot." He cuddled her closer, and she whispered. "Bite me, Harry." Their gazes locked, and he sweetly rolled her under him. Resting on his forearms, he kissed her cheek and whispered into her ear. "I love you, Elizabeth."

Her heartbeat sang a siren's song, leading his attention to her pale throat. The vein that sang to him pulsed wildly as she lay still beneath him. With a practiced thrust, he buried himself within her as he bit. He heard a groan, loud and long that had him worried until he realized it was his own. He was spent.

♦♦♦♦

Tonight, on the chaise, Lizbet marveled at the gamut of physical sensations Harry's loving provided. Last night was heaven, and tonight was wilder. Now, lost in her multi-orgasmic world, she didn't know what her invitation would bring. *I just asked him to bite me.* With the cool feeling of his lips on her neck, her eyes sprang open. *When did his flesh pale to translucent? When did his eyes silver?* She dared not move, her eyes closed.

How did she miss his metamorphosis? Her fear was pierced by her lover's bite. Wave after wave of sensation and emotion overwhelmed them. She opened her eyes and the room, which had been dim, filled with song and shimmering light.

When had he become so beautiful? She felt his soothing hand on her hair; she felt everything. She felt the breeze of his impossibly thick eyelashes, and she basked in his gift. Fireworks went off within her. She thought she should see them; they were so electric. Tears of joy rolled from her eyes as she reached for Harry's face. "Kiss me, Harry…" When he did, he was Harry again and they were spent and sweaty and warm.

Chapter Eighteen

Harry set the head of the chaise to a lower level, pulled a throw from the chair, and spread it over Lizbet. He climbed back onto the makeshift bed and held her close.

She giggled and, in a breathy voice, said, "Wow… I'm surprised you folks don't charge us for that."

Harry's chuckle traveled through his body, and she pulled closer to him, throwing her leg over his. "For you, it's free." He stroked her hair and kissed the top of her head.

She murmured against him. "Aren't you exhausted? I am." He felt her fall limply against him, her eyes fluttering shut.

"I love you, Elizabeth." He closed his eyes to hold her and meditate. The first vision in his reverie was Lizbet pointing to a piano in his living room that he had forgotten entirely. *How is it possible to forget the piano?* Lizbet sat on the velvet piano bench and ran her hands over the Birdseye maple. When she swiveled back around, her manifestation had a genuine 1940s aura. Her hair was a halo of black curls, sea green eyes in sharp contrast to her usual emerald green.

The pages of a calendar floated by, December 28th, 1946. Frankie nearly swooned at the sight of a raven-haired miss sitting at the bar, a Lucky Strike teetering between her index and second finger as she stared into the lounge's grey haze...

Harry snapped out of his visions. *I've never had a character in a book come to me like that. That's writing fiction for you.* Lizbet shifted in her sleep. He recognized the moon's movement in the clerestory windows of his living room. *Time to go to ground.*

◆◆◆◆

Lizbet cuddled to where Harry had been. He was gone, the sun was flowing through the windows high on the wall. She looked around the room for a clock. Eight fifty-seven. She hunted for their discarded clothes, but this dress was not what she wanted to wear on a Sunday morning. *I wish I had brought those robes I bought.* She washed out her cup from last night and nuked a mug of water for tea. *I have to bring some mortal essentials here*. Walking around the room, naked was not her idea of being a proper houseguest. Although Harry might like it. She turned to the large bathroom and began opening doors and drawers, being nosy. Laundry detergent, a stacked washer, and dryer next to a rod with a variety of Harry's shirts hanging. Well, of course, he sends his dress shirts out, but a long-tailed polo hung waiting for her.

After a luxurious shower, she stood at the bathroom's full-length mirror and looked for his bite mark. She felt where it was, but there was nothing showing. Phantom feelings returned when she touched her neck if she stroked it, it tingled.

After all the body fluids, they'd exchanged, what was borrowing a toothbrush? *Humn, cinnamon toothpaste? An odd choice for a species with no sense of taste*. She donned the polo shirt and decided while Harry was down for the day, she'd snoop a little. She checked out his office bookshelf with M.C. Westmacott's books. The Bikini Murders occupied the far right position, his latest release. The hardback and the audiobook stood together. The previous eight books had the paperback sandwiched between the hardback and the audio. She pulled the earliest book and found it was published in 1992. *That old guy has a good gig going*.

Looking down, she noticed four other shelves similarly laid out, each shelf with a different author. Lizbet opened the book on the far left of Westmacott's shelf. Inside the pristine hardback, she read the jacket cover, "M.C. Westmacott is the true-crime writer for the nineties…" *this was a hearty recommendation for a first book*. The New York Times Best Selling Author was a guy by the name of Bernard Quick. *Son of a gun, the bookshelf below was full of Bernard Quick books. Ah, the quick and the dead. Harry was certainly quick and not dead*.

The same recommendations flowed from decade to decade for Harry's collection. *Hey, it worked once!* Of course, he would change his identity with each decade. *Imagine the royalties*.

Lizbet bent to the bottom shelf and pulled out Harry's freshman effort. The 1951 book was mortal Henry W. VanAlt, Jr.'s sole publication. The jacket read, 'Murder in the First is a bone-chilling insight into the mind of a Pacific Northwest upstanding physician driven to murder by his calculating business partner.'

Lizbet brewed another mug of tea to quiet her rumbly tummy and found a place in a curved easy chair. Immersed in the book, she'd just reached the part where the instigating partner, Dr. Leo Krueger, pressed Dr. George to kill Krueger's wife, when there was a knock on the door. *Will Harry hear that if he's gone to ground or whatever?*

She hesitated. The knock repeated. Throwing caution to the wind, she peeked at the security monitor mounted next to the door. It was Matt with what looked like room service. *Matt?*

She swung the door open. "Are you moonlighting as a room service waiter?"

He gave her a charming smile. His teeth glittered. "Just helping out. I had to make sure you have brunch while Harry is unavailable."

She watched Matt warily. "That's nice. Whose notion was this? Do you do this for all Harry's mortal guests?"

Matt pushed the fragrant cart into the kitchen area and stood with a satisfied smile. "I guess so; you're the first."

"Oh, right. Cause Harry's other guests were like him, like you, I mean all of you."

He bowed a confirmation and began placing the items on the island. She held the tail of Harry's polo shirt down as he motioned for her to sit and eat. "You want to eat this while it's warm." He waited for her to relax and take a bite.

"I still don't get it." She poured a cup of coffee from the carafe. "Less than twelve hours ago, you were trying to flip me out, and now you want me to eat?"

Matt leaned against the island and folded his arms over his broad chest. He looked away and then back at her. "Well, I can't hassle you if you waste away."

Lizbet put the coffee cup down. "That's the best you've got? I surmise you don't approve of mingling the species."

Matt's hand scrubbed his face. "I don't get into debates before twilight. Can you accept my kindness and enjoy it?"

Lizbet looked over the cart, pushing napkins and jelly packets aside. "Where is the customer satisfaction poll for me to complete? I'm sure you want Mr. Hiatt to know I'm fed."

Matt leaned into her comment, with his thumbs in the back of his belt. "Look, I don't answer to Rick Hiatt. We're partners."

She picked up a toast point and chewed, nodding. "Forgiveness does not change the past, but it does enlarge the future. I'm ready for a truce if you are."

Matt slowly extended his hand. His nostrils flared, and his lips drew straight.

When they shook hands, Lizbet quirked a grin. She pointed to his face. "I haven't been around you guys long, but I can tell when you're reading the room. Those nostrils of yours have a mind of their own."

Matt's hand flew to his face; he covered his nose. "Of all the mortals Harry could meet, he brings home a profiler."

"That keeps coming up." She gestured with her fork, turned to her plate of bacon, eggs, hash browns, and toast. She drank some orange juice and nodded. "Thanks so much, Matt. Have a nice day."

Matt went to the door and then turned back. "Anything else you need?"

Do I send Matt out for panties? "Oh, could you tell me if there is a lingerie store in the lobby?"

A wry smile crossed Matt's lips. "Mamselle's is a high-end shop. They deliver." He buried a smirk as he closed the door behind him.

Chapter Nineteen

Lizbet shook her head. *It costs how much to buy a basic pair of lady's panties and have them carried up twenty-eight floors?* One pair! She returned her credit card to her wallet and cried alligator tears.

She stood by the door, not wanting to have them ring the bell and wake Harry. When she accepted the package, she saw where her money went. The opulent gold bag held an explosion of pearlescent tissue. The receipt was handwritten, and the panties were folded within more pearly paper. A salesclerk's flowery handwriting thanked her for her purchase with the invitation to shop at any time. Lizbet pulled on the beige panties and crumpled the paper into a ball, tossing it all in the garbage container under the sink.

◆◆◆◆

Just as the defendant was about to go to trial in *Murder in the First* Harry's door opened, and he emerged looking paler than usual. His eyes were half-lidded as he shuffled into the kitchen area. Lizbet sat with the book in her lap, watching him move like a sleepwalker. He pressed the hidden fridge door and withdrew a bag of blood. He emptied it into a tall latte cup, and swallowed a good part of it, walked to the sink, ran his hand under the water, and wiped his mouth. He turned and leaned against the sink. "I'm not an evening person."

"But you're a vampire." She stayed in the chair.

"You know how mortals say, 'I'm not a morning person'?"

"You don't like getting up any more than I do."

He knocked back the rest of the latte mug and did the same sink ritual before he moved across the living room to join her. The lightweight navy silk robe fluttered away from his sculptured legs. Mid-stride, he tightened the belt and buried a grin at the near reveal. "Seeing you in that chair certainly makes getting up worth the world. You won't believe this, Lizbet, but for ages, your soul has haunted me. Perhaps I knew we'd meet." By this time, he was in front of her and held out his hands to embrace her. While he held her under his chin, she wrapped her arms around him and sighed happily.

He led her over to the sliding glass doors and the darkening sky. "Do you know what I've noticed most about you this time?"

"No, what?"

"Your energy. You have this ravishing, full of life, vixen-like energy. I feel like I'm alive when I'm with you."

Lizbet ducked her head. "Oh, Harry, what a romantic thing to say, thank you." They embraced, Harry kissed his two fingers and placed the kiss on her lips. "Come sit with me. I've been reading your book. Wow, you've had quite a few different pen names through the years."

Harry grinned as they cuddled on the chaise. "How would I explain that Westmacott is eighty-two and still churning out a true-crime yearly? As a matter of fact, Westmacott is about to herald a new novelist."

Lizbet knew his artful juggling. "What's his name?"

"She's a woman. Haven't finished the research yet."

Lizbet nodded. "I got the irony of Quick's name cause you're not dead."

He barked out a laugh. "That was Rick's idea. He loves westerns."

"Really, I would never have thought that about him."

"He's from Ireland originally, and the American west enthralls him."

"I guess every vampire has their quirks."

Harry stretched out his legs and repositioned his robe. "Everyone does."

Lizbet narrowed her eyes on a mission. "Hey, you promised to tell me about how you became a vampire. Spill it, handsome. What happened?"

His smiling countenance faded, he looked out the window for a beat, made a considering face and then his lips drew straight. He studied her face and admitted. "I'm drawing a blank."

She felt his earnest confusion by the tension in his brows. "Is this sudden? Has my presence disturbed your orientation?"

His voice was soft. "No. It's all very fuzzy. I remember Matt being like a father to me." He pivoted on the chaise to face her. "When a vampire is left without their sire, the Family steps up. Matt has always been there for me…" His voice trailed to silence.

Lizbet pulled the lapels of his robe closer and nodded. "So, what do you want to do tonight?"

"I want to show off my girl and cut a rug. We both need a good meal. The Gaoler has an excellent spread for the vamps and donors in about an hour."

Lizbet stretched the polo down her thighs. "Ah, after last night, I don't have a thing to wear that doesn't smell like sex and confusion."

"But you look so good in my polo. Call Mam'selle and ask them to send up something in your size that you could wear swing dancing."

Lizbet buried a laugh. "Mam'selle? Aren't they kind of pricy?"

He waved her off. "The residents of these condos have accounts at those stores. Get whatever you want." He pointed at his office. "Those books pay me great money, and you're worth it."

♦♦♦♦

Harry whistled a zippy tune as he slid into the shower. He smiled at himself in the mirror as he shaved. *It's too beautiful a night to sit inside with a DVD. The night is right for a stroll on the pier, maybe some drinks and dancing cheek to cheek.*

He ambled out of his dressing room, adjusting his tie. The sight of Elizabeth in her new sateen dress blew his mind. The bodice hugged her in all the round places, and the front crisscross straps formed a peek-a-boo over her cleavage. *I could stare at her all night.* "What I want to know is, are you or are you not a jive bomber?"

She stood perplexed. "I don't operate firearms…"

His laughter unleashed. "Oh, Elizabeth, I was asking about your dancing skills. After dinner, I think we should make a stop at the ballroom."

"What ballroom?"

"At the pier."

"But, Harry, there hasn't been a ballroom at the pier since the fifties."

"No kidding? *Is* it closed? There must be dancing somewhere."

"Well, there's a concert tonight. It's a big name swing band; that's right up your alley."

"Yeah, I'm in, how about you?"

"I already have my ankle strap heels on."

♦♦♦♦

Harry's classic car drew intense scrutiny from the crowd as he pulled the extended LaSabre into parking spots cleared just for him. He shook the attendant's hand and slipped a crisp bill into the kid's palm. "Keep an eye on my baby, okay?" The kid looked at the car and nodded slack-jawed.

As they left the parking lot, Lizbet looked over her shoulder for another peek. "Aren't you afraid of leaving that beast in a public parking lot?"

"What good is having a car like that if you don't enjoy it? She's my baby."

She faux pouted. "I thought I was your baby."

Harry dropped her hand and wrapped his arm around her shoulders. "It feels so good, being out like this."

Lizbet stopped short, causing him to whiplash back into her arms. "I'm glad you feel that way, I love going out with you." His fingers brushed back windblown strands of her ebony hair, and their lips met lightly to the amusement of the crowds passing them. The ebb and flow of the rollercoaster screams echoed in the background as Ferris wheel lights twinkled brightly.

"Come on, Beth, let me win you a stuffed bear. We have time before the concert."

She gave him an uncertain look. "I've always wanted a stuffed bear."

Harry capped her shoulders with his hands. "I think the rose of your dress perfectly matches your cheeks." He ran the back of his fingers down her soft jaw.

"Harry, my dress is white."

Harry did a double-take. He'd distinctly seen a rosy pink dress. He could have sworn it was rosy pink. "So, it is. Come on, and I'll show you my fastball…" He led the way to the arcade games, outwardly enthusiastic about their play but inwardly concerned that another reality was bleeding into the present.

Harry wound up and let fly the softball into the milk bottles, knocking all of them off the barrels. He repeated the assault until his booty was the three-foot stuffed pink bear. "There you go, Beth." He handed her the stuffed animal. "A pink bear for your pink dress."

Her brows rose, and she bit her lower lip. "Thank-you, handsome. You are an amazing pitcher." She looked down and back up at him. "Ahh, when did I become Beth? Are you having trouble saying Lizbet? My big brother called me that because he couldn't pronounce Elizabeth."

Harry shrugged nonchalantly, but privately quaked with alarm. He didn't realize he was doing it. He knew very well her name was Lizbet, why would he call her Beth? "Speaking of names, what are you gonna call this big guy?" He held up the bear.

Lizbet straightened the bear's bow tie. "I could call him Handsome, but I don't think he's anatomically correct."

Harry chuckled. "He also doesn't have fangs, which is probably a good thing. Art doesn't always imitate life." Harry led her closer to the bandstand where the M.C. made announcements. "And now, ladies and gentlemen, The Big Boys Swing Band." The stage lights flashed brightly, illuminating the eight musicians in full swing with "Chattanooga Choo-choo".

Harry shouted to Lizbet over the music. "You know how to swing?"

"I can hoof it!" She dropped the bear on her chair and fell into his arms. He carried her away with fancy footwork and speedy turns.

At the end of the first dance, when he drew her close, he whispered. "You are one cool kitten." His lips traced the shell of her ear, and she shivered closer into his embrace. Four songs in, the band slowed to "It Had to Be You", and Harry caught Lizbet into an intimate foxtrot. "I could do this all night."

"That's one of the nicest things you've ever said to me." She cooed back. "Can you do this horizontally?"

"You should know what I can do horizontally."

He pressed closer to her slim hips and then turned in annoyance at a tap on his shoulder. An older man in 1940s period clothing, wearing a pencil-thin mustache, grinned at them. Harry frowned. "Buzz off, Mac, no cuts." He picked up Lizbet around her waist and whisked her across the dancefloor. "Can you believe that guy's moxie?"

"Oh, you're so valiant." She purred as she rested her cheek on his chest. They were hip to hip now, and Harry was swept away by her pheromones. His most urgent desire was to drive her back to her tiny bedroom and strip off her nylon stockings. He needed to touch the lace of her garter belt and feel her melt around him.

The band stopped playing to let the lead singer talk to the audience, and Lizbet pulled back from Harry's embrace. Slowly his eyes opened, and he reluctantly let her go. She fanned her face with her hands. "I've got to put my hair up; I'm all sweaty." She giggled. "And look at you, cool as a cucumber." She pulled a large hair clip out of her purse and twisting her long ebony locks atop her head, pinned the mass in place.

"I love it when you wear flowers in your hair." He held her hands in his. "That was one of the first things I noticed about you."

Lizbet's brows knit. "Really? Harry, you don't seem yourself tonight. I'm enjoying the evening, but it's like you're not really here."

"What do you mean, Beth?" He discreetly pulled her into his pleated trousers where his phallus hung heavy. "Is this real enough, because this is what I'm feeling for you."

"I'm not sure what's going on with you tonight."

A flash of lucidity broke into Harry's awareness. *Jesus Christ, this is Lizbet, not Beth. Who is Beth?* He looked down at the woman in his arms. *No pink dress, no flowers. No Beth. Who was he remembering?*

A look of alarm flitted across her face. "Let's stop and get the bear."

"What bear?"

♦♦♦♦

Harry couldn't get Lizbet home fast enough. They rode in silence until he opened her car door and walked her to her front porch.

"Thank-you, handsome. It was quite a night." She turned up her face for a kiss.

106

Harry lowered her chin and pressed a cool kiss on her forehead. "Thanks for the swell time. I'll call you tomorrow when I'm up. Don't let them work you too hard." He watched her unlock her door and close it behind her. The sound of her relocking it was unsettling. It was the smack of reality that drove him to Rick's glass and concrete mansion in Beverly Hills.

Rick's majordomo opened the door and directed Harry to the patio. He floated on a raft, watching the twinkling lights of Los Angeles. When he saw Harry, he raised his tumbler and grinned. "How about a refreshment, you look pale."

Harry shrugged, both hands up in resignation. "That's my constant state of appearance, your Grace."

"Ohh, you wound me. Want some trunks, want to swim? You won't offend my new butler if you skinny dip."

Harry surveyed the home's solitude. "I'm okay for now. Don't let me disturb your swim."

Rick paddled closer to Harry. "You don't look good, son. What's going on?"

Harry ignored his critique and went directly to what was troubling him. "Have I mentioned a memory problem to you?"

"No."

"It began this year when I went to ground. It's like five hundred file cabinets drawers open in my brain."

"Yeah. Kinda like dreaming, which we aren't supposed to do."

"Right. Well, now it's like the file drawers are open all the time. I'm having trouble distinguishing reality from the images. I … I'm going nuts."

Rick frowned. "Have you told anybody else? Matt? What about Adam, remember, he's a psychologist. He would have more experience than I do."

Harry flinched. "Is there an Arkham Asylum for vampires? I'm afraid that's where I'll wind up."

Rick's frown softened to concern. "When did this start? Why is this is the first I hear about it?"

Harry gaped into the night. "Not a subject for casual conversation. Not even something I'd want to email about. It started the day after I met Elizabeth Mitchell."

"Elizabeth, huh? Tell me about that." Rick stretched out on the raft.

"Well, you know she's a... She's a handful with a wicked sense of humor. She's passionate about so many things..."

Rick's lips curled upward in a chiding smile. "Is she passionate about you?"

"That's the problem..."

"She's not?"

"She is, and you know she's mortal; we're coming to terms with that."

"Hmm. You're not worried about her shelf life?"

"No. We haven't had that discussion. It's way too soon."

"Oh. Did I pluck a nerve? Were you thinking about saving this one from the mortal coil?"

"It's not a problem like that."

Rick's brows knit. "Then, what is it?"

"You know I don't usually get involved with mortal women."

"You're a monk. Anyway, go on."

"Yeah, with you. Not with her. When I'm with her, I can't think straight. I get visions. It's like some other life bleeding into now. Is that a vamp thing? Have you ever heard of that?"

Chapter Twenty

Harry glanced over at Rick, wishing he felt as calm and collected. Seeking your adopted grand-sire's advice in this matter was like going to a doctor expecting a cancer diagnosis. No matter how compassionate the doctor, the bad news was bad news.

Matt Brenner swung open the door to his playroom. "Hey, buddy! Come in. Take a seat; make yourself comfortable." Matt gestured to the library atmosphere of relaxed leather club chairs in the conversation area of the room.

Rick perused the liquor cabinet. "What's everyone drinking?"

Harry's voice wavered as he took a seat. "A Positive? Straight up?"

Rick's brow rose, and he glanced at Matt. "Okay. How about you, Single malt?"

Matt delivered the glasses as he appraised the younger vamp's demeanor. "Something's up." Matt sat across from Harry and Rick. "What's going on?"

Rick threw his ankle over his knee and leaned back. "Harry's going nuts. I suggested we talk to Adam."

Harry shook his head. "Thanks…"

Matt poured the rocks glass full of blood into a tumbler and added more, then handed it to Harry. "Could you be a little more specific about the nuts part?"

Harry ran a hand down his face and began slowly. "I feel like some other life is intruding on this one." He shook his head, knowing the explanation was inadequate. "When Lizbet and I began talking about each other, I realized I don't remember my life before the night I was turned. I mean, I know I grew up in LA, and I know my parents were Henry and Rose VanAlt, but I don't remember what they looked like or where I lived. I know I was in the Army, but I don't remember where." He looked into their concerned faces. "What's happening to me?"

There was a moment of stunned silence. Matt leaned forward, hands between his knees. "This is new, right? I mean, you remembered this stuff before…"

Harry wrung his hands. "I don't know. I don't remember."

Matt nodded. "I do know. We've talked about it. Right after you were turned."

Harry frowned. "So, it's not like memories fade the longer you're undead?"

Rick joined the discussion. "No."

Harry swallowed hard. "Is there such a thing as vampire Alzheimer's?"

Rick tucked his chin, and his brow rose. "No." Rick shrugged. "We don't know everything. Maybe we need a Responder specialist."

Matt nodded. "Sounds more medical than psychiatric." Matt's attention was on Harry. "How disabling is this?

"It's getting worse and worse. I missed a deadline; I swore I wrote things that I couldn't find."

Rick inclined his head. "Where are you eating? Any chance of tainted blood?"

Harry sighed deeply. "Since it's gotten worse, I only take blood from The Gaoler."

Rick's gaze narrowed. "Are you concerned that you're dangerous?"

Harry closed his eyes and pinched the bridge of his nose. "Yes, I think I am."

Matt's words broke the tense silence. "To complicate everything, this banging looking mortal is sniffing around him like he's The Bachelor."

Harry's gaze raised from his lap to challenge Matt. "Don't talk about her like that."

Rick took playful offense until Matt glared. "He's got it bad."

Rick paced for a beat. "Are you reading something from this mortal? Could she be a vampire hunter?"

Harry burst out laughing. "A vampire hunter, no."

Matt slid his chair a bit further from Harry. "I don't think it's that kind of hunt."

Matt and Rick hovered over Harry and, in unison, asked. "Tell us about your friend."

♦♦♦♦

Matt joined Rick next door in his dungeon. Rick paced worriedly until he reached the soft leather spanking bench. His hand caressed the smooth leather padding as his fingers brushed the soft suede of the flogger left hanging over it. "Matt, what do you think? How could these images bleed into his mind now?"

"I'm no expert. We need one of those. What about Adam Lachlan?"

Rick nodded. "Adam will be my first resource; his background in psychology should be an asset."

♦♦♦♦

Matt followed Harry back to his apartment, trying not to hover. The minimalist space was filled with the soft trickle of the fountain that separated the kitchen and dining area from the living room. The fountain's soft glow of lighting cast an eerie atmosphere over the awkward silence.

Harry wandered to a chair, and Matt did a short inventory of his blood supply, the apartment thermostat, and the settings in the mausoleum. Every carefully curated item in Harry's mid-century home was exactly where it was meant to be. But everything was wrong.

"Harry, if you missed your deadline, why don't you let me transfer some funds into your account?"

"You don't have to do that…"

"I'd feel better knowing you had a cushion. Your well-being is my concern. We're going to get you through this. Have you paid your bills this month?"

"Matt, I'm not a child. Everything is handled by direct deposit."

"But if there's no money in the account…"

"Please don't make a big deal out of this."

"When did you last get a royalty check?"

"I don't know… three weeks ago, maybe…

♦♦♦♦

Lizbet couldn't help daydreaming at her desk. Naturally, the dream revolved around Harry. She planned her wardrobe's fancy lingerie; she loved it when he undressed her. It was unsettling that he wasn't himself. It was almost as if he was in a dissociative state. As if another lifetime intruded on this one. *Very, very strange.* She planned to look into the literature when her desk phone rang. She pressed the speaker button and sighed.

"Dr. Mitchell, is your go-bag in your office?"

Lizbet threw herself back in her chair and closed her eyes. "In my trunk. What now? Where's Dr. Keith? He's up next." She looked at the on-call rotation on her wall.

"Dr. Keith's wife is at eight centimeters, and he'll begin taking his vacation after the delivery."

"Oh. Hard to argue with that. How long? Where am I going?"

"The rest of this week, Columbus, Ohio."

"Oh, I'll never get home Friday night."

"What's the matter, Mitchell? Got a hot date?"

Lizbet covered her eyes and shook her head. "Not anymore."

◆◆◆◆

Lizbet had to leave her car in the long term lot and call Harry's apartment from the airport. Only one flight out of LAX to Columbus, she would just make it. She got to the gate and called. "Harry, hey, handsome. I've got bad news. I'm jetting to Ohio until possibly Saturday. I'll call you this evening, cannot wait to hear your voice." She trudged to the last seat at the gate and texted Eddie. They had an arrangement, he fed and played with Minka when she was out of town. She sighed, and it was time to board the jet.

◆◆◆◆

Five Days Later

Harry leaned against the doorbell of Matt's penthouse apartment. It's was three in the afternoon. Not typical hours for vampires to be out and about.

Matt eventually roused from his deep rest, hurriedly pulled on a robe, and belted it as he hustled to his front door. He glanced at the security monitor and saw a man's disheveled hair.

As the door swung open, the scent of Harry's decay engulfed Matt's foyer. Matt shook his head at the eye-watering assault on his senses. "You have electricity? Damn, it feels good in here." Matt's forearm covered his nose and mouth as he stepped aside, and Harry wandered aimlessly into his home.

"Yeah, I've got power, don't you? Is your power off? You're not looking so good." Matt went directly to the refrigerator and pulled out a pint of blood. "When did you feed last?"

Harry mumbled as he held a conversation with himself, counting on his fingers. Matt had the glass in Harry's trembling hands immediately. "Hey, buddy. You need to drink this, then get a shower and go to ground."

♦♦♦♦

The twilight sky issued in with the purples, golds, and oranges that hinted at rain later in the night. Rick pensively watched the sky and straightened the outdoor furniture on Harry's balcony. The apartment was a mess, and Rick had never known Harry to be anything less than compulsively neat. Matt had already said he would consult Adam tonight. It couldn't happen soon enough, as far as Rick was concerned.

Chapter Twenty-One

Rick heard the ding of the elevator and walked toward the door, expecting Adam. Instead, it was Harry's ravishing raven-haired woman dressed in a power suit with a slim skirt. He swung the door open while she was still in the act of raising her hand to knock.

"Dr. Mitchell." He eyed her suspiciously.

Her smile was bright and engaging. "Mr. Hiatt."

"Why, yes, I am. Harry isn't here."

"Where is he?"

"He's indisposed."

She gave him a tight smile and said firmly. "That's alright. I'll wait."

"He may not be home tonight."

"It's Saturday. I'll wait. I need to see him."

"Oh? Why is that?"

"No offense intended, but our relationship is none of your business."

"And if I wanted to make it my business?"

"Now, just a minute! You may be Harry's grandsire, but you're not mine, and I don't appreciate the third degree."

Rick narrowed his gaze. "I want to know if you're a vampire hunter."

She stared at him in astonishment. "What is this, the eighteenth century?"

"That's not an answer. Don't make me force it out of you. I assure you, I can."

"Are you threatening me?" She glared at him. "What's going on? Why would you think I'm trying to hurt him? Where is he? He's indisposed in what way?"

"I'm not telling you a damn thing until you level with me."

"Look, I would never hurt Harry. He acted oddly when I saw him last Sunday, and I haven't heard from him since then. I'm worried about him. Is he alright?"

Rick took a deep, assessing breath of her. Her determined frustration emanated from every pore. "He's physically okay, but mentally, we have some concerns. When you say he behaved oddly, what exactly do you mean?" Rick stood back from the door and mutely invited her into the pigsty.

♦♦♦♦

Lizbet's sharp gaze crawled over every aspect of Harry's wreck of an apartment. She turned to stare at Rick with wide eyes. "It is not Harry's habit to live like this." She walked purposefully through the room and stopped at each station of disarray. "I was here Sunday." She tapped the bridge of her nose in thought. "I called Monday to let him know I was being sent out of town for work. I told him I'd call that night, and I did. But he didn't answer. He hasn't answered any of my calls. I came here straight from the airport." Rick's eyes narrowed in disbelief. "Check his answering machine." The machine blinked on the office desk.

"I need to know what you know." Rick ushered her to one uncluttered chair. He paced before her.

"It was his disorientation that threw me. He called me Beth, which could be short for Elizabeth, my given name. But no one calls me Beth. Everyone, including Harry, calls me Lizbet. He said my dress was pink more than once when I was wearing white. I even pointed out I was in white, and he continued to call it pink. Unless vampires have suddenly become colorblind…"

"I thought you knew; we're practically perfect in every way."

"But, that's Miss Poppins's alibi…" The sparkle died from her eyes. "The most disturbing thing, he was extremely demonstrative in public. It escalated into possessiveness on the dance floor when a guy casually tried to cut in."

Rick moved around the room, righting fallen pillows, magazines, and books. He halted at the last point. "Was he aggressive?"

"His tone of voice was a little deep and menacing. He picked me up around the waist and carried me to the other side of the dance floor."

Rick approached her and bit at his bottom lip. "Did Harry mention seeing other vampires there?"

116

"Honestly, he seemed to only have eyes for me."

"And that wasn't welcome?"

"It would have been under other circumstances. In a split second, Harry was all over me and warning off other men." There was a beat of silence between them. "He deliberately held himself against me; he was throbbing-hard. He asked me, 'Is this real enough? Because this is what I'm feeling for you'. He scared me. It was too much power; it emanated from him."

Rick shook his head as if to return to reality. "I'd like to have you meet a friend of ours. Are you available now?"

Lizbet nodded.

"If you're up for it, we need to take an elevator ride to my office. Has Harry ever mentioned Adam Lachlan to you?"

"Yes, I met him at Saturday night's demonstration. Is he like you?"

"Could you be more specific?"

Lizbet snorted. "Is he night shift, too?"

Rick laughed. "While most of Harry's friends are on the night shift, Adam is a horse of different color. But, we're as close as family."

♦♦♦♦

Lizbet endured the customary, uncomfortable silence of two virtual strangers in an elevator. They silently stared at the descending numbers. As the lights dimmed, the ambient sound of a heartbeat thrummed around them. Lizbet shivered, partly from the sudden chill in the car and partly from apprehension. *Where is this vampire taking me?* Her hand slid inside her purse and sought her tear gas canister.

"You're a criminal profiler, right?"

Lizbet cleared her throat, striving over nerves for a normal tone. It came out more a squeak than she intended. "Yes."

"How's this on the creepy meter?"

"I'm bound by confidentiality."

"Do you practice other forms of bondage?"

Her eyes closed to a slit. "Harry warned me about you."

Rick stood over her at vamp speed, a hair's breadth from her, pressing her into the corner.

"Nothing Harry could say would ever come close to the truth."

To Lizbet's great relief, the elevators doors opened, revealing the Viking, Adam Lachlan. His deep voice was amused and casual, cutting through the tension. "Richard, we need to work on our impulse control."

Rick righted his orange and black Princeton repp necktie and smoothed his lapels, and his expression abruptly turned angelic. "Dr. Mitchell and I were discussing fetishes."

The huge man held out a gallant hand to Lizbet, who had the insane inclination to take it and cleave to his side. She drew a steadying breath and felt his detached aqua gaze assess her from head to toe in a notably different way from when he acted as a Dom. She pulled herself together to assume her professional persona. This was not a demonstration night at The Gaoler. Holding out her hand, she said. "Dr. Elizabeth Mitchell."

His confirming voice was baritone and smooth. "Dr. Adam Lachlan." His voice enveloped her, soothing the nerves Rick ruffled. *I'll bet he's a damn good therapist.* He shook her hand briefly, and a smile flitted across his perfect features. "Won't you join me in the office, Dr. Mitchell? I understand you've been as concerned about Harry as we have. Perhaps, together we can get him through this." They walked side by side, Rick leading the way down a corridor of padded crimson leather. The flickering carriage lights reminded her why she called this Jack, the Ripper's place.

♦♦♦♦

When the dark-haired woman fully entered the room, Rick and Matt circled her with vampire perceptiveness. Their nostrils flared, their gazes narrowed, and surreptitious looks were exchanged before their subtone conversation began.

Rick crossed one arm over his chest and rested his elbow in his opposite palm, disguising his subtone speech by stroking his upper lip. "God's nightgown, she *is* 1940s throwback…"

Matt assumed the same posture and sighed deeply. "No wonder Harry is having flashbacks."

Under their scrutiny, Lizbet's head pivoted back and forth, returning their inspection. "Your lips are moving. You're going to quite an exaggerated posture to hide it from me. It's your vampire parlor game, isn't it?"

Adam chuckled. "Gentlemen, Dr. Mitchell is a trained observer, a criminal profiler." He reminded them.

Rick's arms snapped down, and he held them behind his back as he leaned in for a deeper scent. "You caught me, sure. But this is no parlor game; we need to know more about you, Dr. Mitchell."

"Really?" She backed closer to Adam. "How do I factor into Harry's irrationality?"

Rick turned on his heel and gestured to a seating area with a couch and chairs. "We wanted to see you again to confirm it." He sat like royalty in the largest chair. "You bear a striking resemblance to a woman of the 1940s. You could be a replica of one of Harry's sweethearts from his mortal years."

Lizbet withdrew her Blackberry and, within seconds, held up a photo of Elizabeth Short. "The week I moved to Los Angeles, I started getting comparisons. One guy even sent me black dahlias. He was a little creepy."

Rick's brows disappeared into his hair. "He was not a normal man. How old was that guy? Was he into role-play? Did he try knife play?"

"I got he wasn't normal. He worked for one of the studios, and he was into props and forties memorabilia. I set him straight the first night. There was no second date."

"He wasn't an octogenarian, then?"

"Ah, no." She paused. "What's happened to Harry?"

Adam bent forward in his chair; hands grasped between his knees. "He has amnesia, and he's regressing into childhood. These symptoms seem to coordinate with meeting you."

Her lips drew grim, and she nodded. "I saw glimpses of the amnesia. But knowing this, what are you going to do?"

Rick paced. Every few steps, the men exchanged worried frowns. "We understand your concern, Dr. Mitchell. Harry has expressed his infatuation with you and apparently yours for him." There was a beat of silence. "We, his family, have come together to get him through this."

"That's not very specific." Lizbet challenged.

Matt's voice deepened to a Dom register. "Dr. Mitchell, your arrival on his horizon has scattered his marbles. We'll handle getting Harry right again."

Adam stood. "I know with your training; you want to help. This is where the magical and mortal worlds separate. We're unable to accept your help at this time. If you'd like, you and I could keep in touch."

Lizbet's hands dropped on the chair arms, and she planted her feet squarely. "Is this where you pull out a pocket watch and hypnotize me?"

Rick and Matt exchanged uncomfortable glances. "Don't you think we dress far better than those sideshow hypnotists?"

She narrowed her glinting eyes at him. "This is a hell of a time for sarcasm. Are you telling me, don't go away mad, just go away?"

Adam stood close to her chair and extended his hand. "Did you park in the CGI garage?" She nodded. "Let me walk you to your car."

Chapter Twenty-Two

Harry's unconventional treatment team convened in the living room of Matt's penthouse. Matt closed the media room doors and joined Rick and Adam. "He should be entertained for a while. He's glued to the television, watching documentaries."

Adam dropped into the largest chair, and his brows knit. "Makes sense, he's thirsting to fill in his blanks."

Abruptly, the media room double doors bounced open, and there was a peel of childlike laughter. Harry slid into the older vamp's circle brandishing a brass turtle like a badge. "There's no need to fear, Jigsaw John is here!" He posed triumphantly like a superhero."

The regressed vampire stood wearing white sports socks and Matt's customary black silk pajama pants. Harry's glistening dark locks stood wild and tousled; his stubble belied his juvenile behavior. Sturdy fists rested on his slim hips, accentuating the physique of his bare chest. The men sat slack-jawed at Harry's arrival.

Matt's expression turned to caution. "Jigsaw John, who brought him up?"

Harry slid from his pose to stand over Matt. With a child's enthusiasm, he explained. "This guy was the bomb. He caught all the bad guys. He was like The Shadow. He got every bad guy but one."

Rick nodded. "The Shadow? I remember the Shadow."

Harry jumped playfully to Rick and leaned into him. "Did you know the Shadow? He's cool."

Rick leaned back from the energetic and odiferous Harry. "Hey, sport, when was the last time you went to ground?"

Harry bounced on his feet like a five-year-old in Rick's face. "I'm not tired; you're not the boss of me."

Matt hid his face in his hand. "Harry, give it a rest. Did you finish the glass I gave you?"

Harry spun on his stocking foot. "You keep sayin' its good stuff, but it's yucky. I didn't like it." He pinched his nose.

Adam rose and circled the boy-man. With a cutting aqua gaze, he pursed his lips. "Okay, geniuses, what's the next step?"

Matt stretched out, frustrated. "He's been like this since he arrived on my doorstep."

Rick stood and plunged his hands into his trouser pockets, jingling his change. "I have something that should slow him down, and once he's down, his exhaustion will take over."

Adam's head swiveled rapidly. "You're not going to stake him?"

Rick returned the horrified expression. "Of course not. I've got some of the juice we gave the Moreau Brothers in 1922. He might have a little headache, but we'll have some peace while we strategize."

Adam paced the room's perimeter. "That drug is short-acting."

"True, but once the drug knocks him out, he'll be down for a while, at least I hope so."

Adam rubbed at his forehead, deep in concentration. "Is there anything we can tap from Harry's mortal history? He fought in a war, he was exposed to chemicals, and World War II had a high rate of Post-Traumatic Stress; they called it shell-shock."

Rick stood still, jingling his change. "Pull the Responder file on his turn. We'll comb through that."

Matt picked up the telephone and called Giles Paquet. "Giles, long time, how's Luna? Yeah, good. Hey, I got a situation can you drop in… like now?"

The room heard Gile's hearty laughter. "I hear Richard there; I'm probably thirty minutes away at CGI. Are you at home?"

Matt put a thumbs up to Rick. "I'm in my penthouse. We'll be waiting, and dinner's on the house."

♦♦♦♦

Giles Paquet, the polar opposite of Inspector Clouseau, was originally a French gendarme. After being turned in the early nineteenth century, he decided France was no longer the place for him. Giles set sail for New Orleans and joined the 'vampire police' known as the Responders. In the nineteen twenties, at Rick's urging, he relocated to Los Angeles and spent two decades as LA's Chief of Responders. In nineteen forty-three, he established the Quebec Responders and remained there until the nineteen nineties.

When Consort Group International grew to its twenty-first-century proportions, Rick called him back to head special security for CGI. Giles had contacts everywhere.

Rick greeted Giles at the door with a hearty handshake. "Welcome, you've been working too hard, it's been ages. Have I got a great AB Negative for you."

Gile's smile went straight to his eyes at the mention of that blood type. Matt shook his hand and led him to a cleared-off desk.

Adam toasted with his own drink. "Giles, you're looking well as always. What can I get you from Matt's bar?"

Giles grinned slyly. "How about two fingers of Bacardi 151, three ice cubes, and five drops of that AB Negative?"

Adam dropped the cubes in the glass. "These aren't the big cubes."

Rick shook his head. "It's as if your wife, Luna, spoils you entirely too much."

Giles sat at the desk and adjusted the chair. "That is what is wrong with you men; you do not have the love of a good woman."

Matt slapped him on the back brother to brother and held up his thumb and forefinger. "In 1922, I was this close to winning her."

Giles gave him a smug smile. "Regrettably, you are not French."

Matt stood considering and then shook his head. "Well, let me tell you what's going on now."

♦♦♦♦

Giles sipped his second Bacardi when Matt returned from his office with pages from the printer.

"We've got the rape turn report, the mentor assignment ruling, and the Responder's report on his sires' incineration."

Matt flipped through the pages, sharing them on his dining room table. Rick's lips straightened. "There's nothing in here that would contribute to… what did you call it, Adam… disassociation?"

Adam nodded. "Is it possible in a city like LA with so many undead, could Harry have crossed someone earlier? Maybe been exposed to vampire blood that affects him now?"

Giles nodded. "I'll go back and do the last name search." They hung over Giles's shoulder as the search processed. "I've got a Henry V-a-n-a-l-t, Jr., 1947." The room went silent.

Adam spoke. "That's too close to perfect to be an accident. Someone spelled his name wrong."

Giles nodded. "1947 was not a great year for Responder leadership. Armand Polk was run out of town on several ethics charges."

Rick's eyes narrowed, and he pointed to Giles. "Didn't he have an unfortunate guillotine accident?"

Giles placed his hands flat on the desk. "Comme ci comme ça." Giles continued scrolling through the information he found under Vanalt. "La vache."

Rick threw up a hand in chagrin. "Oh crap, is all you've got to say?"

Giles's humor fled. "I have found the root of Harry's problem."

Matt made victorious fists. "Yes. So, what do we do?"

Rick put a hand on Matt's shoulder. "Slow down, I can see by Giles's expression there's not an easy solution. Tell us, Giles, what happened to him?"

Giles scrolled the information and nodded to his friends. "Have a seat." The three men held their glasses and forgot to drink as Giles read.

"1946, Henry Vanalt, Jr., a musician at The Blue Gardenia Lounge, had a brief affair and one-night stand with a female who met with tragedy after interacting with a group of vampires from Argentina."

Rick snapped his fingers. "The Zimmermanns." His lips straightened, and he hung his head. "Damn them."

Giles nodded. "Yes, it was Harry. He was mortal. It's noted here that he was emotionally distraught when a female was murdered. He was a witness to her association with the Zimmermanns, and she was last seen in their company. Because of his unstable emotional state and his ability to testify against the Family, the decision was made to thrall him and cause him to forget the time between December 1946 and February 1947."

Matt scratched his head. "So?"

Giles held up his index finger. "Here's the second part. Harry did well with the thralling as a mortal. We have new evidence in the literature that male mortals who are thralled and subsequently become vampires have about a twenty-five percent chance of experiencing the symptoms you describe in Harry. Our scientists believe it has to do with the physiological change in the brain."

Adam stood and returned to his nervous pacing. "This is not good news. What the hell do you do for it?"

Giles drummed his fingers on the desk. "I don't know, but I know someone who might have an answer. He's a psychology professor at UCLA. He was the 1947 Responder who did the thralling."

Rick's brows knit, and he dialed his phone. "I'll send someone over to get him."

Giles nodded. "I believe he uses a botanical truth serum to penetrate the shielded memories."

Rick swiveled abruptly. "Looks like Braswell's fig preserves?"

Matt's mouth hung open for a beat. "You're five hundred years old and familiar with Braswell's preserves?"

Rick's lascivious grin went straight to his whiskey-colored eyes. "Had a donor who loved their goodies. After she fed me for eight or nine years, I bought her the company. Anyway, you need a silver bladed knife and a certain amount of time. Let me consult my apothecary shelf. Meanwhile, what's the name of your professor?"

♦♦♦♦

The men in Matt's penthouse listened for Harry's slip-sliding across the wooden floor in the media room. It was quiet…it was too quiet. Matt and Giles entered the room and found Harry in the corner of the sectional sofa hugging an angora throw. He stroked it like a toddler as the History Channel covered World War II Pinup girls.

When doors closed behind the vampires, Harry's gaze zipped to the adults. His finger flipped the channel to an infomercial. He looked at Matt. "Those girls have soft pillows." His hands repetitively stroked the throw balled in his lap.

Matt gestured to the furniture. "I'm going to burn this couch." Giles nodded as he took a seat next to Harry.

"Hello, Harry. I'm a friend, my name is Giles, and I want to know if you like grape juice?"

Harry's five-year-old self brightened. "Is it from the glass jug?"

Giles nodded. "How about, I bring you a nice cold glass of grape juice, we'll turn off the TV, and you can dream of those soft pillows all you want." Harry nodded and sat up expectantly.

The door opened, Rick came in with a tall jelly jar of grape juice spiked with blood for flavor and the last of the knockout drops. Rick held out the glass. "It's your favorite jelly jar. Drink up."

Harry's brows knit. "But you guys don't have any. We all need grape juice." The silent signal went from Giles to Matt to Rick that grape juice would be served for all or none.

Within a few moments, all the men held glasses and listened to Harry describe his mother, and how she let him be the first one to drink from the jug if he picked up his toys.

As Harry tipped the last of the glass, the men waited expectantly for him to sink into oblivion. Once he didn't respond to prodding, they carried him to the chilly mausoleum and set up blood transfusions.

By eleven in the evening, there was a knock on Matt's door. It was Harlan Gardner in a tweed sport coat with leather elbow patches and worn Levi button-up jeans. His gold wire-rimmed glasses sat over a bulbous nose and a bushy gray mustache.

Matt opened the door, and Harlan stepped back from the four men hovering in the foyer. "I understand this is about a negative thralling reaction from 1947?"

Adam cleared a path and welcomed the man. "Please come in, Professor Gardner. We do need your help."

♦♦♦♦

Rick filled in the professor on Harry's current status. "He's laid out in the mausoleum. I had to slip him a draught of a sixteenth-century botanical with his grape juice to sedate him. We're on the second unit of blood, and before you see him, we'll hose him down." Rick sat beside Gardner on the sofa, holding a carved wooden box.

Professor Gardner held up halting hands. "I shouldn't be the face he sees. We should proceed with Dr. Lachlan, a neutral party who can unlock the memories."

Adam walked around the owlish man. "How do I unlock memories that you bound?"

Rick opened the long box and revealed a silver dagger and a wax-sealed bottle.

Professor Gardner took off his glasses and cleaned them nervously. "Where did you get that?"

Rick's lips curled. "As a physician in Italy in the seventeenth century, I had cause to collect many ancient curatives." He slid on a leather glove and wielded the silver dagger under Gardner's nose. "Nice dagger, isn't it?"

Pressing back into the sofa, the man nodded silently. "Mr. Hiatt, did that thing come with instructions?

Gardner stood up, a diminutive man in a room of tall strangers. "Without following the lunar timeline, the memories will not unfold."

Adam cocked his head and stood, hands on hips. "Are you telling us this has to be done under a full moon? Any blood sacrifice, naked dancing?" Rick smiled in buried humor at the shape-shifter's suggestions.

Gardner soothed the tall blond man. "The subject must be willing. Their heart and mind must be open to discovery. You must explain what was done in 1947, and they must understand once it is revealed, it cannot be suppressed."

Matt paced, running his hand through his hair. "And what's the timeline?"

Gardner nodded authoritatively. "The incision must be drawn by Civil Twilight; the subject should be provided with nourishment during the revelations. The room should be dim, as silent as possible, no intrusions."

Matt leaned over the back of the couch at the man. "How long does this go on?"

"The formal ceremony will last until sunrise the following morning. That is when the wound will begin to close. Some subjects have a few glimmers that arrive before going to ground. Once at ground, the incision disappears, what's done is done. There is no second ceremony."

Adam sat forward, his hands between his knees. "So, having been informed of the subject of the revelation, I'm assuming the therapist asks open-ended questions to help the patient uncover the missing memories."

Gardner nodded. "That part of the procedure is a fairly simple interview." Gardner stood. "My work here is done. Good luck."

Matt caught his shoulder with a leveling hand. "I have a few questions about your technique back then. I took Mr. VanAlt on after his rape turn, and to give me peace of mind, let's say, I'd like to have a long talk, just you and me." Matt put his arm around the man's shoulders and led him out of the apartment.

Adam cocked a brow at Rick and Giles. "I'd love to know what's going to happen to that man."

Rick closed the wooden case with regret. "I was optimistic this would be this done tonight." He shrugged. "Well, we'll have the opportunity to top Harry off with several units. He'll be in great order by …" He looked at his watch. "By eight twenty-seven tomorrow evening."

Chapter Twenty-Three

Shape-shifter Adam Lachlan was not bound by the rising and setting sun. However, his role as Master Dom for The Gaoler put him on the night shift.

When he left Matt's penthouse around midnight, he opened the moonroof on his Mercedes AMG G-Class and turned up his high tension playlist. Before Gershwin's "Rhapsody in Blue" finished, he made up his mind to call Lizbet and enlist her aid in Harry's interview. When her phone went to voice mail, he punched repeat on the song and drove faster. Not aggressively, just a bit zippier in between the motorists tooling west on the I-10. His car phone's ring punctuated the flute, and Adam answered immediately.

"Dr. Lachlan? This is Lizbet Mitchell, is it too late to talk?"

"Not for me. I should have been more mindful of the hour for you. What are you doing around four this afternoon?"

"I haven't been able to sleep anyway. What's going on?"

Adam pressed the garage door opener on his Sunset Mesa home. "The good news is, we have a diagnosis. The shaky news is the treatment is a sixteenth-century vampire curative."

He got out of his car, waiting for her response as he entered through the garage. He stood in his glass-walled living room and appreciated the smattering of city lights along the California coastline.

Lizbet's voice held incredulous awe. "A sixteenth-century vampire curative? I'd clear my calendar for that."

"There is an element of talk-therapy involved, which is why I'm calling you." Adam slid open the glass door and sought the peace of his hillside patio and illuminated infinity pool. "We have less than twelve hours to restore his memory, and I need an observer and note-taker as I lead him through the process." Adam heard her open a cabinet and run water as he slipped out of his pinch tassel loafers. He sat on the side of his pool and rolled up his pant legs to drop his feet into the water. "We've consulted with a vampire specialist, and I'm confident in the approach, but this is purported to bring out disturbing memories." Adam heard her microwave running in the background.

"I understand the talk therapy, what does the curative involve?"

"Basically, think of it as vampire truth serum." All Adam heard was popping corn.

Lizbet took a deep breath. "Well, I don't know what I'm getting into, but if Harry needs help, I'm there."

Adam leaned back on his elbows and gazed at the night sky. "This is a hard call for me to make. You're the professional I'd call, but you're also the woman Harry loves."

"So, you're wondering if I want to know everything?"

Adam heard her chewing. "It could be nothing, it could be concerning, or it could be macabre. I have no idea what we'll unearth."

Lizbet thought for a moment. "You know, Adam, my practice deals with abnormal psychology. In my professional opinion, Harry is not capable of macabre. Everyone has something concerning in their background. I think I can handle it."

Adam sat up, feeling satisfied. "You and I are the only people who won't be sustained by tumblers of blood. Why don't you come over to my office at CGI, we can eat there while we discuss the strategy?"

"Is this a power bar situation?" He heard her opening kitchen cabinets.

"When I'm plumbing the depth of my friend's psyche, I like a charcuterie board with extra fruit."

Lizbet chuckled softly. "Works for me. I'll bet CGI puts out a better spread than the LA Police Department. See you around four."

♦♦♦♦

Rick shuffled playing cards at Matt's gaming table. "I do wish these cards were more stylishly illustrated. In my day, they were all hand-painted works of art."

Matt looked at Rick askance. "Wouldn't that make it easier to mark cards?"

Rick sniffed in offense. "A gentleman would never do that."

Matt sat back in the chair, stretching out his legs. "So, what are the high cards in this game?"

"Primero was the sixteenth-century precursor to poker. It's similar…"

Matt's gaze narrowed at Rick. "You hold a nineteen ninety-nine World Series of Poker winner's bracelet, and you're taking time to teach me a game you played five hundred years ago? Am I being hustled?"

Rick laid his cards face down on the table. "Did I ask you to open that tight wallet of yours? We can play for donor rotations."

Matt gave him a jaundiced look. "Unh huh, which one of my donors are you cheating for?"

Rick sniffed. "A man of honor…" His nostrils flared, and he looked over his shoulder at Harry wandering into the room.

Harry stood within sniffing distance and scratched at the dusting of hair on his chest. "How did I get here?"

Rick motioned him away with a gesture. "How do you feel?"

Harry shrugged as he wandered in the penthouse. "I think I'm okay. What day is it?" He raised his arm and gagged himself. "I smell like a goat. Was my power off?"

Matt fanned the air with his cards. "It's back on now."

"Can I use your shower?" Harry scratched at his hair, disoriented, and stumbled back toward Matt's bathroom. "Can I borrow a robe? You don't think anyone will mind me riding down to my floor in a robe, do you?"

Rick watched Harry pull the bathroom door shut. "I have one word for you, Matt. Bleach."

♦♦♦♦

Harry sat on the couch, newly showered, shaved, and fumigated, drinking a tall glass of blood. "Do I smell Dakin's solution?"

Matt joined Harry on the sofa. "How do you remember Dakin's solution? That's an old, old disinfectant."

Harry shrugged between sips of blood. "My mom cleaned the bathroom with it." Matt sunk back into the sofa cushions and nodded.

131

Rick came out of the kitchen, a tumbler of blood in each hand. One for Matt and one for himself. "We have some good news. While you were at ground, we discovered what's causing your symptoms."

Harry's eyes grew large. "What is it?"

Rick sighed. "The explanation is a little complicated, but we believe we have what we need to take care of it within the next twenty-four hours. Adam and Lizbet will be here shortly to do their part of it." Rick checked his watch and drank as he paced the sofa area.

Harry's gaze followed Rick's turbulence. "I wish you'd sit down; you're making me dizzy."

Rick nodded to Harry and took the seat across from him. "I don't mean to make you nervous. This is an ancient treatment, and the steps are quite specific. I'm going over them in my mind to be sure we do them in the proper order..."

While Rick spoke, Harry stared at the ornately carved wooden box on the coffee table. "With all the modern stuff in your place, where did you get this box, Matt?" Rick swept it up and held it on his lap.

Matt's brows knit Rick. "It's Rick's."

"Part of the treatment involves something I carried from Italy. You have no idea how grateful I am I've held on to this."

Matt looked at the clock when he heard the elevator outside his penthouse door. "If that's Adam and Lizbet, we'll begin the discussion."

♦♦♦♦

Matt opened the door with Harry lurking behind him. Adam nodded to Matt and Harry and took the chair next to Rick.

Harry searched Lizbet's face for her mood. They embraced, and she rested her cheek against his chest for a moment. He raised her face to his for a chaste kiss on the lips. They held each other's hands between them.

"I'm here to be Adam's note-taker and clinical observer. I'm going to sit by the bar. Forget I'm here." He watched her take out a stenographer's pad and two ink pens and pull a chair next to Matt's bar. She was in business mode as she filled a pitcher with ice and water and placed it along with a tumbler on the coffee table in front of Adam. She put a glass of water next to her seat.

Harry found himself the last man standing. "So, what do I do? Lie down like I'm talking to Freud?"

Rick gestured to the sofa. "You may be more comfortable sitting; however, many of your memories may be accompanied by movement. We don't want to get in your way."

Harry sat, and Rick pulled the coffee table about three feet away to give him space.

"This is a process of giving you back your memories."

"What do you mean by that? What else don't I know about myself?"

Matt offered, "We found out last night you were thralled in 1947. This was complicated by your turning in 1951."

It dawned on Harry; he had very few recollections from the time he entered the Army. His next scant memories were flashes of a party at Chateau Marmont in 1951.

"So, what do we do?" Harry levied a stern gaze at his friends.

Rick reached for the box. "What you will see can't be unseen. Once the curative begins to work, your memories will unfold. Adam will be here to help clarify the events. The start time will be within the next three minutes. If you're in for this, roll up your left sleeve above your elbow and take off your watch."

"How long is this going to take?" Harry stared at his watch and waited for an answer.

Rick set out the wrapped dagger and the wax-sealed bottle on the coffee table. "We'll be done by sunrise." Smiling his most professional smile, Rick put on a pair of leather gloves and uncapped the bottle. Harry was surprised there was no malodor. With all this cloak and dagger talk, he expected a stench from something that old.

Vamp quick, Rick was on one knee in front of Harry. "Let me have your arm."

"What is that?" An unconvinced Harry held back his forearm.

Rick held up the uncapped ancient glass bottle. "It's a catalyst for memories." Rick assumed the posture of a priest, two fingers raised in blessing. *Rick certainly must have been a priest in one of his incarnations.*

The Latin Rick spoke was recognizable, but Harry lost familiarity with the language of his childhood's Roman Catholic faith. He wanted to know precisely what Rick said. "Excuse me?"

Rick repeated. "Be opened for an odor of sweetness. Be thou, devil, begone, for the judgment of God shall draw near." His hands repeated the blessing action.

Understanding, Harry sank back into the sofa and waited for the blade.

Matt announced. "Eight twenty-seven."

Rick bowed his head, lifted the sheath off the silver knife, and recited words Harry recognized. "Receive this burning light and receive thy truth without blame." Rick laid the bar cloth under Harry's forearm on his thigh.

As he drew the dagger's point the length of Harry's forearm, it burned a searing path toward his undead heart. When Rick was satisfied with the area opened, he removed his left glove and cut his thumb with the same blade.

Rick used the spoon in the handle of the dagger and measured the elixir onto his thumb. He smeared the catalyst with his bloody thumb up the length of the open wound.

Harry watched Adam, pad, and pen in hand. Matt's back left his chair, his hands clasped between his knees as if in prayer. Harry waited for the revelation. *Will it come from within?*

Rick rose and stepped to the side and backward until his knees hit his chair, and he lowered himself slowly. "What you will feel will be your memories buried through thralling, Harry. You met Harlan Gardner on January 19th, 1947, a Sunday morning. He listened to you play your guitar on your family's porch." Rick grew silent for a few moments.

Harry felt his head go light.

With a nod from Rick, Adam took over. "Do you remember the man who approached you that Sunday, just before dawn? He asked for directions. Do you remember?"

Eyes closed, Harry shook his head 'no,' and Adam continued. "Harlan sat down and looked deeply into your eyes. He asked you about the past few months, and you told him everything. Your words spilled out like a tapped font, Harry. The pain you harbored was inconsolable. By the time your parents left for ten o'clock mass, Harlan was gone. You rested peacefully that day for the first time in weeks. Do you remember?" No response from Harry, who was falling down into the past. "From time to time, Harlan intersected with you, just to make sure the memory was overthrown, and you were peaceful."

Adam shifted forward intently and used his Dom voice to press on, "Try to remember, Harry."

"Yes, I want to remember. I don't know what I'm supposed to remember." Harry's relaxed posture belied his tense words.

Adam read from the file notes. "Let's see if I have some information that will help you. There was a musician at the Blue Gardenia Lounge…"

I guess by the look on their faces, they're waiting for me to come up with some exciting stuff…

"Yes, Harry, the musician was you. You were a mortal involved in a tragedy. The vampire Family was involved. They wanted to protect themselves, and they also wanted to spare you belaboring the memories and extending your heartache."

Looking at his forearm's incision, with the peculiarly textured gelee, Harry waited impatiently to remember.

Adam's deep, resonant voice carried the tale. "In those days, 1946, some vampires hung out on the strip of sad bars where the ah," he checked his notes, "The Blue Gardenia was."

Harry's gaze narrowed at the lack of recollection. "Pardon me, The Blue Gardenia?" He shook his light head unbelievingly. Harry watched what looked like fig jam soak into the open wound, wondering how it would flow into his system with a vampire's scant circulation.

"The name isn't important. Let's unlock this mystery. Sit back, Harry. Close your eyes. Listen and accept it all, regardless of how unfamiliar it is. Tell me about everything, and we'll transcribe it."

Harry heard Adam's words through a haze as perceptible as gauze over a camera lens. "You're a writer, describe to me what you see. Imagine these are events in a book you're writing…"

A gamut of experiences began to flow back into Harry's mind by way of his heart and soul. He began to narrate the images as they flew to the forefront of his mind.

Chapter Twenty-Four

I was in Los Angeles, November 1946. My first thought when I woke up in my old bedroom was no cold feet. No reveille. No mess hall. No trooping boots outside. No ribald laughter. No cursing. No Jeeps grinding gears through muddy ruts.

The house was warm. My twin bed held me captive under homemade quilts and soft sheets. The smell of coffee perking combined with the sound of my mother humming along with the radio until the Pepsodent ad intruded. At twenty-five, I was a discharged Army Medical Corp Officer, and I was home.

My mind was miles from nowhere; everything about the past few years was eons away. For years, I slaved over a steady influx of war-torn bodies. I managed twelve crises at once under blackout conditions and war-time shortages. I ordered medications, assisted in surgeries, made staff assignments, arbitrated disputes, and calmed the homesick injured with a song or two on a borrowed guitar. I always found a joke or smile to keep the patients and staff in good spirits.

Since I slept in a comfortable bed, a lifetime of clarifying experiences revealed my earnest desires in life. I knew what I didn't want. Now, what *did* I want? The war flew by in a blur of activity at the same time it felt like an eternity.

My bedroom's relative silence was deafening. Between sleep and waking, I drifted. That drift was partial relief, but I was at loose ends. All that was required of me today was helping mom clear the table and dry the dishes.

I lingered in bed and hugged my pillow. In four nights, I'll join my parents for my first Thanksgiving back in the states. But Dotty, my girl-next-door sweetheart, will be celebrating with her family this year.

Why didn't I marry her after I graduated from Officer Corp school? Her dragon of a mom, a military wife herself, told Dotty, "He'll get you pregnant and then get killed. Who wants a widow with a baby?"

Our tears were useless. My rational banker father sat down with Mrs. Hedlund and explained the benefits of insurance and long-term post-war financial planning, especially if we had a child. None of our professions of love or Dad's logic swayed Mrs. Hedlund. She refused to sign for her daughter, and Dotty's eighteenth birthday was the week after her high school graduation. I knew the military would never consider marriage a reason for emergency leave. Those days were chaotic, and all training was accelerated. There was no leave, period.

My bare feet hit the rug next to my bed, and I absent-mindedly scratched at my bare chest. It was heaven to sleep in my boxers and not wear six layers of clothing to bed. I ambled to the bathroom and thought about *not* shaving. I smiled at the sunshine pouring through the window. California winters were mild compared to England's frigid dampness. I slid on an old pair of trousers, which hung slack at my waist, held up by suspenders. I chuckled at muscles earned from hospital work and regarded the freshly ironed plaid sports shirt mom thoughtfully had waiting for me.

I mustered out of the Army and had a new commanding officer, Rose Flannery VanAlt. Dad, Henry William VanAlt, Sr., president of the First Bank of Los Angeles, was preoccupied with the post-war boom. I feared my post-war return would cramp my parent's empty nest romance.

As soon as the ink dried on my DD 214s, I headed home. The house next door, my sweetheart's house, was now separated from ours by a tall wooden fence. Mom complained that Mrs. Hedlund and Dotty perfected the cold shoulder before the wall was even erected along the property line. "I don't understand it. They act as if you jilted *her*!"

There was more separating us than a wooden fence. I expected that, shortly after I left for Europe, Dotty would graduate from high school and go to college while she waited for me to come home.

I heard my mother at the foot of the stairs. "Are you dressed for church? It's only coffee this morning. We leave for Mass in thirty minutes."

Mass? Shaving? A shirt and tie. Who am I kidding? A suit. I miss reveille. "Right, it's Sunday. Give me five. I'll be down."

♦♦♦♦

I sported a piece of bloody toilet paper on my jaw and rode in the back seat with Mom and Dad jabbering in the front. My mind spun at the regression of being driven by my father to Mass at the Cathedral. None of their conversations sank in until Dad called my name at the stoplight.

"Harry?"

"Hum? Pardon me, Dad?"

"I say, I talked to the Dean of the medical school at Loma Linda. You can't get back this coming spring semester, but you can take summer classes. Pick up your electives."

I closed my eyes. "Right." I would rather work as a grill cook. I'd had my fill of bloody bodies and seen enough disease to last me a lifetime. Everyone in med school should go to war first. It would sort the driven from those who thought healing was a 'genteel' calling.

I felt Mom's scrutiny over the front seat and smiled placidly at her words. "You look tired, Hank. Why don't we go by the Biltmore for brunch? Then you can take a nap."

Dad agreed. "When you get up from your nap, we can listen to the radio."

I didn't know if I would actually nap, but some time alone to stare at my bedroom ceiling would bring welcome peace.

◆◆◆◆

Within the massive Catholic Church, parishioners were packed shoulder to shoulder. The incense hung in a cloying fog above us. Lost in the scent of supplications and repentance, I solemnly stood, knelt, and sat in rhythm with my parents. My Latin responses came by rote as my mind flew with the angels on the ceiling. After the service, well-wishers thronged me in the narthex, welcoming me home from war.

My hopes for a rapid extraction to brunch were dashed when Dad dragged me toward a pinched-looking couple with a studious daughter. I nodded and shook hands. "Harry, I want you to meet Judge Wilson, his wife Jane, and their lovely daughter, Joy."

Jane Wilson's matronly powdered face creased into a broad smile when she noticed me over Dad's shoulder. "Oh, Henry, you must bring the family to dinner after the holidays. What are you doing New Year's Eve?"

I stood reserved, hands in pockets watching my parents chatter with the Wilsons. Joy eyed me like I was a prize at the church bazaar. The quintessential college junior was home for the holidays. Was she as severe as she appeared, or was this in deference to the church setting? If we wrestled in a car's back seat, what would that tight bun look like? Between the tightly drawn bun and the white gloves, she was forbiddingly austere.

Dad dragged me closer to Joy. "Miss Wilson roomed with the 1944 Miss America at UCLA. Don't you think she's a far sight more attractive?"

Who was Miss America 1944? I was in England, digging shrapnel out of bellies. I nodded agreeably. "I'm sure you are, Miss Wilson. What are you studying?"

The girl with nothing in particular, smiled simperingly. "French literature."

"Oh, will you teach?"

Her gloved hand covered her coral lips. "Oh, no…" and she laughed. Message sent; she's working on her MRS. Degree.

I stepped back promptly, checked my watch, and whispered discreetly to Mom. "If we want a seat near the fountain, we need to get moving."

♦♦♦♦

The Biltmore Hotel was a landmark destination in downtown Los Angeles. Everyone who was anyone ate Sunday brunch in their elegant Rendezvous Court and had since 1923. Once the server brought steaming cups of coffee, Dad leaned back and smirked. "Last week's LIFE magazine featured party raincoats on the cover. Do you have yours, Rose?"

Mom's smile erupted. "Oh, Henry, you're such a romantic."

He winked at me. "Yes, Rose, the world is such a romantic place without the war. When did LIFE become a woman's magazine?"

Mom began to open her mouth when Dad's attention turned to me. "After the holidays, you can borrow the car if you want to take a ride up to Loma Linda."

I agonizingly regarded my cutlery and place setting. I did not want a public debate on returning to medical school. I muttered a noncommittal,

"Thanks, Dad," desperately wishing we could hold a generic conversation. It would be a conversation free from medical school and the attributes of the several handsome women he paraded in front of me since I returned last Thursday. Each day was a smorgasbord of potential wives and future mothers, each more socially relevant yet less sensually appealing. What do civilians talk about? Raincoats? Someone rescue me.

"Mom, have you heard anything about Dotty Hedlund? Did her dad make it through the war?"

Mom sighed. "Colonel Hedlund died in the Pacific. Dotty is now Mrs. Arnold Craft. Arnold works for Bell Telephone." I felt my face drain of blood. How has Mom not told me this before? Has she been avoiding it? "They married right after she graduated High School in June." Mom bent closer. "Nothing like a little 'prom dividend' if you know what I mean?" My cheeks flushed with angry color. "They hid the child as if she were afflicted. Not often do you see an eight-pound preemie."

My jaw stiffened, and I grabbed for a water goblet. After draining half the glass, I choked out, "Well, that's why Dotty never wrote me back. I never got a Christmas card either."

Mom continued whispering. "Janet across the street said Arnold moved in, and the Hedlunds paid for his graduate school at UCLA. He's got an engineering degree, he works in research, doing …"

"Harry VanAlt, you son of a gun!" I looked up as the devil himself, Arnold Craft, walked toward us. He'd put on about twenty pounds, his face was still florid, and his platinum hair was thinning.

"Crafty, what are you doing here?" I stood and fought for a smile, extending a hand. "Good to see you." I searched over Craft's shoulder for Dotty.

"I see you returned to the scene of the crime." Arnold's words fell on Mom and Dad like a bucket of ice.

"Well, Crafty, I did do a good job of smoothing out things with the house detective. You shouldn't have brought the school mascot into the hotel lobby."

"Who'd a thunk a bobcat would scare a few Saturday night hob-nobbers?" My parents blanched. I changed the subject.

"So, what are you doing now, Craft? You weren't in the service?"

"Nah, flat feet. I did postgraduate work in electronics. I'm gonna build the world's future communications from my drafting board. I'm contributing to the peace effort."

"Commendable. How's Dotty?" I could hear the misery in my own voice.

"Wondered when you were going to get around to the old ball and chain." I winced, and my face flamed. Arnold dismissively waved at Mom. "I'm sure your mister doesn't feel that way about you." He winked at her and returned to poke a finger in my shoulder. "So, are you a Doctor yet? Didn't you get credit for all that work?"

My words came out in a hiss. "That's not how they train doctors, Craft. I'll be using the G.I. plan when space opens."

"If you're looking for work, I can probably get you on as a mail boy at the phone company."

I pulled myself up to stand an inch or two taller than Craft and looked down my nose at my rival. "I administrated a hospital three times the size of this building." Dead silence all around. "I'm not interested in juggling mail."

"Well, Harry, that was the war. The military had to work over their heads."

I sat down and drew my napkin over my lap. "Nice seeing you again, Craft. Have a good Sunday. Give Dotty our regards." Arnold Craft slithered back to Dotty, sitting uncomfortably alone at a tiny corner table.

♦♦♦♦

Listening to his tale, Lizbet realized immediately that Harry had been a child of some privilege. *He came by his heroic instincts naturally. He rescued me, and he'd certainly been a rescuer during the war. I wonder what happened to Dotty?*

♦♦♦♦

It wasn't a week later when Dad bellowed. "I hope you don't expect to wander through my house aimlessly. Music is not a profession!" He shook a condemning finger at me. "You're wasting the last four years of your life."

I tried not to tower over my father. "Dad, why do I have to give you a decision this month? I can't even apply until next summer." Mom sat silently, her crocheting motionless in her lap. "So, I spend a few weekends picking up gigs at clubs. I'll be here for Mom and you."

"You can't hope to put away any tuition strumming a guitar in a club."

"Dad, I'll be going back to school on the G.I. plan. I'll make enough at a club to contribute to the family. Don't you understand what I've faced, day after day, for the last four years? Do you honestly begrudge me a few weekends of music?"

"I know you have to catch up to idiots like Craft. Don't tell me it doesn't bother you that he's ahead of the game?"

I turned away from my father, and then I turned back. "You know, Dad? It doesn't bother me. I know who I am, what skills I have. When I get to where I'm going, it will be the right place." I didn't wait for that to sink in, it probably wouldn't anyway. I wiped the expression off my face and went for a walk.

Chapter Twenty-Five

I felt for the wallet in my pocket and hailed a cab to Sunset Boulevard. Sunday nights weren't the hottest, but you could read the regulars and tap the tone of the club. Was it a good vibe? Was it a down vibe?

I strolled past the quieter club doors and found the loudest at 8852 Sunset Boulevard. The deep blue door swung open, and two sailors danced out drunk, arm in arm. I stood back and slipped into the darkness as the door closed behind me.

A bubbly blonde sidled up to me at the bar and leaned on her elbow. "Where did you come from, handsome, and can I make you a drink?"

It was nice to have a flirtatious moment without ulterior motives. She brought back my long lost crooked grin. I watched the bartender's blue eyes widen. I had to think for a minute. "Gin Rickey with plenty of ice."

"A guy like you's gotta cool down?"

"I'm just happy to be home where there is ice."

While she made the cocktail, she talked over her shoulder. "Where ya been?"

"Merry old England, where the beer is warm, and the winters are cold."

She turned with the tall, frosty drink and placed it on the napkin in front of me. "Welcome home, soldier."

I fingered the blue logo on the white napkin, Blue Gardenia. The room was noisy between sets as my finger tapped the fancy font. "Is there such a thing?"

Her attention snapped from a loud table back to me. "Perhaps as rare as a Hollywood virgin." Her long-pointed fingernails combed through the loose curls around her young but world-weary face.

I wondered abruptly what heartache had stamped itself on her soul. I spun on the barstool and regarded the long room with envy. It was the quintessential jazz club with red half-moon booths and dark corners. Smoky mirrors multiplied the characters drinking, dancing, and telling tall tales without a care. Me? I was still waiting for the next bomb to drop.

The band played another set while I nursed my drink. It really wouldn't do to wind up in front of Dad cured in smoke and spirited by alcohol my first week home. A loose-jointed man with sleeves pushed back on muscled forearms, the drummer, strolled over to the bar on the next break, and requested a beer and a shot of Old Overholt Rye.

I shuddered. "You're a brave man."

The drummer held up his shot and downed it. "It's the same stuff Doc Holliday drank."

"You know, he died of TB. Like I say, a brave man."

"I once ran from an angry goose, so, not so brave." He stuck his hand out. "John Franklin Smith. You just get back home? Your hair is a little high and tight."

I laughed and ran a hand over my hair. "Yeah. Got home Thursday. Trying to figure out what it's like to be a civilian."

The drummer pulled out a pack of smokes and held it out. I took one and nodded thanks. "Living with the folks, right?" The drummer lit my cigarette.

"Do I look like I've run away from home?" I drew in a deep drag of the fresh cigarette, enjoying the burn and sent blue smoke out my nose.

"Cannot be easy going from independence to minding your Ps and Qs for Mom and Dad. What did you do in the war?"

I shrugged. "I ran a hospital in England."

"Ah, head janitor, huh?"

I cocked my head. "No. I was an administrator, but there were times when I was the surgeon's right hand."

Candy slid her elbow closer to me. "How old are you?"

"Twenty-five, going on eighty."

The drummer nodded. "That's a hell of a job, fella. No wonder you're carrying the weight of the world. What are you going to do now, buy a boat and sail the seven seas?"

I smiled, emerging from my dark mood, and winked. "Get new strings for my Gibson ES-150 and strum on the porch."

Smitty shook his head, his cigarette hanging on his lip. "Man, you're gonna get bored with that real quick. Ever play with a band, make some real music?"

"I've always wanted to. I used to play sets at the church carnival."

Smitty laughed. "They let you play the devil's music over there?"

"I cleaned up Cole Porter."

Candy nudged the drummer. "Go ahead, Smitty, ask him."

"Our crooner is our piano player. He's about to take a gig in New York City. Do you play the piano and guitar?

"My keyboard's a little rusty, not a lot of time to play in a war. But I've played enough to keep up with things. I taught myself to play guitar."

Smitty asked. "Why don't you bring your guitar tomorrow night, you can sit in and see if you can get'em dancing cheek to cheek. The tips are better when the guys think they'll get laid."

"I'll do my best. I have to warn you, though, I might be leaving for medical school in the summer."

Smitty waved a hand at the bar's atmosphere. "The Blue Gardenia will work that right out of your system."

♦♦♦♦

Adam leaned forward to interrupt Harry's recollections. "Harry, sounds like you were looking for some emotional relief. Nowadays, we'd say you were suffering from Post-Traumatic Stress, and your dad was stifling your recovery. And piling on the guilt."

Harry shrugged. "When he came home from WWI, he said he had to hit the ground running. Of course, he spent his whole duty right here in the U.S. He had no understanding of what I'd done 24/7. He rode a desk." He sighed. "I resented it. I don't mind saying that now."

Lizbet nodded to Rick and tapped her watch. Adam smiled reassuringly. "I can understand why you'd feel that way. What did you do about it?"

Harry's narrative resumed.

♦♦♦♦

The audition went well with Smitty's quartet at The Blue Gardenia. A month flew by, quicker than I thought possible. I evaded Dad by working nights with Smitty or carrying my gig bag to open sets at other clubs. My improvisations whipped the crowds into applause, and nightly I felt more musically confident.

The day after Christmas, before the evening rush, I leaned against the bar in an intimate chat with Candy. "In the year between closing the hospital in England and settling the soldiers at Walter Reed, I think my Mom and Dad believed I was drifting like a barnacle in search of direction."

I wisely neglected to mention to Candy I actively humped each of her photo gals, coat check, and cigarette girls in the back seat of Smitty's hoopdy sedan. I played sets with a drink on the barstool, next to the reefer in the ashtray. I was on stage nights and slept days in my father's house. Dad wasn't too happy about that. At least he didn't know about any of my other societal transgressions.

♦♦♦♦

Adam tapped his pen and held up a finger. "Harry, it sounds like you had a lot of meaningless intercourse. Did you find a girl you could really care for?"

♦♦♦♦

Oh, yeah. On December 28th, 1946, I nearly swooned at the sight of a raven-haired miss sitting at the bar. She held a Lucky Strike teetering between her index and second finger as she stared into the grey haze. My God, she was lovely, different. Her beautiful green eyes expressed… aloneness.

I sent her a drink and prepared for the next set, a few Nat King Cole tunes, "Mona Lisa", "Nature Boy", and "Stardust". By the time I warbled about the greatest thing is 'to love and be loved in return' she was staring a hole through my crotch, or my guitar, I couldn't tell which. She didn't have that carnal, lustful look. She drained the first drink and sat swirling the squared ice cubes in the tumbler. She wore her hunger for affection like the ebony silk flower in her hair.

Was she craving my attention? 'Cause I wanted to be that guy. I caught Billy's eye and nodded to give her another drink. Perhaps we'd go to breakfast at the diner after we blew out of here? Otherwise, at this rate,

148

she'd be in the bag before I got her home. And I do not put the moves on a drunken gal.

I walked her home. Her name was Elizabeth. She told me to call her Beth. Today, I wonder, what is it about the name Elizabeth? I keep running into them, don't I? Her place was a seedy little walkup a couple of blocks from the bar. Just a room sparsely furnished with the dreams of a 'wanna be' starlet. Pages torn from Movie Story and Photoplay were thumb-tacked into the tired plaster walls.

The stars on the wall watched me lay a tipsy Beth onto dingy sheets on the twin bed. In the cruel light of the bare bulb, her shoes were worn, her stockings snagged, and her dress a bit faded. Somehow, in the harsh judgment of the swinging light, her features were still innocent and wistful. She was a Snow White without seven diminutive friends.

The walk home cleared my head, the night air dialed back the buzz of the weed and sanded the edge off the gin. The scent of her cologne hung on my jacket like an invitation to see her again. At home, I took in a deep breath, then slid out of my coat, and hung it on the back of the bedroom door. Mom quit making my bed, her signal for me to grow the hell up.

The sheets cooled in the uncharacteristically humid night, and in seconds I fell into the arms of some demon, pulling me under warm waves. I wanted to sleep, knowing dawn wasn't far off, yet whatever demon held me kept me roiling through a red river of suffocating flames. It had been a while since a woman cast a spell over me. Was it her dark magic, or was I fucked for life?

At three in the afternoon, I ignored the look on Mom's face as she ran the Electrolux over the carpets. She wore out the design at the end of the dining room rug as her eyes burned through me, eating a bowl of Cheerios over the sink.

I hadn't been right with her since I came home with a cigarette burn in Father's dinner jacket. A damn marijuana seed popped and landed on the lapel. I had two more weeks' payments before I could bring the new jacket home. Hopefully, by then, I'd be redeemed.

♦♦♦♦

I jumped the bus down to the club around eight in the evening. I sat in the corner, tuning my guitar and watched the parade of the broken and the damned. Tonight, the barflies and roués postured for our first set. There were no Prince Charmings with crystal shoes in their back pockets, they were cads ready to slip an ingénue a Mickey. I had to find another gig.

The crowd milled, as it fouled the air with cheap aftershave and cheaper cigars. I sought Beth's face in the audience but, when I did make visual contact, she was on the arm of some painfully effete, European looking guy. He was luminous in the smoky heat of the bar. What afforded him that glow? Was it Beth on his arm? She snapped up a stool at the far end of the bar, and he hung over her like a villain in a fairy tale. His hungry brown eyes took long looks at the lily-white crescents of her breasts peeking out from a sheer black bodice.

I lost the beat of 'Satin Doll,' and Ernie smacked my head with the drumstick. What a bastard. After the set, I turned to put down my guitar, and in the time it took for me to straighten up, the happy couple was gone. I guessed he was better for her than I was. I ambled to that end of the bar. Billy nodded and withdrew a paper note from his back pocket; it smelled like Beth's cologne. That was a far sight better than the air in the lounge.

"Thanks for being a gentleman. There are damn few of them left. Excuse my language; I've been alone awhile.

See you again soon. Got a date with a guy from MGM, wish me luck. -Elizabeth

P.s. Are you playing Saturday night, maybe I'll see you then...?"

So, she scored an after-hours *audition*. I hated the idea that she would buy a place on a stage with her body. I downed a gin and tonic and went back to croon about the woes between guys and gals. My sarcastic streak came out, good for her. I shouldered my guitar and mindlessly fingered the strings. I counted the beats until one A.M. when I went straight home for the first time in months.

Chapter Twenty-Six

"To what do we owe this honor?" My Father, in pajama pants and a tee-shirt, stood at the top of the stairs. His pit boss voice boomed. I stared warily up the steps, hoping to dial down his volume. I didn't want to wake my Mother.

I assumed a chastened posture. I didn't know whether to address him, Dad or Father, it depended on how much trouble I was in. "Hey, Dad, what's got you up at this hour?" I dropped my gig bag in front of the hall tree and leaned on the newel post, half interested in a conversation.

Dad's voice deepened as he shared the news. "Dotty's mother died tonight."

I ground my jaw. "Did the coroner behead Mrs. Hedlund before they took her body?"

"Henry William VanAlt, Jr. that's a hell of a thing to say." Dad chided, but a sly grin snuck out. "I thought she was too evil to die."

I ascended the steps. "How's Mom taking this? She and Dotty used to be close."

"Your Mom is sleeping; I gave her a whiskey."

I nodded. "How's Dotty?"

My father followed me into my bedroom and sat at my school desk. "Dotty's husband bent my ear. I'm going to the funeral parlor with him tomorrow unless you want to go."

I began removing my tuxedo shirt and cummerbund. "That might be awkward for me. I typically handle deaths, but you handle finances." I stared out the window at Dotty's home next door, recalling the nights she and I talked on string and tin can telephones. "I'll make a call to the house with Mom tomorrow while you and Arnold handle business."

Dear old Dad leaned back and sharpened his gaze. "Thought any more about medical school? These hours can't be easy if you want to associate with normal people."

"You know, Dad, during the war, I got used to working all shifts all the time. And you do know; doctors are called out all hours of the night. It really doesn't bother me." I was down to my boxers. "I'm going to catch a shower. See you in the morning, Dad." I left before he was up from the chair.

♦♦♦♦

Mom and I stood on the Hedlund's deep front porch, and I watched the white swing motionless in the December weather. There were ghosts there, necking actively as they giggled. I buried my brief smirk and faced the door, seeing Dotty's shadow through the lace curtains. I stepped to the side and let Mom lead the conversation.

"Oh, Mrs. VanAlt, aren't you the sweetest? Come…" When she noticed me, tears erupted from her eyes. "Harry, how nice of you to come." She stepped back and welcomed us into the large foyer.

I held up a casserole. "May we drop this in the kitchen, is it a good time?" I was polite but direct. The way to the kitchen was exactly the same as it had been since Dotty and I were kids. Now there was a formal wedding photo over the mantle. Dotty, in a tea-length lace dress, and Craft wearing a smirk behind a small wedding cake. I drew in a cleansing breath as I slid the Pyrex casserole into the icebox. I put the soda bread and homemade preserves in the pie safe.

I stared out the kitchen window as I counted for patience in dealing with Dotty. "One, two, three, four, five…"

An active little sprite with luminous blue eyes and pouty ruby lips played with a ringlet of her dark curls and leaned in the kitchen doorway. "I am three." She dropped her hair and held up three fingers. "I had a cake."

I jumped. "You had cake?" I backed into the corner of the kitchen counter. "Who do you belong to?"

"My mommy and my daddy." She pointed a finger toward the front of the house.

I gulped. "Where are your parents?"

"Mommy's sad."

I closed my eyes and counted on my fingers behind my back.

Footsteps approached from the front of the house. "Valerie, baby, don't bother Mr. VanAlt."

Valerie raised seven fingers. "I'm going to be four. Will there be cake, Mommy?"

Dotty caught the child to her hip, bent, and kissed a flurry of dark curly hair. "Maybe, Pumpkin. Where's your Raggedy Ann?" Dotty ruffled her hair. "Better go find her before Cotton finds her."

My gaze deepened. "Cotton? How old is she now?"

"Don't be silly, Harry." She talked to me like I was a child. "This is Cotton Two. Arnold gave him to me on our first Christmas Day."

I nodded. If I was married to her, she wouldn't be talking to me like that. I followed Dotty to the parlor. I was in my second home, but the welcome mat had been pulled out from under my feet. I trailed the scent of Arpege in Dotty's wake and remarked: "She's beautiful."

"She's smart as a whip, too."

"She takes after her mom."

"Righto, Harry." Within each sentence, our tensions mounted. When we entered the parlor, it was an art gallery of family photos. Dominating portraits celebrated graduations and birthdays. All of the family was tall, thin, with pale with icy aqua eyes and straight platinum hair. From the wedding photo, Arnold's blond hair was Brylcreemed into obedience, ensuring precision.

Mom shared the settee with a bag of yarn and a knitting spool. "Valerie, I've brought you a big girl toy. Want to learn how to spool knit?" She tempted the girl to join her.

Valerie was my Mom's miniature. I blinked hard and positioned myself, so I could see the child without appearing to stare.

Dotty took a seat across the room and sat desolate. "Now that Mother is gone, may I go back to calling you, Momma Rose?"

Mom nodded her head forlornly. "Oh, sweetie, you've always been able to call me Momma Rose. Now more than ever, you'll be going through so much, don't be a stranger. Perhaps Arnold will take down that angry-looking fence?"

I slunk back into the chair. *Or build it higher?*

On the way home, I measured my stride so Mom could keep a comfortable pace. She gazed harshly at the six-foot wood fence that ran directly to the sidewalk. "Now, I know why that fence was erected."

I kept my mouth shut and schooled my features to bland.

"Was it because something else was erect, Henry William VanAlt, Jr.?"

"What are you saying, Mom?"

"That sunny little apple didn't fall far from the VanAlt tree."

"Evidently, it fell on the other side of the fence."

Mom waged a level look. "Did you even know?"

My hands flew out in surrender as I ground my jaw. "It was one night, our last night together. We thought if we slipped, that would be even more reason for us to marry. But, no, I didn't know." My face colored in anger. "You and Dad knew we wanted to marry. That ogre of a mother refused to sign for Dotty. But that doesn't explain why she didn't tell you or write to me about her condition." I stopped at the end of their walkway and curled my lip at the Hedlund home. My expression was grim. "You know I would have done the right thing. I loved Dotty."

"I'm sorry, son." Mom hugged my arm. "Unfortunately, what's done is done. The baby's father is recorded as Arnold Craft. You can look at that angel and see she's fifty-one percent VanAlt." I was unmoved, still glaring at the Victorian painted lady I'd considered a second home.

"Obviously, her mother meant more to her than I did."

Mom tugged me toward home. "Daughters are easy to dominate. Elsa Hedlund was alone. You would have taken Dotty away. Instead, she took her from you."

As I opened the door for my Mom, I burned inside. "Forget Dotty. They took my daughter away from me."

♦♦♦♦

Lizbet put down her pen. Inhaled a deep breath and took a sip of water. Her hand covered her mouth, and she felt Matt's scrutiny. She met his gaze, and his expression softened. Matt's lips fell into a sad smile as he shook his head. Lizbet shrugged and straightened her posture.

As loving and giving as Harry's been with me, how will this loss and betrayal affect him now? Will he be able to trust again?

♦♦♦♦

Between then and the thirtieth, I tossed around the idea of asking Beth to the lounge for New Year's Eve. Maybe I could start 1947 with one girl on my arm. As I tucked a note in the door-frame at her place, someone who passed as a landlord stuck his unshaven mug around the corner.

"She moved out." He grunted. The words hit me, and I yanked the folded paper out of the paint blistered jamb and pocketed it.

"Did she leave an address?" I gave him my best earnest look. I didn't want him to think I was an ex-husband.

He scratched at the hair in his jug ears. "The gal said she moved in with a friend, Eva around the corner, on North Cherokee, where she and three other girls room together. The brown building, Eva Jackson's name is on the directory." He didn't care if I was an ax-murderer, so I nodded and tipped my cap on the way out.

The brown apartment building was cleaner, looked like someplace girls would share. I buzzed the apartment, got nothing. I left the note wedged in the mailbox. What's a guy to do otherwise?

Chapter Twenty-Seven

Adam leaned forward for a drink of water and observed Harry was now more casually wedged into the corner of the sofa, one long leg stretched out while one bare foot rested on the floor.

He couldn't help but notice that as Harry became more engrossed in the memories, he assumed more of the parlance of the times and gestures accentuated his monologue.

◆◆◆◆

December thirty-first, 1946, what an electric night! More sequins were shaking than I'd seen before in The Blue Gardenia. More swells with gals in their arms, more champagne flowing than beer. I waited to see if she'd be here before Saturday night, January fourth. I had a shot of courage, wore a clean shirt, and when Beth sauntered into the club alone, I was on top of the effin' world.

Sure, it was an extraordinary night, the end of the war era, the beginnings of hope. I know I had hope, for a steady girl, for a better gig, for some way to turn my life in the right direction. I wasn't even bargaining with God the way you do when your back is against the wall.

I nodded to Beth and blew her a kiss, as the bartender served her a Martini, extra dirty. She sent me back a wave, and I shivered at the sight of her in the ebony satin dress, a black silk flower in her lustrous raven waves. Rubine lips caressed the edge of the glass, and I got into the swing of "A Fine Romance".

She mesmerized me, and the spell hung through the entire set. When we swung into the last song, a sultry blonde appeared behind her. Hurried greetings were exchanged, and they hugged. Then it all went sideways when Blondie locked lips with Beth right there in the middle of "Five Minutes More". I could have been Frank Sinatra, and not kept the crowd's attention around the end of the bar. I guess they hadn't seen two women lock lips like that.

Hell, I had never seen two women get into it. I fingered the strings with sheer determination, as I slid the cool, smooth back of my guitar across my stiffy. I wondered if she'd kiss *me* like that. Most people would pay for a show this steamy. Sly, soft hands roamed over each other's shoulders. Jesus, didn't they need to come up for air?

Then the wiry guy who came in with Beth the other night slid behind the horny blonde and led her away. Beth's blush rose from her cleavage to her hairline as she smoothed her hair and wiped at her smeared crimson lipstick. She flashed a smile at me and blew a kiss at the same time. I was watching the clock, but I actually wanted to watch her undress. It was 10:47 P.M., just a tad more time in 1946.

Ralph stopped the music about 11:55 P.M. He figured he'd go out of 1946 with a full till. I stepped into the bathroom and splashed water on my mug. Beth's little show with the blonde made me rearrange myself. Was she showing her hand to challenge me to step up and show her what I could do, or was she throwing her cards down to keep me back?

My bet was on the challenge. I wiped my wet face on a new segment of the towel from the wall dispenser. I always wondered where the crumpled dirty towel went when you pulled the clean part down. What the hell, I'd find Beth and see if I could make some fireworks between us. She kept her seat at the end of the bar, alone; the party went on around her. I admit I got a rise in my shorts when she brightened up, seeing me strolling toward her.

"Almost Happy New Year." I grinned at her as I leaned my elbow on the bar.

"Same to you, Harry." She craned her neck to pucker a smooch on my cheek; I felt the waxy residue of her lipstick on my stubble and the scent of her cologne. Had I won her approval? The next couple of minutes flew, and before I could shuffle from right to left foot, we had drinks in our hands and our arms wrapped around each other for a midnight toast.

We kissed at midnight, eyes wide open, in a sort of frank and abrupt manner. It was part perfunctory, part exploratory, and a significant part elation at having a new set of lips to kiss.

Then, a switch flipped, and the drinks were out of our hands. She was on her feet, hands splayed under my dinner jacket, combing across my back. I met her action for action, feeling the slick, tight fabric of her evening frock. I felt the rigid structure of her brassiere, and both my hands rode the curve of her buttocks, feeling the garter belt, yet no panty waistband. Holy Lord, she was sans panties.

We caromed off the vertical surfaces until we were outside the club. The night air hit us as we kissed, turning in circles until we smacked into a parked car. I pitched her onto the hood of a sedan, and her hands flew off me to steady herself against the cold metal. I caught her wrists and held them over her head as I bent over her and leaned in for another long smooch.

My knee split hers as I slid her further on the hood, and her high heels left the ground. No talk, just sloppy kisses, and fabric sliding between bodies pressed hard against each other. Did I let go of her wrists, or did she wrestle free from me? I don't remember. We were buried in the throes of that fresh rapture, new bodies making sparks.

Partiers ran past us in the street, hooping, hollering, and clanging noisemakers, it was a rush in the din of the crowd. Somewhere in the background, I heard a guy yell, "Hell, yeah, what you do New Year's Day, you'll do all year."

The thought melted into my mind, to plunder and pleasure this woman-child. My pleated trousers tented, and I rubbed over her thigh. We were so high on each other; we just heaved in deep breaths between kisses.

"Can you come home with me?" I knew it wasn't for milk and cookies. I could get them at my house.

"I have to play the closing set. It's a short one. Then we can get…to your place, Okay?" I stood straight and situated myself, the steel in my trousers wasn't going down. Elizabeth caught my excitement and smoothed it down my thigh. I gasped with the sensation of her hand on me.

My dick sprang back up. "You've got to stop that, or I'll blow right here." I shook my head and sucked in any air I could catch.

"I can relieve that pressure." Her eyes sparkled in the streetlights as her hand grasped me harder. I shuddered at her touch, soft and firm at the same time.

"It's not like I couldn't go for that right now, it's, it's, ah, not the way I want to do it-- give me thirty to forty-five minutes, and we can be alone, okay?" I thought about my New Year's resolution to cover my soldier, fished in my pockets, and came up empty. I didn't need another tax deduction in 1947. Good idea to stall until I could bring balloons to the party.

I cleared a seat at the top of the bar, nearest to the band, while we did the last set. As I played, all the sensations of her body against mine swirled within me. Propelling my fingers over the neck of the guitar, I strummed along, turning away from her to concentrate. I didn't want another drumstick to the head. We finished big with "Deep Purple", and I fixated on deep purple dreams, so dark they were as black as Beth's hair.

The guys in the band saw our expressions. I packed up my guitar and slung it over my shoulder, they winked at me, and I took her hand in mine to walk home. I scored a trifecta of rubbers in the bathroom, and we were on our way. Talking as we walked, it didn't seem too far to her North Cherokee apartment.

"My roommates went to San Diego for New Years, so it's just us," Elizabeth demurred as we sauntered down the sidewalk. The streets were still alive with revelers as we climbed the steps to her flat. It was cleaner than her last place. There was more to be cleaned this time.

Well-kept plaster walls had fakes of famous oil paintings; the movie magazines were fanned on the coffee table in front of a chintz sofa. The tiny kitchen had three liquor bottles on a gay colored tray with small jelly jars waiting. Beth kicked off her platform heels and went to crack the ice tray into a bucket. "How about a drink? I've got gin, rum, and bourbon." She stood in her stocking feet; her hip cocked at an angle -- she looked so inviting even in the fluorescent overhead light. "I've got a lime, some cola here somewhere."

"Whatever you're having, okay?" I slid out of the dinner jacket and hung it over the chair in the living room. I sat to untie my shoes while she made our drinks. Leaning back, knees wide, legs extended I watched her hips undulate under the slinky dress. I felt the heat rise in my thighs. I wanted her all night.

She flicked off the kitchen light and walked to me in a silhouette from the streetlights outside. Her ivory skin aglow against the deep black-red of her lipstick. She handed the tall drink to me, a double, maybe a triple of what looked like lemonade with bourbon. Then she straddled my lap, and all of the past flew out of my mind.

I lay back in the chair and let her engulf me. The skirt of her sleek dress hitched up to her full hips, revealing the garter belt and just as I felt, no panties.

We slaked our thirst, drinking down the liquid courage halfway, and then again, our hands emptied to get to the matter at hand, each other. There wasn't enough water on the earth to put her fire out.

We were wrapped in crazy motions kissing, petting, and pinching at just the right tension of painful pleasure. We worked on all the skin that showed before I broke out in a keen sweat and grabbed her to carry her to bed.

"Where?" I hoarsely choked out as I held her like a bride over a threshold.

"Second door on the right." Beth's black hair fell from its control with combs and silk flowers. She looked like a wild child, totally untamed. I kicked open the door, and the fresh air rushed us. We needed it, we hadn't begun, and we were already overheated.

I dropped her onto a full-size bed with a blue and black striped bedspread so I could undress. She rebounded and knelt on the mattress in front of me. A single painted nail went to my lips as she opened her eyes wide to mine. The windows on her soul showed pain, loneliness, and something I couldn't identify. All I could do was lean into her supplications.

Her slow way of unbuttoning my dress shirt and sliding my suspenders over my shoulders riveted my attention to her delicate hands. She pressed close to reach around to undo the cummerbund when the sweet scent of her cologne sang an invitation to thrust away the sadness. Warm flat palms skimmed my chest, my hair standing up at her touch. Again, she knew how to ring my bell with the smallest effort.

Then the killer blow, she unbuttoned my trousers, slowly unzipping the fly. Each pair of teeth in the zipper registered a loud noise, as I ached to be in her hands. Finally, my trousers slinked to the bare floor, and my shorts followed. Our energy charged the room, and it was finally my turn to undress her. I snatched her by the waist and spun her to stand before me as I sat on the side of the bed.

Unzipping her side zipper and lifting the dress over her head, I tossed it to the chair. There was my reward, the black lace lingerie that covered her ripe, pale breasts. The lace on the garter belt matched the brassiere, yet the only black at the top of her thighs was a thick bush of dusky curls.

I plunged my nose into her, grasping her hips while I inhaled that decidedly feminine tang of a hot wet pussy. She was warm and soft and musky in a distinctive, romantic way. Just the scent of her stiffened me. If I dared sink right in, I'd lose it in seconds. I had to extend our foreplay.

This was fifty-seven varieties of intense, from the corn silk feel of her black hair as it whipped back at me, to the pliant flesh she pressed against me. I had to grab her, hug her hips, and feel the flat of her belly against my cheek. I felt her fingers comb through my hair, down my neck to crawl across my shoulders.

When did flesh on flesh feel like this? We hadn't even fondled each other yet. We were going insane running skin over skin with the expectation of plundering further.

Then she tipped the balance of my concentration, and I fell back on the bed, feeling crisp, clean linen beneath me. The smell of the ironed sheets still fresh around me, a perfect counterpoint to her musky, honeyed aroma.

She crawled up my length and worked me to a dither, so much so, that I couldn't do more than lay back and let her ride me. I never wanted the sun to rise. I just wanted to feel her planted on me, riding until I came undone in a whirlwind of bright lights and a deep throb that rolled up from my toes. I shook as I emptied into her, and she quivered from her shoulders down to her toes, especially her tight pussy clutching my shuddering cock.

She fell on me, a soft brush of hair and sweet lips, finding mine as we whispered our awe for each other. We were bathed in the overwhelming spell of each other's sweet sweat. What a way to start 1947! I wanted to freeze the moment for all time.

We laid there and dozed off and on until we heard the milk truck amble by the open window. The alley cats trailed behind the most influential guy in their lives, waking us with their caterwauling. The milkman sacrificed half a pint of cream in a saucer. We laid on our bellies and watched out the window, affectionately stroking fingertips over each other until we were nearly in giggles.

When the sun peeked between the two buildings across the street, I twirled a strand of ebony hair around my finger and drew her face to mine, seeking her kiss ravaged lips for more. "You hungry?"

"Just for you." And we rolled over and started all over again. Beth had so many misgivings about her young life. It took me back to my days bargaining with God in the operating room. We were close in age, yet decades apart in experiences. Listening to her talking about crisscrossing the continent between her parents, I dug at my conscience to appreciate my own parents dealing with me in my arrested development.

If she had been manhandled, her response to me didn't show it. Beth was eager and sweet and pleasing to me. Sex threw us into wild waters. Coming together to know each other in those early hours of January first, we swam to a stranger shore than we had known singly.

Earlier in the morning, we tore at a loaf of bread, seeded rye, while she carved at a few inches of Genoa salami and provolone cheese. God, we had hungry bellies, but hungrier libidos.

Drink fell short of the high we were found in each other. Later in the day, I taught her a few tricks about scavenging a kitchen, and we settled for a sort of homemade quiche. Bellies full, we showered and retreated to the aired out sheets.

"I, ah, brought these, and I didn't get them out in time." I proffered the trio of wrapped condoms, and she playfully grabbed them, holding them by the ends of the packing like an accordion.

"Only three?" It wasn't a sneer; it was a smirk at underestimating our lust. "Doesn't a guy like you, buy them by the case?" Her gaze shot sideways as she dropped them on the bed table and fell back against the headboard, knees drawn to her breasts.

◆◆◆◆

Lizbet blinked back tears listening to Harry's ecstatic descriptions of his time with Beth. *Did he date The Elizabeth Short, The Black Dahlia?* Whoever she was, she was long dead by now, so how do you compete with a memory? Harry longed for that woman. By the time they tasted each other's passion, the longing was a high tension wire. *Did he feel any of that with me? If someone interviewed him about us in fifty-six years, would I be Beth or lumped in with the girls in the backseat of Smitty's sedan?* She sighed and refocused.

♦♦♦♦

I left her around sunset. I showered and dressed, knowing I needed to be home. Home for dinner, for apologies, for epic conversations with my parents about what 1947 would see me doing.

If Beth could travel and make life alone at twenty-two, I should be able to do more than stumble into my parents' home and tumble out to play music. I was nearly whistling when I turned the corner on my street. I wasn't avoiding the Craft's stretch of the block anymore, but I spared them the sight of a single guy walking back from an all-night bed fest. I needed a shave, a change of clothes, and I wanted to share an earnest drink with my Father.

Chapter Twenty-Eight

"Aye, look what the cat dragged in? Do you know this one, Mother?" My Dad sat back in his easy-chair, reading the afternoon paper, a stub of a cigar in the side of his mouth. I shrugged, and my lips instinctively mouthed a silent apology as I stowed my gig bag and hung my dinner jacket up. "You want to get cleaned up before dinner, son?" He gave me an 'out' of facing Mom when I smelled like bed sports. One shower wasn't going to wash Beth off me. Hopefully, there would be a semblance of decorum at the dinner table if they were going to take me to task.

I took steps two at a time to shave, shower, and change into fresh clothes. I trotted back down to a table set with a pork roast, red cabbage, black-eyed peas, and a cast-iron pan of cornbread.

"I see you made it home for dinner. I guess I should be glad." Mom grabbed me by the jaw and did her best to crush a kiss on my chin.

"Oh, Mom, if you had a tattoo, it would say 'Son'." I winked at her and hugged her around her waist, nearly picking her up.

"Right, and the pain of gettin' that said tattoo would be less than how my heart bleeds for ya', Harry." Her eyes were about to narrow when something snapped, and she shook her head as if remembering it. I saw the table set for six. That meant the Crafts would be joining us.

I dropped Mom on her feet and clapped my hands together in mock anticipation of the meal between all of us. I followed her lead with the water pitcher to fill the goblets.

Within moments there was a knock at the door, and Dad held it open wide for Dotty, Arnold, and rosy-cheeked Valerie. The dimpled child stared up at Dad. "I'm Valerie. I'm three!"

Dad looked down at her, with his fists on his hips as he darted a gaze to Mom and me and back to the child. "Humph."

Much to my discomfort, they took seats around the dinner table after making New Year's small talk in the entry hall. Mom watched every expression and bit of conversation, especially Valerie's. Truth be told, I was watching her too.

Dotty proudly smiled at Arnold. "Arnold is next in line to lead a top-secret project."

I choked on my wine. "How secret can it be if you know about it?"

Arnold frowned dismissively. "Of course, she doesn't know the particulars." He stared at his wife, imperiously. "Dotty, we've had this discussion before…"

"I'm so proud of you; I can't help myself. I can't believe you're mine." Dotty reached a gentle hand to Arnold's, and he eluded her, slipping it quickly back into his lap.

I gazed at my parents in disbelief and nodded. "Well, we can't either." There was a lagging silence around the table when Valerie clapped her hands and squealed. "I'm the luckiest little girl in the world."

Arnold beamed at my kid. "Because that's what your Daddy tells you every night."

Mom buttered a piece of cornbread and handed it to Valerie. "You are, sweetie, your mommy and daddy love you very much." She glanced surreptitiously at me, and my cheeks colored. Valerie bit the buttery treat and nodded, her dark curls offset by the bouncing pink bow.

Even a social imbecile like Arnold must realize a family full of Norwegian blondes isn't going to produce a child who looked like Valerie. Does he even let Dotty touch him? He may be a good provider, but does he have a wandering eye? He was a bit of a perve in high school.

"Aren't you, son?" My mother glared at me.

"Sorry, what was the question?" I blinked. I was thinking about Arnold, the perve.

Dad's voice lowered. "Arnold asked you when you are going back to medical school?"

I chuckled. "You folks need a new family doctor? Too bad, I've spent the last four years as a military sawbones." I put my napkin on the table. "Did I tell you about the field amputation I had to do on a gangrenous foot?" My folks glared at me. "How about the sucking chest wound that never made it past the front door? Want to talk medicine? I've got plenty of stories."

Mom interrupted quietly. "Little pitchers have big ears, Harry. We'll talk later." She gave me a shriveling look, and I smoothed my napkin back on my lap.

"Oh, then it's back to school?" Arnold asked snidely.

"That's the big debate in this house. I'm waiting for that G.I. plan they promised us, and I can't get back in till next fall anyway." Again, the table sat silently, eating as Valerie hummed between bites.

"Valerie is so talented. Before Mother died, she made me promise to take her to the open studio auditions. She just knew Val would be snapped up. Elizabeth Taylor and Shirley Temple are too grown up!"

My silverware clattered to my plate. "Dotty, absolutely not! Do you know what those young ladies are put through?" The dinner guests stopped mid-bite. "I'm seeing a young woman who is currently auditioning. It's not for children. Not for little girls."

Dotty shook her head at me. "But, Harry, look at her…"

Arnold's palm tapped the table. "Dotty, I have to agree with Harry. Moving pictures are a dirty business. Your mother is deceased, and so is the idea of your daughter in movies."

"What's dezeesed?" Valerie asked, her little face scrunched up.

Dotty glared at Arnold and me. "Gone to heaven."

Valerie bobbed her head.

While Mom rinsed the three one-gallon milk jugs in the laundry room to put them out, I waylaid Dotty as she carried a stack of dirty dessert plates back to the kitchen. "What hairbrained idea did your mother plant in your head? I thought I knew you. The Dotty I knew wouldn't put a child through a Hollywood meat grinder."

"That child is filet mignon. She'd go through the system and be a star. She'd be set for life."

That flipped my switch. "When did you become consumed with the idea of security? When did money and notoriety take over your life?"

"When a G.I. left me pregnant without a dime."

I leveled a harsh gaze directly into her icy blue eyes. "I wrote to you. I telegrammed you. I even called before my ship sailed. I got nothing back for years."

Dotty's face went translucent, and her knees buckled. I caught her before she hit the linoleum. Mom walked in to see Dotty across my lap, recovering from the faint. She rushed to dampen a dishtowel. "Oh, sweetie, are you in a family way?" I glared at Mom as I sat Dotty on the chair and stood holding the damp dishtowel to the back of her neck.

Dotty dropped her chin. "How would that happen? It would be a miracle. He never touches me."

Mom and I blinked hard. "Mom, Dotty just found out all my cards and telegrams never got to her. I guess I should have sent them to you and had you slip 'em over the fence?"

Mom slid the kitchen door closed and turned her back against the pocket door. "The two of you are going to have to let that go. You'll have to offer that up to the Lord. What's done is done." Mom scrutinized our fallen expressions and pulled a chair between the two of us. She took Dotty's hand and sighed. "What your mother did was a terrible thing. I'm sure she answered to the Lord for that sin of omission. But two wrongs don't make a right. You have vowed before God to honor Arnold." She took a long gaze at me. "You, Harry…" She shook her head. "You will need the grace of God to overcome this. There's an innocent child out there who should never know the truth." Mom fingered the rosary beads in her apron pocket. "No, the two of you go out there and act as if nothing has happened. Subject closed." Mom stood, slid her chair under the breakfast table, and went to do dishes.

Dotty wiped at her nose. "May I help you, Momma Rose?"

My ears ringing, I entered the living room alone. "So, you're not out gallivanting tonight?" Dad's voice was hopeful, as he set the seventy-eight RPM record on the turntable and began the first cut of an evening of Glenn Miller.

Arnold leaned back with a newly lit cigar. I wanted to smack the grin off his self-satisfied face. This punk knows Valerie isn't his. He used Dotty's pregnancy to marry into the Hedlund's money. Dotty listened to her mother. Now she's stuck in a loveless marriage, and where does all this leave my daughter?

By the time Arnold stubbed out the end of the cigar, Mom and Dotty emerged from the kitchen with reserved smiles forced from sullen lips. Valerie spent her after dinner time asleep on the love seat.

"Well, now that my wife has helped with the dishes, I'll take her and her daughter home. I have some people to visit this evening."

I rose and exchanged glances with Dotty. That son of a bitch. Who does a family man visit on New Year's Day?

Mom shook her head, watching them go and carried her crochet tote to her chair. She sat for a moment and then stood to open the parlor windows to air out the cigar smoke. "He's no bargain."

Dad frowned at me and back to Mom. "You get no argument from me. He's a showboater, but at the funeral parlor, he poor-mouthed the entire appointment. If it hadn't been for me, Elsa wouldn't have had any flowers at all."

"Harry, I hate to say it, but I'm glad you didn't marry that girl. She's got no backbone. She floats through life, letting others lead her around by the nose." Rose glowered over her crochet project.

Dad snapped open the sports page. "Hopefully, the child won't turn out like her mother."

I barked back. "She won't!"

Dad shrugged with a humph. "1947 is off to a roaring start, and I'm considering moving to Switzerland, a nice neutral place."

"It's a new year," I admitted as I found a seat on the sofa and held the throw pillow in front of me. I nodded at Mom and Dad. "I want to start in a new direction. I've been playing fast and loose since I came home." Silence. I guess they're waiting for more. "I thought being a musician would be liberating, but it's a grind. It's the same playlists every night. I could be a lot of things."

My dad pushed his glasses back on his head. "Harry, everything is a grind after the shine wears off."

I swear my Mom dropped a stitch. "Everything, Henry?"

"Oh, Rosie, I mean work, work is a grind."

"Harry, Dr. VanAlt has a glorious sound to it." I grinned at my mother's reverence for the title. When I broke into a laugh, she nodded more adamantly.

I held up a cautioning hand. "After that war, I don't want to see one more drop of blood." I pressed my thumbs into my closed eyes, vanquishing the thought of blood-splattered ground and shattered bodies. "I applied to UCLA, pre-law. I'll go on the G.I. plan, but, just like everyplace else, there's a waiting list. I guess playing music will do until my spot opens, the tips are good. Dad, I was hoping for your blessing."

Dad closed his newspaper, blinked, and then pursed his lips. It was his 'tell'. "Is that what you truly want, son?"

I nodded. "When I eliminate everything I don't want, it's the last choice."

"You ought to have a word with your cousin. He just made Detective over at the LAPD." He smiled broadly. "Law is a wide-open field—quite a few avenues to pursue. I'm proud of you. I think it's a good choice." I closed my eyes in satisfaction.

"I'd like to count on you to be with me more in the day." Mom prodded. My eyes flew open. My mom constantly fished for time to chat, time for me to open pickle jars, and do small errands. Time well spent together. Her hands returned to the Granny square while she peered over her glasses. "It will be a while before you can register for classes, and meanwhile, you can get back to better habits. Sobriety significantly aides your decision-making process."

For an Irishwoman, it was odd; Mom never gave up Prohibition. So there I was getting the sermon I asked for, making the obligation for self-development in 1947. I threw away the note about my cousin. I'd never become a cop. Then I got the lecture about virtuous women, and the implication was stressed by both parents that I needed a wife and a career, in that order.

Chapter Twenty-Nine

On January 2, my New Year's resolutions rolled out. No nights of drinking. No dope. Always wear a raincoat. Save what money I was spending on a loose life. It was time to firmly focus on what career I'd to follow.

True to my resolutions, I played clean, no smoke, one beer, albeit it was a tall one. Reggie didn't look too hard at me; in fact, he thanked me for keeping up with the band.

Beth didn't show, so I could either go by her place and embarrass myself or go home. After the pledge I made the other night, I chalked it up to giving the lady the night off, besides -- what if Beth was entertaining someone else or washing her hair? I planned on retiring by three in the morning.

The door stayed open while several people bumped in. The first gal was the honey-blonde who laid the lip lock on Beth. She was with an equally handsome guy. Beth trailed them, holding his hand.

Following them was a towering, husky man in a white dinner jacket and a bright pleated shirt. He would have been the perfect foil to Bogart complete with a black patent leather eye patch. His woman had the smooth oval face of a ballerina but dressed like a temptress in blood crimson velvet. She could have been Mata Hari with a chin-length bob, the shade of the richest, the deepest red of them all. On her long stems, she was mulled wine waiting to be enjoyed.

This crew looked like something out of central casting. Were these swells from Paramount? Were they slumming? The five of them slid into our largest, circular booth, and Candy advanced to earn their good graces. She leaned in and got their drink orders and was back to their table post-haste.

The band got a card with a fifty-dollar bill folded into it. They requested "Till the End of Time", a little ditty by Buddy Kaye, and "You Keep Coming Back Like a Song" from the musical film *Blue Skies*. The last was a corny one for our joint, "Puttin' on the Ritz".

They didn't look like posh partiers from the last decade, but their taste in music spanned that era. For fifty bucks, we'd play "Happy Birthday".

Right in the middle of "Puttin' on the Ritz", Beth planted her hand flat on the table in front of Mr. Movie Idol. The blonde reached across him to cover Beth's hand with her own. The spoiled looking Movie Idol caught each of their hands in one of his and kissed their wrists with equal fervor. This was the guy she had the 'audition' with last week.

Was I jealous? Sure.

Each time "Mr. Patch" wanted something, his right hand rose slightly with a folded bill between his index and second finger. Candy sniffed at the gesture promptly and worked it for all he was worth. At the break, Candy sidled up behind me. "Mr. Patch wants you to join them for a drink."

"That's his name?" I chuckled.

"His name is Lorenz Zimmermann, he's Eu-ro-pe-an, now from Ar-gen-tin-a." Candy accentuated each syllable as she leered at me. "So, order a single malt and make it worth our while." She shuffled from one sore foot to the other in her high heels, balancing her tray on the flat of one palm. She winked and headed for the service bar.

Single malt? I blanched at the thought of spending that kind of coin for a belt of booze. Sure, Candy, as long as it's his tab. I'll take a leak, and head over.

Around the circular booth, I spied five of possibly the most beautiful people on earth. The strangers were dressed to the nine's. Mr. Z's cravat held a gold Fleur de Lys and ruby stickpin, and his pinky ring was a similar design. He winked his good eye at me and pulled a chair close to him, patting it for emphasis as I neared. He rose and extended his hand. "Lorenz Zimmermann, pleased to have you join us, Mr. VanAlt."

I shook the coldest hand I'd touched this side of the morgue and dropped it, as he introduced his date, Lita Braun. *Another Kraut?* Lita wore a gown that draped her pale shoulders and caressed her as if it were a living garment. A gleaming ruby sat cradled seductively in the hollow of her clavicle. She wore her arrogance like perfume.

Mr. Movie Idol liked his women on opposite ends of an erotic spectrum. He was dressed almost as gaudily as Zimmermann.

Beth sat demurely with them wearing a 'How do you like me now?' look on her face, very much impressed with her new friends. I wasn't. Her date outfitted Beth for the evening in head to toe ebony. Nothing but a miracle held up her chiffon strapless gown. Jet teardrops bobbled at her ears, and her magnificent raven hair was pulled up to reveal her graceful neck. I couldn't afford to dress her like this. Nope, I had the lettuce for breakfast at the diner, but not hobnobbing with the fat cats.

His blonde confection, the sun in his galaxy, shimmered in gold lamé, claiming every one of her curves. She suckled on a gold cigarette holder with bright red lips.

I noticed the jet bead bracelets on each of Beth's wrists when I caught her hand.

Mr. Z spoke up. "I believe you know Augustine's protégé, Miss Short?"

Protégé? The next thing they'll tell me is he's her Uncle from Philadelphia. Mr. Z nodded with a haughty grin, I nodded back to him and caught Beth's slim hand, warm in comparison with the others. I held it for a beat, and then thought, what the hell, I saw a guy kiss a girl's hand once, so I did it. Right there in front of her date. Did that guy growl at me?

Mr. Z verbally bumped me along. "Allow me to present Augustine Fielding and Desiree Hearst."

They nodded regally to me, and what else could I do but put on my best hayseed drawl. "Folks."

A rocks glass of single malt mysteriously appeared at my hand, and we began chatting about music. Mr. Z's favorite topic was American Jazz and the accommodations at The Biltmore, someplace I'd never have the coin for.

Beth sat silently, lighting her date's cigar, and then her hands folded primly on the starched white tablecloth while Mr. Movie Idol ran a well-manicured finger over the bracelets on her right wrist. It was distracting as hell, watching him touch her almost reverently. Hadn't I been between her legs a couple of nights ago? I guess he could do more for her than I ever would.

"Are you a pure-blooded Californian, Mr. VanAlt?" Lita queried as she sipped a dry double martini, her delicate eyebrow arched in my direction. Deep red waves cascaded over her ear, and a brilliant oxblood colored nail snagged it back behind her ear to reveal a hefty ruby earring.

"Second-generation on my Father's side." I was amazed at a foreigner's thirst for the genealogy of a Californian she'd just met.

"And your Mama?" Lorenz posed, cigar aloft, the same style brow cocked at me.

I wondered how he lost his eye, and I found myself staring at the patent leather patch. I blinked into my drink and washed down more than I planned. "Irish by birth. Met Dad when her family migrated in the Great War." Why was I spilling my guts to these folks, for the price of a glass of single malt?

"And she's the musical one, isn't she?" Lorenz's eye nearly glazed over in rhapsody, as if he remembered some tune, then he snapped back. His eye set on me, he reached out and touched the back of my hand. "Harry, may I call you, Harry?"

Lita spoke up in the process of ignoring her drink. "Harry, do you ever play anything 'gritty'? Something that gets right under your skin and burns?" Her dark black eyes smoked.

I was mesmerized by the ruby earrings bobbing on her ears. I was drawn to nod, and I swallowed down my scotch. "About as rowdy as we get is Cole Porter, he's racy."

She rolled her eyes at me. Is this high school?

I turned my attention back to Lorenz, his one good eye held my attention, and I don't exactly remember what he said with the din of the club whirling around me.

My gaze panned the table as his date's hand disappeared under it. Lita's shoulder movement implied she was stroking his thigh or higher. With her other hand, she held a gold cigarette holder. She inhaled and lingered in the flavor of it, leaned her head back, and blew rings of smoke that rose above her head as if she were the entertainment.

On the other side of the booth were Beth and her date, Mr. Movie Idol and their sidecar, Miss Hearst. Is she really a Hearst? Beth stopped looking at me, nursing her drink. I wondered if she was thinking about our New Year's revelry.

Then, I felt a tap on my shoulder. "Hey, Harry, it's time to pick it up and start playing again," Reggie muttered, keeping a few fingers on my shoulder to pull me back to the stage. He was the top dog in our little group. I guess he had a vested interest in my performance with this generous table.

"Could you play, "I've Got You Under My Skin", and Harry, could you sing it for me?" Lorenz slid me a fifty-dollar bill folded twice.

I cocked my head. What could I say? I shouldered my guitar, as the guys gave me that look of curious envy. I began the first line, "I've got you under my skin." Yeah, Beth was deep in my heart. Mr. Z nodded in rhythm as his lips pursed around the burning Churchill. As the Porter lyrics described a painful romantic confession, I watched Mr. Z suck on his cigar. The ash was perilously long as my singing continued. Mr. Z was that mesmerized by the lyrics, or me, I didn't know which.

Beth was the one under my skin. Tonight, she made it clear it was going to be a long while before it happened again. Was I looking for the 'one'? I wasn't in any position to offer anything. Mom was right, a career first, and then a woman.

There should have been a warning shot across my bow about smoky-eyed women you meet in bars. Mr. Porter knew how to ram it home about waking up to reality. Thanks, Cole, you're a couple of years too late. I sang, eyes closed, as I envisioned two of me: the proverbial Boy Scout and the penultimate sinner pulling in opposite directions.

When my eyes opened, I spied Lorenz, his head back, his eye closed, and taking a luxuriantly long draw on the Cuban. His redheaded goddess now made lazy circles on his shoulder as she cuddled closer. He broke the pose, gripped her free hand, and walked his lips from her fingertips to her wrist. With élan, he kissed her ardently over her throbbing pulse point. They looked like they needed a room. I felt like a voyeur. I was sure he wanted it that way.

Somewhere in the last set between "Night and Day" and "If I Loved You", my eyes left the enigmatic group, and when I sought Beth's smile, they were gone. The table was clean with new music lovers in their place.

Chapter Thirty

The lounge was quiet on Tuesdays, and January ninth was no different. I waited for Beth to drop in, either with that weird group or by herself. What a bust. Our set cruised through by rote, and before I even gave it a second thought, I was strolling home, too late to catch a bus, too cheap to hail a cab.

I heard the solitary hum of an automobile over my shoulder, it could have passed me, yet it lurked, the engine glub-glub-glubbing in time with my footsteps. I went to crush my cigarette butt under my foot, and I turned to see the sleek, blood-red Mercedes stop hard.

"Harry, is that you, Mr. VanAlt?" It was Lorenz, in his white dinner jacket, was he alone in this pristine automobile?

"You must be slumming in this neighborhood." I declared as I got closer to this piece of art on four wheels.

"Not in the least, this car is made to enjoy, as so many things in this world are." His hand flourished, and the streetlight caught the glint of his ring, his gold watch. "Would you like a ride to your home?" His tone was ingratiating as if I'd turn down a ride in that auto.

"You going that way?" I pointed military-style with my full hand in the general direction. With almost unseen speed, he leaned across the passenger seat and threw the front passenger door open. I went to open the back door to drop in my gig bag, and the door light revealed the backseat's occupants but obscured their faces. I inhaled sharply at the smell of whiskey and pussy, two of the world's most efficient solvents for direction and goals.

The sharp in a sharkskin suit cradled a gal. This guy's jacket was broad-shouldered and screamed money, even in the dark. With a commanding posture, he held the woman like a god would hold a sycophant. She withered against him, head covered by a cloche. Her face tucked into the niche of his neck and shoulder. Wrapped in his arms, her lithe body melted to his. Her extended legs lay across his thighs, frothy petticoats foamed around her shapely calves. The shoes hung delicately off her toes, and in that split second of laying down my gig bag, I swore I'd seen them before.

"While we're young." Lorenz wittily invoked, throwing the car into drive, and letting the brake off and on, prodding me to get in. I settled in for the ride, not prepared for the power of his foot on the gas. He offered a cigar from a leather case he extracted from his breast pocket, I demurred. We were closer than he knew, and I wasn't going to sit up the rest of the morning to smoke the gift.

"Do you play private parties?" He kept his eye on the road, and I wondered how a one-eyed guy drives.

"Sure, especially when the checks clear." I snorted. I was tired, yet if he anteed up half a yard for one song, what would he pay for an evening?

"I would pay cash, of course." He snorted as if that was the only way he did business. As I pointed out the turns, we chatted about his tastes. He loved show tunes and ballads based on classical movements.

"Give me Katherine Grayson or Patrice Munsel, any evening. They breathe the life of the lyrics right into the melody." He struck the flat of his hand on the steering wheel. Man-o-man, he was really into his songbirds.

"Well, we don't have a gal with us, they always want to fall in love, get their MRS. Degree, you follow?" I scratched at my neck and loosened my collar. Was this guy an art patron? He seemed that type, a bit of a lightweight, his face soft, and when he touched me, his hand was smooth, cold, and uncalloused.

"Ah, yes, the old till death do us part vow, wouldn't it be monumental to not deal with that entire death thing?" His voice was silk, a rich tenor waiting for the venue to perform. Had he been an opera singer before the war? The car purred down my street, and as much as I enjoyed holding a half-intelligent conversation without Reggie's comments about tits and ass, it was early in the morning, and I was bushed. Honestly, Lorenz and I would never run in the same circles, but I was grateful for the lift.

As I exited the car, I heard the guy's voice from the back seat. It was Augustine, Beth's date the other night. "Good night, Mr. VanAlt".

Yanking the back-door open, I bent to retrieve my gig bag and return the bidding, the woman in his lap shifted in her sleep, her face falling away from his shoulder. My sociable words caught in my throat. Augustine held Beth in his arms. "Good night." I choked out, unable to even say his name. She let go of a breath-hyphenated sigh as her head lolled left and right. Then I turned on my heel to face Lorenz. "Is she alright?" I guess my eyes were shooting daggers. Augustine hitched in his seat at my query.

"She is just fine. For your information, tonight, we enjoyed ourselves at The Biltmore. Perhaps she enjoyed herself a bit too much. Of course, the entertainment wasn't as earthy and gritty as The Blue Gardenia Lounge, yet we head home... satisfied." Augustine's clipped European accent drew more bitterness out of his comments, and then he extended the last word as if he could exclude me from satisfying her.

Stepping back haltingly, Beth looked asleep. I didn't see torn clothes or bruises. I closed my eyes hard, conjuring a different vision when I reopened them. There wasn't one. I slammed the door closed and leaned in the window to make my goodbyes. I don't even remember what I said. My gut had a riot inside fighting to get out.

The peace of the neighborhood was broken by the sound of a child's cry. I turned to see the light go on in Valerie's bedroom, the silhouette of Dotty raising the window sash. Bright white eyelet curtains fluttered in the night breeze. Valerie was fussy all day. She must really be sick. Should I check in with them?

Mr. Z leaned over the console to stare at the window. "Harry, is that your child? You never mentioned a child."

I was stunned for a beat and shook my head. "A neighbor, we're very close."

Mr. Z sniffed, and his brow arched. "I understand."

"Well, thanks again for the ride, don't let me keep you." I watched the car slink down the road.

I yanked open our unlocked front door and flew up the staircase, regaining control or something that passed for it once my coat dropped on the bed. I stared at my reflection in the dresser mirror. The image was white-faced and haggard. The man I was looked a million years old.

Beth was woman number two who betrayed me. Not really, we had no agreement. I had been with enough women to think I knew when there was a special connection. What was it about me? I guess some women were no different from some men. Some people could have one night together and be done. Was it the woman I picked who saw me as disposable, or was I wearing a sign?

I'd gone to sleep with the cries of a plaintive child in my ears, and I awoke to the same. Dressing hurriedly, I went to the kitchen. "Mom, do you have any of that Paracetamol I brought home from England?" I frantically opened and closed doors.

Mom pointed to a far cabinet. "It took every bit of my restraint not to go next door last night. Arnold was an oaf. That child was ill, and he expected dinner on the table at six on the nose." She handed the bottle to me.

"My mortar and pestle?" I stood lost in the large kitchen.

Mom brought them to the counter and then reached into another cabinet. "You won't get that past her lips unless you put it in this blueberry syrup." She watched as I made medicine to carry next door.

I loped up the Craft's front porch steps and raised a fist to bang on the door. Arnold opened it, stunned by my fist in his face. "What are you doing here?"

"I… I have medicine for Valerie." I held up the brown glass dropper bottle.

"Dr. Jackson didn't order medicine for her."

I looked right and left, annoyed. "She has a fever? Throwing up? Not sleeping?"

Arnold shrugged. "She's sick."

"I have something from England. It's better than aspirin." I stepped toward the open door.

Arnold thrust his chest out. "Last I knew, Valerie isn't a soldier. We don't need your help. You can go back to tuning your guitar."

I heard heavy footsteps down the stairs and the hiccupping sobs of Valerie in Dotty's arms.

"What is it? Arnold, go to work. I've... Harry, what are you doing here?"

I held up the brown bottle. "Something to relieve Valerie's fever and headache. She needs restful sleep."

Dotty shot Arnold a dismissive look and bumped him out the door. With a jerk of her head, she invited me into the entry hall. The home was in odd disarray. A tea kettle cried from the kitchen.

"Dotty, get the teapot, let me have her." I rested my cheek on the feverish child's face. "Come on, baby, let's get you in the bathtub."

"No..." She rubbed at puffy eyes and cried some more.

"I know it's horrible. Do you like blueberries?" The child frowned. "Momma Rose said you do. I brought blueberry medicine to make you feel better." Valerie curled into my arms and blubbered.

I changed the child's bed while Dotty soothed her in a tepid bath and gave the medicine a chance to work. Once she was in a fresh nightgown and a clean bed, exhausted, she quickly went to sleep. I felt her pulse and knew it had stopped its bounding, frantic pace. It was now approaching normal as her fever lowered.

I stood in the upstairs hall. "She'll sleep for a while. It's your turn now. Go grab a shower, and I'll make some tea and toast downstairs."

Dotty slumped against the banister. "You're a godsend, Harry. Mother wouldn't even do this much for me." She turned toward the master bedroom, and at the doorframe, she shook her head and paused. "It feels so odd to be the parents in this house. When I married, and Daddy died, Mother gave Arnold and me the master bedroom. It feels wrong."

I had no response. I held the banister, fingers blanching white at the idea of Arnold sharing her bed. I nodded and took the steps quickly down to the kitchen.

Everything in the kitchen was exactly where it had been years ago. Where it had been all the time I was growing up. I listened for the shower turning off and scrambled eggs, fried a piece of ham, and made toast. I imagined I could thank Arnold for the large percolator, still plugged in and almost full of aromatic coffee. At the sound of Dotty's approaching footsteps, I was at the stove and asked, "Is she still asleep?"

Dotty wore a towel wrapped around her wet hair. "Out like a light." Her housedress was freshly pressed and colorful, reflecting roses to her wan cheeks.

"You need to eat, then have a nap." I plated her breakfast and aimed her to a chair at the kitchen table. "I can make chamomile tea. You don't need this coffee."

"Leave it plugged in. I might need some sludge later on." She smiled weakly as she buttered her toast.

I leaned on my elbow, watching her eat. She swallowed and feebly smiled. "So, what have you been up to? It's been a long time since we've just talked." I watched her eyelashes flutter as she ate.

"Just working at The Blue Gardenia, helping out around the house." I leaned back and stretched my legs out, instinctively crossing my arms over my chest, as I described my tedious life. "What's the deal with Arnold's traveling? The cabs come and go here frequently."

"It's this project he's on, they keep flying him… I don't know where."

Curiosity bit me. "You think he's a spy? Something out of a Hammett novel?"

"Haha." Dotty deadpanned and swept the toast around the liquid egg yolk on her plate.

We made small talk. She spun a few yarns about Valerie coloring on the walls. "Your mom's a treasure. I know she keeps an eye out for me."

"Does she need to? He doesn't hit you, does he?"

"You don't have to hit a woman to break her." She didn't make eye contact. "Are you seeing anyone?"

"I thought I was. It's… complicated. I thought we were tight, and then Beth disappeared. I haven't heard from her since our New Year's Eve date." I shrugged and sat up, drawing my feet back under me.

"Whoa, that's a poor way to start the year. I'm sorry, Harry." The corners of her succulent lips turned downward with empathy. We were quiet for a bit, both sipping tea while I watched her drag the glass's sweat down to the napkin.

"Dotty, if I ask you something about us, would you tell me the truth?" I pushed words out through tight lips with a quiet voice.

She played with her towel, twisted in her chair, and tucked her ankles over each other as she drew them in tighter. While her chin was tucked, I heard her let out a long breath. "Truth about what?" She downed her tea and rose quickly, whisking herself to the sink to rinse her glass and tossed the rendered lemon into the trash beneath the sink. I watched her look out the kitchen window at nothing, and then she turned, her backside against the cabinets.

"Who's Valerie's real father?" Leaning over, I sat, elbows on my knees, hands in prayer for the truth.

Dotty's breath drew deeper, and she wrung her hands up to her chin. "Do you really have to ask?"

"I guess so because I'm asking."

Why was she uncomfortable talking about this? Hadn't we roamed over each other's bodies with eyes, hands, and tongues?

"You and I were only together once, Harry." Her words were devoid of romance or passion.

"So, were you pregnant when you went to prom with Arnold?"

Dotty hid her face in her hands. "It wasn't supposed to turn out this way."

I laughed sarcastically. "How was it supposed to turn out?"

Dotty stared over my shoulder at nothing and began to talk. "Once I missed my monthly, I told Momma you and I had to get married. I thought if I was under eighteen and pregnant, that would do it." I shook my head. "Momma told me we weren't waiting for you. She thought Arnold was good stock, even though his father lost the family fortune. She called Mrs. Craft and suggested Arnold take me to the prom." My jaw worked in anger. "He had a deferment and was already in college, but he wanted to go to grad school, and our parents sat in the parlor and arranged our marriage." I groaned. "We were married the day after my birthday."

I bolted up from the chair. "When you could have said no."

Tears filled her eyes. "You were already gone. I had no idea where and I was starting to show."

"You could have walked next door. My folks knew where I was. Your mother diverted all my communications."

"I had no idea, Harry. I was eighteen and scared. Before Valerie was born, we got the news about Daddy in the South Pacific, and there was no going back."

"I don't want to make trouble for you, but I'm going to be in my daughter's life. She doesn't need to know why except I love her. I'm Uncle Harry." There was a beat of silence between them. "Does Arnold know who her father is?" Before Dotty opened her mouth, the telephone on the kitchen wall shrilled. We both stared at it before Dotty jumped to answer it.

"Craft residence, this is Mrs. Craft." Pause. "Hello, dear." Pause. "She's asleep, and I've just eaten breakfast." Pause. "Yes, thank you for making the coffee." She rolled her eyes at the empty used cup Arnold left. "No, he's gone. He left shortly after you left." She sighed. "Again, Arnold? How long this time?" She controlled her breathing. "Of course, the black suit with the green tie and pocket square. I'll have your bag packed with a fresh razor in your kit. When is the cab coming for it?" Another pause. "It will be ready. Yes, by three. Didn't I say that?" Her eyes squinched closed and she turned away from me, hanging up with a soft click.

"So he knows, doesn't he?" I persisted.

"Yes, he knows. Everyone knows, thanks to Janet across the street. She was here the next morning raving about Valerie's size and her deep brown curly hair. It doesn't help that she has your cleft in her chin and your lips."

I shrugged. "There are two ways this could work. Arnold could be a prince of a guy and let Uncle Harry and Momma Rose be generous, or Arnold could be a prick, and I could be one too."

Dotty held her cheeks with her hands. "Arnold was born a prick. Good luck."

"So, if he left you, he's leaving his golden goose. You'd win. Valerie would win. I'd win. Unless you think he'd hurt you or kidnap Valerie for spite."

"I don't know what he'd do, but I'll never be a divorced woman."

"You'd better find a way to make it work with your traveling man because I will be in my daughter's life."

Dotty sighed dejectedly and shook her head. "Go home, Harry. I have things to do. Thanks for bringing the medicine."

I rose to leave but turned in the doorway. "I'll check on Valerie later."

I meandered somberly back home and to my bedroom. Toeing off my loafers and sitting heavily on the bed, I pulled the covers over me and tried to sleep. Falling asleep, I acknowledged my mother was right. It was a good thing I hadn't married Dotty.

Chapter Thirty-One

My dreams were wild. The fires of hell danced down Wilshire Boulevard and took a turn to Pershing Square toward The Biltmore Hotel. The grounds outside were salted, the land was damned. Hands grew from the flames, squeezing the breath and life out of the hapless people on the street. They fell to the pavement and were spontaneously consumed as ash.

I shook myself awake around noon. Once I drank a few handfuls of water from the bathroom spigot, I shuffled back to bed and slept like the dead until one forty-five in the afternoon.

I shelled peas on the porch, watching the laundry whip itself dry on the line. While counting every blessed hour of my day off, I made myself available for any chore, anything to keep busy, to keep my mind off Beth.

Then, dressed in slacks and a sports shirt, I went back to the kitchen. I hugged Mom extra tight. "Want to take a ride to that new toy store?"

"Oh, Harry, your father hasn't caught a baseball since his back went out."

I grabbed a stem of grapes and grinned, wagging eyebrows as I chewed. "I'm in the market for a tricycle with streamers. A bright pink one for Valerie."

"Why in Sam Hill? Do you have any idea the arguments you're going to start?"

"It's a gift from Momma Rose."

She dried her hands with a dishtowel and untied her apron. "Are you sure they make those in pink?"

I slid into a sports coat and winked. "If they don't, I'll have it painted."

Mom picked up her purse from the closet and followed me out the front door. "I don't give you long before you're attending tea parties."

On the drive, Mom raised the delicate question. "What about that young lady you mentioned Sunday?"

I didn't want to go into it. Why should I spill the fact the girl who stole a piece of my heart was a foil for some ne'r do well from a film company? "She's working." I made something up; "She's getting an audition over a Paramount." Mom leaned against the car door and nodded but gave me her knowing gaze.

"Well, then maybe the two of you'll be a Hollywood Tour de force!" She nodded and turned her attention to the road.

♦♦♦♦

It was Thursday before I stood strumming at The Blue Gardenia, and I had given up seeing Beth. No phone on her end and she hadn't been in the most receptive mood to take a message in the car. I'd forgotten what it felt like to 'pine', so I sang my heart out all night, or at least until our break. Then, I slipped a coin into the payphone and called The Biltmore. "Lorenz Zimmermann?" I asked, and the desk man didn't hesitate,

"Mr. Zimmermann is not receiving guests, would you like to leave a message?" One part officious, one-part snooty, and one part bored, he waited for my answer.

"I'm trying to reach …my sister. She's visiting him. Elizabeth Short, black hair with a flower in it, she usually wears all black? Has she been there at The Biltmore?" Did he catch my desperation? Did he suspect I was a spurned lover, or worse, her father?

"We respect the privacy of our guests, sir. Perhaps you'd leave a message we could deliver to Mr. Zimmermann's suite?" His voice turned empathetic; maybe he had a sister. I left my number, actually the number at the club, and then shuffled back to the stage where I plucked out a little Stephen Foster. I'm sure they thought I had lost my mind, I was about to agree with them.

By the time I finished the little ditty, the mostly alcoholic crowd had gathered their beverages and settled down. Couples were nestled in each other's arms. Even the horny guys had settled to cuddle their 'Miss Right Now'. Reggie thumped me on the shoulder. "What kind of funeral music are you playing, Harry? Did some girl cut your heart out and eat it in front of you?"

♦♦♦♦

January tenth, I didn't see Beth that night. I didn't get a phone call either. After the set, I sat at the bar, flipping the Zippo I bought at the PX

188

before I mustered out of the Army. In my periphery, I saw Candy tilt her head toward the new bartender, and within a minute, he had a double shot of single malt before me. The good stuff, the stuff I had first tasted at Mr. Z's table. The taste was growing on me; I wondered how much this habit would cost me throughout my life.

Candy tapped my shoulder. "Your buddy in the white dinner jacket is here. He wants the table in the front." I caught her cigarette breath and the 'Midnight in Paris' cologne she slathered on a few hours ago.

I snubbed out the Lucky Strike and inhaled the last of the riveting smoke before I spun on the barstool to see Zimmermann giving a salute from the brim of his black Homburg. That quickly, he removed the hat to reveal slick and shiny black hair. He looked freshly shaved and ready to go all night. Where was everyone else? Candy paraded him right past me, her back to him, she winked as she moved. Tableside, she did her little backward lean to afford him a view of her cleavage. "What's your poison tonight, Mr. Z?"

"What's your best Irish Whiskey?" His voice purred in the din of the lounge, and I knew what Candy was thinking as she stared into his eye, wondering what was under the patch. Was he disfigured? Was his eye mangled or missing? I nearly snorted as I saw her catch herself holding her breath at his crisp white jacket, the blood-red rose boutonniere in the lapel, so dark it hardly seemed real.

She shook her head to come back to now. Then I watched her hips sway as she headed off for the one Irish Whiskey we had. She brought two glasses and the fifth to his petite round table. His gaze followed Candy as she worked her few tables around him.

I figured he'd be a real hound by himself. Surprisingly, he sat back and watched the crowd and the band. The tilt of his head, the way he held the cigar, he seemed lost in the lyrics of the set. Nothing like a string of Cole Porter hits to tempt the most reserved soul, between the bounce of the score and the double entendres, I grinned just a bit along with him.

The first break, he waved to me with a loop of his cigar in the air. I strolled the few steps, loosening my tie, I scanned the crowd for Beth, even if she was with that guy from the back seat. Zimmermann rose and came right up to me as if a hug was warranted.

For me, a handshake would do, trust me. Then Mr. Z held the cigar in his left hand, out from us, and he stepped toward me, leading his hand toward my face. I thought he was leaning in to pick some lint off me, then as his fingers passed my line of sight. I felt the pad of his thumb skim my jaw, and then his hand looped around my sweaty neck. Unexpectedly I was drawn right to the starched bosom of his dinner jacket. I thought I was going to suffocate in the embrace. It all happened so road-runner quick that I thought I had imagined it. I stumbled back, moved by his release, as fast as the embrace. "Good evening, Harry." His voice was cold honey, slow and sweet. "A cigar, or perhaps you are saving that melodious voice of yours?" I deferred the smoke and sat, knees spread, elbows on them to keep a certain distance from him. "A drink, perhaps? Nothing like getting a bit of stiff Irish, right?" His pour completed, he slid the glass in front of me before I could decline it. I nodded a thank you and sipped. The Jameson went down slippery and hot. I nodded, waiting for the point of tonight's visit. "You were upset the other night. It was…evident by your…demeanor. I wanted to assure you that Miss Short is alive and kicking, as you Americans say. Perhaps Augustine was a bit abrupt." He dipped his chin down to peer up at me through black lashes on his good eye.

"Right, I was a bit abrupt myself." I had to learn how to get along better with strangers. Somehow that night clicked through my head like an eight-millimeter projector when the end of the film left the teeth of the back reel. I flew loose after seeing her passed out in another guy's arms.

"So, no hard feelings for Miss Short's choices?" He was on his third rocks glass of whiskey and not the least bit slurred or affected—what a guy.

"We dated once, that's all, and I don't like to see women in that situation, passed out." I'd be more polite in the future, yet I wouldn't backpedal on being concerned for Beth.

"We are harmless, simply enjoying the company of the exquisite young women of Los Angeles. I promise you we only take was is… freely given." That made me trust him even less.

"So, Mr. Zimmermann, did you have a gig to book with us?" I wanted to change my clothes after his last comment—what a sleaze meister.

"Regrettably, not at this time, Harry. My lover is jaded and wants to return to Buenos Aires. Augustine has business in the Orient. I lament that I will be traveling home also. I abhor being alone."

I was glad to see a departure in the future for Mr. Z. I was hoping he'd forget The Blue Gardenia. Yet, I found myself nodding slowly as he spoke, my body language turning more open to him, even mimicking his posture.

I got the two-minute wink from Reggie and shuffled my feet to stand. Just then, Mr. Z's hand caught my wrist. "Harry, how about a song for me?" He slid the bill, tented lengthwise across the table, another half yard for a few moments of a song, a few moments of his hanging on every lyric.

When my fingertips grasped the bill, his hand was upon mine. His splayed fingers covered the back of my hand. Cold tendrils left his body and surged up to freeze me, not so much from the temperature, but from his stare.

I shook off the moment and became the performer I knew I could be. He wanted me to sing "Night and Day", only where was his woman? Is that the kind of song a man sings for another man? From the way he focused on me? Yeah, he looked like he had a hungry yearning somewhere behind that eye patch. I got the creeps.

My heart rendered the words theatrically for the benefit of the audience. I ricocheted back and forth from being fascinated with Beth to being repelled by her behavior. As I sang about romantic torment, I felt Zimmermann's gaze paint me with his pain and abandonment. Once the song finished, my eyes opened, and characteristically, Lorenz was gone. The table empty, the bottle empty, another fifty-dollar bill was waiting for Candy to scoop it up. The rest of the evening escaped my memory. I was weary and needed sleep. I wanted a peaceful night's sleep.

◆◆◆◆

Saturday, January eleventh, my folks told me they were heading out of town. As I drank my coffee, all I could do was nod, mouth full. I knew I cramped their style, the older I got, the more I knew I had to grow up and give them space. Dad was still a vital guy for his age. Mom was one of those timeless beauties. One day I wanted to be just like them, in love forever.

◆◆◆◆

Candy slid sinuously off the bar stool as she watched Lorenz glide through the door. "Your boyfriend's back."

"Stop that." I shot back at her and spanked her on the left cheek of her tight ass. She brushed by me, bumping her shoulder into mine. Candy's a swell gal to work with. I'd just never want to wake up next to her, that prospect is a little frightening.

'My boyfriend' slid into the round booth, the size of it dwarfed him. He appeared lonely, forsaken. Candy was there in a heartbeat bent over, giving him a sneak peek at her cleavage while she took his order.

"He wants you to come by for a drink." Candy pooched her lips like a kiss and uncorked the Jameson's, setting two old fashioned glasses on her tray. I turned on the barstool and gave him a nod. He waved the Cuban cigar at me, and I waited until Candy had it lit before I approached the table, hands deep into my pleated trousers. I hadn't tied my bow tie yet, that was the last thing I did before stepping up to play because the damned thing strangled me.

"Good evening, Mr. Z, I thought you were leaving. Any changes in how life's treating you?" I rocked back and forth on my heels, casually scanning the rest of the room, checking out the crowd filling in the smaller tables near the stage.

"Ah, Harry, I extended my stay a few nights. Tonight, things are -- Fine."

Yet, the resigned way he pronounced the few words led me to believe he was indeed FINE-- Fucked up, insecure, neurotic, and emotional. This guy was an attention-seeking, fixated, overly expressive middle-aged man. He needed either a girl or boyfriend. I couldn't figure out if he wanted to impress and seduce me or just bend my ear at fifty dollars a visit. Look, I'm making psychiatrist money already.

Saturday night evaporated into a Jameson fog of grand Irish proportions. I remember the first break, paying attention to Mr. Z's confessions of enjoying too much dining and drink in LA. The second break was less coherent, more jovial. I had actually gotten Mr. Z to laugh, even though his eye seemed to hold itself back from joining the smile on his thin lips.

By the last call, it thrilled me to be going to an empty home. Mr. Z left in the last set, after enigmatically sending his ornately scripted note with the customary gratuity. This time he wanted to hear, "I Get a Kick Out of You".

I felt naked under his gaze as I crooned. I ducked him as I sang lyrics about being bored and unexpectedly seeing his face. I sang to a new couple in love directly in front of me. I paid my respects to the crew, split the fifty dollars amongst us, and headed home.

This time, there was no lift in a vintage automobile. I slid the key into the door and rejoiced at being alone. The silence of the Frigidaire cycling off and on, the old frame home settling in the early morning calm, and it all pleased me.

◆◆◆◆

I stripped in my room and enjoyed the cool bathroom tiles beneath my weary feet. Would I soak, or would I shower? I showered and paid myself a little extra attention. I'd say the soap got the best of me.

I craved Beth; it had been days since I had her, sharing the pleasures of meshing hard flesh into supple, hot flesh. Alone, a single physical release only reinforced my lost heart. I dried off deliberately and fell to sleep naked on top of the clean linen to be thrown to hellish dreams in torrents of confusion.

By dawn, I had awakened three or four times, not understanding what I dreamt. Craving rest, I punched my pillow and rolled back to sleep. Mother Nature played a cruel trick; she sent her songbirds after me. If music kept me up into the wee small hours of the morning, then it would be music waking me. Well, at least it wasn't a cock crowing on the mornings after my wild nights in bed.

I shuffled down and made coffee. Sure, I could wrestle the percolator into making a couple of mugs of java. The fact that I did it naked, at least trudging and scratching behind the lace curtains, gave me some sort of silly rush. I could get used to living alone.

Then the activity on the sidewalk picked up, families walking to church, some walking to the café for the pancake special. I jaunted upstairs for a pair of boxer shorts, claimed the paper on the porch, and set out with my coffee for the shade on the back porch. Somewhere between the later birds who still managed to catch a worm and browsing the front section of the paper, I dozed off, feet up on the railing.

◆◆◆◆

Sunday evenings at The Blue Gardenia were usually sublime. Smooth music rolled from set to set without any harsh crescendos. We'd go off on some easy roll, then some southern California voice called from the dark. "Play, That's Why the Lady is a Tramp". I didn't see a cigar burning in the darkness or a hammy hand holding a folding note. That's okay, I played like gangbusters, leaving the rest of the guys in the dust as Reggie sang a la Frank Sinatra, rousting me to pick some string time. You know, wind out and play an extended solo to give Reggie a chance to chill his pipes. While one side of my head fell into the groove, my other side fell apart.

After a quiet walk home, my solace was a shower. I wouldn't dare conjure Dotty's form with me in the tile temple, I went the route thinking blonde, and all I saw was Candy's snarky face as I soaped myself liberally. I shook my head to scatter that thought. It would be a while before I'd go for blondes thinking of the fallout from two platonic dates with Candy.

Could I even remember Lita Braun's face? Not that she'd be able to pick me out of a crowd, either. So, I was back to Beth, all ebony hair, and red lips. I wanted to fall hard into the fantasy of a crime of passion with a woman who thirsted for Gomorrah.

The clock struck four A.M., and I still wandered the dark house, ice swirling in a glass of Irish Whiskey usually summoned for birthdays and anniversaries. My lips were hot for a woman branded for spreading creamy thighs for the right guy. I was Mr. Right Now, seeking Miss Right Now.

My quest was a pathetic attempt to get some sleep, perhaps to dream of what had happened to Beth. Post-War America bred a generation with a fair share of misfits, and I wondered if maybe I was their poster child.

Was there any fear in a Monday the thirteenth? I woke late, danced the push-mower back and forth across the lawn when I saw Dotty waving at me. We caught some shade on her porch with glasses of lemonade. We watched the breeze while we shot the shit, and then she spoke up. "Harry, you know Valerie isn't quite right. She's still got a cough."

"Oh, she's got to see the doctor, Dot. She could have bronchitis or even pneumonia."

"If I made an appointment, could you give us a ride? Our car is here, and Arnold's out of town again."

"You trust me with Arnold's car?"

♦♦♦♦

Monday evening, January thirteenth, my ears were assailed. "Hey, Harry." Candy wailed as I came from the back of the lounge, dropping my gig bag to warm up.

"What have I done now, Candy? Left the toilet seat up? Stolen your last cigarette?" I was always on her shit list for something.

"Letter came for you this afternoon, some guy in a uniform, you know like a chauffeur, here, have a look-see." Candy sailed the heavy envelope down the bar into my hands. I wished it had come with whiskey.

> *Dear Harry:*
>
> *Got a great "in" with Augustine over at Paramount. He says if I had been there in 1938, they wouldn't have hired a Brit to play Scarlett O'Hara, how do you like that? I'll be traveling with Augie, we're seeing Mr. Z and his girl tomorrow night. It's looking like a big party, wish you weren't working every night.*
>
> *Love and special kisses,*
> *Elizabeth*

♦♦♦♦

The truth was, I didn't work every night. I conjectured when that pansy-ass Lorenz came in tonight I'd slide the fifty-dollar bill back toward him and buy my invitation to that party. So, I tied the bow tie, slipped on my dinner jacket, and smacked Reggie's back before we opened the first set. It was going to be smooth sailing straight on to the morning star, or so I thought.

The crowd was deep, clapping when they should, wailing when they should and definitely sending up unlimited drinks. The jazz virgins here tonight ate up what we laid down, and when the night was done, it felt more significant than any of the nights in the past months. Had Beth been down in front, it would have been the icing on the cake.

The Victorian house, proud and painted, stood outlined in the waning moon, just scant nights ago it had shown itself full and glorious. Now many things were waning as I imagined Beth slipping away from me. Stripping down in the laundry room, it was a little harder to negotiate the hallway. I stubbed my toe and instinctively covered my package, didn't want to bounce that off the furniture. This time, I showered and fell into bed, sleep covered me like the chenille coverlet. Burying my face in my pillow, I fell into a fog.

Chapter Thirty-Two

The Biltmore was brightly lit, awash in a golden glow, a throng of party goers bumping shoulders navigated between cocktail soirees. The tuxedoed staff made polite hand signals toward the Emerald Room as the guests emerged from limousines; it was glamour and glitz as if there had never been a war.

Damn it all, Mr. Z was holding court at the table nearest the band. Now our lounge group was a righteous twelve-piece band that could swing and sway like Sammy Kay. Mr. Z's usual guests were doing what came naturally for them. Beth was enthralled by Augustine's stoic attention to her, and Mr. Z's date was the jaded Queen of Sheba. How could anyone that loaded be so bored?

I had no seat, no place card in a Spenserian script assigning 'Mr. Henry VanAlt, Jr.' to even a back table. I played and stared as the figures danced by the mirrors, and their grace drew me to gawk. That never made for manners, or so my mother claimed. From the velvet draped corner of the room, it was up to me to eavesdrop, stare, and wonder at the event and what would happen next. Was I here to see the future, or learn about the past? Other than Beth, what was I here to witness?

As our group took a break, the music took on a gypsy edge, and it could have been a scene out of musical, circles of dancers moved within larger circles, arms raised, as they sang exuberantly in a foreign tongue. The musicians fiddled as if their existence depended on their briskly increased cadence, then as the music stopped abruptly, Augustine and Beth appeared as the wall of dancers split for them.

In a way, the dance is known as 'the dance of the underworld', the Apache took on darker tones through Augustine's expressions and intense strength. I was aghast at his grace and facility with portraying sex and violence as they acted out passionate embraces with fierce segues to their next steps.

Beyond the speed and implied violence, I was totally mesmerized with his gaze; those whiskey hazel eyes burned like a hound from hell, and Beth ate it up with voracious gusto.

They were primitive, not vulgar. They were passionate, not overtly sexual. Augustine's slender fingers wrapped around Beth's throat as he controlled her sway. And then his focus zoned to her arms, where his ivory hands glided to catch her wrists and entwine their arms as they pranced in a predatory circle, caught in each other's hypnotic gaze.

They reenacted a violent discussion. When had that occurred? Augustine delivered mock slaps and punches. He picked up Beth and threw her to the ground gracefully as she elegantly struggled or feigned unconsciousness. This was stage combat disguised as dance. At no point did she fight back.

Not a soul spoke or moved from their tables. They reverently observed, worshiping the dancers. My heart caved as she revered him, then in a flash, Lorenz Zimmermann cut in. All that the dance had been was eclipsed by the music's end and her body held between these two men as if she were expired, lifeless.

The crowd focused entirely on the men, not a drop of perspiration on either of them. Their cool ratio was through the roof. Their eyes sparkled as her head lolled. Then Lorenz dropped his preternaturally curled lips to her white throat. I gasped as blood sprayed from between the three of them. It rocked me from what I thought was a sound sleep. In my sleep, what had I seen?

◆◆◆◆

Wednesday, January 15, 1947

The staccato of the alarm rousted me; it had been a while since I had been up at sunrise. After the inferno of a night terror, I welcomed the calm morning birds and the familiar clink of milk bottles at the side door. Showered, shaved, and wearing my old man clothes, my dress trousers, sport shirt and jacket I felt responsible. I drank a cup of coffee and took brisk steps to get next door.

Dotty held Valerie in her arms in the back seat of their 1941 four-door Ford sedan. The child fretted and gave a honking cough while her mother held her, smoothing feverish tendrils of hair away from her florid face.

We rolled down the road while I pondered the mendacity of me playing house like this. It settled in the pit of my near-empty stomach. I knew if I was the husband, I'd have been home. I would have breakfast with my loving family before I drove them to the doctor's office. Things would be different.

The road was open and smooth. I whistled Cole Porter all the way, turning off the radio that was a cacophony of static that irritated Dotty. I parked at the clinic entrance and held the rear door open for her. "If you stay in the car, I'll carry her in." I offered, but Valerie's dark brown brows knit furiously.

"I can walk." She clung to Dotty.

Dotty smiled shyly, walking out of my sight. The street-level parking bunched directly around the clinic, and I found myself driving in circles looking for a place big enough for this boat. When a wife trusts you with her husband's car, you should return it in pristine order.

"Make a hole; make it wide." My sergeant major would harp while he pushed through inspections. I wished he was here to clear my path. There was no warm morning sun to heat the car, as I pulled right onto Norton Avenue between 39th and Coliseum streets into the Leinart Park neighborhood. With no buildings, there should have been yards of curb to cozy up to.

It was a grey, overcast morning as I straightened the wheel and killed the engine. I inhaled deeply, thinking about walking back into a clinic and sitting with Dotty and my daughter.

I should bug out, move up the coast, and set up a bank account in Trust for Valerie, definitely not at my Father's bank. Valerie gave me an unlimited scope of reasons to live.

The neighborhood was new, this street austere except for wild outgrowths of waist-high weeds. The breeze was heavy and sadly aeolian as it moved sluggishly over the patchy wildflowers. I was alone except a woman and her toddler daughter ahead of me. She had the particular pace of a woman on her way somewhere when something caught her eyes. Her gaze dropped into the grass, and she jumped back to the other side of the sidewalk. What had she seen?

Shrieking, she clutched her toddler and covered her little eyes. The identical brown curls on their heads shook, I couldn't hear words, just the wailing of a distressed woman and confused child. I dashed there in seconds, grabbing both of them, pulling them away from whatever had set them off.

"Monsters, it had to be monsters…" Her brown eyes were pie wide; her lipstick smeared from holding her daughter to her face to shield her from a brutal view. I turned them to the street, trying to comfort them as much as a perfect stranger could.

I had to see what she was talking about. "Call the police over there." I reached in my pocket for a coin and pushed her toward a phone booth in the next block, away from the field.

When I heard her feet hit the street, I turned and took heavy steps toward whatever it was. 'It' appeared to be a discarded store mannequin, taken apart and splayed as if twelve-year-old boys had pretended to have sex with a 'model' from the department store. Two steps closer, and I knew it wasn't. The mother was right; it had been a monster's handiwork.

I froze at the body's gray pallor. I had seen war, bloodletting in uniform, bodies strewn by shell blasts -- I wasn't prepared for deliberate death, posed for shock value.

What stunned me first? This woman had been cut in half, the two halves separated by less than a few inches. Her body had been flagrantly placed with her legs spread eagle.

No blood. No blood? My medic eyes sought the one familiar thing from my training, blood. There was no blood. This was a brutal murder. The victim was carved and then scrubbed clean before being dumped.

My hand flew to my heart, and I prayed she hadn't known what was happening while they did this to her. Every attempt to make this sexual had been a twisted victory; whoever bound and tortured her had been a sadist and misogynist of the highest order. Ghastly as it appeared, her lower torso seemed to be trying to sit up as if she had been sitting at the time of her murder.

This wasn't the spoils of war; this was the ultimate in expressed contempt for women or at least this woman. My eyes hadn't even traveled to her upper torso, where more taunting cuts had been exacted. I swallowed and turned to the sidewalk, watching as the poor lady cried into the telephone across the street.

My head spun, as I lost the cup of coffee I had for breakfast, I doubled over and upchucked until I was light-headed and dry heaving. I yanked the handkerchief out of my pants pocket, frantically wiping my mouth. I spit what bile was left, and I blinked to make the horror go away, yet it didn't.

With a cautious step, I turned to see what the butcher had done to her upper torso. The cruel slices advancing up her breasts were a prelude to the hacking cuts from the corners of her mouth back to her ears.

In war, I had heard of 'The Glasgow Smile' or the 'Chelsea Grin' exacted by pillaging miscreants who had gone renegade from their units. They'd inflict savage cuts, slashed from the corners of their mouth to the dying invader's ears. If battle wounds didn't kill them, they'd likely bleed to death.

With this disturbing discovery, I shook by way of outrage that the devil left his victim for some unsuspecting citizen to find. I turned to see the poor woman collapsed to her knees. Still holding her young child, she laid shaking hands, framing both sides of the child's petite face to hold her attention away from what the adults had found.

I lost track of time, not wanting to leave until the police arrived. I was rattled, wondering if Dotty would need help with Valerie or if perhaps they were done and wondering where I was. The morning swirled around me, a vicious torrent of stark images.

I was hypnotized by the sight of the girl's ravaged face, trying to imagine her age or her beauty in life. Her black glossy hair, a rage of waves framed her unnatural death mask. I was again repulsed. This butchered woman was Elizabeth, my Beth.

It was my turn to break down, fall to my knees on the sidewalk, my face in the crook of my elbow. I couldn't reconcile my shock, not right now. Cops swarmed, reporters pushed, photographers, spit on light bulbs, and swiftly shoved them into their camera flash units.

Voices, all questions, and orders overwhelmed the three of us as we huddled between two men in blue. Without our noticing it, the lady with the child and I had been danced over to a black and white unit. I remember saying something about being needed around the corner.

The detectives didn't see me as a person of interest. Sure, they had a jaundiced eye at my chosen profession, musicians seem hinky, unstable, given to fits of drug-induced mania. Then, when I thought they'd cuff me and haul me down to the station, they looked at my full name. Some guy in the back shook his head as he chewed on a toothpick. I was dispatched to join Dotty at the clinic. I'll take that 'get out of jail card'. I never want to be headed where they'll send Elizabeth's murderer.

♦♦♦♦

The clinic bustled with pacing mothers, colicky babes, and hacking children. Crisp nurse's caps cut their way through the room like shark fins, escorting the patients down long linoleum hallways into exam rooms.

I didn't see Dotty, so I fingered the business card and sat. I sat picking apart what I thought were Elizabeth's last days, was she with *them*?

The other night, had she really sent me the note? Did I even know her handwriting if I saw it? I sat there, lost in a shit storm, feeling totally out of place until I felt Dotty's hand on my shoulder.

"Hey, champ, I thought we lost you." Her large eyes sought mine, and I looked up, leaving her hand on my shoulder because it just felt so right.

"There was an, an--" I stumbled on words, an organization so pure as a pediatrician's office should not be sullied by the mention of murder so foul. "Accident, another woman, and I had to give our statements." I lowered my voice, speaking closer to her ear than socially acceptable in public. Her light cologne calmed me immediately.

I couldn't drag the two of them back to the spectacle around the corner. I slipped back to the car unnoticed by the police and attempted to be polite company for the ride to the café to pick up lunch.

♦♦♦♦

In my shallow sleep, the Army Chaplain prayed over me. The men I'd treated at the hospitals held me down on the muddy ground as I thrashed. "I exorcise thee, every unclean spirit, in the name of God the Father Almighty. In the name of Jesus Christ, His Son, our Lord and Judge, and in the power of the Holy Spirit, that thou be departed from this creature of God, Henry William VanAlt, Jr..."

The morning dawned golden and glowing. Has that devil departed? The priest couldn't cleanse what I'd seen. Someday, a long time from now, if I live to be an ancient man, all the terror I saw on that mother's face, perhaps, will be replaced. It will take decades of the smiles of my wife, my kids, and the satisfaction of a job well done in a calling I cannot even foresee to scour away that image.

How long will I have to live, to forget what happened to Elizabeth Short? She's gone down in history as 'The Black Dahlia', each hour the radio repeated the same gruesome news.

I moved through our familiar home grief-stricken wrapped in cotton wool. I flipped the radio off and forgot about eating. I sat alone and smoked half a pack of Lucky Strikes on the back porch in my undershorts.

When the silence was too much, I set a stack of records on the turntable. I opened the window to listen to the frying bacon snap and pop of a phonograph needle on the turntable as George Gershwin tickled the ivories.

Eventually, the moon climbed behind the trees, and I realized my eyes were cried dry. With every breath, my lungs burned from drawing in hot smoke, only to forcefully expel the captivating nicotine through my nostrils. I hung the back yard in smoke rings, the haze attaching to the dew damped foliage. There wasn't a thing for me to do; not that I could concentrate anyway.

I could contribute nothing, so I cracked the lever on the ice tray and emptied it. I sullied Mom's favorite iced tea glass with gin and tonic, a triple, in fact. If I was going to hell, I might as well ride the polished handbasket.

The last sounds I remember were Debussy's waterfall of melody against the backdrop of my heavy breathing. Wrapped in cotton sheeting, I rode the dream highway past the Zimmermann's and that character that held Elizabeth in the back of the Mercedes.

Sure, I had spilled all about them to the detectives. I was certain The Blue Gardenia would be crawling with flatfoots handling glasses of tonic with a wedge of lime, passing for gin drinkers while they assayed the crowd in the lounge. I told the cops Zimmermann, and his crowd were taking a plane out of the country, I figured they watch us all for a few weeks.

♦♦♦♦

The following evening, somehow, in the middle of the last set, the squidgy looking guy holding his tonic and lime with both hands got on my nerves.

The entire night Reggie hadn't burned one joint, for fear the homicide mopes would bust us for weed. I was on edge and could have enjoyed the smoothing smoke of a few puffs.

Bozo, the mope, shifted his eyes one too many times, as I sat my guitar down and headed for two fingers of gin.

"Harry, my man, how do you play away when your New Year's Eve babe is laying on a slab getting the once over by the morgue crew?" The weasel's lips barely moved as he bugged me.

"Excuse me?" I wiped the sweat off my lip with the back of my left hand, my right hand grasping the chilled bar glass so tightly it nearly shattered.

"Tell me, didn't this joint entertain a few rogues from across the Atlantic, you know those with high dollar habits?" He supposed we had some sort of secret club here? That Zimmermann and his clan signed some agreement to hold some 'membership' at a joint like The Blue Gardenia?

"Don't think so, Bub. Anything else you want to get the skinny on, walk it out the door. The only thing we investigate here is who's wearing panties and who's not." I eyed Candy as she slithered by, her empty tray carried behind her, obscuring the sight of her ass cheeks as she vibrated on to the next table. Discourse, chat, whatever you call it, you don't come into this joint for intelligent conversation and epiphanies.

"Sly dog that you are, Harry, what did you have to do that night? You said you weren't with Elizabeth Short." His lips twitched after he uttered her name.

204

That was all it took. I swigged down the gin, felt it hit my empty gut, and dragged my damp hands down the hips of my trousers. My fingers fisted and released a few times, and then I caught the mope's shoulders, lifting him to his toes.

"You don't know how close you are to landing on the pavement." We were nearly belt to belt, while I breathed hot gin breath down his face, his eyelids closed and his lips quivered. "Let me induce you to find another club tonight. What's your name, Bub?" I was shuffling the two of us through the crowd as they noticed our brouhaha. The drinkers parted like the Red Sea. Then, I let the little man down on his heels right next to the door.

"They should be looking at a boyfriend scorned, shouldn't they? Some guy who was a sawbones in the Army, who could scythe off a gangrenous foot in a barn?" He mewed the words out as if he had been beaten to say them. I looked out the door at the sidewalk to see if he was operated like Edgar Bergan's dummy. I wondered if he really was a cop.

"Are you a cop?" My brows knit over dark eyes as I watched him nearly wet himself.

"Naw, who'd work for that kind of dinero?" He pulled at my grasp, his paws too sweaty to move me, and that just riled me more, that was it.

"How about, we take your sorry ass out, stick a wick in your mouth and use you for a gas lamp?" I had to pull him up a few inches for our eyes to meet. The thought of my lighting the fool on fire must have extinguished whatever burning desire he had to crack the case of the century.

He wiggled like a twelve-year-old girl as I threw him across the hood of the nearest car. When his jacket fell open, I saw the press pass from the Los Angeles Examiner, William Randolph Hearst's rag. He scratched away from me, his rubber-soled shoes grabbing at the car's contours.

I couldn't help it. Was it his cowardly retreat, or his mentioning the field amputation I had to do in a Dover barn? The slimy bastard researched me.

Ripping the windshield wiper off the car, I beat him. I dealt him the beating of his life. I was vicious. I whipped sideways and hard, starting at his hips. I loosed the change from his pockets as dimes bounced off the car hood. I can't even remember what I said, as I worked out my life's frustrations on this stooge. By the time I got to his head, he was curled up like an armadillo, and all I got was a few swipes at his neck. I wanted to bloody his nose, but all I accomplished was marking the backs of his tan sleeves with black streaks.

A crowd didn't gather. They gave me solitude to banish my demons. When I walked back into the club, nobody even noticed I was missing. I slicked back my hair, tucked my shirt back into my trousers, and swigged another two fingers of gin.

Chapter Thirty-Three

Some providence comes shielded by beauty, some by stark brutality. I overslept. The Baby Ben clock on my bed table hadn't been wound tightly enough to ring the alarm. I woke after sunset. Stomping angrily down the stairs, I bellowed. "Mom, what'd you let me sleep for? For Christ's sake, I'll lose the shit-can job at the shit-can lounge for this…" I was talking to myself. The house was silent. Only a single parlor lamp burned, Dad and Mom had slipped in and then slid out for dinner.

I picked up the phone to call the lounge. The call wouldn't go through. I jumped into my clothes and took off on foot. The night air was heavy, and a few blocks from there, I caught the scent of smoke.

It made me think of the scant fires we lit in England. I thought about a barn and Sonny's blood in the hay. I was sick to my stomach between tardiness and the nightmare of what I'd had to do to save a soldier's life. I bent over, panting, and threw up a little, then recouped and bolted at the first break in the traffic.

I wasn't prepared for the hive of activity when I blew around the corner, finding The Blue Gardenia ablaze. Three, four stories of flames and smoke danced above the heads of the crowd milling around. Were they waiting for heroic rescues from the apartments on the upper floors? I doubted it.

"What happened?" I guess I sounded this side of a half-wit.

"Firebombed, the place was gutted before the firemen got here." A bum nodded, sucking his near toothless gums while he shuffled from foot to foot.

"Gutted? Where is everyone? Anyone get out?" My feet fought to cover ground, find the guys, find Candy.

"Just a few people around the door; have you seen the place? It's a dive. The old place was a fire trap." The bum sniffled and hacked, as he dug for a smoke in his pockets.

I grabbed him, making him focus on me. "Why aren't they bringing them out?" Why was I asking him?

When the smoke cleared and the firemen left, the place was burned to the ground. The firemen couldn't or wouldn't go into the burning building. The smoke was too thick to see.

Survivors, people sober enough to move in the right direction, reported a character of some odd behavior shouting something about "Die, murderers." They were too smart to hang around; they vamoosed.

I sat on the curb across the street, watching the blur of activity peter out as the fire turned to smoke, and the smoke dissipated in the three A.M. breeze. Silently, I cried into my folded hands, my gig bag at my feet.

The Red Cross set up a truck, feeding the firemen coffee and doughnuts, their universal cure for any loss. I took a bite of one doughnut that tasted like ash itself, and I hurled it to the pavement.

All those hours, there was no sound, only the slow movements of people in a surreal setting. I closed my eyes for a quick minute and then out of wet slits; I thought I saw that fuck-sack, Augustine. I started to rise to my feet, and in that split second, he was gone, vanished. I never saw a guy move that fast in my life.

♦♦♦♦

To say I had a baptism by fire would be succinct. So far, in 1947, I had discovered a lover hacked in pieces, and my buddies at work burned to cinders. I wondered how much more I'd be up for this year, as I wandered the hospital. An orderly caught me and guided me to Emergency Admitting; there is an upside to looking pitiful because people help you.

The efficient nurse in the starched cap glared at me. I had that unhealthy mien people with demons occasionally exhibit, and I smelled like Lucifer. "My friends were in a fire, The Blue Gardenia Lounge." I stood waiting while she shuffled through paperwork.

"We've had one admission, a woman." Her eyes never met mine. I waited for a beat before I begged the name and got an icy response. "Gladys Collins, an employee, she's being treated now."

I didn't know any Gladys, yet I wasn't ready to let go. I retreated from the desk, waited till no one was looking and skulked behind the ER swinging doors. I grabbed a white coat and an empty clipboard and acted like I knew where I was going, so nobody bothered me.

The smell of burnt clothing and acrid flesh drew me to the end of the hall. The empty silence frightened me. Was this the end of the road for the person behind the curtain? Had they rolled them there unable to do anything? I almost recognized a hint of familiar cologne, and I cautiously stuck my nose between the two drawn curtains. Candy lay there in an opiate daze, bandaged at her elbows and knees as if she stumbled through the debris. Her eyes were closed, her face obscured by the oxygen mask. I slid to the side of the bed.

"Gladys?" I wanted to make her smile, if for no other reason than we both needed to break the cycle of unrelenting pain.

Her eyes opened with a butterfly flutter, and she gritted through her teeth. "Not on your life, buddy." She coughed mercilessly and managed to choke out. "Haven't been Gladys since eleventh grade, got it?" She coughed desperately again, and then she smiled weakly, and I guessed I was welcome to sit beside her bed.

"What happened, Candy?" I caught her hand, and she let me hold it, she usually wasn't this warm with me when tips weren't involved. I looked around for water and a cup.

"Some drugstore cowboy comes in and starts jacking his jaw about where were the sheiks and shebas? He was looking for a doll he saw with a musician on New Year's Eve."

My heart tightened, he was looking for Elizabeth Short.

"So, when Reggie says she's passed on, the lounge lizard goes off the wall, he blows out of the place. When he comes back, he's got a bag, and he tosses it right into the center of the club. I never saw a match; all I heard was the explosion. I had scooted into the office. That worm gave me the heeby-jeebies; I didn't want to be around the guy; it seems that saved my life." She hacked violently.

"What about…" I had to know. This was the curiosity that would at least skin the cat and leave him terribly uncomfortable.

"The band? They got burned up bad. I got out through the office door to the alley." She coughed some more. "Then you walked in here." She was resolved to rest. I didn't blame her.

"Look, you take it easy." What more could I say? Out of a job, skinned up and burnt in places that didn't show, Candy was one lucky gal, all things considered.

"I'm being admitted, can you pick me up when they toss me out?" Her smile was weak, forced, resigned.

"Sure, I will. I'll borrow a car to ride you home in style. Till then, don't start any card games without me, okay?" I stood and brushed the singed blonde hair off her forehead and gave her a little wave as I stepped outside the curtain and padded down the hall to look for a way out. I was done here.

At five in the morning, the sidewalk had the sad task of listening to my reflections as I dragged home. Instead of going inside the house, I sat on the porch glider and strummed the last bit of my old life, my guitar. Right now was 'grow up' time. I strummed quiet chords as I thought about tomorrow. What had these days in 1947 taught me about being a man?

It's one thing to march through war, taking orders, operating like there's no tomorrow. It's another thing to come home and find the rest of the world thinking it had all gone back to normal because there isn't a wartime death toll on the radio.

I had to get straight. No dope, no liquor, behave like a gentleman. Who was I kidding? Could I get by with minimal alcohol and getting some skin on the third date? Yeah…I hope so because that's where I think I need to head."

♦♦♦♦

Harry shook his head and ran both hands through his hair. He blinked and looked at Adam. "And that's where I headed. I applied to teach a hospital administration course at the VA until I finished my undergraduate classes at UCLA."

Harry looked at Matt. "Is there any more A Positive left?"

Matt eagerly brought a tall tumbler back to him.

Adam referred to his notes. "Did you continue to live with your parents?"

Harry nodded. "Remember there was that huge housing shortage after the war. Plus, it gave me access to my daughter."

210

"How did your relationship work out?" Adam asked.

"As predicted, Arnold was a prick." Harry grinned wickedly. "But I gave as good as I got. Eventually, Arnold was rarely there. Valerie came over for piano lessons with my mother, but I was the one teaching her." Harry winked. "She had a good ear." Then Harry's expression sagged. "My senior year, a professor asked me to submit a story I wrote to a contest. During the summer between graduation and law school, I found out I won." Harry stood and began pacing while he stretched. He looked over his shoulder at Adam. "Winning was the beginning of the end. My dad hit the roof when he found out I postponed law school to write a book."

His friends exchanged looks. "How exactly?" Adam prodded.

"The contest set me up with an agent in New York and a book contract with a small advance. My editors were local. My professor was my mentor. My dad strongly suggested I suffer for my craft. When I came home from the beach one Sunday, all my stuff was packed and sitting in the foyer."

Adam blinked hard. "Did you have someplace to go?"

"I had hinted I had a line on a room in a Victorian mansion near the college. I had to move in sooner than I expected. But the tension at home was unbearable. Mom and Dad were at each other's throats over my decision. It was better to leave."

Adam flicked a glance at Lizbet. "Were you able to repair that relationship? What happened to Valerie?"

Harry sat again and stared at the wound on his forearm. "Dad eventually loosened up, and most Sundays, I had dinner at their house with Dotty and Valerie." Harry tilted his head with a frown. "I need you to fill me in on this Responders thralling thing. I get that I was eaten up with grief over Beth's death and the fire at the bar. But how did thralling me about that affect me now?"

Adam calmly explained. "It was agreed your mortal life would be enhanced by forgetting the incidents. The Responders acted on their decision to use thralling because of the traumas you experienced."

Harry whispered to no one in particular. "Damn it."

Rick leaned forward. "They lost your thralling report by misspelling your name. When there was evidence that thralled males who were later turned could have issues, there was no connection."

Harry met his lean and ground his jaw. "A clerical error?"

Rick nodded. "We never connected the two incidents. Since 1900 a file has been kept on every vamp, how they were turned. Where they live and their identities. Think of it as a census."

Adam drew in a deep breath. "Back to Lorenz Zimmermann. Most of his little group were vampires, including Lita Braun and Augustine Fielding. Of course, they all knew Elizabeth Short and Desiree Hearst."

"So, it's still a cold case?" Harry arched his back and stretched on the sofa. "Jigsaw John never cracked it…" Harry thought back to the detective, his cousin, who heard his name and dismissed him as a suspect.

"Let's not digress. Lorenz and his playmates had a wild time on coke, booze, and blood the night Elizabeth and Desiree were killed. It was a feeding party gone out of control."

"Augustine was apparently the only one with any sense. He consigned Miss Hearst's body to a sea burial. She was never heard from again."

Harry's voice was a grave whisper. "And Beth?"

Adam let out a huff. "Lorenz Zimmermann always had a ghoulish flair for the dramatic. He was convinced the evidence of their feeding frenzy would be disguised by mutilating her body as if she was mauled by some crazed killer."

Chapter Thirty-Four

Harry groaned and picked at his cuticle. "Do you know what has been lingering in the back of my mind for decades?"

Adam watched him quietly. "What's that, Harry?"

"I've always wondered if somehow I was the Black Dahlia killer. I know that's crazy. I had no conscious memory of Beth. But I knew I was the right age, and I knew I was in Los Angeles at the same time. I knew I had the skills to do that kind of dissection. I always felt guilty about her death, and I never knew why."

Lizbet looked at her notes. "Do you believe meeting me close to the anniversary of her death may have aroused suppressed memories?"

Harry blinked hard and sighed. "I just don't know."

Lizbet knelt before him and took his hands. "Harry, I want you to remember that I deal with sociopaths and psychopaths every day. I assure you, if you had killed someone in such a macabre way, you would not have guilt about it." She glanced up at Adam. "Isn't that right, Dr. Lachlan?"

Adam gave them both an understanding smile. "I concur, Dr. Mitchell."

Harry's blue-green eyes were a haunted deep teal. "Are you sure about that?"

Rick stood and paced, his head shaking. "God's nightgown, Harry…We have it in black and white from the Responders that Zimmermann did it."

Adam soothed. "Let it be a relief to know you weren't responsible." Adam flipped more pages and continued. "The Council demanded Lorenz and Lita go back to Argentina and never set foot on North American soil again."

Through the hours, Adam pressed a tissue into Harry's hand from time to time as he wept with sadness or joy. Harry paid keen attention to each of Adam's questions. His head tilted to the right or to the left as if seeking direction at times.

Adam rubbed his forehead. "We're up to 1951, Harry, do you remember your turning?"

"The night of the book release party? 1951? No, I don't, but it's coming up, isn't it?" He wiped his lips; they caught a little more saliva than usual. Harry's head fell back, and his eyes closed. "Chateau Marmont. It was after this huge party. Cocktails, reporters from the New York Times. Afterward, in a mountainside bungalow, my agent was there, playing the piano."

"Did he seem familiar to you?" Adam asked.

Harry sat up and walked to Matt's Knight-Brinkerhoff player piano. He sat down on the bench, and his fingers began a tune. "No, I'd been dealing with him long distance from New York. We just met in person that evening. He and his secretary flew in for the release. It was their bungalow. He was playing Cole Porter's, "In the Still of the Night", but he was in the wrong key… I sat down to correct his playing."

"And? What did he look like? Do you remember the secretary?"

"His name was… Loren Carpenter… His secretary was Lena Browning."

Rick buried his face in his hands and then removed his fountain pen and notepad from his breast pocket. He wrote 'Zimmermann = Carpenter. Lita Braun = Lena Browning.' He slid the note to Adam.

"Lena was one of those fiery redheads. She comes up behind me, and right in front of Loren, she runs her hands down my shoulders and leans into me. I felt… cornered."

Harry played the Porter song like a dirge. "I told her I didn't play with women from work. Loren spoke to her in German, I couldn't decipher what he said, but he left and turned down the lights. Lena sat next to me, her back to the piano and her arms around my waist. She was the strongest broad I ever wrestled. She started licking her red lips and nibbling on my ear. Her hands went into my pants, and I wasn't drunk… I didn't know what was happening." Lizbet shivered and shook her head. "I told her I wasn't into one night stands anymore, and her words ground out on breath like death. She said, 'I can turn you any way I desire. I can bend your will'."

The room was silent for a beat.

"The next thing I knew, I was in her bed, stripped to the waist. I was exhausted, worn out. Couldn't remember what she'd done. I heard her call out to Loren in the living room, and he walked toward the bed, untying his bow tie. What little adrenaline I had surged, and I shrieked at her to call him off."

Matt's forehead dropped onto his fist, and his eyes closed tightly. Rick walked behind Matt and placed his hands on his friend's shoulders. "Remember, it's not happening to either of you right now." Matt turned to meet Rick's gaze and nodded straight lipped.

Harry continued. "She stripped down to nothing and told Loren, 'We're ready for you'. They each took one of my hands, and their faces went demonic. Icy white eyes, pale blue-veined skin… Fangs, long, sharp incisors, and they dove into me. I was their meal.

"Loren loomed over me, his nostrils flared. He threw back his head and with a menacing laugh he ran his hand over his undead heart. 'If he's delicious, imagine the sweet purity of his virgin daughter'.

"I lost consciousness. I fought to come back from hell. I felt their fangs move up my arms to my neck, and the two of them fed on me there. The stench of their breath knocked me out, or maybe it was blood loss?"

Lizbet touched a tissue to an errant tear as she blinked and kept recording his words.

"The next thing I knew, both of them held their wrists over my mouth." Harry played Frédéric Chopin's Funeral March. The song's stunning emotion blanketed the room as he recounted waking to the taste of two distinct blood types flowing down his throat as he twisted and fought the feeding.

"This was my death." He wept as he played the classical piece and described the assault. "The first quarter of this piece is slow and sad, like the brief premonition I had of my end. I couldn't fight off both of them. The second and third parts of the music illustrate my bittersweet memories of my life after 1947. Reconnecting with Dotty and my daughter."

In the music's last quarter, he played the slow and morose movement. It droned woefully. "This illustrates my fear they would reach Valerie before I could. I was lost, but I couldn't bear them dragging her into their hell. This piece has become a classic evocation of death, but I see it fitting for a transition to the undead. I came to in the blood-stained bed between Loren and Lena. Their peaceful, mortal appearance belied their evil indulgence in my living blood. I feared the worst, I looked around the room for my daughter."

Lizbet's hand covered her lips, and she wiped her nose.

"I crawled to the end of the bed and out to the living room. All the lights were off, but it was like daylight to my new senses. Valerie was nowhere to be seen. I broke off piano bench legs like it was nothing, and I staked Loren first, and then Lena." Harry clawed at his chest, reliving his new undead senses and fears.

"Even though I didn't see Valerie, I had to be sure she was alive. I called Dotty and wouldn't let her go until she confirmed that Valerie was alive and well, asleep in her bed.

"I went to the bar cart and rounded up every bottle of alcohol. No matter what I drank, it tasted like ash. I knew it would still burn. I poured a bottle of liquor around the bed, on the bed, and sprayed another on the curtains. I doused the devils in alcohol and stood at the bedroom door." Harry gestured, pounding the stakes, and tossing a lit bottle, his eyes clenched closed.

"I put on Loren's jacket and used a dinner napkin with the last bottle of vodka as a Molotov cocktail. I tossed it onto the bed. The bungalow's interior went up in flames, but the building itself was essentially fireproof." The music piece ended, and Harry's head hung.

Matt wiped his mouth, catching his words before he sought permission to speak from Adam. Adam waved his approval, and Matt rose, pacing to finish the evening's narrative. "Do you remember what happened when you headed toward your car?"

Tears streamed down Harry's cheeks, he wiped his face and turned to Matt. "You were there. Coming to my bungalow with a package for me."

"What did we do?" Matt's baritone was smooth and soothing.

"You took me to your car. I sat alone for a few minutes while you went for help. Then you told me you had been commissioned to do my cover by your artistic agent. That you were bringing me a print of the cover as a gift."

"When I saw the blood, what did I say?" Matt stood at the penthouse window, streaks of purple crossed the sky.

"You asked me if they bit me, and I showed you my neck and wrists. Then you took me to Richard Hiatt's home. You explained what I was. You got me cleaned up. Got me fed. Then you put me in a dark room, on a marble slab."

"What do you remember after that?" Matt's voice exhibited gentle paternal strength.

"By the time I woke the next night, you had already sent people to clean out my studio. You brought back my records and books. You secured my passport and important papers. You explained Henry W. VanAlt, Jr. was dead. Now I was Harrison VanAlt if I expected to stay in Los Angeles. Your lawyers drafted paperwork to will Henry's mortal estate to a cousin, Harrison VanAlt."

Adam queried. "And what happened to your book, Harry?"

Harry turned on the bench and sat with his hands splayed on his thighs. "Runaway bestseller. Die in a fiery blaze, and your real crime book shoots to the top. My mom found…" Harry made air quotes. … "the account you set up for my daughter."

Adam's gaze traveled from Matt to Rick and Lizbet. "How was your transition, Harry? Do you remember your family's life after your passing?"

Harry stood and scratched at the back of his neck. "Matt was right. It was hard for me to watch from a distance. Once I knew Valerie and Dotty were safe and financially secure, I was able to let them go. My parents retired in 1962, moved to Sun City Center between Tampa and Sarasota. I wanted to go to the realtor's open house to see it one last time, but Matt kept me busy."

There was a beat of silence between the five of them. "Do you remember your parents passing?" Adam folded his hands over his knee and waited.

Harry wiped at his face as sadness swept over him. Adam held out a box of tissues. Harry plucked out a couple, and he spoke from behind them, rubbing his eyes. "Dad's obituary was in the Los Angeles Times, June of 1972. It said he was predeceased by his son, Author Henry W. VanAlt, Jr. It mentioned how he grew his bank before his retirement. Mom passed away in her sleep in 1994. She was one tough Irish woman." Harry wiped his mouth with the wrinkled tissue and turned away from his friends.

♦♦♦♦

By the first glow of dawn, all the flattened, flushed images held somewhere else had been reanimated. Harry came out of the last bit of a haze with a glass in his hand, a particularly lively A Positive, and he swallowed it down in one smooth swallow.

The gash was raw, just beginning to knit. Adam silently watched, sitting across from Harry. "I don't know what else to say…" He ran a hand through his unruly hair and felt the scruff on his chin.

When the men heard mortal Lizbet's head sink to her forearms, their attentions turned to the woman with the little whistle in her snore. She was slumped over her notepad, fast asleep. Rick's lips curled up wryly. "Poor mortal, can't run with the pack." He walked over, carefully picked her up, and headed to the door. Over his shoulder, he whispered. "I'm taking her to your Murphy bed, okay, sport?"

Harry nodded. "I know she's in good hands."

Chapter Thirty-Five

Adam closed his notepad. "While that wound is open and we're together, more things may come to the fore. Once the sun rises, get yourself cleaned up."

Harry watched Matt and Adam linger over a freshly poured tumbler of blood and mug of coffee. He stretched as he strolled around the room. "It's something about going through this process; I'm too antsy to go to ground."

Matt nodded. "Being behind these blackout draperies and having consumed so much fresh blood all night, you might be up all day."

Adam retrieved a business card. "You should call this therapist." He held it out to Harry. "The Responders have some excellent counselors. You may find weekly conversations to be helpful as you process this experience."

Harry slid the card toward his watch on the coffee table. "Thanks, I'll do that."

When Rick returned to Matt's apartment, Adam was on the way out. "Thanks, Sparky. You deserve a night off. However, it's the high season, and The Gaoler is double-booked."

Adam narrowed his gaze, and his smile spread wide as he dug for his car keys. "Your thanks are underwhelming. But, you haven't gotten the bill for overnight therapy yet."

Rick rocked on the balls of his loafers. "Seriously? Thanks, old man."

Adam turned and waved good-bye.

When only the undead remained, Rick raised a brow to Matt and gestured for Harry to have another seat in the center of the sofa.

"Now you're going to find your time as a vampire has always been compromised by your peculiar neurophysiology. It's time for you to see the power you inherited from your sires. You were innocent in all this. We need to talk about your future."

Harry chuckled darkly. "Why?"

Matt pulled a book from over his desk. "This is the sire-lines, what mortals would call your pedigree." It looked like a massive Altar edition of a Catholic missal. He slid the red ribbon bookmark to open the ornate hardback and placed it in Harry's lap. Rick joined him on one side with Matt on the other. "These pages reflect the Zimmermann line. It goes back to Five-forty-two A.D. and the Plague of Justinian. By some fluke, your forbears escaped the damning plague and headed into the Fall of the Western Roman Empire. It's an ancient bloodline. Very strong."

Harry looked to each of his older cohorts. "Do you guys have anything like this? I mean, how will this make me different?"

Matt's expression brooked no humor. "We'll get there in a minute. However, you were co-sired. That's extremely rare. Lita was from a Spanish line…" Matt gazed in Rick's direction.

Rick threw up both hands. "I'm from Romani blood. She's not in my line."

Matt's finger moved from the top of the illuminated pedigree. "It turns out her mortal father was an Interrogator in the Spanish Inquisition. One of the vamps of that time thought it would be hysterical to turn a member of his family. That led Lita to high-tail it out of the country on Vespucci's ship to South America."

Matt flipped through her pages and pointed out where she sired quite a few undead among the first families of Argentina. "You're damn near vampire royalty, and you've been living vampire-lite."

"The meaning is lost on me. Is there an income from this?" Harry gestured to the pedigrees.

Rick's chest shook with a hearty laugh. "Oh, Matt, I can tell this one is your stepson, he's asking about money."

"No money, Harry. Only phenomenal power. Once you've gone to ground and risen at the next twilight, your perceptions will be sharper; your strength will be greater, everything about you will be more… potent." Matt slid back to the end of the sofa and folded his arms over his chest. "Any questions?"

"Potent? As in more sexual?" Harry's brows rose humorously. "I thought we were king of the hill, or at least that's how I've always felt.

Never had any complaints there." Harry shrugged, sliding the book closed and placing it on the coffee table.

Rick nodded with unflappable recognition. "You may be more into the activities of The Gaoler. Your vigor will be many times more intense, along with your demands and your drive. With Lizbet, you will truly need to temper your strength."

♦♦♦♦

Lizbet bolted upright in the strange bed. She was in Harry's apartment; it was eleven in the morning. Everything was pristine again. She didn't remember walking downstairs from Matt's place. Her curiosity had to be fed. She stood and slipped into her shoes, straightened the bedsheets, and pushed the bed back into the wall. *Well, don't I look like Medusa?* She twisted her wild waves into a chignon and clipped it loosely. Grabbing her purse, she had ground to cover. She wanted to find her own copy of Harry's first book.

She stopped at a diner and borrowed their phone directory, making a list of vintage book stores. Once she ate a hearty breakfast and took a paper cup of coffee to go, she was on the hunt.

Her third stop, The Wayback Machine, was a treasure trove on Alameda in the Arts District. A bell rang when she entered the orderly and brightly lit store. Somehow she was expecting a grandma's attic atmosphere. Lizbet took in the assemblage of mannequins posed around the store. Some in military dress, some in authentic flapper regalia, a few Haight Ashbury Hippies complete with love beads. She didn't know where to begin. Making a three-sixty turn in place, she sought a sales clerk and gasped when the mannequin seated on the edge of the bay window ledge blinked at her. She squealed and clutched her heart.

The tall, pale, dorky-looking kid laughed. "I get that a lot. Welcome to The Wayback Machine. What eclectic piece of memorabilia are you seeking?"

"I'm looking for a book from 1951, *Murder in the First*, by Henry VanAlt, Jr. Do you have that?"

Sliding from his place, he came from behind the counter. He eyed Lizbet suspiciously as he drew closer. "How did you hear about that book?"

"From a friend."

His dark head of curls bounced with his nodding head. His voice, intense, he demanded. "Who's your friend?"

"I don't think I like your tone. You deal in vintage. I'm looking for a vintage book, do you have it or not?"

"I have it, are you sure you can handle it? Or you could just buy one of those glossy reprints, but it wouldn't be the same."

"Why wouldn't it?"

"You know this book was based on a true story?"

"Was it?"

"Oh, yeah. The two doctors were arrested, jailed, and got disappeared."

"Got disappeared?"

"Yeah. The theory is the Pentagon had them removed to a more secure area." He made air quotes on his words.

"Why would they do that?"

"Some people think they discovered alien abductees, some think they discovered some Commie plot, but me? I think they found out the government was contaminating the psych medications. They were psychiatrists, you know."

Lizbet winced. "Isn't the book about a murder trial? One doctor killing the other doctor's wife?"

"Her death was accidental. The doctor was framed when he didn't play along."

"Okay, I'll take that original book."

"It's your funeral." He clipped his turn and headed to the back of the store. On a top shelf with other framed VanAlt memorabilia, one copy stood. "You know the guy who wrote the book died under mysterious circumstances, right?"

She lowered her voice. "No, I didn't. What happened?"

He held the book to his chest and surveyed the store. In a hushed tone, he began. "The night the book debuted, there was a fire. Of course, whoever tried to start a fire at the Chateau Marmont didn't realize they were built to near bunker specifications." He lowered his gaze to her as his brow rose.

"So, a fire…"

"They never found a body."

"Maybe he got away?"

"Got away and disappeared?"

She shrugged. "It happens."

"But it wasn't just the author, his agent, and secretary, they all disappeared."

She reached for the book. "That sounds about right."

He took a step back. "You've talked with someone about this? We have the Con Club on the first Thursday of every month. Perhaps your friend would like to meet with us?"

Lizbet headed toward the cash register. "I think I'll just take the book. But I'm curious, what are all those framed things?"

The store owner's lips curled. "I've got a whole scrapbook on him. He was a musician, and you know tragedy followed him everywhere. The club where he played, burned down."

Lizbet bit her lip. "Fire, again? Perhaps he's Lucifer incarnate?"

The young man sneered as he pulled the scrapbook from the shelf and walked to the counter. "Laugh if you will." He spun the album around for her to peruse. It held copies of Harry's military I.D., his Officer's Training graduation photo, newspaper archive copies of the lounge fire, and headlines of Harry's blazing demise. The most obscure image was an actual photo folder from The Blue Gardenia. The indigo folder was stamped in tarnished silver foil. "Our Night at The Blue Gardenia."

Lizbet hesitated. *Do I want to see the picture?* "Will you flip this open, please?"

The kid chuckled and removed it from the covered page and held it from her grasp. She leaned in to see a Post-War newlywed couple being toasted by the room as the band watched. Their small table was at the edge of the stage. The groom wore a Navy uniform, and the bride wore a dark suit with a carnation corsage. Everyone held a glass aloft.

High over them on the stage, Harry's grin was the broadest. Some of his slicked-back hair escaped order as it fell over his forehead. *He should have been in movies, my God he's handsome. He out-Elvised the King.*

"How much for the photo?"

"In for a penny, in for a pound. I might as well sell you the entire scrapbook. You won't live long anyway." He nodded knowingly.

Lizbet's lips rose with inside humor. *That's an option. I hope I don't.*

Back in her car, she sat buzzing with the pride of owning something from Harry's mortal past. Now it was time to get home and do some computer research. *Minka's probably hungry.*

♦♦♦♦

Hours of back and forth discussion filled the day, and the rousing conversation circled back to the initial thralling. By sunset, the wound was a thin red scar, and the door was closing on retrieving more palpable hidden treasures.

Harry sat back, thinking about Lorenz Zimmermann skulking off in 1947 only to reimagine himself as Loren Carpenter in 1950. "That man wanted me. Did I ever stand a chance?" The feeling of being hunted over the years was haunting.

"No. I think Zimmermann was one of those twisted minds who took what he wanted. You and I are like this because of vampires like him."

Harry shook his head vehemently. "Matt, I hope I didn't inherit that trait. I never want to be like that."

Rick bolted to his feet. "There's not a chance in hell you'd be like that. Zimmermann was born that way. You were born with compassion. That doesn't change when you're turned."

♦♦♦♦

"So many things make sense now, certain nagging feelings, gut reactions." Harry slugged at Matt's shoulder, and his step-sire moved vamp fast to evade the playful punch.

"You opened my eyes to more than my past." Harry stood, staring at the open leather-bound books.

224

Sketchbooks lay on a drawing table under a lamp simulating natural light. While Harry recounted the moments of his past, Matt had sketched vignettes. The faces of the mortals in his life were featureless like Amish dolls. "You did these while I jabbered?"

"You didn't describe their features well enough to finish them. They have a weird vibe without the features. Maybe I can start an art movement?" There were Runyonesque images of nightclub scenes and Harry lost in his music.

"I had no idea…"

Matt gathered the different sketchbooks and stacked them on a high shelf, where they joined others. "Well, do you have any ideas about what you are now? Are you feeling more positive about being… undead?"

"Yeah. But it still doesn't answer my questions about mortal women." Harry looked over his shoulder as he headed to the humidor.

Rick met him and held the lid open. "Matt is a stick in the mud. He doesn't realize how hard it is to find a woman you want to spend fifty years with, much less eternity. Dr. Mitchell has …"

Harry corrected. "Lizbet."

"Lizbet, a rose by any other name, would still be intriguing." Rick's arm caught him round the neck and whooshed him to the edge of the balcony. The rising lights of the city flickered, and he whispered in Harry's ear. "Welcome to the wilder world of the undead, officially."

Chapter Thirty-Six

By twilight, twenty-fours after the beginning of their journey, the scar faded to nothing; the door for discovery was closed. Rick and Matt followed Harry back to his apartment. As Harry unlocked the door, he asked in subtones. "Do you think Lizbet waited for me?"

Rick stepped forward, stood in the doorway and scented the room. "Gone, been gone a while. We just wanted to walk you down and see that you had what you needed. Perhaps you'd like a little privacy between now and going to ground?"

◆◆◆◆

Matt closed Harry's front door and gestured Rick to go ahead of him toward the elevator. Rick pressed the call button and looked at the thumb he'd sliced to administer the curative to Harry. He raised a sorrowful gaze to Matt. "You know? That curative is basically a truth serum…"

Matt stood with his hands splayed on his hips, his head back, giving Rick a half-lidded gaze. His lips straightened and grew to a lopsided grin. "Yah got something to tell me, Pops?"

Rick hung his head and shuffled one foot. "I've had my eye on Heather, your patrol woman donor…"

"You're into uniforms now?"

"The way she wears it, yeah. I think she's given me some, you know, eye contact."

"Eye contact? I see."

"So, if you could give her up on your rotation next month, I'd throw in two dozen roses for your next demonstration…"

Matt placed a considering finger against his lips. "Meh? What else you got?"

The elevator door opened with mortals inside, Rick and Matt stepped back and let it pass. Rick shrugged. "Are you talking yachts, cars, donors for a weekend?"

"Flying lessons."

Rick began to nod in agreement until Matt finished.

"And a helicopter."

"What?"

"I'll have to find a whole new donor. It's not like Heather will want to leave once you've had her…"

"As long as we run it as a business expense, you've got a deal."

Matt dealt him side-eye. "Anything else you want to confess?"

Rick bounded on the balls of his loafers. "No, I can't afford any other confessions."

♦♦♦♦

Lizbet sat entranced by every detail of Harry's eight decades. *How incredible would it be to live all this history without growing old and feeble? Harry's as vital now as he was when he came home from the war. He could be anything he wanted to be, Doctor, Lawyer, Merchant, Thief.*

She stacked carefully printed info beginning with census records showing his parent's Angelino Heights address, the marriage license for Dorothy and Arnold, birth record for Valerie Craft, Henry VanAlt Jr.'s death certificate, and property records showing the Craft family residence.

She was there as Harry recounted his memories, but these documents proved it was not imagination.

♦♦♦♦

Harry regarded the perfectly cleaned apartment, each item back to its usual perfection. The Murphy bed was back in the wall, although he caught Lizbet's perfumed aura. He showered while listening to his nineteen forties playlists. Now the songs meant something. They conjured faces, events, and more powerfully, images.

Once he was in his robe, Harry pulled his first book from the shelf. The slipcover was worn, and the musty smell made him sneeze when he sat down beside his fountain wall to read.

He read the dedication to his parents and chuckled. *Sure, Mom was okay with my writing, but to Dad? This was putting off my adulthood.*

The week he began the book, Harry moved into a dingy studio befitting a starving writer. In his mind's eye, he walked through the small room in a converted mansion near the university. The landlady had only two rules, no women above the foyer and no hot plates. If he wanted to eat, he had to be at the table at six on the dot. He was happy to comply

228

with both rules, and he was pleased to be out from under his father's thumb.

He finished reading the book by four in the morning. After the last couple of days, he wasn't going to make it until dawn. He was a new vampire, and this vampire was going to ground early. His last recollection was seeing the clock at '4:07'.

◆◆◆◆

Harry felt the pull of twilight and sat upright in his mausoleum. The apartment was graveyard quiet. The refrigerator cycled off. The air conditioner picked up. There was the musical sound of the fountain that separated his kitchen from the proper dining room. Evening traffic scripted an odd song of horns and engines as vehicles coursed up and down Wilshire. Dressing quickly, he quietly slid open the door of his mausoleum.

No time to be involved at Consort Group International's Gaoler. *Or is there time to trade tricks for a meal from a willing donor?* He took the blood from his fridge in a glass over to the sofa. *Okay, where's this power Matt and Rick talked about?* He waited for any extraordinary perceptions.

◆◆◆◆

As he stared through the dancing water, sipping his dinner, Harry leaned back and tensed. He was prepared to restrain himself if he caught certain vibes off Lizbet. She was too precious to hurt, or worse, frighten off.

It would be an extraordinary experience if they pulled the trigger on continuing their relationship. *But tonight is talking, getting the new rules out in the open.*

Harry always sensed Lizbet felt comfortable in his mid-century flat. His manner seemed to turn her on, especially since Harry wasn't stuck in the era's chauvinism. Yes, he did enjoy Lizbet in her luscious vintage undergarments as much as she savored the sight of his suits, and yes, his sock garters.

Sensing her leaving the elevator, his hand flew to his heart at his overpowering awareness. *Between the new 'skills' and her magnetism, she twists me up.* He stood there in his jeans and a cashmere sweater, catching a view of himself in the hall mirror. Harry hadn't even put on socks when he slid into his loafers. With a stroke of twisted optimism, he was commando.

The high definition security monitor appeared even sharper as he watched her on the screen. Lizbet's dark hair shone like she carried the sunset. Building her courage to press the doorbell, she bit her bottom lip.

Harry opened the door. "Hello." She didn't move. He had to extend his hand out to her. "You left a message you wanted to talk?"

"I'm sorry I flaked out on you. I wasn't prepared for the marathon." She stood there in an outfit he'd never seen. Navy stilettos, white linen crop pants painted over her curvaceous legs, a navy and white French-style sailor's sweater, and a chunky chain necklace. Tiny gold anchor earrings swung as she stood, waiting to be invited in.

"Come on in." He stepped aside and scented her optimistic apprehension. "Wine?" He led her to the kitchen, where she leaned a shapely hip against the island.

"Will you join me?" She held her purse in front of her, like a pointless shield. He extended his left hand to her in an invitation to join him over at the shelves of wine bottles. "You pick tonight."

"You look fantastic, Harry. Like a new man." She turned to the wine rack and chose a jammy Malbec. He felt her contemplative gaze as he opened and poured the wine in silence. Harry paused and rested both hands flat on the counter, his head down.

"Everything okay, Harry?"

His aristocratic nose twitched, and he ran a thumb over his full bottom lip before he raised his head.

"Lizbet, you were there for the majority of my recollections. But afterward, it was just the undead, Rick and Matt sat me down and explained that I've been using a small percentage of my vampiric powers. The man you knew was Harry Lite. Now I'm Harry 2.0."

Her brow raised, and she held her wineglass without drinking. "How different can that be…"

"I don't know. I guess it's something we'll find out together."

She put down her wine. His ornery woman wrapped her arms around her waist, and her gaze danced at the intrigue of their discussion. "Your eyes turn the most incredible color. You get a wild look in them, too."

"That was the old me. You're telling me you didn't notice the grave pallor or the marked roadmap of veins?" He retreated against the back counter, his muscled arms folded over his broad chest.

She waved it off. "Not really. I was absorbed by your command of my body."

"The night I rescued you, that rogue genuinely scared you, there was no turn on."

"That night, he was trying to kill me. There was no romance."

Harry nodded his head. "You had reason to be afraid. He was intimidating."

"To put it mildly. I thought I was going to die until you pulled him off me. Harry, what's the subtext here?"

His voice darkened as it dropped a register. "This discovery I went through. I'm going to be a different vampire now. More…"

"Unleashed? More aware of your power?"

"Exactly, and we're only sexy in the movies." His gaze traveled to the double doors at the far end of the flat. "Here, without the special effects and the film soundtrack, my strength can cripple you. My cries can terrify you." His voice was barely a whisper as her expression sobered.

"And I need to know this because?" After she drew in a long breath, she swallowed a long draw of wine. At his silence, she drained the glass, poured more, and guzzled it.

"What stresses you, Lizbet?" His gaze pierced her bravado.

"You keep saying this." Her posture toughened up, and she took a step toward him.

"I realize that. It's in your sweat, your saliva, and other places…" Harry circled to the other side of the island.

"I'm drowning here, Harry. If you can scent me, I can only assume you're flat out ignoring my acceptance."

Harry exhaled unnecessarily and flinched. "I'm getting that through both nostrils, Lizbet. Your scent is enough to send me into an ice-cold shower. I thought it was intense before, but now… Anyway, every time we're together, I'm awestruck."

"So, we're talking… after everything that happened, did you invite me back to…"

"To ask you to be with me… to be my lover?"

Lizbet let go of the breath she held. "I was worried I wasn't the mortal you want to get horizontal with. Oh, Harry, you had me worried."

Harry bent his head and pinched the bridge of his nose. "But is this sex, or is this romance?" He wasn't a fan of casual sex. He'd done that before.

"You can scent me, you tell me." Lizbet's eyes watered, and she held herself tightly. "I've tried to not connect you saving my life to my feelings. I've tried not to crush on your looks and your manners. But deep inside this progressive and uncompromising woman, is a girl who wants her car doors opened for her. She wants that gentle hand at the small of her back when we walk. I want the Rat Pack era gentleman, who's just the other side of dangerous."

"The other side of danger? You make me sound like an action film star." Harry demurred.

"I do like your brand of action."

"Well, that's a relief."

"Seriously, Harry, how long do marriages last these days? Three? Five years? What if I was a vampire? Would it be different?"

"I'm getting mixed signals, Betts. You quote disappointing stats on marriage, and then you talk about turning? What do you want from me?"

"I've spent the day researching you. Do you know there are several Harry VanAlt conspiracy theories?"

Harry cocked his head. "No, I didn't."

"I realize you didn't ask to be this…" She pointed to her canine teeth. "But your life could be phenomenal. If it hasn't been, you have new opportunities. You could live a lifetime in every place that has ever fascinated you."

He shrugged. "I suppose I could. I never thought about it. My friends are here… Believe it or not, vampire travel takes some preparation."

Lizbet poured more wine and shook her head, her long black hair danced over her shoulders. "News flash, dude. Mortal travel takes some preparation. But time is not on my side like it is for you."

"Leading me to wonder if you might ask for that turn…"

"I've been thinking about this all afternoon."

Frustrated, Harry raised a hand. "How long did you take to make a decision about your college major?"

"I don't know. I was headed into law. I took a class on abnormal psychology, and it was like I opened a door. I knew profiling was for me. In a way, I guess you could say I've been majoring in 'mortal' for thirty-four years, and a door has opened."

Harry frowned. "I think you need a few more afternoons to think about it."

"Since your teams don't go door to door with pamphlets, who can I talk to if it's not you?"

Harry scrubbed his hand down his face. "Not Matt." Lizbet drained the wine bottle into her glass and pointed to another bottle on the rack. Harry nodded. "Yeah, we don't have a welcome wagon. There's always Venus, your friend in leather."

"She's not as big and bad as she thinks she is. Men are intimidated by women in leather. I'll bet she has a gooey center."

Harry gave her a jaundiced look. "Okay."

"So, knowing what I've said tonight, have I frightened you off?" She looked up at him through coal-black lashes.

"Me? No. I was worried I'd frighten you off."

"We're on the record, neither of us is frightened."

Harry smiled blandly. *You should be.*

"Let me show you what I found out today…" She picked up the bottle of wine and spread the contents of her large purse on the coffee table.

"You scrapbook?" Harry circled the coffee table and sat on the sofa next to her.

"Oh, no, but your conspiracy theorists do." She opened the book to reveal his military history and photos. She sat back for him to take his time.

"Where did you find this?"

"A quirky place in the arts district. The man seemed to think I'd take possession of these artifacts and be dead within a week. Now that I think about it…"

Harry lifted the book into his lap and laughed. "Abducted by aliens? I hate it when that happens. All that probing."

"How about taken to a dark opps prison, ever done that over a weekend? How are you on formulating Commie plots?"

"I've never even bitten a Russian."

Lizbet turned to the back of the scrapbook where the things she printed were in chronological order. "Your parent's home is for sale. Would you like to have me schedule a private showing? Just for old times' sake?"

"I think everyone has a sentimental tug when it comes to seeing the house they grew up in. Other than that, I haven't been in that house for fifty-two years. Sure, schedule it."

Chapter Thirty-Seven

Lizbet scheduled the home's private showing at four in the afternoon on a Saturday. The day was mercifully cloudy in deference to Harry's 'allergy' to sunlight. Lizbet drove her SUV down the street Harry had traveled thousands of times on foot. Large trees almost hid the majority of the houses. Their roots heaved the sidewalks.

"The houses are so colorful." Harry gasped as they drove along.

"I thought painted ladies were always colorful."

"Trust me, not like this." As they pulled into his home's driveway, he pointed to the house next door. "Colonel Hedlund would never have approved of a purple home." He gestured to his house. "For that matter. My Dad would have a conniption with all those shades of blue. When I grew up, the house was beige and white."

"That's so wrong. All those architectural details stand out better with vibrant colors."

They climbed out of the car, and Harry stared at the kaleidoscope of colors along the street. "I can't argue with you there. What a difference." He pulled down his baseball cap and adjusted his dark sunglasses. Holding out his hand, he asked, "Ready for this, Betts?" She nodded, and they walked silently up the wide walkway to the broad front porch steps.

The Realtor came to the screen door. "Mr. and Mrs. Mitchell?"

Harry stopped mid-step, and Lizbet pulled him along. "Yes, that's us."

Harry stood on the porch and turned slowly, regarding all the patched gingerbread. He could tell where pieces had been copied and spliced by the thickness of the paint. Within his reverie, he hadn't noticed Lizbet walking off with the Realtor. In a few minutes, the nicely dressed woman walked to the porch swing and said, "Your wife is waiting for you, Mr. Mitchell. I'll be out here if you need anything."

The haunted vampire pulled open the door of his past. The foyer that ran from front to back had refinished wood floors showing wear from so many trips to the kitchen. His grasp on the banister proved it was repaired and tight. The walls were freshly painted; his Mother's carefully chosen ornate wallpaper was a memory.

Lizbet met him in the kitchen, holding a house fact sheet. "All these light fixtures have been rewired, and the appliances were refurbished so they could keep the original look."

Harry walked to the back screen door and recalled his Sundays with the newspaper. "They did a nice job on the granite countertops; we had linoleum." He tapped his foot on the pine floor. "I expect these wood floors were under our linoleum."

Harry felt a peculiar disconnection. He was born in this house, yet it was no longer his home, and he was accepting of that.

"Do you want to see anything else?" Lizbet tilted her head sympathetically.

"One more place." Harry turned on his heel and headed up the back stairs. His parent's room was smaller than he remembered. His bedroom was downright claustrophobic. He went to the window and drew back the drape. Aside from the bold purple, the house next door looked much the same as it always had. Directly across from his window was Dotty's childhood window; it had become Valerie's room in later years. He looked inside the small closet, and the inscription HV + DH was still carved into the closet's sidewall. He ran a finger over it and scoffed sadly.

He took the front stairs two at a time and called out. "Honey, I'm ready." Lizbet smirked and shook her head as they walked outside. Lizbet excused herself to talk to the Realtor reading on the porch swing.

Harry stood, hands in his baseball jacket, cap pulled low, his memories flying through his mind, a video on fast-forward. He heard Lizbet make polite excuses about the home, but he saw her slip the Realtor a business card. They silently descended the porch stairs, and he guided her to the large sycamore in the front yard. "I wonder if my treehouse is still here?"

Lizbet looked straight up the tall branches. "I see a plank thing up there."

"Yeah, that was my treehouse. You have to have an imagination."

Lizbet shook her head at him. "Sorry."

A reedy call from an elderly voice floated across the lawn at them. "Harry!" He turned toward the Hedlund home. "Harry VanAlt."

Harry's undead heart stopped. She would be eighty years old now, but Harry would know her in the dark. "Dotty." He mumbled.

Lizbet gasped. "The Dotty?"

Under Dotty's spell, Harry sunk his hands into his trouser pockets and walked across the grass to the porch railing. She sat on an outdoor rattan sofa wearing a light green velveteen tracksuit that matched her eyes. Her once platinum hair was in a silver bob to her chin. She wore a rosy pink lipstick and orthopedic sneakers.

The home attendant walked to the porch railing as Harry approached. "I'm sorry, sir, our Dotty gets confused some days. We don't mean to interrupt your tour."

"It's alright. I love meeting neighbors. Would she mind if I visited for a bit?"

Lizbet caught up to Harry and spoke to the caregiver. "Is the homeowner here? Could I talk to them about the neighborhood?"

The attendant smiled. "As long as you folks will stay here with Dotty, I'd be happy to ask Miss Valerie if she has a moment to speak with you."

At the mention of Miss Valerie, Harry's chin tucked to his chest, and he bit his bottom lip. He did not expect to find Dotty there or face his daughter. Lizbet followed the caregiver to the settee near the front door. Harry walked to Dotty on the couch and sat beside her.

She looked up at him with still clear, peridot green eyes. "Our little girl is all grown up now."

"It's good to see you, Dotty. You look well."

"You've been gone a long time, Harry. What brings you back? Are you here to take me home?" A shadow of fear passed over her eyes.

"What do you mean?" Harry slipped his sunglasses into the neck of his sweater and tucked his hat into his jacket pocket. "I'm not like that, Dotty."

Dotty reached up and finger-combed his hat hair. "You're wearing your hair a little longer these days. Is that what the men are doing?"

Harry grinned. "I guess so. Your hair is different too."

The years dropped away from her as she fluffed her hair and gave him a flirty smile. "Do you like it?"

Harry kissed her parchment cheek. "It's beautiful."

The screen door creaked, and Lizbet and Valerie emerged. Harry's jaw dropped embarrassingly as his grown daughter approached him. He rose as the image of his mother stood before him.

"It's so kind of you to spend time chatting with Mother."

Harry nodded his head. "It's my pleasure."

Valerie's head tilted in recognition. "Do I know you?"

"I don't believe we've ever met."

Dotty caught her cane in her hand and tapped it twice on the floor. "Valerie, you can catch handsome men anywhere. This one is mine. Now chat it up with his wife while we sit a spell." Lizbet and Harry buried a laugh. "Bring me our photo album."

Valerie smiled at Lizbet. "This time of day, Mom and I have tea, why don't you come in and we'll choose one." She turned to Dotty. "Mom, I'll have Mary bring you the album."

Harry sat back at the end of the sofa so he could take in all of Dotty's mannerisms. She playfully barked at him. "Now that you're here sit closer to me." She patted the cushion closer to her.

The caregiver brought the album, and Dotty held it to her chest. "Let me show you what's been happening..."

♦♦♦♦

Two hours later, as they were making their good-byes, Valerie held Harry's pre-warmed hands and stared into his blue-green eyes. "Do you narrate books on tape? I swear I recognize your voice from somewhere."

"You're correct, I do. I generally read for the Author M.C. Westmacott. Do you read true-crime?"

Valerie stepped back and smiled confidently. The tilt of her chin, her upright posture the same as his long-dead Mother's. "I write murder mysteries. Maybe I could convince you to narrate some of mine."

Dottie tapped her cane. "Someone help me up. I'm not going to let Harry leave without a hug."

Harry lifted her in his arms, and she stood solidly with his arm around her. He felt her hand resting naturally around his waist.

With a thin birdy finger, Dotty pointed to her daughter. "Your father always had a wonderful voice. You should hear him sing," Dotty turned to Harry and drew her fingertips affectionately down his jaw. "Thank you, Harry, for your visit. Can I talk you out of a kiss?" She lingered in the embrace when Harry kissed her cheek. "I may be old, but I know handsome when I see it." She turned to Lizbet. "Don't let this one get away."

Chapter Thirty-Eight

Lizbet drove in silence as she watched Harry absorbing every image from his old neighborhood. Once she entered the freeway, she spoke. "Do you think Dotty really knew who you were?"

"Oh, yeah. The old girl knew exactly who I was. Time dropped away like a towel at the beach. With her dementia, she's living in 1946."

Lizbet spoke with grim determination. "I never want to go through that. I never want to be old and look at you thinking I'm still young."

Harry watched her pinched expression. He removed his cap, ran a frustrated hand through his hair and sighed. "Can you break that down, Betts?"

"Maybe I never want to grow old at all, whether you're in the picture or not. I've always worried I wouldn't have enough time to do everything I want to do."

Harry nodded judiciously. "You want to be turned."

Her agreement was immediate and firm. "Yes." She took her eyes off the road to search his face. "Can you do that?"

"I've never even thought about turning anyone. I wouldn't know the first thing."

She raised one hand off the steering wheel now that she focused fiercely on the road. "That building you live in is crawling with the undead. Somebody has to know something." Her hand flew in a frustrated gesture.

"I could ask. I have friends who are Responders."

"Great, the people whose clerical error stole your last fifty years are going to begin my eternity?"

"One, they are different people. And two, after this week's fallout, those folks are out of a job. But nothing is foolproof."

"Good, I won't ask a fool to turn me."

♦♦♦♦

Harry waved good-bye to Lizbet as she drove off grim-lipped. They hadn't spoken a word since she said she wouldn't ask a fool to turn her. He was no fool, but he wasn't a recruiter for the undead. Who cuts a diamond perfectly on their first try? It was like pancakes. He remembered standing on a chair as his mother showed him how to pour the right amount of batter and good Lord, have the patience for the batter to set before you flipped it. No wonder they called childrearing, 'The Pancake Method', the first kid was the throwaway.

Harry bolted for Rick's penthouse. His fist nearly went through the door. *Dang, I've never done that.* The speaker beside the door crackled to life. "VanAlt, what do you want at this hour?"

"Open the door, Rick." His usually cheerful voice sounded a register deeper in his command. The door flew open, and standing in the foyer, Rick and a sweet young vampress swapped spit.

The brunette unlocked lips and coyly sighed. "Call me, okay?" Harry watched Rick tighten his robe belt as the lady shimmied past him.

"Coitus interruptus is a crime punishable by staking. Why are you banging on my door while I'm pre-banging the lovely Delores?"

Harry stood his full six-foot-two height and folded his arms over his chest. "She wants me to turn her. Go ahead, stake me, and I'll be unavailable."

"Could be sticky. A relationship as a sire is a good deal more serious than a boyfriend." He ushered Harry inside. Rick walked to the fridge for dinner, hands dancing over his head as if working equations in the air. "After the week you've had, this is the takeaway?"

Harry leaned on the kitchen counter. "It's her takeaway. I told you she was intense."

Rick's brow rose as he slid a glass of blood toward Harry. "If you love her and you want her, her bond in this undead family will be stronger if she has a different sire." Harry shook his head in denial. "Harry, you're spreading her connections broader. If something were to happen to you, she'd still feel included..."

"I don't want anyone else to turn her. If she wants this, I'll be the one!"

Rick pointed at him and smirked. "A minute ago, you were ready to hide. I mention her building relationships in the family with a different sire and bingo; you want her."

The two men stared each other down as they drank. "I lost the love of my life when a parent stood between us. There will be no one between us in our relationship."

Rick's measuring gaze bore into Harry a moment longer, and then he lightened with his customary grin. "Then, you'll need this book." He walked into the living room and pulled a pocket-sized leather-bound book from a top-shelf. He held it to his heart. "Today, you are a man." His grin crooked, and then he shook his head. "Seriously, lad, I've never had the occasion to do this. I'm no authority. But I understand the process is not that difficult."

Harry looked doubtfully at the book in his hands. After a few moments, his brows knit. "This looks too simple."

Rick shrugged. "Right, the earth should be crawling with undead. But it's like making a baby; there's the fun part and then the next lifetime to worry about. And you will worry about her because you'll have a blood bond."

Harry ran a hand through his hair, and he stood tall. "I'll take her to Big Bear."

Rick walked back to pour another glass of dinner. "Matt's place? Are you telling him what you're doing before or after you ask for the keys?"

Harry tucked the pocket-sized book into his breast pocket and grinned. "I'm not stupid."

Rick bent over with laughter. "Yes, indeed, today you are a man. But seriously, place your order for plenty of … what's her blood type?"

Harry gave a thumbs up. "A Positive, I'll order plenty of it."

♦♦♦♦

Harry rode down to the twenty-eighth floor, feeling the weight of his thoughts propelled him to a few hours of reading. Within his apartment's silence, he poured over each page printed in 1860. On paper, none of it is difficult; her education and her socializing into the family would be the tricky part. This was his last thought as he went to ground.

Harry spent a day in seclusion contemplating the implications of turning his lover. The silence went both ways, there were no phone messages between them. He knew he would have to take the first move.

243

The next evening when he rose, Harry showered, shaved, and dressed in her favorite suit, the royal blue double-breasted. He caught his keys off the hook and left to claim his destiny.

He dropped the top of his beast of a car and headed toward her bungalow. Her neighborhood street was relatively silent at nine-thirty when he pulled into Lizbet's driveway. Harry winced at the thought of his next trick. *Hope Eddie understands romance.*

He cued up every version of Cole Porter's, "At Long Last Love", on his iPod. Then he dialed up the car's powerful sound system and pressed play.

At Julie London's sultry voice, Lizbet's porch light went on. Her home was dark. Harry clearly saw her silhouette in the living room window.

House lights along the street came on. People looked from behind draperies. Some came out on their porches in their robes with disapproving frowns.

Harry's decision to sit on the car's hood until she acknowledged him looked worse with every verse. With his new awareness of sounds, by Frank Sinatra's version he realized the sentiment perfectly described the uncertainty of falling in love. He hoped she came to the door before the seventh recording artist, or he'd have to restart the playlist. He'd be damned if he got off this car hood without her running to him.

He watched her move within the house. *Damn, this enhanced vampire vision is coming in handy.* By the time Lena Horne had his undead heart fluttering, Lizbet's door flew open.

She leaned against the doorframe, shaking her head at him. "Is this song supposed to mean something?"

Harry's hands flew up in surrender. "You tell me. What do you think?"

Eddie stood in his bathrobe at the side of his porch. "Not to butt in, but Lizbet, I think the man is proposing. You need to answer him before ten P.M., or someone will report you." Eddie shook with laughter.

Harry dialed down the volume. "Am I a fool, Betts? If I am, I'm your fool."

She ran to his arms, nearly knocking him back flat on the hood of the car. He had her in a loving grip and rolled her into his lap. "I never called you a fool." His lips smothered hers. "I never thought you were a fool." She squeaked out.

"Will you spend a few lifetimes with me? You know until you get on your feet and decide what you want to do?"

Her hands caught his handsome face, and she rubbed noses with him. "Yes, Harry, I will. I get to pick the first destination, right?"

"Our first destination will be Big Bear."

She smiled, nodding at the portent. "When?" Her emerald green eyes flashed lovingly.

Harry nodded toward her neighbor's home. "You have some arrangements to make for Minka. Want to ask Eddie while he's watching us smooch?"

Lizbet jumped off Harry's lap and ran across the yard to Eddie's porch railing. She was back in a flash, and Eddie waved goodbye as he went inside and turned off his porchlight.

"What'd you tell him?"

"I told him you were sweeping me away for a lifetime of extensive travel, and Minka needed a new home. He was delighted to have her. He has keys; he'll move her over."

"How about tomorrow? That will give you time to quit your job."

Lizbet shrugged. "That's an email. They'll be fine without me."

Harry caressed her soft cheek with the back of his hand. "Pack your warm clothes. You have to look mortal. After tomorrow the cold won't bother you anymore." He lovingly kissed her forehead as she hugged him with all her might.

♦♦♦♦

On the evening's ride up, Lizbet was a bundle of nerves despite trying to appear nonchalant. Harry was electrified by the intensity of her vibrations. He reached across and caught her hand. After kissing her fingertips, he rested her hand on his thigh. "We're going to stay here until you're comfortable with feeding. This community is relaxed enough for you to get used to mortals with your new enhanced senses and abilities. You'll enjoy the cold…"

"Well, how long will that be? Days, weeks?"

"You'll know when you feel it. No rush. Mortals may get on your nerves until you learn to block out the heartbeats, their breathing, their constant chatter, the sounds of appliances, dogs, all the things that make a community."

"Wow. Did I ever ask you if you could walk across a ceiling?"

Harry cocked his head and buried his laughter. "Even Frank Langella needed special effects for that. We're not spiders or bats."

Lizbet nestled closer to him, "I can't wait to find out all the things we can do."

♦♦♦♦

Harry parked his car and led her to the front door. "Matt told me he sent us a gift. I have no idea what it is. He said we have to find it before we get started."

Lizbet hugged him sweetly. "Matt's an outstanding sport about all this." She followed Harry as he walked from room to room. At the end of the hall, the door to his usual mausoleum opened to reveal a commercial double-wide freezer on its back on a platform. The double glass doors wore exquisite fresh snowflake patterns of frost.

Harry opened one side. "Matt listened to me, and he had everything built exactly the way I described it to him a few weeks ago."

"Wow, is that a mattress? Do we do stuff in there? I thought you said you lay down and turned off."

"We do, but now, we do it in temperature-controlled comfort."

Chapter Thirty-Nine

Harry brought the luggage from the car and dropped it in the standard mortal bedroom. He returned to the living room and emptied his pockets, dropping his keys, watch and wallet on the bar. As he walked to the refrigerator, he asked. "Need something to unwind? Perhaps a cocktail? A snack?"

Lizbet stood, pulling off her gloves, hat, and jacket. She shook out her long black hair and hugged herself. "No, nothing, let's get this done."

Harry closed the fridge door, repeating her demand. "Let's get this done?" His brows drew together, and his head inclined sharply. "You're counting on all my instincts, instincts that have just been unlocked." Harry caught her sweetly, tucking her head under his chin as a muscle quivered in his jaw. "I love you, Betts. I hope you know doing this proves how much I love you."

Lizbet's body melted into his embrace. Lightly, he fingered a tendril of her hair. His undead heart, previously unheard by her, now thrummed deeply like a song's bass line. "I can tell you sense my anxiety from the way it's twisting you up here." She tapped his chest.

"Right. You're right." He nodded, not seeking her gaze. "I felt you. We can eat afterward." His fingers strummed her arm tenderly.

She turned a slow circle surveying the beautifully appointed lodge home. "I read the book while you drove." She walked from window to window watching the moon's reflection ripple on the dark lake, and then and turned back to him. "I know you have to be well-fed, are you well-fed? The anticipation is driving me up a wall, without special effects. Can we get this done, please?"

Harry looked at her sympathetically. "Wow, let me grab a tumbler for me, and let's go relax." He held up his glass and caught her hand in his. "There's a lovely garden tub back here. It's comfortable and a perfect place for you to transition. We can begin with warm water and then cooler water afterward."

"Relax…" She snorted. "Not till this is over…" She pressed into his arms and grabbed his lapels. "I know I've made this decision freely, but until I come out on the other side, I'm a wreck. Thanks, handsome, for understanding my jitters."

Harry held her gently in his arms. "Then let's get this done." He rolled the stainless steel cooler into the expansive bathroom and dialed down the lights.

"Is this happening in the dark?" She halted undressing.

"When you wake up, the lights will be too bright. You wouldn't want it brighter than this."

She nodded somberly. "Okay…"

Harry ran warm water and sprinkled organic lavender and clary sage oils into the tub. "Just for you, a few stress-fixers."

She watched him undress. "Were you in this good of shape before you were turned?"

"All we consume is protein. I'm a lot leaner since 1951. I've never seen a chunky vampire." He dropped the last of his clothes in the hamper and pulled towels and robes out of the linen closet.

"I have fixated on these last five pounds for weeks. You have no idea how good your news sounds." Her clothes dropped off faster than he'd ever seen her disrobe.

He held out his arms. "From the moment I met you, you've been perfect. Absolutely perfect." Lizbet glided in, and they kissed affectionately, but without the urgency to make love.

In her mind, Lizbet was overcome with the thought that he would be the man who would love her after death. His waist was such a comfortable place for her arms.

Their gazes swept over each other in silence as he led her down into the tub. He stood, one foot in the swirling water, his hand out to her. "Let me take you into the night…"

She took his hand, and their bodies melded like yang and yin. They nestled in the swirling water and looked out the broad picture window. The moon was high over the black water; trees were silhouetted against the indigo sky, and snow shimmered on the mountain caps. "What a beautiful sight to behold -- I'll always remember it." Harry caressed her, moving her in various positions to see what would be the most comfortable for the turn.

Lizbet wore her long dark hair twisted up in a clip, and she made faces while he maneuvered her. "Hey, are we swimming, or are we getting this done?"

"I don't want you uncomfortable."

"Handsome, please, I read the book. I know that right before I die, I'm going to panic. You're bigger and stronger, and I know you'll take care of me. Let's just get this done."

◆◆◆◆

My God, I've never seen her so anxious. Does this mean it's the right thing or the wrong thing for her? Maybe she's right; I should just do this."

Harry drew her into his lap. This wasn't getting done without some of the pre-feeding pleasantries. He knew how to treat his donors. This was going past donating. "Let me hold you, won't you kiss me this last time, your warm lips against mine? It's going to be different the next time we love, Betts."

Her hand glided down his cheek as she found a comfortable position in his arms. "That's what you promised me. Besides, I always made you hot." Their lips melded in her last mortal kiss, and then she watched as his features chilled. His long eyelashes fluttered open to reveal opalescent eyes, his smile revealed long, ivory fangs. She reached toward one fang and pricked her finger. "I'm going to have to bite more than that, Betts." He suckled that finger and released it with a reverent smile.

Harry caught her neck in his hand and tilted her head to the side. Her veins were a delightful throbbing presence to his enhanced sight. His lips descended for a tasting kiss, and when his other hand caressed her body and pulled her to him, he bit.

True to his education, her initial response, without a sexual preamble, was panic. He held her tightly against his chest and drew steadily. Her heartbeat bounded, and with his careful suckling gradually diminished. He felt her life force flowing within him, warming him, and delighting his undead heart with her love for what they would be. Her body lay heavy in his arms, and he paused, his lips over his punctures as he listened for her heart's last beat.

The silence rocked his psyche. *I have to get this right.*

He bit deep into his wrist, jumpstarting an almost mortal blood flow. He pressed his bleeding wrist to her full lips and prayed. *This better work.* Harry looked at the two of them, naked and vulnerable in a place that was usually a sensual playground. Silence. *This has to work.*

Chapter Forty

Lizbet lay back in his arms and closed her eyes. *Wow, what was that?* The bite was harsher than Harry's nibble for sexual release. *Whew.* It was electric, and it sent her down a thick warm river. She was caressed and coddled into another cosmos. No sound, no light, just floating in warmth and well-being.

A pinpoint of light expanded, and she saw the tunnel with many other mortals headed away from her. She'd read about this and knew it was vital to her vampiric eternity to resist the tunnel's magnetism.

How would I explain to my family that I was trading eternity in the clouds with them for a vampire's immortality?

She mentally shrugged. If she was flying to London, she wouldn't begrudge the people flying to Paris.

The ripping at her throat sent her into a rolling sensation of chills as Harry withdrew every warm drop of her blood. Still, this slide toward death was euphoric. Her soul shuddered with the power of a cosmic orgasm. She soared past stars riding new ecstasies.

Lizbet heard, or did she feel Harry's prayer 'I have to get this right'? Celestial energy surged through her, stirring her bit by bit. Heavenly vitality filled every atom of her being. With exceptional grace, her spirit drifted toward her body.

She blinked at Harry and realized her lips suckled at his wrist. At the flutter of her eyelashes, he caught her closer to his chest, and he kissed her forehead.

"I wish I had a picture of you right now. You are devastatingly gorgeous." She tried to say thank you, but he shook his head. "Drink, keep drinking." He smoothed back a loose tendril of her hair and blessed her forehead with so many kisses she lost count.

Her body was weak, but Lizbet felt an endorphin rush surge through every limb. She didn't feel cold—quite the opposite. Harry's blood wasn't just sustenance; it held their emotional bond in every drop. His blood strengthened her. Now his confidence, kindness, and appreciation flowed through her veins. She wrapped her hands around Harry's wrist and drew it back, her tiny fangs emerging for the first time.

Harry's nose crinkled with a grin. "Aren't you the cutest little baby vampire?" He cuddled and rocked her in the tub, splashing water over the sides.

"I've been described many ways, but never cute. Also, you bite my neck, and I have to chew on your wrist?"

He held her back and regarded her in totality. "Same snarky Lizbet, now in an immortal form."

She worked on sitting up in his arms. "Whoa, I've got a little disconnection here." She startled like a newborn and then settled into his embrace. "Head rush." She stretched luxuriously. "I feel wonderful. Do you feel like this all the time?"

"Having had a complete blood transfusion, I'm feeling pretty fresh myself." Harry's expression was triumphantly smug. "Of course, I've never had this much estrogen flowing in these veins, and you're getting the testosterone rush."

"Whatever it is, I like it." She leaned over Harry to climb out of the tub and floundered like a baby giraffe.

"Take it easy there, grace, let me carry you to bed." He rose with her in his arms as she caught his face in both hands and covered him in kisses.

"Put me down, I feel like running…"

"Have another drink, then tell me what you want to do." He wrapped her in her fluffy robe and nestled her in the mountain of pillows on the king-sized bed. He came back with two glasses, and she was out of the bathrobe, looking at her hands, her feet, her belly.

"Everything looks so different. I can see every vein in my body…"

Harry passed her the glass and listened to her litany of questions. "This must be what parents go through with the terrible twos."

"You're telling me I'm terrible? I don't think I like that." She stalled before she drank her glass of blood. "Am I going to like this? Will it taste like you?"

Harry sat on the side of the bed and inclined his head closer. "I tasted like you because I consumed all of your blood. This tastes like a twenty-two-year-old soccer player from UCLA."

She crinkled her nose. "Will I taste his secrets?"

Harry shrugged. "We won't know what your unique ability will be for a few weeks. With your career experience, you might just feel more of what makes you a good profiler now." They settled together on the bed. "I'm hoping you don't become a telepath. That's a grind."

"The cold feels so good." Her eyes widened. "Let's go build snowmen, naked on the lawn."

"Naked snowmen?"

"No, us naked."

"When I said the neighborhood tolerated vampires, I didn't mean we had free run of the place. About as far as we can push it? Walking from the house to the spa tub naked."

"Bathing suits then?"

"We have to pass. Jeans and a sweater, don't forget your shoes."

"Well, you're no fun. I might as well stay in bed and wait for you to ravish me."

Harry tipped his cup up to drain the last of the blood, and his brow wagged at her. "That's my Betts. I'll open all the windows, so we get a fresh breeze."

She finished her cup. "This soccer player is very boring. Is anyone sexy in the fridge?" She slid to the end of the bed to dig in the cooler.

Harry leaned back and watched her take her wobbly first steps. "Take it easy."

"You told me we couldn't fly. Why do I feel like I can?" She took quick steps and ran into furniture. "Damn, I'm a clutz."

"Within an hour or two, your coordination will kick in. What are you digging for over there?"

Lizbet dropped to the floor and went through the cooler. "I don't know. An FBI agent? I always wanted to pick their buttoned-down brain." She read the labels on the bags. "27-year-old mixed martial arts instructor, grrr." She dropped the bag back into the cooler. "No ballerinas?"

"Some mortal donors exchange blood for cold hard cash at The Gaoler. We've found it's more flavorful if mortals have rip-roaring sex and then have their blood drawn. That means every bag of donor blood is a delicious wild card for jump-starting erotic adventures. I think I saw a pole dancer…" He crossed his hands behind his head and stretched his long legs out on the bed.

"As great as you look to me all buff and naked, I shouldn't drink pole dancer."

"Are you truly hungry, or are you just excited? You don't want to stuff-gut yourself. That isn't pretty."

Lizbet pulled herself up to her feet, and her hands flew out to steady her walk back to bed. "Yeah, Matt would probably charge a cleaning deposit." She fell back into Harry's arms and caressed his face with both hands. She sighed. "If there's a list of things I can't do, why don't I lay back and let you have your way with me?"

Harry winked at her. "If you insist." His arms encircled her and flipped her within a half-second. She squealed. "Vamp speed, remember?"

She lay on her back; her luxurious hair spread over the bedding. "You won't do everything fast, will you?"

"What I do fast, I can make up for with frequency." He balanced over her on his forearms and moved between her legs. His lively erection tickled at her sex as it glanced over her.

"Whoa, you're ready in a hurry, and I'm still figuring out my wiring."

His hand covered her sex. "Let me help you with that." He nuzzled her neck where he had bitten her, as his palm brushed lightly over her.

Sensations jolted her, and she shook. A wordless stream of sounds erupted from her lips. "That's the wiring I'm talking about. How am I going to walk without coming? Holy Mother."

"Why do you think vampires are portrayed as sensual? But remember, you'd have to bite to come."

"Right, right. You know, the first night you sat in my living room across from me, and you put your heel on your knee?" Harry's lips spread in a mischievous grin. "I saw that manspread of yours, and I just about melted into the sofa."

He rolled his hips over her teasingly. "I know that."

"What?"

"Vamp appeal works every time. Back then, I was just a vampire-lite. After what I recently went through, brace yourself, Betts, we're going to be in bed -- a lot."

She wiggled underneath him, and in a blink, her legs wrapped high around his waist, and she flipped him on his back.

"I see your coordination is coming in." Harry's hands roamed her soft skin. "Does this mean you want to be on top?"

♦♦♦♦

"I thought we'd share the billing. This is 2003. Let's see what these new reflexes can do."

Harry felt Lizbet's fingers playing in his hair, down his neck, and over his chest. The pressure of her hands sliding over his eight pack was heavenly frisson until she glanced over his nipples. She hesitated for a moment, gliding her palms over him. He lay, mesmerized by her loving curiosity, allowing her to do whatever she chose to do. Her hair tickled him as she hovered to kiss his nipple.

"Ummm." Her vibration rumbled straight to his cock. She moved her mouth to the other nipple and sucked it gently. He raised his arms in surrender. Lizbet smiled wolfishly at him. With two manicured fingertips, she outlined his lips. Her undead heart beat faster as she moved to straddle him. She rested her elbows on his shoulders and made lazy circles on his jaw with light strokes of her nails. "You're so pretty."

His expectant smile melted to a grimace. "You want to rephrase that?"

"No. With my new vision, you're beautiful. The better to see you with... and I want to see every part of you, now that I have that clever vamp sight."

His hand buried into her wealth of ebony hair. "God, you're so ..." He inhaled her transformed scent hungrily; her heart and body were ready for the epiphany of their eternal communion.

"Isn't it crazy how kissing is such a turn on?"

255

"It's our unperishing breath. Our blood bond connection. Each kiss unlocks our hearts." His fingers wrapped around the back of her neck as his hips bumped up. "Imagine everything else?"

Chapter Forty-One

Lizbet's lips parted beneath his. Both her hands splayed through Harry's expresso-dark hair, and her tongue ran over his lower lip. He savored the taste of her mouth. Her sighs reminded him of her appreciation of dark chocolate. He ran his tongue over one fang and shared the flavor of his intentions.

Harry carefully maneuvered out of her embrace. They gazed into each other's eyes in dreamy discovery. She made him burn in that particular way high school girls did under the bleachers. Her soft, rich lips were velvet sugar against his. Her body was strong and soft in all the right places.

His magnetism pulled her back to the mountain of pillows. Her thigh pressed against his groin, and his erection pulsed. She pushed in tighter and smiled against his lips as his hips pushed back of their own accord.

Harry began to pant. "Oh, God. Lizbet. Are you ready for this…? Maybe we should…wait. You need to know that this will be one wild ride. We've never had full out vampire sex."

She threw her hands up, rolled out of his embrace, and clapped her hands over her ears. "You just made me. This is what I was made for. Us, together like this."

Harry climbed back into the pillows. "How do you know? I'm not even prepared for what I can do. Will terrifying be appealing?"

Lizbet climbed back into his arms. "Nothing between us will be terrifying."

His eyes didn't meet hers for a second, and then he sought her gaze. She pouted at him intently, her face serious. *Is she hearing anything I'm telling her?* "Lizbet, you're a scamp. Get over here, right now."

Their playful clutches snapped into wrestling, full out. There was nothing hesitant about their familiar dance because every sensation rippled wildly. Rather than her A Positive scent alone, she was the fragrant blend of all the donor blood he'd consumed and fed her.

Lizbet's fingertips slid down his hip. She laughed when he quivered. "You have a few live-wires, too?"

He felt the grazing tickle of her long hair as she bent over him. Her invitation was undeniable. She moved her mouth to his nipple and sucked it gently. Lizbet smiled shyly at him. With two manicured fingertips, She pushed Harry back to his throne of pillows. "I want to go out, see the sky, and feel the night air."

"You think you're steady enough?"

"Well, if I'm not, you can always fuck me up against the wall."

"Will you bite me with that mouth?" Harry drew back with a raised brow. He heard her slow vampire heart beat faster as she moved off the bed.

Lizbet turned when she got to the door. "I can hear your heartbeat, that's so cool." She hesitated on the back porch, scanning the tall pines and a long staircase down to the lake. She bounded out, following the milky moonlight creating her path.

His fledgling's body glowed like a fae angel as she ran down the steps two at a time to reach the moon-bleached beach. He chased her with a pang of primal hunger. They ran, invigorated by the light of the night's full silver orb sensually illuminating their preternatural bodies against the dark forest.

When he caught up to her, she coyly turned and summoned him with a tweak of her finger. They collided and tumbled into the icy water. Harry caught her legs to wrap around his waist as he nuzzled her intently. "Betts, you know what?"

Her response was muffled by her lips on his earlobe. "What?"

His lips caught hers for a split second and then nose to nose he growled. "No prisoners."

Harry dove head-on into the lake, pulling her further into the depths. Their splashing, their shrieks, and their laughter, all of it summoned the wildlife. A lone wolf howled in a solitary effort and was rapidly answered. The responding pack howled together in chorus. Owls hooted their melodious calls, the music reverberating off the cliffs. Eagles skimmed the treetops, shrieking as they dove into the lake.

Lizbet and Harry wrestled joyfully without the need to breathe, their lips locked. Submerged, they rolled like sea creatures becoming one. As they broke the surface of the water, arms wrapped around each other, they moaned in pleasure. The water caressed their newly awakened senses as they moved toward the floating swim dock.

Harry backed up to the dock, half hanging, half floating. He held on as Lizbet wrapped her legs around his waist and floated luxuriously. Her dark hair moved in the water like a halo.

"Handsome, I'm in heaven." Harry sighed in agreement, moving his hips from side to side, admiring her floating right and left, her graceful arms extended joyfully. "We woke everyone up, have you ever heard anything like this?" She stroked, making angel wings in the tranquil lake.

"We did this. They're celebrating us. We sent out the vibration, and nature sensed it." He winked at her. "Ah, the children of the night." She squeezed her legs tighter and giggled. "Our happiness was a territorial claim, a declaration of who we are now. They won't come near us, but they're out there in solidarity, celebrating us being together like this."

◆◆◆◆

Lizbet broke away from Harry and bounded up to the swim dock. Like a nymph in the glen, she whipped her hair around as she spun. "Come get me, handsome. Let's celebrate some more."

He was up and out of the water, and over her within a mortal's breath. "Everything about our meeting fell into place so ironically. And you, you were like a terrier after me."

Lizbet growled like a puppy. "You were *my* prey!"

"You unleashed me. You conspired with the universe for all of this."

"I did. I wasn't going to settle for anything less than the unexpected, and there you were pulling the door off the cab. That was unexpected. What's more unexpected than a vampire?"

Harry moved with her in his arms until they both lay on their backs, facing the starry sky. "I was half asleep until I met you. You stuck with me, saw me through that nightmare." He abruptly rolled over her, his arms out to the side to pin her. "I want to spend eternity thanking you, one stroke at a time."

She reached for his hands to thread their fingers together, "God, you're so …" He breathed hungrily, her heart and body were ready to play. "Isn't it crazy how…."

She grinned. "Kissing is …"

Harry's knee split her legs to take her. "All these sensations, everywhere. You're the woman who drew me out of darkness, let me send you into the stars."

She leered, her tongue skating her top lip. "Ready for lift-off."

Chapter Forty-Two

Harry rolled away from his fledgling, grinning. He pointed a steady hand at her. "Hmm, I believe you'll be delicious." Harry's chest rumbled with a hungry growl.

So seductively, she lay there, arms out. "Will you kiss me?" Her eyes half-shut, aflame with desire.

Propped on his elbow, Harry smiled down into her adoring gaze and kissed her lips. She let his mouth wander over her face, gently kissing her eyelids, her cheeks, the corner of her mouth. He nibbled gently on her jaw and nuzzled her ear. His hands explored her too, caressing the hill and slope of her hip. Inky black hair splayed over her shoulders. He twirled a hank of it tightly and pulled her closer to him. His lips moved down her throat to her shoulders.

Lizbet's fingertip traced his treasure trail, from his chest to his navel, and below. "Can you believe it? No more condoms." Her hand skimmed his muscled thigh and caught his thick column of flesh. Her strong fingers cast stars behind his closed eyelids. *So much pleasure.* Unrelenting, she turned him on as she stroked the thick stalk of his erection, running her fingertips softly over the contours of his shaft as his back arched into her hand.

"Let me tell you something. If seduction is music, I feel like your perfect instrument, because you're a hell of a musician." His two fingers trailed softly over her mound, teasing her petals of flesh. She madly enjoyed his rambling fingertips. Her hips rose, thrusting into his strokes.

"No matter how fast I want to get inside you and claim every inch of you, I don't want this to be…"

"Slam, bahm, thank-you, M'am." She sang it like David Bowie, and his grin spread across his lips. *She has a sense of humor during sex.* With delicate fingers, she caught his hand and brushed his palm across the delta of her thighs.

He gasped humorously. "A pierced clit? When did you do that?" Harry sat up abruptly, drawing her with him, her legs wrapped around his waist. He caught her heady scent, unleashed by his question.

"I don't wear the ring all the time, but tonight's special."

Their embrace shared the burn as he rocked her over him. "Oh, Betts, hold on…"

"Hold on?" Her voice was a soft whisper. "Tell me what you've always wanted to do with me? Remember, I won't break…"

He smirked, thinking about the clit ring. "Okay. If taking you is an amusement park, I consider this an 'E' ticket ride

Lizbet giggled as she wiggled over his hard flesh. "Well, it's definitely not "It's a small world"."

"Glad to hear that. These days I'm not sure what turns the ladies on. I've been told I can be annoyingly mid-century." Harry kissed her smiling mouth, holding himself over her before dropping the weight of his lower body onto hers. The length of his hard-on pressed into her thigh.

She smirked into his eyes. "Harry, what is it about waiting?" She bumped her hips up to him.

"Patience, Betts, that old fashioned mentality combined with vampire abilities means my lady will be well satisfied." Harry lowered his chest to graze hers. He brushed himself slowly from side to side across her hard nipples. She threw her arms around his back and pulled him all the way down, nipping his neck.

Burying his face in her neck and thick hair, he inhaled every spark of her allure. He ran his tongue along the shell of her ear, down to the lobe. He murmured in her ear, "Please keep your hands inside the ride at all times." Resuming his tongue's journey along her jawbone, he kissed toward her chin. He nipped his way up to her mouth and captured it with a slow, deliberate kiss. Their moans excited the night.

He pursued her, traveling down her neck to the hollow of her throat. He nipped it and inhaled her scent again. "Do you smell this good just to tempt me? You're enticing, good enough to eat." She swooned at his words and tangled her hands in his hair. He kept kissing his way toward his reward.

She gasped and arched into his mouth. He reached her left breast, circling the nipple with hungry kisses before suckling and teasing it with his tongue.

"Oh, handsome, that is so hot. I love the way you take… what you want. You do the most exciting things." Lizbet gasped.

"Do you know how long I've wanted to taste you in your new… form? This is my reward for patience." Harry lifted his head to grin at her and then returned to teasing her breast. When he repeated his favors on her other breast, he felt her body respond, and her pheromones rise. Her heart thumped, and her breathing increased with low moans.

He reveled in the delicious fragrance of his aroused vampress. Harry resisted the urge to abandon her other breast before it received his full attention, and Lizbet's little gasps told him he exceeding her expectations. Her needy fingers massaged his neck, where it met the base of his skull and tugged gently on his hair, thanking him wordlessly.

He continued his journey down her body, kissing the underside of her breast and nuzzling his way to her navel. "Mmmm, delicious." He hummed into the thatch of ebony curls at the base of her belly. Sniffing again, he was overcome by her desire. Their bond connected her need, and he noticed the hitch in her breathing at his delay. "You want mid-century romance? Well, having this lush bush, God, Betts, that does it for me. I can't tell you how thrilled I am you haven't waxed this to nothingness."

His palm skirted over her thick curls. He hadn't fingered her or laid his tongue on her, and she fell apart. He lifted her knee to nestle between her thighs, and her eyes closed. He glanced the flat of his hand over her belly. "Is this good?" He blew a chilled breath over her.

Lizbet opened her eyes in surprise. "Yes. More than you know…" His smile split as his tongue ran over his bottom lip. "My dear…" He gently parted her flesh to reveal her sex. Scenting her lusciousness within, he lapped at her, consuming her intoxicating taste and scent. Her thighs spread wider in invitation. Hungrier than ever for her pungent sweetness, he slid his hands under her to lift her closer to his mouth. Lizbet's cries quickened. "Please, please…"

"Stop?" He grinned, the word muffled by his lips on her. The vibration made her moan deeper as he teased her along a sensual journey.

"Are you insane?" Her body quivered beneath him, tensing as he built her climax. She was so close he could taste her body's response. She spun tighter under his tongue, quivering. He added the right pressure, his fingers within her. His loving attentions built the perfect storm for her.

Harry thrust his wrist toward her as he saw her frantic grasping at the air. "You'll have to bite, Betts, when you're ready to come, bite me." Once the deadly combination of his lips, tongue, and fingers cast stars into her dark heaven, she bit.

Her soulful, muffled wail was music to his ears. He placed his cheek on her bush as she shuddered and gasped his name. He kept a soothing finger on her swollen bud until her shuddering stopped, and then he kissed her there, once more, reducing her to twitching.

"Over the top, nooo… Harry, give… me… a… second." She groaned. Harry caught her clit ring in his teeth and chuckled. The vibration arched her into his mouth. She slapped the dock boards three times. He smugly crawled up her body until he lay face-to-face with her again. Lizbet opened her eyes as she shook her head. "Well, that makes any space ride look tame." She caught his lips and kissed him, tasting herself.

"I didn't even get inside you." Harry curled two fingers over her belly. "I want a do-over."

"Ahh, I'd be catatonic. I wouldn't be able to give you yours."

"Betts, remember who we are. Taking it slow is gone."

She reached for him, her words short and husky. "I feel like I owe you for that ride you gave me." She leered mischievously at him.

"What did I say about you coming first? It's what I want for you." Harry pulled her over him to cradle her head on his chest. "Time is on our side."

Lizbet answered, kissing him, blowing his words right out of his mind. He lost himself in her taste, and her silky body pressing against his so deliciously. "Touch me, Betts. I need your touch." She slid to his side, and her hands captured his cock. Pressing her palms together around his shaft, she stroked him masterfully, rhythmically. He reached for her breasts and urgently rolled her nipples to bring them to hard pink peaks.

She leaned into him, and his thrusts answered her. *It was too much.* He had to take her. He rolled her over, and she fell open to him. He felt the aura of her heat, and the shock wave traveled down his spine. Harry bit his bottom lip just before making that first thrust into her. Her legs caught him high on his hips, and his strokes became shorter, not wanting to leave her honeyed heaven.

Lizbet watched him with a curious gaze as he felt his fangs aching to drop. Looking at her body beneath his, Harry felt the welcome urge to bury his face in the curve of her neck and bite her where that delectable artery pulsed.

Instead, he pulled his hips back and thrust into her tight heat with unrelenting force. He pulled her willing legs over his shoulders, soldiering deeper and faster, giving him time to relish their first real intercourse. Lizbet watched in awe, his beauty translucent in the moonlight. Harry felt every aspect of Lizbet's second orgasm building while he felt the force rising within him.

His body electrified their joining. Every sensation was exulted as he increased the rhythm further. *Bite? Not bite? Bite? Not bite?* His circular argument went up to the sky as she threw back her wet hair and offered her pale, heavenly neck. He dropped to the beckoning vein and caressed her lovely jaw. He offered his wrist anticipating her climax

Harry cherished her new undead appearance, and he smiled proudly as her eyes silvered to opals, and her baby fangs elongated for her bite. "Oh, Betts…"

He felt her adoration of his full-tilt undead appearance, the blue-white skin, his glowing eyes, his fangs only turned her on. *Let's do this.* His bite broke her skin. *Oh, what a heavenly bond we share.*

They bit in unison, and her orgasm fed his own. Overcome with spasms of discovery and joy, his forthcoming rumble and growls made her giggle.

She ran an index finger over his still descended fang. "Ah, handsome, this is the good stuff for sure." She pressed her finger, and he met in a halfway bite to draw another drop of her delightful blood. "How long will we stay like this?" She waved her bleeding finger at his face, and his gaze followed that finger hungrily. He caught her hand and collapsed over her, panting as he suckled it.

"Betts…" Her nickname rode his sigh. He couldn't speak, even undead, he was utterly spent. She still held him within her, and they rolled whimsically. "You're just as brave as the devil on Saturday night." He panted and kissed her face, his rowdy cock throbbing within her as he pulled her over him. Her face was wet, and he realized that he was the one crying. Enjoying her knees alongside his hips, she wiggled as he took a steadying breath.

"Well, hell yeah." Lizbet grinned at him and wiped the tears from his eyes. She hugged him gently.

Harry pulled her down. She crossed her arms on his chest and put her chin on her hands, looking into his face.

"Oh, woman, I'll feed you again just so we can do this over and over." He sat up, holding her in his lap, rocking her to reinitiate their congress. "We need to swim back and check the cooler. We may have to call out for delivery." His words were smooth and even as their titillation built.

"Oh yeah." She arched to rise and drop, fiendishly riding him now. "The problem is, Harry, we'd have to… stop… doing… this…" Her words dissolved to moans as he let her work toward her own orgasm. He rocked with her rhythmically as she dragged her nails across his back.

Her moans, her heavenly scent, and the brisk bite to his shoulder told him she'd risen to the skies with another lengthy orgasm.

Chapter Forty-Three

Their playful shrieks echoed off the cliffs as Harry chased Lizbet back to the house. She tore into the shower and lathered her body and hair, dancing under the spray head's icy rain the entire time.

Harry threw open the glass door and laughed. "I brought towels. I'll wash your back if you wash my front."

"Oh, you think I'm falling for that offer? I'd be a silly vampire if I didn't." She handed him the bubbly bath puff and offered her back for scrubbing.

♦♦♦♦

Two weeks later

Lizbet ducked her head out the front door into the twilight. "This is the hardest part, getting up with the sunset." She slid on dark glasses.

Harry came up behind her with a consoling hug. "With age comes power, within a month or so you'll be a day-walker. Just not a sun-bather." She cuddled into his embrace and turned to rest her cheek on his chest.

"I cannot wait to show Matt my fangs."

"I'll bet you can't wait to show Venus your fangs."

"Venus and I will be thick as thieves, believe me." She hugged him fiercely. "I checked all the rooms. You packed the car. I'm ready to go back to LA."

♦♦♦♦

When they arrived at Harry's apartment, he put down his bags, unlocked the door, and swept Lizbet up like a bride. She squealed as he carried her over the threshold. Harry put his fledgling down, and they walked through his now cramped apartment stuffed with most of her furniture pushed against his gear. The two pianos stood side by side. "Well, Betts, you better learn how to play that thing. We can have dueling pianos."

She walked to the flashing red light on his answering machine. "You have a message."

"*We* have a message. Go ahead, put it on speaker."

"Harry, this is Valerie Craft. I'm calling because my mother has taken a bad turn and she's asking for you. If it's not too much of an imposition, could you please call me when you get this message?"

Harry saved the message and looked at his watch. It was nine in the evening. "Betts, do you think it's too late to call?"

"No, time is precious to mortals. Call her."

◆◆◆◆

Traffic wove them to Angelino Heights just before ten. The porch light burned brightly as Harry and Lizbet approached, and Valerie stood silhouetted in the front door's glass. Before they climbed the steps, the door opened, and Harry hastened to embrace her.

Valerie apologized. "I hated to call you. I know you don't really know her, but she was so insistent, and the hospice nurse said it would make the end easier for her."

Harry patted her back and tucked her head under his chin. "In the last month, how many people have sat with her on the front porch and talked about old times?" He drew her chin up to share a gaze, her eyes so like his mother's. Valerie looked down and wiped a sniffle.

Lizbet stepped up and gently hugged her. "Why don't you take Harry to see Dotty, and you and I can have some of that delicious tea."

Valerie gestured them into the front parlor, where a hospital bed was set up with the foot facing the bay windows. The head of the bed was elevated, and Dotty gazed out at the gayly lit veranda. When Harry and Lizbet looked from Dotty's perspective, they noticed the line of potted plants up against the porch railing. Each plant had a colorful windmill or whirligig moving in the night's breeze. Harry and Lizbet shared a solemn moment.

Harry slid into the chair, sitting at Dotty's bedside, and thought again how cruel mortal aging could be. He noted the oxygen concentrator and tubing, remembering her as bright and vibrant as she had been in 1950.

Dotty winked as she extended her left hand. "My boyfriend, where have you been?"

"I've been out of town, just got Valerie's message that you were sick, so I hurried over."

"I have not had any of Momma Rose's chicken stew, is she out of town?"

Harry nodded. "They went on vacation. She's going to be sorry she didn't have some I could pull out of the freezer. What can I do for you?"

Dotty strained to look at the parlor door and stage-whispered, "Is that dark-haired woman your secretary? She's with you every time you come."

Harry's head dropped back, and he muffled a grin. "Yes, she is. She's great at what she does."

"Maybe she could go over to your house, get Momma Rose's recipe and get cooking. I miss that chicken stew."

◆◆◆◆

Lizbet sat with her hands folded in her lap. "What does the doctor say?"

Valerie busied herself gathering the implements to brew a pot of tea. She turned and leaned against the counter. "She's had a stroke. It affects the right side of her body; it affected her heart; that's why she's on oxygen. Mom needs thickened foods because she has trouble swallowing, and the stroke has made her dementia worse. She and I and the doctor have decided she wants no parts of a hospital. She's on hospice now."

Lizbet nodded. "They're great. How are you doing?"

Valerie placed the tea kettle on the burner, and Lizbet saw her shoulders quiver. When she turned, her smile was gone, and she wiped tears from her eyes. "I was an only child. My parents didn't have a happy marriage. When my father died, I was ten. Have you ever had a family member die by accident?"

Lizbet's head cocked inquisitively. "No, that had to be traumatic."

Valerie brought the sugar and creamer to the breakfast table. "It seemed to free Mother. I wasn't supposed to hear, but the Momma Rose she talks about was the lady who lived next door. I heard her and Mother talking one time. I used to have an Uncle Harry, who was Momma Rose's son, who I think was the great love of Mother's life." Lizbet had been warming her hands in her lap just for this moment. She reached across the small table and slipped a tissue into Valerie's hand. Valerie wiped her eyes and continued. "The thing is, Harry died in the spring, and Mother was bereft until my Father died in July. Then she became a different woman, but I think she's always mourned for Uncle Harry. I believe when she saw the two of you leave the house next door, she settled on your husband as 'her' Harry." Valerie shook her head. "Isn't it amazing they're both named Harry?"

The phone rang, and Valerie took it in the hallway's phone nook. Lizbet exercised her developing vampire hearing to eavesdrop on Harry's conversation with Dotty. She tuned in just in time to hear Dotty's remark about his secretary. She had to smother her laugh as the tea kettle whistled, and she busied herself, making tea.

♦♦♦♦

Dotty held their high school yearbook and pointed a birdy finger at Harry. "They told me you died. I bought your book, but I couldn't bring myself to read it. It's up there somewhere." She waved at the bookcases flanking the fireplace. "What happened to you?"

Harry took her cool hand in both of his. "You could say my life took a turn, an unexpected turn. I never wanted to leave you, Dotty. I never planned on leaving Valerie. I didn't have a choice."

"Did you go off and get involved with the wrong crowd?" Her white brows knit, scandalized. "You were a musician once..."

"No, it was more a medical condition. I have a dangerous sensitivity to sunlight, and my diet is extremely limited. For a long time, it was risky for me to mingle with the general population. The powers that be decided it was better if everyone thought I was dead."

Her head tilted in his direction. "Your hands are as cold as mine."

Harry nodded and smiled. "It's part of the condition. Thankfully. things have improved enough that I can finally have a life."

"What about that woman? Why can't you move back and spend time with me? Better than that, you move into the spare room, and we can read and play cards, and you know..."

Harry bit his lip. "Think of Dr. Mitchell as my physician. She has to go everywhere with me."

270

"Well, that would cramp my style." Dotty pushed the yearbook away. "Ever since that son of a bitch husband of mine fell down the back steps, I was hoping you'd come back."

Harry sat straight up in the chair at that news. "I heard Arnold had died. I didn't know how. What happened?"

"The only time he touched me was to threaten me." She pulled her fist up to her chest. "That day, I fought him off." She shook her fist at Harry. "Arnold was a cheap bastard and never fixed the back stair's top step. You know that tread was loose." Harry nodded. "Arnold went ass over teakettle straight to the first floor. I never heard another foul word in this house."

"How did you live, with a young daughter and no income?"

Her green eyes sparkled. "Remember me talking about Arnold's secret projects?" Harry nodded. "He was heavily insured by the U.S. Government. Back then, a million dollars established a good income for life. Your father saw to that." Harry tucked his chin and nodded. "The day your book's first check arrived, Arnold had a fit. He was about to rip up the paperwork when I challenged him."

Harry sat back and folded his arms over his chest. "Was that what did him in?"

Dotty chuckled. "Yessirree, bob. I know he always irritated you. It seemed fitting somehow. Those checks saw that your daughter had the best of everything. Dance lessons, private schools, Smith College, and her year abroad."

Harry's smile broadened and spread to Dotty. "That's exactly what I intended. I wanted to be here to give her my love, but since I couldn't, at least I gave her opportunities."

Dotty leaned forward in her bed. "You know, she's a writer, she's published in twenty-eight countries in twenty-six languages. She writes murder mysteries."

Harry felt his smile all over. "I've recently read some of her books. Perhaps one day, she'll write my story."

Dotty pressed the bed control to sit up further. She waved at the railing, and Harry dropped it for her. She gestured for him to sit beside her.

When he settled next to her, she leaned into him, and he caught her in an embrace. "Harry, a part of me died when you died. You are the love of my life. Being with you right now gives me the grace to make it home."

Harry kissed her white curls on the top of her head. "I'll always carry you in a special part of my heart." He drew her hand to his undead heart.

Dotty gasped and turned as white as the linens. She clutched her good arm to her breast. She stuttered. "I need to lie down." Harry read dread in her eyes at the thought of their separation. He scooped her up, placed her comfortably in the bed, and tucked the bedclothes around her. Her eyes drooped, and her breathing eased. "I'm sorry, Harry. I want to talk more, but I'm so tired…"

He leaned over and kissed her lips gently. Her fingers covered the kiss when he straightened. "Anything you need, have Valerie call me, please?" Dotty nodded and closed her eyes with an angelic smile. Her cheeks were pink, and her breathing relaxed. Harry stepped backward out of the room. He stood, holding on to the doorframe, watching, listening in medic mode. *She's got perhaps a month, six weeks. Valerie will always have me.*

◆◆◆◆

Harry turned and ran into Valerie, standing wide-eyed with the landline telephone buzzing a dial tone in her hand.

"You alright, Valerie?"

She muttered as she tucked the black phone back into the niche. "Umm, it's kind of you to pay so much attention to a woman you don't know, Mr. Mitchell."

Harry nodded and sunk his hands into his trouser pockets. He shrugged boyishly. "Did you get that tea made?"

Valerie seemed disoriented and gestured vaguely toward the kitchen. They walked silently back to see Lizbet serving up three perfectly brewed cups of tea.

"Well, there you all are. Harry, one lump or two?"

"I've had plenty of lumps today." He waved off the tea and dug for his wallet. He produced his calling card and handed it to Valerie. "I haven't been honest with you, Valerie."

She read the card. "Harrison VanAlt? Are…?"

"Dotty means a great deal to me on a personal level. Should either of you need anything, call me. No hesitations. Promise?"

Valerie's complexion blanched as she looked toward the parlor, then Harry and the card." Her gaze swept Lizbet.

♦♦♦♦

Mother was asleep. The porch light burned if she woke and wanted to see her whirligigs. Valerie locked up the house and went into her first-floor office. She thought, *they were both so pale. So pale… Didn't Lizbet purposely keep her hands in her lap, and yet her touch was as cold as Harry's?* His conversation with Mother was unbelievable, but what explained it? She turned on her computer.

♦♦♦♦

The Los Angeles night air played over their heads as Harry drove the LaSabre on a roundabout route along Mulholland Drive. Lizbet watched him as shadows crossed his face. "You had quite a history with Dotty. How do you feel about seeing her again?"

He pulled the long convertible into a parking space and leaving the car, held out his hand to Lizbet. "Walk with me." They climbed the steps to the overlook above the Hollywood Bowl, and he pulled her to the railing. Standing behind her, he relished her cachet and embraced her tightly. "I made my decision about Dotty a long time ago. As in B.V."

Lizbet turned her head inquiringly. "B.V.?"

"Before vampire." He grinned. "I told her the truth. I'll always have a fond place in my heart for her. She gave me a daughter who, thank God, I'll be able to know for a time. But nothing compares to a woman who decides her destiny to be with me."

Lizbet turned her head again to grin up at him. "You mean your secretary?"

Harry chuckled. "Yeah, didn't I tell her you're with me every time I come? I testified you're great at what you do."

"Hah. You only love me for my body. What happens in two years when you're bored with me?" Lizbet planted her feet on the path, ready to debate."

273

"Betts, I love you now. I'll love you forever. You can hold me to it." He squeezed her tighter in his embrace. "Go ahead, ask me in two years."

◆◆◆◆

It was four in the morning before Valerie finished her research. She flipped through the myriad pages she'd printed. Unsolved mysteries related to exsanguination, symptoms of death, and random photos from an alternate lifestyle website fascinated her.

Quietly she slipped back into the parlor to grab her mother's yearbook. All of this fascinated her. *The clincher?* Once she dug back thirty search pages, there were candid color photos from 1983 celebrating the renaming of a jazz club opened in 1923. The Phoenix was reborn as The Bridge. The images revealed a coterie of devastatingly handsome fanged men with gorgeous women costumed as flappers and Prohibition-era showgirls.

In one closeup, Valerie zoomed in to view black and white photos of the 1923 opening. They were traditional film photos printed on paper involving silver emulsion. The women were in perfect focus, and the men were blurred — s*ilver film emulsion.* By their postures, Harry was not there.

In 1983's digital photos, one 'vamp' in particular caught her eye. Harrison VanAlt. She opened the yearbook to Henry VanAlt Jr.'s graduation photo. She stared dumbstruck. *Occam's razor?*

Valerie moved to the rollaway bed in the office and slipped her diary from under her pillow. She bit the end of her ballpoint pen and then wrote.

March 10, 2003

My father is a vampire…

The End

Other Books by Amber Anthony

Paranormal Romance
Appetite for Blood
Blood Rising
Blood Emerald
Blood Dragon

Metaphysical Fiction/Romance
Arise, My Darling

Contemporary Romance
Becoming Gabriel

Action/Adventure Romance
Roman's Revenge
Roman's Rules

Seasoned Romance
Roman's Rules

Where to follow Amber Anthony

https://www.facebook.com/WriteAmber/
https://twitter.com/WriteAmberA
https://www.instagram.com/writeamberanthony/
https://www.goodreads.com/author/list/17062164.Amber_Anthony
https://allauthor.com/author/amberanthony/
https://www.bookbub.com/profile/amber-anthony
WriteAmberAnthony@gmail.com

Now Available at Adagio.com

Custom Tea Blends reflecting Harry and Lizbet

One Night at The Blue Gardenia

Chocolate and Cherries.. yummy as
our Vampire, Harrison VanAlt

Blended With Black Tea, Honeybush Tea, Cocoa Nibs, Natural Chocolate Flavor, Natural Hazelnut Flavor & Natural Vanilla Flavor. *Accented With Chocolate Chips, Cocoa Nibs & Cherries*

My Favorite Profiler

A Honey of a Tea like
Dr. Lizbet Mitchell

Blended With Black Tea, Honeybush Tea, Natural Almond Flavor, Natural Creme Flavor & Natural Vanilla Flavor. *Accented With Cocoa Nibs, Safflower & Cranberry*

Search our teas in the BLEND sections

Search under 'Tags', Amber Anthony

Praise for Amber Anthony

Arise, My Darling

"Being an intuitive myself, I was hooked from the beginning."
-Amazon Customer

Roman's Revenge

"Amber Anthony generously doles out steamy romance, heart-pounding action, and edge-of-your-seat suspense."
-Amazon Customer

Roman's Rules

"Great characters and setting, with plenty of humor, fill another fun read for these terrific authors."
-Amazon Customer

Becoming Gabriel

"The romantic buildup between Grace and Gabrielle was priceless. Multi-dimensional facets of the protagonists' personalities made the plot come alive for me.

The book has an old-world charm. There's a special kind of magic that happens when two people fall in love within impoverished settings. Their dire circumstances created a delightful tension which magnified their romantic encounters."
-Amazon Customer

Appetite for Blood

"A paranormal romance that has it all and then some! When a prequel has you itching to read the trilogy, that's superb storytelling!... I'm a fan! Kudos, Amber Anthony!"
-Amazon Customer

Blood Rising

"Great world-building and complex characters add to an interesting story. Matt and Cat's attraction is deep and powerful. Their chemistry is very hot, and the love between them sweet, touching, and spicy. A plot that offers plenty of drama, suspense, danger, and passion."
-Amazon Customer

Blood Emerald

"Rick Hiatt is a hero to die for in this stunning standalone. Literally. We were first introduced to this devilishly handsome vampire in the first book of the Blood series. Now, Rick is the leading man in this second installment, and readers are going to melt as his story unfolds."
-Romantic Times, Top Pick 4.5 Stars

Blood Dragon

"Amber Anthony writes paranormal characters you'd like to have as friends. Bound by fierce loyalty, Adam and his colleagues, vampires Rick Hiatt and Matt Brenner (previous books), engage in the kind of good-natured ribbing and witty repartee that had me laughing out loud. Their devotion to their mates and the sizzling love scenes had me wistfully sighing."
-Amazon Customer